TIME AND SEASON

TIME AND SEASON

ODI IKPEAZU

AuthorHouse™
1663 Liberty Drive
Bloomington, IN 47403
www.authorhouse.com
Phone: 1-800-839-8640

First published by AuthorHouse   10/13/2011

ISBN: 978-1-4567-9668-6 (sc)
ISBN: 978-1-4567-9669-3 (ebk)

Printed in the United States of America

Going back east

By his reckoning, he was probably born in the basement of life's lowest station but most certainly, he was bred between *the* rock and *the* hard place.

Even as a toddler, he had needed to grow up fast. As a mere boy, he already had to be a hard man with no illusions about what a wonderful world this could be.

Not surprisingly, a sardonic outlook marred what might have been a childhood and on adolescent shoulders quickly grew the head of an untimely adult. Very little made him happy, although he most likely derived some pleasure fuming at Fate for dealing him a bad hand.

Very early on, he discovered that treasure chest of the poor, that ironic strength of the weak: *the knowledge that there was nothing to lose and nowhere further to fall*. He was always a moody, lean and hungry boy and naturally grew into a broody, mean and angry teenager. His taut, handsome, chocolate-brown face was the tightest screw.

No one would ever describe him as well behaved as he exhibited a remarkably premature inclination to the bad life. He drank, smoked pot and went to brothels and other seedy places from the earliest age. He was a natural truant, who cut classes just as soon as he started school. He quit attending mass at around the age of ten and raped his first girl when he was about twelve.

'Thou shall not steal' was a sick joke to him, much like *'Good Morning'*, that banal cliché that totally lacked any meaning. Another gut-churner, he thought, was *'Welcome to Lagos'* or some such other corny city limits sign that actually sucked you into a big, bad place.

One clammy night in March, he boarded the bus in Lagos, sulkily reflecting on his young life. He was heading back East to his hometown, Onitsha, while convinced it was by no means the most sagacious thing to do.

He had left home two years before, challenging his parents he was going to make out good in the big city. The old folks had balked at the idea but never ever really had much leverage with which to impose their will on him. They spent most of their time pinching the pennies, which they pinched so hard, the tough metals almost bled.

Not that his father had not tried to instil some fear in him during the earliest years. On the contrary, the lacerations on his back were evidence of the old man's efforts by way of a steady supply of bamboo canes. He whipped him for the slightest misbehaviour and since the boy was impetuous, that meant constantly.

It did not help that the old man was a locally celebrated inebriate. In the neighbourhood, he was fondly indulged as the favourite drunk but at home, a violent streak often accompanied his inebriation. He would stagger in home at nights and invariably have something to take out on his family. All too frequently, he laid the rod on his poor, dear wife, a frail and sickly woman. He also did on his children, the two boys and the girl. One night, he whipped their mother so badly and although it was routine, the elder son thought for some reason that it was also the last straw. He hit back at his father with a mortar pestle, making a gash on his forehead, from which he nearly bled to death. The testy boy was all of thirteen at the time.

Tonight, the prodigal was going back home, nineteen years of age now, and his tail stiff between his legs. He had only scraped through some secondary education, finally dropping out in third form after some dreadful results. The high point of his school career was being in the football team, where he had been one of the better players. At fifteen, he was picked for the State's schools selection. Soon after that, he got an invitation to the national Under-17s in preparation for the following year's FIFA championships in Venezuela. Increasingly, it appeared that his only hope of a decent future lay in football. There was a growing number of Nigerian players in the European football leagues earning fat sums and feeding the fantasies of youngsters in the country. In his own case, he imagined that his ambitions were not far-fetched and so frankly did a number of observers.

However, one stormy night, as the school team returned from an away game, those dreams got shattered. The driving rain thrashed angrily at the bus windscreen, the driver squinted desperately through his befuddled sights and almost inevitably, they plunged into a gorge at a hairpin bend.

The leg injury he suffered ruled him out of the Venezuela tournament, towards which he had lately channelled all his energies. More bitterly, it ended all his football ambitions forever because neither the school nor his parents could give him the specialist treatment he needed for the leg. As a result, he was left with the permanent limp and a formidable conviction that he was up against the world.

After he left hospital, he dropped out of school in exasperation. He searched fruitlessly for jobs, which was difficult enough for bright youngsters with good grades and all. People were pauperised by years of bad governments and school leavers often wished they had never left school. Since there were no jobs, it was better to be a bad student, remain in school than a good graduate, and be without a job. What was more, the rotting economy could only get worse, no matter how hard anyone stared in a crystal ball.

So, along with droves of idle youths, he roamed the rude streets, his parents being in no position to give the unemployment support that the state could not. To make matters worse, he had a huge appetite, which, by the way, was one funny thing with hard-up people. They, who could least afford food, had the most hunger for it; or perhaps they had the most hunger for it *exactly* because they could not afford it. On the other hand, rich folks seemed set to starve themselves to death with all manner of diets, moaning about calories, cholesterol, and the rest of it. Anyway, food was always a subject of altercations with his mother. She never had enough to offer and *he* never could eat his fill.

Once upon a time, a job opening did present itself, which he jumped at. He was sixteen and the national elections had come around once again. A friend of his took him along to see a local politician, who needed thugs for the hustings. It was one of the few times that youngsters were assured of a paying occupation, albeit for a few, short, suicidal weeks. He enlisted.

The job detail was simple enough, if not quite so easy. They were to put as much violent behaviour as they could at the service of the politician, for whom the election was a straight matter of life and death. Thugs were indispensable to the Nigerian politician. With them, he could intimidate his opponents and rig the votes. During election campaign, the thugs encamped at the politician's home, well supplied with guns, slugs and bucks. They thoroughly exploited the situation, knowing his desperation to win and the shortness of the romance.

During this period, there was a curious truce between the underworld and the law. The politicians had an unspoken license to employ known criminals. Police officers looked the other way as wanted gunmen cleaned their guns on front porches. Drug enforcement agents drifted tamely past as gangsters smoked giant spliffs and freebased crack with cocky contempt. The thugs had a right to anything that would fuel their rashness and the ambitious politicians bankrolled their lawlessness for the period.

On Election Day, the frenzied thugs invaded polling booths, put scare and confusion in the air and intimidated voters, election officials and even cops. If they sensed that the voting was not going their patron's way, they would seize or destroy ballot boxes and shoot in the air or at people if it was called for.

The silver-tongued politician promised them jobs in the event that they won but the wily hoods understandably took this with a pinch or two of salt. First, there could only be so many winners. Secondly, even if their man did win, how many jobs could there possibly be? Sure, a few might get on the state payroll as official hoods but the truth was, most would return to the regular underworld once the election was over, won or lost. The hardened pros naturally would go back to their old beats, while amateurs usually drifted on to more serious crime, now finding themselves with bad company and lethal weapons. They knew from experience that down the line, those same politicians that put the guns in their hands in the first place would hunt them down for it. Crime control was always on the agenda for corny, new incumbents.

He left for Lagos shortly after the farcical election, which, by the way, his man lost. He thought he might learn a legitimate skill if he could and the easiest he could think of was automobile mechanic. It seemed for some reason to be the natural choice of dropouts. There was an illogical popular notion that little or no brains was demanded by the job. He was to discover how dreadfully wrong it was. Nothing on earth was easy.

He apprenticed for months, barely managing in the end to tell the difference between a crankshaft and a spark plug. He was understandably not the boss' favourite, who, as a result, never promptly paid him the pathetic pittance. Therefore, since he needed to eat, he set his mind inevitably to more familiar occupations such as picking pockets and shoplifting. By so doing, although he did not exactly meet with resounding success, he did manage to keep from starving. *That* was no mean feat in the city. Just the other week, a friend was nabbed and hacked to pieces with *matchettes* by vigilantes while scampering with a snatched mobile phone. Another was lucky to escape with only a grazing from a police bullet.

Remarkably, the chief drawback to his calling as a felon was not the police. Fortunately, there was a bent cop born every heartbeat. Criminals could get away with just about any crime if they could pay the price on the tag. At the precincts, desk sergeants traded all day and in truth, there was quite a supermarket feeling to the place. The only things missing were cash tills on the checkout counters.

One irritation for sure was that there were far too many other felons milling about. Also, victims had become not only quite vigilant but very paranoid and manic. The streets were full of ostensibly normal people but with a perverse sense of justice. At the drop of a hat, perfect gentlemen would gladly join in the lynching of an urchin for as little as pinching pringles.

He attempted to get into the organised gangs. However, organised gangs did not merely pick pockets or snatch mobile phones. They went into the heavy stuff such as arson, armed robbery and assassinations. Therefore, members were required to kill now and then.

Killing. Now, *that* was the chief drawback to his career as a felon. Along the way, he had subconsciouly drawn the line at taking life. That was about the only inhibition he had but what a crucial one it was for someone who wanted to make it as a bad guy. He owned a handgun and God knew how much money he might have made if only he would have squeezed the trigger with the barrel actually levelled at someone. He was frequently tempted but he found out about himself that he just could not bring himself to kill. He just was not bad enough, he thought ruefully. Therefore, even as a felon, he was a failure; at best, he was second rate.

Tonight, as the bus hurtled furiously down the eastbound highway, this kind of fretful retrospection pre-occupied him. To add to his vexation, he also had to put up with an itinerant Christian preacher, who kept whining about the end time.

The preacher inspired a deep curiousity in him. These days it seemed there was no business like the Jesus business. New churches sprouted and festered, while pushy preachers scrambled for market share in the booming enterprise. There were more churches and preachers in the country than food and water. That was odd. How could people be so pious, yet their country so odious, everyone so much on the take, the rich getting richer and the poor poorer? The rich built grand churches, filled them with the poor and took from them even the little they thought they had. The venerable preachers preyed on the fears of the poor vulnerable creatures, poached on their phobias and offered themselves as sanctuary. They fed the paranoia of these paupers and took advantage of their superstition. They never let the poor forget their poverty, while putting themselves forward as the means to prosperity.

This particular preacher looked uncannily like a dope pusher he knew in the Campos ghetto. Certainly, he dangled his pious fix the same way the pusher did his dope before the hooked drug fiends. He was a stringy, pipe-voiced man in a green suit and he sermonised with annoying aptness about accidental death, yelling about how people should be ready at all times to meet their Maker. With the driver plumetting the bus through the pitch-dark countryside, the terrified passengers could certainly connect with the message. Soon they were resonant with nervous and dissonant hymns.

To aid the preacher's cause, there was a gory accident near Sagamu. It was a head-on involving a trailer and a coach like the one in which they were travelling. Mangled bodies, body parts and baggage were flung all about the wreckage. Dazed and bloodied survivors groaned and whimpered in anguish as a makeshift rescue team formed from among the gathering sympathisers.

"Thank you, Lord," cried the preacher. *"That* might have been us!"

"Alleluia!" chorused the mobile congregation gratefully.

"The Lord is good!" he whined.

"All the time!"

After about twenty minutes, they moved on from that sorry scene, the passengers pervaded by a very somber mood indeed. Before long, the preacher was doing brisk business selling tracts, pamphlets and books to his captives, who snapped them up as if their lives depended on it.

The young man marveled as the preacher plucked money out of the outstretched hands of eager givers. He soon lost track of how much the man stuffed in his leather brief case, intrigued at how easily it had come. The preacher had not even needed to put the fear of the Lord in the travelers. The homicidal driver did it for him. As he wondered if he should not take to the evangelical line of business, an idea formed slowly in his mind and he smiled wryly to himself.

A few hours later, Onitsha loomed in the dark horizon, its outline darker still in the near distance. The boisterous trading town looked deceptively tranquil after what would have surely been another day's hurly-burly. The glow of the full moon reflected surreally in the calm Niger, across which the majestic silhouette of its famous bridge stretched. Shortly, the driver would be pulling the bus up to a final stop at the terminal, Upper Iweka. As it was still very dark, the passengers would prefer to wait in it until the safety of dawn. The town was notorious for robbery.

He saw the preacher get up from his back row seat and come towards the exit, by which he sat. The man probably was going to piss outside, he figured. If, on the other hand, he was making bold to head home at this hour, about four a.m., then he truly practiced what he preached and really feared no evil; in which case, good luck to him. Old Daniel did make it out of the lions' den and Jonah out of the belly of a whale, would you believe! He watched intently as the preacher passed by him and descend the doorsteps. He got up and followed him discreetly.

As the man of God pissed in a corner, he had a quick, furtive, look-around and then swiftly pounced on him. He kneed him hard in the back and felled him to the red earth.

A grunt escaped the man as did the briefcase his grasp and he grabbed it. The little commotion alerted someone, who riveted towards them but the youth beat past him and dashed for the dark street.

A burst of machine-gun fire came from somewhere behind him, the sound of a startled police guard surely. He sprinted frenziedly, gripping the precious briefcase with all his strength. He cursed as people pointed helpfully to the police guard in the direction of his flight. Another burst of gunfire cracked the night and slugs ripped frightfully into the rusted iron roofing of a shed ahead of him. In a right state, he was glad to see a thicket of bushes, into which he gratefully plunged.

He emerged in an earthen street and galloped through the darkness, relying on instinct to navigate his progress through its peppering of potholes. The speed of his flight belied his limp and his anxious face gleamed with cold sweat. He skirted garbage heaps, vaulted smelly drains and darted past pesky mongrels. He ran for what seemed an eternity before he dared presume that his pursuers might have given up the chase. For this, he was thankful because he was going to die from exhaustion.

He slowed down to a fast walk, still not daring to stop and catch his breath. He hurried all the way to *Enu Onitsha,* proceeding carefully and hugging the bushes as he did so. *Enu Onitsha* was the section of town where the native people like his family lived. On Okosi Road, he froze at a passing police patrol but exhaled gratefully when they did not pick up his shady figure in the headlights. A while later, he turned into their street and not long afterwards, caught sight of their little house, which in spite of its familiar dilapidation, was a curiously warming sight after all this time.

He regarded the cluster of banana trees by the backdoor. In their childhood, its relative shade served in the daytime as a play area. By night, it was a venue for their father's drinking bouts. Here he would duel with gin or beer, usually both. Almost nightly, he took the fight to the bottle, gamely giving of his best until he succumbed and passed out. He always boasted that he would never throw in the towel, tough nut that he was. Frequently, he was counted out and carried off to bed by his obliging family.

Curious nostalgia, the young man thought dryly, snapping out of it. He sat down by the bananas and set down the preacher's briefcase. He felt his racing pulse come gradually back to normal. He opened the briefcase and in the dim light, saw that there was even more money in there than he had imagined. It had all been well worth it, he thought with new satisfaction.

In addition to the loot of bills that the preaching fox had received for his literature, there were three virgin wads of ten thousand each, tucked in a corner. There was even the almighty dollar, all one thousand of it. He beamed with insane delight as he rummaged through the rest of the contents, of which there was nothing remarkable except a packet of condoms and a brand new *Raymond Weil* watch. He tossed the condoms away. Fucking preacher. He pocketed the fine watch. The godforsaken man of God would have to get another piece by which to tell the end time. He went up the road and tossed the briefcase in a ditch.

When he returned, the back door of the house was ajar. He paused, expecting to see the gaunt figure of his father, who was likely to come outside at this hour to savour the first gin of the day. Rather it was his younger brother that emerged through the doorway, about which he was very pleased. His name was Otito, which meant *'Praise be to God'*, a phrase he could very well yell right now. That was yet another weird thing about lowlifers, he thought. They, the most godforsaken gave the most praise to God.

"Tito," he whispered. When he was a toddler, he could not quite say Otito's name correctly. Tito, he managed and the name had stuck since then.

The younger boy turned to and peered in the darkness.

"Who's that?"

"Me. Elo"

"Elo?"

"Yes. Remember me? Your big brother."

The boy's jaw dropped in surprise and then he hurried over. He adored his elder, though always standing slightly in awe of him. Elo took offence quite easily. But right now there was no one else on earth he would have loved more to see. He ran into his embrace.

"You're back!"

"Not for long, I hope," Elo smiled. "But I am so happy to see you, man. You're up early." He was three years older than Tito. They were not exactly opposite characters but there were some marked differences between them. For one, Tito was not as bad a student as he had been. In addition, the younger boy did not share his anger at the world nor his desperate inclinations. Tito was much closer to their parents because he always chipped into the family piggy with one bob-a-job or the other and did chores. One the whole, Tito worked hard while Elo hardly worked.

"I haven't slept all night," Tito said.

"Why's that?"

"Ma. She's very ill. She really needs to go to a real hospital."

Elo felt more than a pang of guilt. "Is she awake?"

Tito nodded and they went into the house. In a tiny bedroom, their gaunt middle-aged mother squirmed as her eyes shuttered in listless sleep.

"She does look bad," the homecomer observed quite needlessly. Their mother had always been under the weather as far as anyone could remember. He turned and went back outside, Tito following faithfully after. At the cluster of bananas, he groped about at the base, and then turned to a wide-eyed Tito with two wads of ten thousand naira and ten one hundred-dollar bills from the preacher's collection. He favoured the younger boy with a skewered smile. "Keep it aside or I'll spend it. We can take her to a good hospital tomorrow."

Tito looked with as much suspicion as thankfulness at his brother. Everyone knew Elo was no altar boy. Certainly, he was no magician and money did not normally materialise from banana trees.

'I've been saving a little myself," Tito finally said, taking the money. "But it's nothing compared to this."

Elo placed a re-assuring hand on his shoulder. "I know how hard you've always worked trying to help. I'll pay you back some day, hear?"

"I know how things would be if things were fine with you. This will really help."

"You still play football?" Elo asked, getting uneasy with the emotions.

"Yes."

"Really well? Like I used to?" Elo smiled. He recalled that Tito used to play sometimes for the juniors.

"I play when I can. I don't have much time these days."

"Don't sound like an old man, kid," Elo snorted and had a wistful look about him. "You're young. You must play."

Elo's great regret naturally was the accident that invalidated him from the game. He could never get over it. He was going to be a useful player someday and help the family escape this bleak existence. He might have played for a local league side, then hopefully gone abroad and made a living of it.

From inside the breast pocket of his denim jacket, he produced a patent leather wallet. He slid a creased photograph out of it.

"Here, take a look at this."

Tito looked at the picture, a shot of Elo and a familiar-looking stranger in a tracksuit.

"That's you—."

"That's me four years ago *with* Bashir Hassan," Elo said proudly. "Recognise him? You remember the time we were both selected for the Under 17 trials and we played against Ghana?"

"How could I forget? Tito enthused. "It was on TV and you scored the only goal!" He looked again at the picture. Elo had cause to be both proud and sick of it. Bashir Hassan was now in Europe playing professionally. He had gone with German scouts after a good performance at the Venezuela tournament that Elo missed. He had joined *Bundesliga* club, Volksgaden but had recently made a great career leap, moving to English Premiership champions, Kingford for a huge fee.

"Do you still keep in touch?" Tito asked, quite starstruck.

Elo crinkled his nose. "He was in Lagos a few months ago. He came to play for Nigeria against Angola. He stayed at the Sheraton with the Nigerian team. I tried *every day* to see him but he made sure I didn't."

"That's bad." Tito remarked glumly with a tut-tut.

"That's life." Elo clenched his fist and sighed, beating against his left leg. "Can't blame him, though. If it wasn't for that goddamn accident."

"Did you ever come across Kosi?" Tito switched the subject after a sensitive pause. Kosi was their elder and only sister. She had run away from home some three years ago. Someone had her pregnant and their father threatened hell. No one knew now for sure what had become of her. She simply disappeared and no one had seen or heard from her ever since. Neighbourhood rumour had situated her in Lagos, which was not so ingenious since that was the logical destination for every runaway teenage girl from the provinces.

"Never saw her." Elo never really did get along with her. She always was on his case due to his errant ways and so he had felt a wicked elation when the little scandal of her pregnancy occurred and she got into neighbours' bad books just like him. But he was very fond of her in his own grouchy way. "Besides, Lagos is a very big place. You don't run into folks often."

"I think if she came home, Ma would feel a lot better," Tito said. He was thirteen at the time she ran away. It had taken a little while to dawn on the family that she was not coming back soon. He in particular had taken some getting used to it, because she used to quite dote on him. She liked taking him around and showing him off. She said he was the cutest boy and gave him as much confectionery as she could make her boyfriends buy. "Ma mumbles all the time about her; even in her sleep."

Blood in the street

In their neigbourhood lived a very wealthy man called *Chief* John Kafara. He was boyhood mates, as well as second cousins, of their father's. A week after Elo's return, there was a buzz of activity in his home, which was just down the road from theirs.

Funny that the two abodes could both be called *homes,* as though they had anything in common. While the Tansis inhabited an ugly, crude, little, mostly mud igloo, the Kafaras lived it up in a cool, modern, sprawling mostly marble mother ship. The fence walls were so high, only little other than the red-tile roof of the mansion was visible from the street. Within those walls was just about every leisure facility. There was an electricity generator, swimming pool, fountains, lush lawns, luscious gardens, tennis and squash courts, sauna and Jacuzzi. And this was only their country home.

Inheritance had left Kafara a great deal of real estate quite early in his life. To his credit, he used his assets well and set himself up in business that included fisheries, textile and oil. Some whispered loudly that he also had links to international narcotics. Anyway, he became fabulously rich, a major political party contributor and so a regular beneficiary of government contracts. Naturally, he veered into politics, having picked up friends in high society. It was making the rounds these days that he had his sights set on becoming the next state Governor. If that was true, he certainly stood a great chance since he was rich enough to rig the votes when the election came. He lived mainly in Lagos and Abuja, from where he ran most of his businesses. He also had homes in London, Miami and Porto Allegre. He was meticulous about the education of his two sons and a daughter, who were all in expensive European schools.

Today, he was getting initiated as *Ajie,* an ancient and exalted peerage of Onitsha, third in line to the King. This was good news for neighbours and relatives, as there was going to be a big to-do at his place. Though eminently pre-occupied with himself, he could quite throw money about whenever he needed to make a show of it.

By morning, there was already a crowd outside his gates, dozens of brightly dressed middle-aged men and women. The celebrations would not get into full swing until late afternoon, so this group clearly wanted to have a head start. Many of the local folks lived for just this sort of day. Apart from it being the high point of their tedious lives, there was the practical benefit of free food and wine.

A large, gelatinous woman, whose silken *buba* enhanced her ample curves, was shaking the locked steel gates. Two Doberman Pincers pranced fearsomely in their luxury cages.

"These wealthy types!" the handsome woman remarked breezily, peering through the gates. "Imagine having themselves locked in on a day like this."

"If being rich means being a prisoner in my own home," offered a lean, dark male member of the party. "I'll gladly stay the way I am: poor and free!"

At this, the party of about twenty broke out in eager laughter. From the look of things, the man was their chief jester; he went on to cause them more rib wracking with caustic wise cracks about the ways of the rich. This man was Obi Tansi, father of Tito and Elo.

•

Obi Tansi was in his mid-fifties, roughly the same age as his second cousin, John Kafara but any parallels ended just about there. Obi had certainly not come into any form of inheritance, his father having been chronically poor. What he did have was a fabled incapacity for holding down his drink as well as a job, both of which he had had quite a few.

At the beginning, he had worked as a chemist's dispenser but in the end, his employer decided that his drinking and temper was ruining his trade, and so paid him off.

At a further time, through the influence of John Kafara's father, he got into the Nigeria Police as a driver but that job had a short life. One day he was to convey some detainees to court in a Black Maria. On the way, he figured that there was just about time for a quick drink. However, one drink led to another and by noon, the detainees were passing out in the heat of the steel bus, while court officials fretted and flailed at their wits' end.

Many of his folks, for whom he was the butt of most jokes, thought him lucky to get his next job with the Railway Corporation. His duty was to supervise the rowdy passengers on the ancient coaches that snaked between Lagos and Kaduna. It was quite a stressful job, tending poor and irritable people through the arduous journey. Obi sought relief in the bottle.

He had a battered Spanish guitar at the time, with which he played some criminal chords, though he fancied the sounds he got out of the instrument. He thought he had a good baritone but was surely the only person of that opinion. As the train chugged along uneventfully enough through the tropical country and he was plastered as usual, he would then dare to subject his rowdy charges to his Nat King Cole *repertoire*.

'*Darling, je vous aime beaucoup,*' he would croak to either great amusement or considerable irritation. '*Unforgettable*' was best forgotten, though his drunken renditions could be quite infectious in its own way.

When thankfully he got weary of his own voice, he would seek to relieve the tedium by finding something to say to his star-crossed audience. So, Obi the taleteller became pretty as much a feature of the rail journeys as the creaky wagons.

He would tell a tall tale and if prodded further, would spin an incredible yarn. He told heroic stories of the Nigerian civil war, contriving always to have been in the picture of all the great events of it. He had survived a direct mortar hit, shot down a MIG fighter, rescued his platoon leader from behind enemy lines, single-handedly ambushed a Federal convoy and sunk a destroyer off the coast of Oguta. He often whipped his audience into incredulous frenzy but never did explain to their satisfaction why such a valiant soldier never made it to lance corporal.

"I did much of this kind of work undercover," he said. "I was really a secret agent."

Too secret obviously, the listeners agreed and their sarcasm would incredibly be lost on him. One day, on a southbound train, he had perhaps done more booze than usual and sung a lot as well. In his last moments of lucidity, he attached to his big toe a luggage tag requesting to be offloaded at the terminal in Enugu. He then fell into deep sleep and hardly stirred until he was was indeed offloaded at the terminal station by none other than the stationmaster himself! He later swore that it had all been done in jest but the stationmaster failed to see the joke and made an easy case for his sack.

He headed back home to Onitsha after that. One good thing down there was the insurance of the extended family. If you were out of pocket, uncles and cousins of every distance might be prevailed upon for help from time to time. Also, there was always one cause or the other for a party and the freebies that came with it.

The folks of home seized almost every opportunity to make a loud party. However, funerals had an edge when they really wanted to have a good time. There were not too many fun places in the town such as nightclubs, discos or cinemas and the few that existed were hardly worth the name. Because of that, it was at funerals that people could really catch some fun. Often, it was usually a safe bet that many people present at a funeral knew hardly a thing about the dearly departed, sometimes maybe not even his name. If men stood speechless or sat stunned at a wake, it was less by the death than by the surplus of comely women. These women came in every contour and went coquettishly back and forth, all too aware of their primeval appeal. Gaily got-up in some of their best clothing, the women competed keenly with the bereaved for the empathy of the guests. They turned and twisted with a delightful lack of choreography to the intricate beats of the percussion *troupes* and the live bands, unabashedly seeking the admiration of on-lookers. Children would be on the sides or in the shadows, winding their torsos and aping the elders' gaudy gyrations to the funky funeral beats. The elders would sit sipping their drinks in the shade of the canopies, acknowledging with glee the continuation of the bacchanal customs.

Elo and Tito, like everyone else in the neighbourhood, looked forward to Kafara's celebrations. He was a contented man, who frequently had something to celebrate, making him a celebrated island in a sea of malcontent, which made him all the happier. A few days ago, his sons, Charles and Peter had arrived from England and his daughter Mary from France. They fascinated the locals at how so much western culture had shaped them differently from them. The Kafara children spoke in dainty English and by their easy condescension impressed and intimidated their country cousins.

Whenever they were around, Tito and a lucky handful of the local boys could expect to get a present or two out of their luggage. A pair of Marks and Spencer boxer shorts and some super-hero comic books were what Tito got this time from Charles. He was Charles' natural local chum. They were cousins after all, unbelievably and roughly the same age.

Charles schooled in Eton and was soon going to university o study law, most likely Cambridge. He was an obsessive football fan and knew amazing details of the English league. Peter was a much more uppity lad who was getting his own education at Harrow. He was two years younger than Charles was and kept pretty much to himself. He rarely mixed with the local boys, clearly thinking them contagious. He always gave the impression he could not wait to get on the plane back, just like Mary, who though only twelve, was a haughty, right little *mademoiselle.*

Not surprisingly, the threesome was the pride and joy of their parents. The couple showed them off like entries at a flower show, yet firmly sheltered them from their uncouth cousins, who crept and crawled all over the neighbourhood.

"My daddy says every kid's got a gun here," Charles said to Tito the night of the party. Tito had had the privilege of being admitted upstairs on the massive balcony of the mansion, from where they had a grand view of the entire carnival scene. "Do you have one?"

"No." Tito was very conscious of the difference in their English, wondering often if they always understood each other. The Kafara kids were not encouraged by their parents to carry on conversation in the native Ibo and had perhaps permanently lost touch with their mother tongue. But *that* was yet another symbol of their superior breeding.

"My daddy says all you get to hear in this town is: *'Give me all your money'* and *'Bang!'*"

Tito laughed. "Like in the movies; like in America where you live?"

"I don't live in America," Charles snapped. "I live in England. It's more civilised there."

"Anyway, it's not true that everyone carries a gun here."

"He's lying?" Charles looked seriously at him. "My dad's lying?"

"No, no," Tito said quickly. Being locally bred, it was taboo in the native custom to say that elders were lying, even when they were spewing them like lava. "He's just exaggerating. It's true some of the boys carry guns; not everybody."

"Do *you* own a gun?" Charles asked again.

Tito shook his head with restrained annoyance. "Me? No. Never."

Below, by the front gates, briefly illuminated by the fluorescent lighting, was a group of minstrels entertaining on a makeshift stage. Not far from there, Tito saw Ona, a flirtatious but extremely likeable girl of the area, on whom he had the most excruciating crush.

"Your brother, Elo. *He* has a gun." Charles did not ask but stated.

"No," Tito declared touchily though his attention was really on the girl, Ona. She was about fifteen and lived not very far from here. Her mother ran a modest grocery shop just up the road. He saw a lot of her and though they had never spoken, they occasionally exchanged glances.

"Are you sure about that? Elo doesn't have a gun?"

"No, he doesn't." Tito was watching the girl raptly as she talked with a boy he also knew. The boy was touching her and whispering playfully in her ear, about which he was extremely envious. She threw her head back and laughed a few times, seeming to enjoy the boy's company, to Tito's annoyance. The boy whispered some more in her ear, this time for longer. Then he took her by the hand and they slipped into the darker fringe.

"Tell me, I hear Elo is a robber." Charles said, leaning closer and lowering his voice confidentially.

"Never talk that way again about my brother," Tito snapped, turning sharply to. He was peeved enough at Ona's disappearance with the boy. He was deeply infatuated with her.

"Well, everyone seems to be scared of him."

"I am not." He was getting weary of Charles' line of conversation. He had come to hear stories about life in England and America, about football and rap stars and hopefully learn to play some computer games. Moreover, if Kafara had helped Elo get the right treatment his leg required at the time, the poor lad might have made a career of football yet. Piqued, he was making to leave when the crowd on the street suddenly broke out in a stampede. As he tried to figure out what the matter was, he heard the sound of light arms fire and people screaming. There was another burst and then things seemed to fall quite quiet.

Mrs. Kafara appeared shortly at the balcony and anxiously motioned her son back in the house, while simultaneously shooing Tito away without actually speaking a word to him! Meekly, he hurried downstairs and out of the house. It was routine getting the brush off from the Kafaras and usually no offence was taken. It was a prerogative of their status, since almost everyone in the neighbourhood ultimately crawled to them cap in hand for favours.

He soon joined the people that were drawn towards the scene of the shooting. A little down the road, about half a dozen police officers pranced menacingly about. They wielded their

Kalashnikovs, trying without too much success to keep the curious crowd at bay. A police pick-up truck pulled up urgently and its headlights provided a helpful illumination of the muddled scene. He watched police officers lift the limp body of a young man and toss it into the open back at which in one enervating, never-to-be-forgotten instant, he stiffened. Even though one side of the face had been blown away, he immediately recognized that the victim was his brother.

He held his head. It could not be. Why, both of them had eaten the afternoon meal together, the perennial staple of *garri* and *egusi*. Elo had left with a friend of his, saying he would be back for the Kafara carnival. There was nothing to suggest any imminent tragedy, nothing by way of the slightest premonition, not even now on hindsight. It was all he could do to stay on his trembling feet. In a daze, he waded through to the top of the crowd, wanting to make a little sense of exactly what happened.

"This boy you see was a wanted murderer," a police inspector was telling some of the crowd, then spat at the corpse. He was clearly awash with a sense of achievement. "We've been trailing him for some days now. When we finally caught up with him, he tried to escape and we shot him. Just the other day, he robbed a pastor."

At this last piece of information, a gasp escaped the gathered crowd. They shook and bowed their heads. Evidently, if the boy had robbed a pastor, he twice deserved what came to him. He was guilty and did not merit the rigmarole of a court trial. What he merited was going straight to hell. People were pious in these parts. They were also used to summary public execution and the police officers were especially justified in this case. No one robbed a pastor.

Tito stared in disbelief at his brother's body and then at the slaphappy cops. They were like poachers just made a kill at a safari and showing it off. For a mad moment he thought he might lunge at them, scream, kick, bite, do something to vent his rage. Finally he did nothing, took the path of discretion rather than valour, as they say. He knew how little it took for a kid to land himself in the police cells and how little more for him to get an execution in the sorrounding bushes.

Still rooted to the spot, he watched the police van soon speed away with the body. He gaped at the patch of blood where Elo had fallen. He tried in vain to stifle the sobs, his body convulsing with the effort. Yet he did not dare utter a whimper of protest or his goose was cooked as well.

The crowd soon began to disperse, leaving him to his lonely grief. No one comforted him, though he was aware of neighbours and relatives hovering at a discreet distance, their eyes boring into him with curiosity. None of them dared to grieve or show any sympathy with him but he could quite understand that. Everyone was self-conscious about the cops and their informants. No words could ever describe the sorrow of that awful night. The sadness was profound, the sense of loss infinite and the helplessness total.

He knew that by now the eyewitnesses could barely restrain their urge to narrate the episode in the gossip rounds. After all, Elo *did* have a reputation in the neighbourhood and not everyone must have known that he was no more than a common thief. Even those who did would be keener to tell the tale of his shooting and the size of the fish increase with every telling. If it was not for the grievous hurt, he might have felt the burning shame.

His thoughts turned nervously to their mother, who was at home in bed. She had been to the hospital the day after Elo's return but was still very ill. She was not in any condition to attend the ceremony at the Kafaras'. Soon, one of the many busybodies around would surely take the news of her son's shooting to the sick woman. Even though she always frowned at Elo's willfulness, she dearly loved her first son and this might finally kill her.

"Elo! Otito!"

From the tiny bedroom came the woman's languid voice. She had heard the sound of gunshots and naturally wondered if her sons were all right, though without undue apprehension.

Tito was home in time to hear her weak calls and quickly rushed to her bedside. He looked at her and yet another knot came to his throat. Beads of sweat had the appearance of warts on her face, which was gaunt from the endless fevers.

Thankfully, it was dim in the room and he could hide his tearglazed eyes from her. In her fitfulness, she had pulled her cloth to her waist and her breasts hung down both sides of her spare chest. He flinched and pulled the cloth reverently back up. She said something but the sound of Kafara's electricity generator only a few yards away muffled her weak voice.

"What did you say, Ma?"

"I had a dream," she whispered. Her breathing was laboured. "I saw Kosi. She did not look well. I am so afraid. I hope she is alright."

"She is fine, Ma. I'm sure."

"I heard gunshots," she recalled. "Where is Elo?"

"He must be somewhere around," he lied and turned his face quickly away.

"You two must find your sister," she charged.

"She'll be back one day, Ma," he mustered, still averting her eyes. He was going to break down in tears. It was all getting too much for him.

"For my funeral obviously," she riposted with attempted humour. "It's been three years now. Only God knows if she's even alive."

Tito nodded somberly, blinking back a tear. "God will keep her alive."

The woman paused to gain sufficient wind and went on.

"I dream these dreams all the time. I'm sure they mean something . . ."

"They're only nightmares, Ma. It's the fever." He wanted to leave the room the way he had never wanted to leave a room before.

"But they're signs, my son," she maintained and then squinted for few curious moments into his face. He looked askance, but even in the poor light, she appeared to notice the glistening in his eyes. "You don't look fine yourself." She adjusted her self upwards. "What is it?"

"Ma . . ." He was losing control, feeling the umbilical pull, the not-so-distant memories of her warm embrace when he had had cause to cry and seek her bosom.

"Are you alright, son? You know if anything happened to you, I should kill myself . . ."

"It's not me, Ma. It's Elo."

"What about him?"

If he did not blurt it out, talebearers were sure to beat him to it. With tears suddenly streaming as from a broken dam, he threw himself into her frail arms and told the suffering woman how her son been shot in the street and died.

A short while before the shooting, Obi Tansi had been providing hilarious entertainment for an inner circle of John Kafara's friends. Obi commonly did this sort of thing simply by being himself, an honest to God alcoholic with an irreverent, giddy, good humour.

He was mates with most of those gathered there in the private lounge, which included quite a few prominent men of industry, the professions and government. The chief judge of the state, Jonas Malife had been a primary school classmate. Incredibly, they were said to have been inseparable in early boyhood. A small, dapper man in a Savile Row suit and bowler hat, gripping a cane and a Havana, Malife was seated next to Kafara. He was now many worlds removed from the lean, drunken man in the faded *ankara* jumper.

"I'll tell you something about old Jonas," Obi had been saying to the indulgent VIPs, who chortled tentatively but were game for a laugh. His tobacco-browned fingers held a cigarette that had burned to the butt. He swayed like a willow tree in the breeze, an emptying cognac in the frail clasp of his armpit.

"What now?" someone mirthfully wanted to know.

"I will tell you what you need to win your case in his court." A ripple of laughter came from all around the room but the listeners were more bemused than comprehending. "Don't get me wrong. Old Jonas will never accept bribes. He is not the sort of man that money will buy. No way." The chief judge smiled patronizingly and sipped his drink. "But a woman will do the trick."

"How do you mean?" Kafara prodded impishly from the edge of his seat.

"I mean a big, fat woman," Obi said waggishly. "Big bum, massive udders. *That* will get you the verdict even against his mother."

Jonas Malife stiffened, turning as grave as the proverbial judge. He clearly did not relish Obi's sense of humour anymore, boyhood mates or not, drunken or not. If you asked him, he had never really had much stomach for the man's inanities and certainly did not appreciate the ready guffaws that came from the other men. Looking quite piqued, he made to leave but Kafara was quickly on his feet to remonstrate with him.

The chief judge was indignant, perhaps unnecessarily so because, as one man pointed out, they were all friends after all. Most of them went back a long way and the fact that Obi might have lost a few marbles down the line was not news to any of them. Besides, regarding his proclivity for big women, Obi had not said anything they did not know already.

Still, Malife was at the point of leaving and his police orderly was officiously stepping to, when a group of women burst in, excited and rattling all at once. Everyone turned to the lippy talebearers, who managed in the end to inform them about the shooting of Obi's son. The men had heard the gunshots a while ago, though it was muffled in the cosy seclusion of the private lounge. They had been reeling from laughter listening to Obi, preferring to get on with the burlesquing efforts of their bawdy, drunken old buddy.

In spite of his fogginess of mind, the message that his first son had been shot pierced through to Obi sharper than a burning spear might. For one long, painfully sober moment, he held his head and let out a pitiful, chilling cry. Then he crumbled and passed out.

Age of discovery

The giant, old bells pealed their final calls just as Tito turned into the school gates. The elderly, grey-haired gatekeeper was uncommonly punctual about shutting them, but not exactly because of his application to duty. On the contrary, his favourite students were the latecomers, who he took bribes from and let past. The latecomers were very glad to grease his callused palm rather than get the flogging from callous form masters and so he made good gate takings. This morning, Tito managed to slip through the shutting gates in the nick of time, a feat that upset the old man no end.

Christ College was all bright and gay today when usually it was quite dim and gray. It used to be a well-heeled school back in the days, the creation of Irish catholic missionaries. It was set in a vast expanse of land, about which there was some grace that induced an illusion of seclusion from the wild town outside. Those early fishers of men had to have been in real estate too.

The missionaries and colonists were long gone and like with most institutions, standards had taken a nosedive since the country's independence. The school was a shadow of itself now but a lot of whitewashing had gone on in the past few days. Today was the regional secondary school sports finals, which begin on these grounds in a few hours. The country's flags of green and white fluttered in the breeze and almost everywhere one looked, banners, ribbons, buntings and garlands hung. Ten schools would be participating in the fiesta, competing in athletics, volleyball, basketball and football.

Tito was disappointed not being picked for the school football team. The strict coach always complained about his irregular attendance at training. The man was unimpressed by Tito's wistful narrative about how he had to work after school as an apprentice mechanic to put a little money in the family piggy. The boy explained in vain about his invalidated parents; how his mother had been diagnosed with osteomylitis and needed some advanced treatment; how his father had suffered a partial stroke and now morosely sat out the days under his beloved banana trees.

"If you are not training, you're not playing!" the coach would rap.

School uniforms were suspiciously clean today. Almost to the last tot, students turned out in sparkling, bleached, starched and blued whites. Belts and sandals gleamed with polish, while many seniors wore after-shave. Clearly, the hopeful encounter with the visiting girls was responsible for much of this sartorial obsession. Otherwise, most of the students were about as keen on the games as they were on calculus or manual labour!

Last year's games, hosted by rival Metropolitan College, had seen some violence, and the Ministry of Education had threatened to call this one off. However, some officials, especially the influential principal of Christ College Mr. Dazie, pleaded and eventually got the benefit of the doubt. Mr. Dazie, being practically the guarantor of the games, spent much of the morning assembly decreeing the best behaviour.

He was a very stern man with deep-seated facial wrinkles. The gravity of his *visage* was however offset by a rather comical gap in his front teeth, through which he forever hissed invectives at the students. The frolicsome students nicknamed him *Red devil* because he was partial to a crimson safari suit that was threadbare in places. Also, he could get tempestuous and was known to have once bitten a student in anger.

"The reputation of Christ College is at stake today!" he cried. "Our integrity is on the chopping block! Our whole future is at a crossroads!"

Many clenched fists shot up in the air—the tender and the sinewy—saluting the theatrical principal. Much of the ovation was prankish but most of the students were genuinely grateful for Mr. Dazie's championing of the games.

"Any one," he warned relentlessly in his quivering high pitch. "*Anyone* caught acting in any way to bring the name of this school to shame shall be expelled! And *that* is a guarantee." He paused cannily as the assembly considered his decree in rumbling murmurs.

"He is very serious about this," vouched Tito's class prefect.

"I am sure he is," Tito shrugged. He had no opinion on the resolve of the red devil one way or the other.

"Mr. Dazie has done so much to keep the games alive. Last year at Metropolitan was a disgrace."

Tito looked curiously at the prefect. He was a studious and bespectacled chap, who he knew not to be particularly keen on sports. "Were you at Metro last year?" he asked suspiciously.

"No," replied the prefect. "Were you?"

"Yes."

"What unspeakable things happened there," the prefect went on nonetheless. "Students even indulged in *sex*."

The principal was still wading through the morning's admonitions. ". . . and God save that student I find leading any of our female guests astray."

"I can't wait for the football game against Metro," said Tito. He was barely listening to the principal.

"I couldn't be bothered with you sporty types," snorted the prefect. "You get too big for your boots, breaking school rules and all."

"We sporty types do a lot for the name of the school," Tito said advocatively.

"You get poor grades," insisted the prefect.

The principal had just concluded his piece and as was his habit to do, stalked off. With both hands clasped behind his back and head grievously bowed, he painted an ominous picture indeed.

It was the turn of Housemasters to take centre stage, after which came the prefects, each one attempting in various degrees to replicate the principal's depiction of stern carriage. Shortly after this customary parade of strong men, the gathering of students dispersed to the classrooms.

It was an unspoken privilege in the unwritten constitution of the school that on this day, no formal classes were had, although the students were still required to stay as much within the walls of the classrooms as possible. There, they huddled in cliques and in youthful voices, engaged themselves in animated conversation.

The prefects found it a most taxing day, having the very daunting task of streamlining scores of exuberant rascals into the accepted behaviour. At Christ College, tradition was venerated and things were supposed to be done in the old ways as much as they could. Under the watchful eyes of fastidious Mr. Dazie, it fell on the officious prefects to refresh the students' memories in matters concerning the school's canons of conduct. However, it was not easy following in the genteel Victorian pretensions of the school's founding fathers. It was in fact impossible. Nigerian society was no longer an experimental farm of the British Crown with the local elite of public school alumni as guinea pigs. Trying to replicate Eton here was a grand illusion. Law, order and the economy had all but broken down in the bad post-colonial society. Bad society produced bad men and bad men bad boys. Bad boys filled the schools and they certainly did their level best to buck the system—or the lack of it. They did all the unthinkable things that Mr. Dazie railed against, graffiti writing, bounds breaking, pot smoking, girl-chasing and much more.

The contingents began to arrive by early afternoon. The considerable overhead sun was warded off from the makeshift stands by roofs of freshly cut palm fronds. In the relative shade, the students arranged themselves behind their school flags and standards.

The students were in high spirits, no doubt mostly for the respite from boring classes. Two lads from Victory High clowned around on the freshly marked track but shortly, one of their prefects chased them off. If those had been Christ College boys, they would be feeling the end of Mr. Dazie's rubber whip on their behinds at assembly on Monday.

There was a great deal of wagering among the students. Though the popular currency was soda, ice cream and yoghurt, some of the *bad* boys bet real money. The smart money in the 100 metres was on a sprinter from Victory High called Chuka. He had won it last year and the haughty hint from his schoolmates was that he was pre-occupied, not with this local meet, but the upcoming national championships.

Tito was sure that Ona would be here somewhere in the red cluster of her school's contingent. The girls of Rosary College sat properly in their section of the stands, demure in their red pinafore over white blouses. It was a well-regarded school, esteemed far beyond the municipality. People of superior breeding favoured it for its pedigree. The *nouveau riche* and successful gauche local traders simulated high class by wangling admission there for their daughters. For male students from all around, however, Rosary College was less an academic haven than a romantic paradise, where they might indulge their adolescent fantasies. Since the girls were the plums of the region, there was naturally some intense rivalry among boys to pick them. Understandably, girls from the other schools were quite piqued about this.

"Tito!" someone called and when he turned to, it was to see the school's athletics captain. "Do you think you can get changed?"

"Into what?" Tito looked at him with some hostility, still smarting that he was not in the football team.

"I want you to run in the 100 meters. Our chap is down with malaria. He can't make it."

Tito shook his head. "I can't, either." He was disappointed that it was not a chance to play in the football match, at which he would have jumped. "Man, such short notice. You want me to make a fool of myself?"

"I'm not asking you to *beat* Chuka," the captain quipped. "Just stand in for our boy. I know you are a decent sprinter."

Half an hour later, he was careening off the marks with seven others. It was a field of strong runners and the crowd roared them on. Even staid Mr. Dazie broke protocol, rising from his seat to root for his boy.

"Go on, boy!" he exhorted. "Go on!"

"You just watch our Chuka go now!" yelled his Victory High counterpart to him over the din. "Watch him go!"

However, it was Tito the Christ College boy beginning to catch the eye at sixty metres, visibly cutting the early lead of the favourite from Victory High. By seventy metres, Tito was doggedly at Chuka's heels and the star from Victory High was glancing anxiously over his shoulders.

A great excitement befell the crowd as the underdog first gained on, then caught up with and then gradually began to inch away from the top dog. The students of Christ College raised their voices to fever pitch, urging Tito on. Chuka kicked with all his strength, his pride and status thoroughly threatened.

Tito's temples pounded and he grimaced with supreme effort. He could see the tape now. It was probably five meters or so away but from the threshold of pain, it might have been five *kilometers*. He glimpsed Chuka from the corners of his burning eyes. They were almost shoulder-to-shoulder but he was possibly ahead by a hair's breath. He sensed he was on the verge of something and curiously had time to be amazed at himself. He had to be virtually flying to stay in stride with a known hare like Chuka, who was making a desperate fight of it.

Seconds later, he was striding over the finish line ahead of everyone. He had conquered the invincible Chuka. He cocked his ear to the riotous cheering coming from the Christ College end and could not believe it. He threw himself to the turf as much with exhaustion as incredulity. He knew he was a decent sprinter but just how had he managed *this?* He lay there, trying to get his breath back and take it all in, thinking that though he would rather have been on the football team, this sprinting thing would do just fine right now. A jubilant crowd of Christ College boys was soon milling all around him. Then suddenly, the sight of Ona in their midst took him completely by surprise.

"Hello," he mumbled, scrambling ponderously to his feet.

"Hello," she smiled. She glanced over her shoulder. She was in the company of another Rosary College girl. "I am taking a big risk coming over like this. I just had to make sure it was you."

"I have to make sure too!"

"Didn't know you were a star."

"Thank you." A star! He was chuffed and tongue-tied. He noted yet again how incredibly pretty she was. "I don't know what to say. We have never really met but I feel as if I have known you all my life. My name is Tito."

"Mine is Ona."

"Who doesn't know Ona?" he gawked unabashedly. He was really looking at her feet, averting her curious eyes. He took in her beautiful legs and her very well turned ankles.

"This is my friend Adeze," she said about her pretty, light-skinned companion.

Just then, the games master and the captain materialized, both most unwelcome if you asked him. They wanted him over where the rest of the contingent was and so with the greatest reluctance, he excused himself of the girls.

"Will I see you later?" he asked quickly.

She nodded and he watched her turn and hurry away, his heart skipping beats in worship. His eyes trailed after the statuesque hourglass figure, ogling at the dainty balance of her carriage on perfect legs. She was surely the cutest girl he had ever seen. He wished that the brief episode had lingered.

Another great roar came from the crowd. No doubt, someone had scored a victory in some event and would soon be the object of everyone's affection, however briefly. *The whole world loved a winner.* Appreciative of that and not resentful in the least, he enjoyed his cameo and waved back to the people waving, including Mr. Dazie, who few had ever seen quite so animated.

●

He had a friend named Francis, a professional automobile mechanic, with whom he worked after school hours at *"Papa Joe's Mechanic Workshop."* They were the same age and shared the tacit brotherhood of the hard up although Francis always managed to convey an ironic self-assurance, a near cockiness quite unexpected of a peasant son. Tito admired him greatly for this, presumably because Francis's *sang-froid* was the very opposite of his own self-effacement.

Francis worked in the mechanical section and although he was a junior mechanic, he was regarded as the most knowledgeable of his peers. Anytime he had a job to do, he would seek out Tito and make him watch as he went expertly through the motions. Tito himself was no slacker at getting the hang of things. He was a very eager learner and keenly watched the older hands as they tried to give new life to ailing automobiles. Increasingly, he looked forward to the constant clangs, whines, whirrs and roars of engines, machines and tools. It was becoming the very stuff of life.

Papa Joe, the owner of the works, was a genial giant in his mid-fifties. He was a very dark man with red lips and a head as bald as a baby's butt. He had lived and worked in Germany, about which he was extremely proud. He was always quick to point to a framed diploma in his name from a polytechnic in Stuttgart. Through a combination of people being genuinely impressed with his credentials and an actual knack for the job, the workshop received constant custom from up-market patrons. He did little work himself lately, except when his experience was particularly required, or if he needed the exercise. Mostly, he would be seen walking about the works in his blue overalls, chain-smoking cigarettes.

All the sections of his works were under roof, which meant that work went on whatever the weather. This was more than could be said of most of his competitors, in whose *al fresco* garages work usually halted when the rains were heavy.

Francis had a friend called Skido, who he could never speak highly enough of. Tito had never met him but from Francis' account, Skido was not much older than they were. He was only eighteen but owned *three* cars and lived in a large flat with proper bedrooms, rug on the floor, cable television, stereo and air conditioning. One evening after work, Francis finally took him along to see the rich, young fellow. A sign outside told them to take off their shoes and walk onto the rug bare feet. He was in the living room with three young girls playing rap CDs, sipping drinks, eating pizzas and generally lounging around. One of them was Adeze, Ona's friend from the other day at the games.

"Hello," Tito said cheerily to her.

"Hi," she replied without much spirit, which he took to be a sign that she was self-conscious.

Skido was pre-occupied watching a football game on ESPN and appeared considerably distracted, if not exactly irritated, by the arrival of the mechanics. He waved them perfunctorily to seats.

"What's on?" Francis asked breezily, sinking into a sofa.

"The Champions' league," Skido replied tersely.

Skido was obviously the big hero and acted so grown-up. He was even starting to grow a little moustache, which would hopefully put some welcome macho in his cherubic face.

"Who's playing?" Tito asked. He was keen on European football like millions of Nigerian youths, though he could not keep abreast of it as much as he would have wanted.

"Kingford versus Conquista," the host replied without looking at him "Bashir Hassan scored for Kingford but Conquista just equalized."

Tito's mind went inevitably to Elo and that photograph with Hassan. After Elo's killing, he had searched for the picture among his scanty belongings but didn't find it. As it was obviously of great emotional value to him, it was possible that Elo had it in his pocket when he was gunned down. Each time Hassan had the ball at his feet, Tito imagined how easily Elo might have been out there too and soon he was getting more misery than enjoyment out of the game. Still, he tried to focus on it. It was a fine international game of football and Skido was very absorbed in it.

Skido owned an automobile workshop himself but specialised in body jobs and since it seemed people would always hit each other's cars, a lot of work apparently came his way. The amazing thing was how young he was, Tito was thinking but the resentful thing how so patronizing he acted. He got the distinct impression that Skido did not care too much for Francis and barely tolerated his intrusion. He discerned that Skido would rather have been alone with the football game and the pretty, pizza-eating girls. However, if Francis noticed this, he did not show. On the contrary, he made himself very comfortable and helped himself freely to the freebies.

They watched the gripping game, instinctively taking sides with the English champions Kingford, since they had a Nigerian in their side. They were therefore crestfallen when Conquista took the lead and further so when the Kingford manager substituted Hassan.

"What a stupid thing to do!" Skido yelled, kicking the air in front of him. *"Now* they'll surely lose the game."

Nevertheless, Kingford were a fine team and near the end, they scored through their famous forward Wayne Starr, forcing the crack Spaniards to the draw.

With the tense game finally ended, Skido eased up and for the first time, gave them both more than a glance. He looked quite intently at Tito.

"Oh." Francis said, taking the cue. "That's my friend, Tito. We work together at Papa Joe's."

As Skido grunted an acknowledgment, it took Tito completely by surprise to see none other than Ona emerge through a doorway. She was yawning and rubbing at her eyes as she had apparently been sleeping. He watched her stumble over to Skido and fall pertly in his lap. Skido's eyes lit up as much as Tito's stared.

Ona exchanged wry smiles with Adeze. Skido kissed her cheek and ran his hands fondly down her smooth back. She did not betray more than the vaguest acquaintance with Tito. No one would guess they had ever spoken.

He had seen her just once since the day of the games. They had arranged a date at Macky's, a rundown joint that young people favoured. They had sat down to some hot dog and ice cream and then played snooker and listened to some loud faddish music from the busted speakers, all of which entailed quite a financial sacrifice on his part. He had told her of his long-standing admiration, how he longed to be her lover. She had accepted his propositions and assured him of her fondness for him. She was soon entering boarding school, she had said. She had joked how it was probably her parents' idea to keep her chaste. He had held her hand, walked her a little distance and then given her fare for the bike hike home. It was impossible to imagine that this was the very same girl. He got a trifle petulantly to his feet.

"We are leaving," he said to Francis.

"We are leaving?" the latter shot him a quizzical, uncomprehending look.

"Yes."

"Aw." Francis was very much at home. He was chomping on a large morsel of pizza and seemed quite puzzled by Tito's sudden decision but got slowly to his feet nonetheless. Skido dug in his back pocket and produced a leather wallet stuffed full of bills. He slid out a few and extended to Francis.

"Here," he said benefactorily and acted friendly for the first time. He appeared more than pleased with the idea of their departure. "Go find yourself a nice time with your friend."

The boys took their leave, Francis doing so reluctantly. He had obviously not had enough of Skido's place, quite understandable in view of the hole called home into which he would soon be crawling. Still, he welcomed the warmth of the street after the freezing air-conditioning of Skido's living room.

"This is the last time I am coming here with you," Tito told him sulkily as they walked.

"Why?" Francis was counting the crisp spanking-new bills.

"God! You don't even notice when you are not wanted," Tito grumped. "Just look at the way he paid us off in front of those girls."

"You might have declined the money then," Francis riposted, done with counting it.

"I *would* have," Tito snapped with a rising voice. "If you were not so quick to take it."

"It's not too late," Francis said, cannily offering him half of the money. "Here."

"Keep it."

"What-?"

"Keep it." Tito quickened his pace to put some distance between them.

"Alright, I'll keep it," Francis called after him tauntingly. "But don't change your mind and ask me for it."

"Not on your life," Tito swore. He had felt like dying from the minute Ona walked into that living room.

"What's wrong with you, anyway? Are you jealous of Skido because he's rich and only our age?"

"He's not our age. He's eighteen, you said."

"We're almost seventeen. What is the difference?"

"And you haven't said how he makes his money."

"Who cares how anyone makes money? Grow up, my man. *This* is Nigeria."

Tito waited to cross the street. He was never one for a shouting match and never had a glib or caustic turn of phrase.

"Just go away," he said wearily.

"Perhaps," Francis said with a stinging laugh. "If your father had been as smart as Skido, you might be enjoying the good life now. If he wasn't such a hopeless boozer-"

A bee might not have stung Tito more and before Francis could say Skido, he was on the end of a crashing punch that felled him to the dirt road. Dazed but dogged, he scrambled to his feet. He shook his head to clear it; he was game for a scrap but Tito was going to press his advantage and did so with a stiff fist in the belly. The blow took Francis' wind right out and brought him to a cringing crouch. Remorselessly, Tito proceeded to upend him with an uppercut to make a prizefighter proud.

A thin crowd had started gathering to form a cauldron for the street fighters, not attempting to step between them. If anything, there was manic expectancy in their faces. Tito glowered down at Francis, who was now on his fours spluttering and spitting some blood. Seeing his pal that way, he felt his tenseness slowly begin to dissipate and decided that he had made his point. Maybe from now, Francis would learn a little respect for his father, who a *hopeless boozer* though he may be, was still his father and commanded his loyalty, however undeserved.

"Come on." He grabbed Francis by the arm and hauled him to unsteady feet. "Let's go."

The crowd began to dissolve, evident disgust in their manner that a potential duel to the death had petered to a pantomime of soppy camaraderie.

Francis winced with pain, feeling his stomach and temple. Tito was suitably sorry but clearly, no apologies would be forthcoming.

"Are you alright?"

Francis did not answer. They did not speak until they reached the doorsteps of Francis' home, where he fished out Tito's share of the money that Skido had handed out.

"*You* keep it," Tito said, declining it once more, but this time with less acrimony.

A Season of goodwill

Coming into Onitsha, the stranger had to really tune into its unique wavelength. That might be said of just about any other place on earth but in this case, it really helped to be forewarned. One certainly needed to be forearmed to resist the shocks of living in the rude, old, riverside town.

Approaching the town west by Asaba through the steely majesty of the Niger Bridge, the stranger might be impressed at far sight. A jungle of medium-rise buildings formed a jagged, low skyline in the distance, which might perhaps suggest a somewhat chaotic order in the imminent town. About that, he would only be half-right; right about *chaos* but dead wrong about *order*.

The grandness of the mile-long bridge in the near horizon might cause him to anticipate an elegant boulevard at the end of it. He was likely to imagine a graceful entrance that would not be out of place for a town of its age and history. But he would be sorely disappointed when the first thing he saw was a legion goats bleating and blahing in captivity. His welcome party would also include scores of poultry and a swarm of timid nomads trading them roadside. The stench of it all would hit him with the force of a gale and it showed his single-mindedness if he did not turn back there. He might later regret his tenacity when he discovered that this ugliness was not one-off but enduring.

In Onitsha, money was not just the stuff of life but the whole reason for it and the means of 'making it' knew no bounds. People did anything to get their hands on it. They craved fame and fortune in the most disingenuous ways. Sure, the same might be said of most other places but again, it paid to keep it well in mind. A merchant hit paydirt adulterating baby food and the fawning public glorified his success as much as if he had invented the wheel. Tales were common of how people offered servered human heads to witchdoctors so that they could turn them into treasure by some voodoo chemistry.

People would hardly venture out after dusk. If they were not mugged or murdered by marauders, they might be decapitated or disemboweled by *vigilantes*. Talk about the devil and the deep blue sea. Certain places were very no-go after hours and the visitor was intrigued how casually people reeled off these theatres of crime as if they were tourist landmarks. He was bewildered how people rushed to beat the dusk danger line as though the underworld issued official notice of its itinerary. He might almost imagine the hoodlums readying themselves in front of mirrors, even dabbing on some after-shave while sprucing up for the evening's rendezvous with victims. Talk about *organized* crime.

A tiny kingdom of the West African savannah, Onitsha was founded in the seventeenth century. By the nineteenth century, it had become an important missionary and colonial outpost of the British. Converted by priests of the Catholic and Anglican churches, then commercialized by merchants of Bristol and Liverpool, it promised by the turn of the twentieth century to be a pearl in the West African sun, a showcase of the British resolve to civilize the crude African native. But in the very end, it turned out a disappointing cement jungle, populated by carefree people dwelling conveniently among pollution and corruption and resigned to the onset of disease and decay. It burst at the seams with coarseness and all the early promise went sadly down the smelly, open drains. Trade practices went the same way, very different from the days of John Holt & Sons of Liverpool. Even though the colonial merchants did exploit the natives, there had been a hint of honour among the thieves. Now commerce was in the hands of the basest cutthroats, most of who would make Shylock shy. Morality was optional while piety was obligatory. There were probably more churches here than anywhere else on earth.

Fugitives from across the Niger fleeing the feudalism of the Benin king had settled the town in the seventeenth century. The love of liberty, they liked to claim, brought them here. However, by the turn of the twentieth century, aboriginal Ibos from the interior bush began to arrive and encroach on the newfound freedom. Mainly crass traders and menial hustlers, they were later to profit so much from Onitsha that six decades later they had outnumbered the landlords. The latter seethed with resentment at this and turned up their noses at the intruders, blaming them for all their woes. They condescended to them and barely tolerated their presence, peeved that they were only here to suck the udders of their fecund land. They likened the strangers at best to leeches. Now, leeches were a nuisance but they were not totally without their uses. Who might otherwise have been their drawers of water and hewers of wood? Still, they would never be forgiven for deforming their picturesque town, filling the place with chaos and a wreckage of artless apartment blocks. The collapse of social order was total but to native dismay, this gaudy state of affairs seemed to be the *very* pride of the crude strangers, which all made for a marriage of great inconvenience.

The landlords saw themselves as divine people, not unlike the way the Hebrews of old Judea did. The puniest native like Obi Tansi sat nearer the kingdom of Heaven than the mightiest of the immigrant denizens. Yet in reality, they groaned under the dead weight of the immigration and by the 1970s, they were drowning in the unceasing stream. They strained against their despair and tried to fight it off by their haughtiness.

In desperation, they prayed to guardian saints and the long-dead Irish priests that had brought Christianity to the kingdom. *What must old Bishop Patterson be thinking now in the heavens? Bishop Heerey would surely be rolling over in his grave.* With such pathos, they missed the old days. They pined for the colonial times, which had given them superior breeding and the head start, which was the envy of the neighbouring hordes. The colonists and missionaries had raised elites of *civilised* Africans to advertise the benefits of European values. In Spanish and Portuguese colonies, they called them *assimilados* and *emancipados*. In English territories, they were more cuttingly dubbed *trousered niggers*. They trudged to school on weekdays and mass on Sundays. They used cutlery and aped the Queen's English. The natives of Onitsha were proud to have been among the first guinea pigs of Victoria's experiments. They duly went to school and served mass, learnt to speak English and Latin, used cutlery and drank tea with their pinkies up. They became catechists, teachers, doctors and lawyers when the aborigines were still beating their first paths out of the mangroves.

They sure were an opinionated lot, these people of Onitsha. They shrugged it off as only natural that the first President of Nigeria, Dr. Azikiwe should be a native son; that he should inspire the entire African race, help deliver them from colonial rule and give them a sense of pride. They used to say he was a superhuman. He did not merely walk on water; he visited the ocean depths and hobnobbed with aquatic deities. They likened Onitsha to Jerusalem. They were emphatic that they were the chosen people and that Azikiwe was the *messiah*. When the white catechist was not within earshot, they equated him with Jesus Christ.

The immigrants, on the other hand, were greatly gifted in graft. More servile to Mammon than to Jehovah, they soon attained economic superiority over their more scrupulous but supercilious hosts. As soon as their ship came in, they could not wait to get their own back, having suffered the latter's disdain for so long. Still, a bitter suspicion stayed with them that nothing could ever assail the massive ego of their landlords.

For all the money in the town, people lived in frightful conditions. Gleaming Mercedes cars and new-fangled Japanese autos crept out of virtual cesspits. State-of-the-art gadgets graced the most dingy mangers. A roasted pear seller would tend her delicacy right next to a garbage heap and fight doggedly for space with wretched mongrels. A health worker was as likely as anyone to be her best customer.

For years, people dumped garbage in the open drains and by now, most were clogged for good. Therefore, when it merely drizzled, intense floods followed, swirling in places like rapids and tumbling in some others like falls. The floods ran fast due to the town's being on a steady slope to the Niger. All the rubbish in town was washed onto streets and drowned bodies were a common find. It was one place, about which it was especially apt to say that it never rained but poured.

•

Once the stranger had adjusted to the ragged rhythm of the town, its calm at Christmas time, instead of serene, was rather eerie. It was a national creed that Christmas had to be spent in one's native town and as most of the inhabitants of Onitsha did not really *'come from'* there, it turned into a ghost town during that time. Still the landlords treasured the ghostly calm and every Christmas they wished the evacuation was permanent. Only days later, their hopes were dashed, for by the second day of the New Year, the immigrant host was surging back, laden with the same loads they deserted with on Christmas Eve.

Obviously, not every immigrant made the Yuletide trip. A handful usually stayed back, though most certainly because of hardship. Onitsha was the land of milk and honey and so if the immigrant did not have enough savings to justify the sojourn, they would rather not face the folks back at home. Christmas was less the season of goodwill than stocktaking time. It was the period when those who had gone in search of the Golden Fleece rendered an account of their odyssey.

Among the folks who frequently stayed back was Francis' family. They had not made the trip in many a year. Francis' father was a mason by profession but even without the depression in construction, he hardly merited the description. He lived a penurious life with his wife and seven children. Francis was the eldest child and practically the breadwinner, although his mother sold minor foodstuff street side.

Tito was always happy to have Francis' company through the season. Despite the skirmish on the day of the visit to Skido's, Francis was still perhaps his only real friend. Ona being in Skido's arms had really been the cause of his short fuse. He had felt some guilt afterwards that he had made Francis the scapegoat for his jealous fit. Anyhow, working closely regularly and getting filthy together everyday in the pits, ensured that their friendship soon returned to normal.

One afternoon just before Christmas, they were working at the bay when a silver grey Mercedes pulled up. Papa Joe leaned out of the passenger side and beckoned to Francis.

"Mr. Taylor's car needs an oil change," he announced.

"Yes, sir."

Papa Joe alighted, as did the owner of the car, a podgy, middle-aged white man.

"We can wait in my office, Mr. Taylor," Papa Joe said to the white man and they went in that direction. Mr. Taylor apparently had a great sense of humour because every now and then, Papa Joe threw back his great baldhead and bellowed with laughter. The boys looked at each other and exchanged wry smiles. They knew the boss was quite a jovial fellow but did not know him to be so forthcoming with the hee-haw. Francis hoisted the car with the ramp.

As it was a routine job, it did not take them too long to get to the end of it. Francis gave it a final once over, nevertheless. Papa Joe was a very meticulous worker and weaned them on that virtue. Francis fine-tuned behind the raised hood while Tito sat in the driver's seat, letting the car idle and watching the gauges. His eyes fell idly on a glossy golf magazine, which he picked up. As he surfed it, he saw a colour photograph tucked somewhere between the pages. In the picture, there were two white men, one of who was Mr. Taylor, sandwiching a black girl. They were all in swimwear obviously enjoying a sunny day at some beach. Something about the girl roused his curiosity and he took a closer look.

With a little flinch, he observed that the black girl in the picture looked uncannily like his sister, Kosi. It seemed improbable but the closer he looked, the more it had to be her. The girl in the picture was a little bigger, a shade more flared out perhaps but there was no mistaking her face with the peculiar heavy-lidded, dark and plaintive eyes. He was getting really excited when he heard the footsteps as Papa Joe and Mr. Taylor made their return to the bay. He grudgingly slipped the picture back between the pages. He looked now at Mr. Taylor with fresh interest. Was he Kosi's lover? Taylor was wearing a pair of jeans and a T-shirt. For his relatively young years, he looked in bad shape with the paunch. However, Africa seemed good for his skin as it was nicely browned.

"All correct?" Papa Joe asked of the boys. It was a pet phrase of his.

"All correct," they chorused.

"Good boys," Taylor smiled and glanced at his watch. "I'm still in good time, Joe."

"Should I make out the bill now?" inquired Papa Joe politely. "Or send it along later?"

Tito thought what a good thing it was to be white. Papa did not mess with his money and most of his customers would never get the feel of their car keys if they did not pay up in full.

"I'll pay now," offered the agreeable Taylor. "Don't want you to come chasing after me."

Papa Joe's great frame rumbled with laughter and the boys seemed not at all sure if Taylor was *that* funny. Meanwhile, Tito squirmed for an acceptable manner in which to bring up the topic of the picture. Papa Joe was around and when he was, there was no getting too chummy with the customers. The big man did not trust his mechanics not to corner them and divert their custom. He normally did not trust anyone. He most likely did not even trust himself.

As Taylor paid his bill and appeared on the verge of leaving, Tito felt a sense of panic. Here was a rare moment, a vital lead to Kosi and he might lose it, so he stepped rather audaciously up to the white man.

"Pardon me, sir but I have something important I would like to talk to you about."

He told the man about the picture tucked inside the magazine and why it was of interest to him.

"She is a girl a friend of mine goes out with in Lagos," Taylor let on, indicating the other man in the picture.

"I want to know how I can reach her," Tito entreated. "My parents are both ill and are dying to see her."

"I'm sorry I can't help you," Taylor said uncertainly, getting behind the wheel.

"Please *do* help me, sir," Tito pleaded but Taylor was revving his car to go.

"Tito," Papa Joe called out sternly. "Leave Mr. Taylor alone."

Taylor waved and drove off, while Tito watched despondently after him. Then, at the exit of the bay, the silver grey Mercedes stopped and the white man beckoned to him.

Taylor squinted up. "May be I can help you somewhat," he said.

"Please, sir"

Taylor scribbled on a piece of paper and spoke as he did so. *"The Mona Lido. The Pub."* He handed the piece of paper to him. "You can find her at these nightclubs. Some nights Jim goes with her."

"Jim?"

"That's the other chap in the picture. You'll find the clubs in Apapa. You can't miss them," Taylor said, and then winked. "Not at nights, anyhow."

Tito read the writing, feeling exhilarated.

"Thank you, sir," he said profoundly, looking up to see Taylor already driving off. "Merry Christmas."

•

On Christmas Day, he summoned the will after much procrastination to go and deliver a greeting card he had bought Ona a week earlier. It was the usual card with the lasting white images of Christmas. The more he looked at the illustration on the card, the more discrepant it seemed. How peculiar thoses images of bob sleighs, fir trees, partridges, pine trees, pudding, reindeer, Santa Claus and snow. Everything hinted that the Christmas season was never conceived with the African in mind. Yet, the most famine-stricken African villagers would emerge from mud huts, exchange these cards and say to one another, *'Merry Christmas.'*

Ona was not home, so he dropped off the card with her younger sister and promised to call later. He had been avoiding her, still smarting from that day at Skido's but ultimately *he* was the worse for it. In fact, it did not even look as if she took any note of his pain. He had seen her a couple of times with different guys, with whom she looked agonizingly carefree and seemed to be having a great time. Now, all he just wanted was to be able to talk with her once again. He would meekly seek a place in her queue of admirers. As they said in an Onitsha proverb, *better to get a hold of just the tail than to lose the entire cow.*

Their Christmas Day treat at home consisted, as it had always done, of rice for breakfast, lunch and dinner. He had made sure to buy two live chickens, both of which he slaughtered quite ceremoniously last night and so there was a bit of lean meat to gnaw at today in memory of the Lord.

His mother, having regained some health but by no means well, had traveled to Awka, thirty miles away. She planned to convalesce there with her only sibling, a sister who was married to a lowly civil servant. As a result, there was only his father for him to take care of over the period and that was surely some respite.

On Christmas evening, he found Francis wrestling with the hood of a beat-up car some distance up their street. Its owner, an obese fellow, was standing by, hands akimbo, impatient and distressed. At length, Francis succeeded in jerking the hood open, which caused him to lose his footing and fall over.

"And *that* is not even the problem!" Francis laughed, wiping sweat from his brow and getting to his feet.

"Get on with the job and quit bantering, you two," snapped the owner. "I have a hundred miles to travel today."

Francis coaxed the engine into hesitant life, shaking his head ruefully. It was in a bad state. The owner leaned in at the window and scanned the mechanic's face to detect his car's ailment from there. He had a bundle of unwashed clothes in the backseat, presumably having made a very late decision to make the Christmas trip.

"Well?"

"I'll test-drive it and see."

"I hope you know your job," the grouchy man growled. The fact was he that was fortunate to get a hold of any sort of mechanic today and would not have if Francis had not happened along.

"Get in," Francis said to Tito.

Francis managed to coax the engine to some form of life and with further determination actually got it to start moving. As it ambled along, the noise from the backfire came in tiny, crackling expositions.

"Engine's dying," Tito shook his head.

"Engine's dead," Francis snorted. "The clown has to abandon his trip."

"He's banking on going with the car, as you can see," Tito said, jerking his thumb at the junk in the back and laughing.

"He'll never get clear of town."

"Adapters?" Tito suggested.

"Where are we going to find those to buy today? Besides, you know what Papa Joe says about adapters."

"Like a man bleeding inside."

Francis soon turned the jalopy around in a wide U-Turn. The engine was losing steam and finding it difficult pushing up the road's incline.

The owner was waiting anxiously for the prognosis, arching his brows inquisitively at the mechanics. As best he could, Francis explained to him the state of his car.

"But I've got to be with my family today!" he protested.

"I understand, sir," acknowledged Francis. "But you may have to go by other transport."

"And leave my car at your mercy?" snarled the man. "You mechanics are always looking for the fast money." He gruffly demanded his keys and all the while cursing, he soon set off on his way. The car was noisy and slow; the smoke from it was a hideous black.

"Nothing for us, sir?" Francis called after him.

"God punish you!" spat the prickly man and went on.

They watched him disappear eventually from their sight and then went resignedly in the direction of Francis' house, chatting and laughing.

Francis' parents, for all their penury, were having a little celebration at home. They were clearly determined to capture a little of what was apparently the essence of Christmas: to be merry, whether there was reason for it or not. They had invited some of their friends over, desperately poor folks like they, who could not decline the offer of a drink, some rice and a piece of beef. A gramophone of the Precambrian epoch cranked out high life music from scratchy, old, vinyl records, to which the low lifers danced with heartbreaking merriness. There was enough drink for everyone, all things considered. Everyone at least had one or two, and although it was nothing compared to what it would be at the Kafaras later, it could have been worse.

"I'll buy a CD player next year," Francis swore almost pathetically, to which trouble Tito did not think he needed have gone. Their own gramophone at home served these days as a rather majestic home for mice.

A live band soon very audibly struck up a tune at the Kafaras in the next street. The amplification effectively drowned out the little party at Francis' but it did not dampen their humble spirits and they generally had a good time. Nevertheless, there was an unspoken understanding that things would be hastily rounded up to allow everyone try to get into Kafara's fortified grounds. It was there that most of the men hoped to get drunk and go stumbling merrily home later.

"Man, can't you drink something stronger than Coke for God's sake?" Francis teased Tito. He himself had been drinking a mixture of stout and palm wine. "This is Christmas."

"You know I hate alcohol," Tito declined.

"*Jew man,*" Francis chortled. "You hate to go with girls too."

"No. I have done a couple of times," he protested. It was not fashionable to tout your virginity.

"You don't talk much about girls."

"Talk is cheap, man," Tito shrugged, managing to convey sufficient ennui.

"Well," Francis raised his glass to his friend's face and winked darkly. "This drink is great in case you want to go with a girl."

"I don't plan to go with any girl," Tito stuttered.

"Are you out of your mind? Everyone goes with a girl on Christmas day."

"I broke up with my girlfriend," Tito lied. "I don't want to get involved with anyone else just yet. You know, to let things cool."

"Funny, you never told me about her."

"I don't kiss and tell," Tito said with convincing maturity. "Do you have a girl today?"

"Are you kidding? I have a girl any time I can pay for one."

Tito's eyes opened wide. "Prostitutes?"

"Yes," Francis nodded. "No rejection, no heartbreak."

"You're not worried about AIDS? It could kill you."

"What are condoms for?" Francis whipped a packet out of his pocket, seeming like a fledgling contraceptives salesman. "And one thing or the other's got to kill you, anyhow. Listen, I'll mix you a drink."

Meanwhile Francis' father, who was passably spruced up for the day, was saying something about Jesus Christ, water and wine. He was tipsy and unsteady on his feet but not completely plastered. He would hope to accomplish that at Kafara's bash.

Francis appeared shortly with two glasses and a plastic jug of the touted aphrodisiac. He set these down and poured the foaming brown broth for both of them. He raised his glass to Tito.

"Merry Christmas."

"Merry Christmas."

Tito sipped and contemplated the taste, a sweet-sour tang that was not very disagreeable. He sipped again and set the glass down.

"What do you think?" Francis wanted to know.

"Maybe I shouldn't really drink this," Tito suggested feebly.

"Aw, come on."

"It's not bad," Tito conceded and his friend seemed pleased.

By the time the party broke up, they had used quite a few more glasses of the broth. Soon they were high enough that the adults took notice but today was Christmas and they had considerable license. In any case, the adults were light headed themselves and preoccupied with their adolescent scheme to sneak into the party next door. Although admission rules to Kafara's annual Christmas bash were relaxed and neighbourhood people and the odd passer-by could get in, it was not exactly a free-for-all.

In Kafara's floodlit front lawn, high society mingled and mixed, some already swaying to the music of a uniformed band. Many of the guests were ranking 'government *people*' who did not let anyone fail to note the fact. Even more of them kept arriving as indicated by the wailing sirens of their motorcades, which seared the night. Their details of fearsome police guards were dressed in combat mode but their incongruity at the party did not appear to bother their masters. Rather, they beamed expansively as the guards heralded their comings and goings with bursts out of *Uzis* and *Kalashnikovs*. Whenever they did so, the gawking, slaphappy locals scampered, but not altogether in fright. They did not take the harassment in bad spirit; not even when the guards got more animated and flogged them with horsewhips or stomped them with jackboots. They were far more impressed by what a very important person Kafara was and basked in his reflected glory. It did not matter if they took a beating from the bodyguards. They were star-struck by the important and famous visitors, who had come to show their solidarity with him. It was now confirmed that he was running for governor in the May elections.

The commoners did not think or perhaps even know what a skewed version of the social contract there seemed to be here. In this variety, apparently, an elected public servant was lord and master and his chief function was to act high and mighty. Aloof from the commoners, decked out in finery and cocooned in luxury, he surveyed the sorry subjects with a mixture of indulgence and disdain. From all indications, he got ample satisfaction from his high office and certainly appeared consumed with his self-importance and sense of well-being. In this, the Nigerian politician was infinitely fortunate because it seemed all right with the commoners.

One by one, the VIPs made their way to the bandstand, aides trailing after them with briefcases full of money. With great flourish, they pasted the lead singer's forehead with bill after bill from wad after wad. After just a short while, the euphoric lead singer was almost ankle deep in a pond of cash. The crowd was spellbound. Politicians traditionally told people to tighten belts, how there was no money in the country but no one here tonight would believe that.

"Man," Francis whistled, eyes wide with wonder. The two boys were standing at the front gates observing the revelry. "There's big money in this government business. I think I am going to be a politician one day."

"I don't think so," Tito shook his head. "You're not bad enough."

"Don't be so sure," protested Francis. "I'm quite bad."

"This is all supposed to be our money, man," Tito wondered aloud at the brassy show on the dance floor. It was cruel seeing that pile of loose cash when you were unsure of your next meal.

"Go grab some then," Francis challenged him and laughed. The cheering of the audience heightened. A well-known politician had upped the ante and was tossing crisp dollar bills the way of the band leader, who was now going berserk and singing the man's praise in full throat. "This is insane! Come on, man, let's go inside."

"No," Tito shook his head and swayed badly. The night that Elo died was never far from his mind. It was a festive Kafara night just like this and he felt an unwelcome sense of *déjà vu*. He recalled that Charles Kafara had been speaking very cuttingly about Elo just minutes before the tragedy. What was worse, Charles had had the last laugh, so to speak. After that horrible incident, the Kafara kids and their snooty mother had put even more distance—if that was possible—between the disparate families. As for Kafara himself, he always seemed preoccupied by grand things. He had his businesses to deal with. He had his numerous foreign associates to tend to. There was his political ambition to nurse. He had his children to maintain in public schools in England. He had not the time to get too personal with his less fortunate cousins and nephews. It was sufficient to throw a periodic party and saturate them with food, wine, and music.

An influential politician next took his turn at the bandstand. He was a rotund man costumed in a sequined lace robe that trailed on the ground a couple of yards after him. He caused a commotion by ripping wrapper after wrapper off wad after wad of new banknotes, which he flung high up in the air. It was all too much for the commoners, who stampeded and scrambled after the money as it drifted back down like confetti.

"I'm going to try and grab me some, old boy," Francis said and snickered. "You did say it was our money."

"See you later," Tito said, going down the street and Francis into the grounds. Francis, he could see, was in the mood to party and from all indications, would end up in a cheap brothel. There was a lot of money flying around in the grounds and those politicians would end up paying for his philandering. If so, good. He might have tried to scramble for some himself if this was any other place than the Kafaras'.

He began to feel sick from the drink and realized that he was going to puke eventually. If only it could wait until he was clear of the floodlights. There were so many neighbourhood folks about. He could imagine the amusement it would cause them: Obi Tansi's son, retching from booze in the street, true chip of the old block. But he could not fight down the nausea for much longer and had to hurry to a walnut tree, where he threw up. His head swam and his temples pounded, the veins in them sticking out like live snakes but he was relieved no one had taken any notice. He wiped his mouth with the sleeve of his shirt and straightened to continue home.

He heard his name but lacked the presence of mind to place the voice. Then he turned around slowly to see *her* standing there. She was wearing a mini skirt of black suede and a turquoise Lycra blouse that desperately hugged her body. Her pretty, dark looks were accentuated by the freshness of youth, a picture-perfect mid-teenager *a la mode*.

"Ona," he whispered, embarrassed.

"Merry Christmas."

"Merry Christmas."

"Looks like you have been celebrating quite a bit," she taunted.

"I'm sorry. I had a little to drink. I'm alright. Are you at the Kafaras' party?"

"As a guest," she said pointedly. Many of the people at the party were uninvited. "We are family friends."

"You are?" Tito sounded surprised.

"Well, we are really one of his tenants. He owns the building we live in."

He stole furtive looks at her, feeling shy and tongue-tied. "I was about to leave," he said.

"Do you have a date?"

"Oh, no," he vouched quickly, which seemed to amuse the girl. "Why?"

"Just asking," she shrugged.

"What about you? Where is Skido?"

"Gone to his home town, I suppose."

"You suppose? You broke up?" he inferred rather hopefully.

"Broke up!" she parroted with an infectious, wheezing, little chuckle. "You make it sound as if we were engaged."

"Engaged? You acted very much like *married* people," he grunted with guarded accusation, alluding to the day at Skido's.

"Skido gives me money," she explained offhandedly. "He buys me things, you understand?"

He shook his head. "So what does that make him? Financier? Fiancé?"

"Just provider," she said after a thoughtful pause. There was a transcendent maturity in her manner, which made it futile for him to go on about the other fellow. She could not deny the affair, not that she was about to, and he would only hurt himself talking about it. "A girl needs to have things."

He nodded acquiescently. "I wish I could buy you things too."

"So do I," she said and sauntered on while he followed faithfully. "Do you mind walking with me?"

Did he mind? He was over the moon, although it was a colder and darker night than the bustle at the Kafaras' suggested. Once the floodlights and music had receded sufficiently, it was a night like any other, with nothing to hint that folks had been living for it since exactly one year ago. It was an awkward walk with spells of silence, remarked mainly by the clip-clop of her high-heeled shoes and the chirping insects of the African night. It took them about thirty minutes to get to her place, which ordinarily would be achieved in fifteen or less.

Ona's family lived in one of a dozen apartment blocks owned by Kafara in the neighbourhood. The premises looked quite stark and desolate, as most of the occupants had traveled for Christmas.

"Will you come upstairs?" she asked.

"Your family?" he wondered.

"They are all still at the Karafas'," she explained. "My sister is spending Christmas at my aunty's."

She led the way to their second floor apartment. He followed almost sheepishly, watching her raptly and thinking there was no person on earth he liked better.

It was a fine apartment, much more so than the stolid exterior let on. The walls were freshly painted and hung with some bric-a-brac of lower middle class living. There were wedding pictures of mum and dad and portraits of Ona, and her two siblings at various stages of their growth. Her older brother was studying at the University of Benin, as his matriculation portrait on the wall showed.

She turned on the television and a barrel-chested American evangelist filled the screen, beating his bible against the lectern and preaching in a nasal whine. She switched channels only to be confronted with a dour, pimply-faced sports presenter *with* a speech defect, would you believe it! She acted horrified and turned the tube off.

"You should have a bath," she said.

"Why?"

"You need one."

"And what will your parents say if they were to come back?"

"If you are quick," she said. "They won't meet you here. You smell of drink and you have been sick."

"I'm sorry," he muttered, fazed.

"The bathroom is on the right," she directed. "My towel is the yellow one."

He went snappily into a bathroom so clean that he could eat his meals there. It was very different from theirs, which was an outdoor four-foot square rusted zinc enclosure with a dwarf door and no roof, so that as you bathed, you could chat with passers-by! If he ever made some money, he would buy his parents a ceramic bathtub like this one.

He lathered himself with her soap, images of her raging in his head. Finished bathing, he dried himself with the yellow towel, swooning as he buried his nose in its agreeable fragrance. He looked at his reflection in a wall mirror, wondering just how attractive she found him. He made faces at the mirror, turning this way and that, frowning, smiling, pouting, winking and deciding in the end that he was not bad looking. He was fooling around in this manner when she walked into the bathroom. But for her tender hairs, she was as bare as the day she was born.

Red lights

He left Onitsha in the middle of January by cheap night bus, bound for Lagos. Lately, a foreboding beset him about his parents and tonight as he took leave of them, he had a nagging premonition that he might never again see either or both of them alive. It was always at the back of his mind that they were both as likely as not to kick the bucket anytime.

Ironically, the health of the old folks had quite stabilized in the last month or so. His mother had come back the week before from her sister's and the visit seemed to have done her some good. She was in the best spirits he had seen her since Elo's death. His father still attended physiotherapy at a hospital since he suffered the stroke. Kafara picked up the bill naturally, which made Obi Tansi feel quite important. So Tito's ominous mood tonight was perhaps more down to homesickness than common sense. He had never really left home all sixteen and a half years of his life, which explained the deep attachment he had to his parents.

The dark night did not help his presentiment. A starless night, its blackness was starker still due to a power failure. In a town mortified and sent to early bed by the equal menace of police and thieves, every silhouette raised the goose bumps. The sounds of crickets, the flapping of bats, the languid hooting of owls, all quickened the footsteps.

Few things were as chilling as the Nigerian night when there was a power cut as there usually was. Its eeriness exhumed the horror buried early in folks by folklore. Tales told to tots by moonlight ran deep and stayed with them all the days of their lives. Ethereal fables of the otherworld and its denizens, witches, gargoyles, incantations and potions were taken literally. They set the tone for the African child, much as the Old Testament did for the Jewish, namely that he wrestled not with flesh and blood but with principalities and powers. His pre-occupation on earth was with the schizophrenic battle that pitted *him* eternally against *them*. Life was a war against Death.

The journey to Lagos was long and tedious as the bus was not the best there was. It barely managed not to break down on them only because the wily old driver took it incredibly slowly. After an eternity, Tito looked out his window and watched both dawn and the big city unfold. Already, cars filled the streets. People milled about the sidewalks, spilling onto the streets at the bus stops. Street traders and hawkers were up early doing brisk business.

The nauseous bus eventually vomited them at the Mazamaza terminal, where it seemed all the commotion in the world was taking place. Early voyagers were already buzzing about the busport, the loading vessels blaring their loud horns to announce imminent departure.

Lagos sure was very different from Onitsha but although he had never been to the famous city, he almost felt as if he knew the place. He had heard so many fabulous accounts of it and being of healthy imagination, gleaned so much from its reputation. He knew it was a city of dreams and nightmares and that lives were made and lost in the most dramatic ways. It was still early but he could confirm from the outlines that it was big and sprawling. He felt a rush of excitement, proud that he had undertaken this mission and thinking how happy his mother would be if he did succeed in finding Kosi. He felt very grown up.

His leads to Kosi were the two clubs, whose names Mr. Taylor had scribbled. By now, *The Pub* and *The Mona Lido* were imprinted firmly in his memory. He took it that she was in the prostitution institution, a fact he was not inclined to moralise about at the moment. For girls, prostitution did present a natural escape from the bread line, the same way that stealing did for boys and it was not entirely their fault.

It was daylight when he got to the Apapa district, with no clue where to turn. He however found some pre-occupation in sauntering about the area. Cranes and ship masts stuck out in the near skyline. A great many trucks plied about, ferrying ship containers and surely, the wharf was in the neighbourhood. There was such a number of white people and Asian types. In one hour here, he had seen more of them than he had done in his entire life.

He emerged in a busy high street, which from the look of it was the main shopping area. He gaped at the big stores and the fancy products in the windows. Most of them were closed but even if they were not, he would have no business going inside. He would certainly raise suspicion, fish out of water that he was. Besides, he had to hoard the very little money he had. He turned a corner and saw a building, newly renovated from the look of it, with *Roxy Cinema* emblazoned at the top in red neon. It had been reopened the week before, because the banners and posters proclaiming that fact were still on the walls. He was attracted by the film posters and spent time looking at them. A Western would be showing later on, *The Outlaw Josie Wales*. He loved westerns and watched them whenever he could. He might come back and see this one.

He went by a big hotel with a legion *malams* hanging about its front, hawking international currencies. He curtsied to a cheery, elderly *commissionaire* dressed in a smart green uniform with gold epaulettes. Foreigners came and went. So did an unusual number of young women, all savvy-seeming and used-looking, sex workers from the look of things, who had presumably come to exchange the previous night's take of dollars.

In a clearing a distance further, he saw a group of Middle Eastern type men playing a game of football. Most of them looked in awful shape and were clearly larking about on the Sunday morning. He sat down and watched the hilarious game, in which the players made up for their poor condition with enough spirit, chasing about until their faces were beetroot red. Afterwards, he watched them talk gregariously among themselves, toweling away the sweat from their bodies. They even backslapped one another, gave high fives and congratulated themselves on a great game! Their wives and girlfriends passed them cold drinks from iceboxes. He watched them drift gradually roadside to their parked cars and depart noisily.

He had never had so much time to spare. He would have to pass the hours somehow until nighttime when the clubs might have opened for business. He was unaccustomed to idleness. For almost his entire life, he was used to running a tight schedule between school and sundry jobs.

Finding himself back at the Roxy, he went on in, bought a soda at the counter and drank it quickly. There was a group of youngsters about his age off to one corner, two boys and two girls. They were all decked out in American hip-hop mode—oversize baseball shirts, fake gold chains, Timberlands *et al*—way above the heads of provincial hicks such as him. He moved self-consciously away, feeling no guilt at all, at how envious he was of them.

He submerged himself in the film posters, scrutinizing every line of the credits, wondering what a director did different to a producer, what a gaffer and a key grip were, the distinction between *panavision* and Technicolor. Dominating the poster was a picture of Clint Eastwood, his grimacing tan face of wrinkles and crow's feet like a map of contours on old parchment.

The crowd that was already inside the theatre soon began to exit. They were mainly whites, Arabs and Asians. Carefree children were closely shepherded by doting parents and he glared at them with genuine jealousy. He did not need any reminding of the childhood he had hardly known, the way that these kids would not know what it was to want. If they cried, it was not because they were hungry but probably just to exercise their lungs. Even then, Mummy and Daddy would ask what the matter was, kiss them and buy them candy and toys. They lived in fairylands, Disney lands and wonderlands. *He* lived in reality's bone-dry woodlands.

Testily, he wrestled with the fact that he had no business here. However, as the new crowd queued up and he sized up the alternatives to wandering about the neighbourhood some more, he made up his mind to get in the theatre at least to take the weight off his feet. He had never been in a cinema like this one, dark, cosy, and air-conditioned. He flopped into an upholstered seat not far from the youths he had seen earlier in the lobby.

The Roxy was very different to Broadway, the one cinema back in Onitsha. Broadway was open roof and if it rained, the rowdy patrons stampeded for any kind of cover. They sat on benches of crude concrete slabs that left the buttocks feeling as though they had been administered local anaesthetics. Patrons who arrived late at the Broadway usually made life unbearable for the early birds inside, hurling sticks and stones over the walls at them. Those inside would hurl back the missiles and more rabid action than in a Jackie Chan film would begin.

Tito fought the chill of the unfamiliar air-conditioning, yawning, stretching and wringing. Bravely though, he tried to follow the flick, the story of an outlaw with a score to settle. He managed to still have his sanity by the time the outlaw, nursing a bullet wound but with vengeance wrought, finally rode into the sunset to stringy soundtrack. As the credits rolled off, much of the crowd was already shuffling towards the exits.

"Race you to the door!" shrilled a blond boy to a bigger one, presumably his brother. The smaller boy ran clumsily down the aisle and the bigger one chased half-heartedly after him.

"Do be careful, love," their mother cautioned, a string-beanie, freckle-bound woman. She and her husband looked at each other and smiled with pride. Tito grabbed his bag and in playful leaps, bounded down the sloping aisle alongside the smaller boy. The boy looked up at him and grinned, showing his braces. The mother noticed this and went to great trouble to break up the budding game. She grabbed her son proprietarily, chiding him lightly and brazening out Tito with a most forbidding stare. The small boy looked at him, then plaintively up at his mother. He had been enjoying the game. Then he was lost to Tito in the exiting crowd.

Like an zealous observer at an observatory, he arrived early at the Mona Lido to take up position. It was about 9p.m. Things did not really get swinging until midnight, someone said, but he was not leaving anything to chance.

The club was a converted warehouse on the corner of Calcutta and Creek Roads. In the daytime when he first passed by, it was a very busy crossroads. It was choked full with the criss-crossing traffic of the bristling habour district and no number of traffic wardens could control the comings and goings in the area. Yellow passenger buses—actually converted light goods vans—hustled ferociously for the endless stream of commuters. They were given a good run for their money by commercial mopeds and rickshaws, which buzzed about the area with the nuisance of bluebottle flies. People actually fancied the mopeds more because only they could get around the notorious traffic gridlock.

By nightfall, the crossroads underwent an amazing transformation. The partying inside the Mona Lido had spilt into the wide, lit street and it was now one big pleasure plaza. Across from the club, there were about a dozen crude woodsheds, in which cheap drinks were sold in deliberate competition with the expensive liquor offered inside. Thrifty clubbers would shake their bodies to their hearts' content inside the club and then emerge outside for drinks that had a realistic price tag.

Girls came in droves and an unlimited variety. They dressed to flaunt their bodies, many stopping just short of stripping nude. Some of them were astonishingly gorgeous but that was to be expected, since Apapa was a Mecca of the sex business.

The girls' main concern was the whites and Asians, whose favourite hangout the Mona Lido was. Sailors were highly prized. They regularly came ashore from the ships, still quite all at sea from every indication and sorely needing the girls to help them adjust briefly to life as landlubbers. The girls, needless to say, were up to it and as one batch of sailors departed, another berthed and famously willing to pay for the play. Girls who had made a catch proudly showed them off before leaving, exhibiting a touchingly genuine sense of professional achievement.

Tito bought a soda from a matronly woman at one of the sheds. Girls came to the shed with handbags or a change of clothes for safekeeping. They sat around briefly and threw back a few tots of cheap local spirit. They gave themselves a once over in a cracked wall mirror before stepping across into the club for the night's work. Anxiously, he scanned every face in his vista. He was mindful that he had not seen Kosi for a long time and she might look a little different from before.

He watched a fight break out between two girls. It was over the rights to a Dutch sailor, who stood aside looking quite bemused and flattered at being the cause of the affray. A Dutch sailor was a great catch here, more so than a Thai sailor was, for instance. Shortly, a passing police patrol settled the matter by picking up both girls. The policemen would extort some money from them later. It was a food chain, the sex business. As the police patrol left with the duo, the sailor was immediately besotted by a fresh bevy of luscious, solicitous girls.

Dope sellers made brisk business just down the street and users enjoyed a relative freedom to indulge their habit. They were given some latitude by the neighbourhood cops but occasionally there was a raiding patrol from outside the precinct to keep them honest. Girls took a break from dancing and soliciting to go over and smoke a joint or two. Pimps, thieves, junkies, gigolos and gays mixed, chatted, argued and flirted. Good-naturedly, the guys took the mickey out of the girls, with whom they shared a close fraternity. They danced on the street, the music from the club's high performance speakers coming loud and clear.

A tall, dark, busty girl stepped out of a taxi, in which there was a white man in the backseat. She leant in to kiss the man's cheek and shortly the taxi left. She then came across to the shed where Tito was. She acknowledged quite a number or warm greetings from boys and girls before ordering a cheap gin and lime. She was striking, breezy and effervescent and seemed well liked. She lit a cigarette. Her close-cropped Afro glimmered with the sheen of hair oil, while large, philtery eyes smouldered in the dark. A short, gold lamé wrap barely skirted her rampant hips and a plunging, black jersey blouse permitted a brave look down a precipitious, gleaming cleavage. She presented a very stirring sight indeed. No wonder folks back home spoke of Lagos in the same vein as Sodom and Gomorrah. With girls as riveting as this on the loose, it was easy to see how a young man might lose his way.

He eyed her furtively. Somehow, she reminded him of Ona and this made his mind wander back to the unforgettable Christmas night in her bathroom. It had been his first time. Ona, on the other hand, had obviously been at it for a while. She had led him on and he had followed. She had guided him to the climatic conclusion, at which he was certain the earth moved. Moments later, her parents had come home from the party and he had leapt into his clothes, out the back door and disappeared like a thief in the night. He still relished the encounter, wishing it would happen again soon. How he loved Ona.

"May I ask you something?" he spoke at length to the night girl, forcing himself out of the reverie. She eyed him coolly. "There is a girl I am looking for. I wonder if you might know her,"

"Wha' she call?" She spoke with a *patois* of some sort.

"Her name is Kosi. Kosi Tansi."

She cocked her ear contemplatively, and then shook her head.

"Sorry, dunno anyone like dat. Wha' she look like anyhow?"

"Like me," he declared, at which she was amused. "She looks like me. She's my sister."

She laughed indulgently and regarded him sidelong. *"Let me see. Do I kno' any girl da' look like you?"*

"Do you?"

She pulled on her cigarette, exhaled slowly, shook her head again and smiled. *"Nuh."*

Someone caught her attention across the street. He followed her gaze, which rested on an Asian type man getting into an SUV. She hurried to her feet and quickly crossed the street to the man. They seemed well acquainted and spoke for a couple of minutes. She got in with him and they left.

He stayed at the shed all through the night, although his vigil was sprinkled with snatches of sleep. As day began to break before his heavy eyes, his disappointment mounted at not having seen his sister. Oddly, he also felt downcast that the girl with the *patois* never returned.

The silvery hue of early dawn and the quite sudden appearance of heavy traffic jolted him into the new day. He had witnessed night turn to day and he had blended along. In Onitsha, that would surely be because of a funeral wake. Here in Apapa it was because people were celebrating life and the living. He was impressed with himself that he had recorded a worthwhile experience.

Already the yellow buses, mopeds and rickshaws had begun their rowdy rounds. Together with the streaming commuters, they would ensure another chaotic day, if the day before was anything to go by.

His duffel bag slung over his shoulder, he joined the early risers and started walking in the general direction of nowhere. He had even less money today. Staying the whole night across the Mona Lido had been at some cost. He had bought drinks and some food to give reason for his stay in the shed. He had to be thriftier today, since there was no knowing when he might see Kosi.

Monday morning and the city were bustling. Lagos people did not waste any time getting going. At the big department stores, shoppers were already calling. *Even* at a jewellery store down the road, there was a considerable crowd. What sort of people bought jewelry first thing on Monday morning?

Getting to the field where he had watched the Middle Eastern men play yesterday, he set his bag by an orange tree, which provided a groovy shade and looked inviting for a quick nap. He sat there gazing idly at the traffic, the shoppers and street people. A subtle breeze was blowing and he soon dozed off.

When he woke up about an hour later, his bag was gone. Looking around fretfully, he saw a pair of urchins who looked just like they might have done the deed. He thought about accosting them but then saw another couple of scamps who did not seem up to much good too. The whole neighbourhood was crawling with rough boys. Cursing, he advised himself to keep that in mind. Now, he really *needed* to find Kosi. He had lost all his money and had no change of clothes. If he did not find her, he was in for a tough time in the big city. Even going back to Onitsha would pose a real problem.

That night, at the end of the longest day in his life, he made his way to the other club on his short list. The Pub was a groovy dive on Marine Road run by an English couple. It brimmed with lively white patrons, whose faces glowed from both the lighting and the drinking.

Coquettish black girls worked the saloon and set upon the coveted white men. The latter rummaged gleefully and enjoyed a leisurely pick of the bevy, among who were some truly outstanding beauties. The white men knew what life was like in Nigeria, what one solitary dollar meant to these local girls, who looked so alluring in the night's coloured lights but lived in unbelievable deprivation by day. They knew how the girls would literally kill for a white sailor and his dollar. As a result, every ruddy-nosed, bleary-eyed white man here felt not just like a king, but the entire International Monetary Fund.

The sounds of laughter carried over the loud music, to which a dozen or so girls moved sensuously on the small dance floor. They danced facing a mirror wall and admired their own figures and steps. They had their backs to the on-lookers, presenting them with a great view of their suggestive forms.

The place was filled with smoke from the cigarettes. Servers clad in skimpy skirts went back and forth with the stream of orders. A blond, red-faced man was smooching a girl in a corner, running his short, thick hands all over her. Tito, square hick that he was, found it notable that no one took more than a glancing notice of them.

He mingled with a number of boys he recognized from outside the Mona Lido the night before, pimps, pushers and junkies. Even though none of them knew him, he took some shelter in their midst and ducked any prying server, who might note that he was not buying drinks. The drinks were expensive as might be expected anywhere in Africa dedicated to the pleasure of white expatriates. The cost of one beer here could feed him an entire day.

He saw her walk in, the girl with the *patois* from last night. Tonight she was mesmeric, dressed in a strapless, red, silk chiffon evening gown. The dress may not have been *haute couture* but how the men gawked, the way it clung in a skin-tight fit to the sensational swells and curves of her voluptuous figure.

A tall, white man tailed proprietarily after her. His manner suggested an intimacy with her that obviously left him a pleasantly disposed fellow. They went to the bar, the man seeming very chivalrous and inquisitive after her needs. They chatted warmly, touched and laughed and one might easily forget that their relationship was that of prostitute and client.

At a point, she glanced his way and saw him looking at her. She furrowed her brow and then flashed him a look of recognition, for which he was grateful. About twenty minutes later, her escort rose to take his leave. She walked him outside and was shortly back in the club, presumably to be in position for the next proposition.

"Hi, handsome," she winked and sat down at his table.

"Good evening."

"Yer no' drinkin'?"

"No," he shook his head.

"Why?"

He averted her eyes. "I don't have any money," he said candidly. Apart from this girl, he had no one to talk to.

"Why yuh here, then?" she chided lightly. *"Dis a night club, my man."*

"I told you yesterday I was looking for my sister."

"Yeah, right," she said tongue in cheek. *"Yer sista, dat's right. I rememba."*

"You don't take me seriously?" he asked dispiritedly. "Well, someone said I should try looking in this club."

"Wha' can I say but wish ya the bes' luck?" She seemed to take a good, long, almost studious look at him. *"Wha' yer name?"*

"Otito," he said. They had not introduced. "But everyone calls me Tito."

"Das a nice name. Drink sumthin', Tito," she offered. She extended her hand and they shook. *"Name is Precious. I'll pay, don't ya worry."*

"Thank you," he mumbled shyly and averted her eyes again. "But what I would truly like is some food. My bag got stolen and all my money."

"Poor boy," she purred. *"In dat case, ya've to go somewhere else 'cos the food 'ere is no' for us, kno' wha' mean? Very expensive."*

"I would never dream of eating here," he swore.

She looked at her watch. *"Am expectin' to meet someone in about fi'teen minutes. If 'e don' show, I'll take ya somewhere ya can eat."* She fished in her purse and gave him a few bills. *"But if 'e does, ya take care o' y' self an' see ya some other time, right?"*

"I don't know how to thank you."

"Forget 'bout it," she said, lighting a cigarette. "'ow old are ya? Let me guess, eighteen, right?"

"Yes," he nodded, even though there was still ten months to his birthday.

"An' 'ow ol' is yer sista?"

"Twenty one."

She all but choked on her smoke.

"Older sista? Ya lookin' fe yer older sista?" She beat her breast and stifled the cough. *"'ad the impression ya migh' be lookin' for a baby sister jus' run 'way from 'ome!"*

"She did run away from home," he said undeterred. "But that was more than four years ago and we haven't seen her since."

A waiter came over to her and said something in her ear. Quickly she went to the phone in the corner. She spoke for a couple of minutes and hung up. She was back shortly and motioned that they leave, explaining that the person she was expecting could not make it.

She took her to a place in front of the Excelsior, where people ate *al fresco* at any hour until the morning. He saw many of the girls he had seen at the Pub. Here, they looked less prohibitive. At the club, they had flirted with the white patrons and sipped with phoney coyness from fancy beers and exotic cocktails. Here in front of the Excelsior, they let their false hair down and dug into the cheap food without the affectations reserved for working the saloon.

Hungrily, he ate up his meal of rice and chicken, drowning it with a soda. As it was considerably late, about two a.m., Precious said she was stopping for the day, which made perfect sense to him. With an openness that was either very admirable or thoroughly despicable, she said how it had not been a bad night overall. She had earlier worked a couple of clubs on Victoria Island with some success, she disclosed. Tito could sleep over in her place, she said, and tomorrow they could talk about how she might help him. There were many young men his age that made a bit of change in Apapa pimping for the girls and the sailors, running dope errands for them and in the process fleecing them with all manner of minor scams. It was more worthwhile than looking for a missing older sister, she implied. *He* did not think so but did not say. He needed first a good sleep.

She lived in the back house of a neatly kept *duplex*. Her room was a trifle untidy but quite clean. A heap of unwashed clothes was on the sofa, a good number of CDs strewn on the carpeting. The tea set that had seen service at breakfast was still awaiting her return.

"Moved 'ere after ma roommate wen' off to live wid 'er fiancé," she said wistfully. *"Couldn't bear livin' all by m' self. We 'ad such good times back there."*

With that and without warning, she unzipped her eveningwear and with such expert languidness, let it slither to the floor. She wore not a stitch underneath and he had to catch his breath at the awesome spectacle of her sculpted bareness. For a moment, he thought he might pass out and to his embarrassment, she seemed very much aware of his discomfiture. A smile twirled about her up-curled lips.

"Y' should git changed y'self," she said and tossed him an *Ankara* wrapper.

A knock came at the door and she hurried to peep through the curtains.

"Shit!" she muttered. *"It's Hans. Wha' he wan' now?"*

She gathered an *adiré* wrapper about her comely body and went to answer the caller. Tito heard the tones of a Caucasian voice. Although he could not make out the conversation but how many reasons could there possibly be why a man should call at a call girl's after midnight? When she sent him on an errand to buy cigarettes, knowing she knew *he* knew she had bought a pack back at the Excelsior, he bashfully took the hint.

He went out of the room and slipped past the white man, who was leaning patiently on the balcony railing. He was a swarthy man with intricately tattooed arms, who he had seen at the Pub. The man smiled conspiratorially and even winked at him, much to his annoyance.

Hans—damn him—stayed over an hour at her place. Tito had to sit around in the dark street across from the *duplex*, fighting off the mosquitoes while waiting him out. He felt a curious resentment, about which he was quite bothered at himself. Precious was all right but wasn't she a whore?

He thought about strolling off to the Mona Lido, where he might as well sit out and keep an eye out at the same time for Kosi. Just as he was about to do that, he saw Hans—*ugh!*—emerge through the front gate and get into a car. Seeing the annoying man leave, he went back quite gratefully into the house instead. He was sleepy, not to mention sulky, which Precious did not fail to notice.

"Sorry," she said. *"Hans' an ol' frien'. We jus' talkin'. He likes to talk."*

"He likes to *talk*," he echoed tartly, his mind on a famous word that made a rhyme with that.

"Yeah."

"Where can I sleep?" he asked sullenly.

"Why you so uptight? I don' really kno' ya, y'kno?" she said, somewhere between irritation and contrition.

"Can I sleep on the sofa?"

"Aw' right," she shrugged. *"I'm sorry, but here in bed with me is more comfortable, I think."*

"It's fine here on the sofa. Thanks. Good night."

"O.k. Be talkin' to ya in the morn', I guess. Good night'."

He was peeved at the blatantness of her calling, wondering how much Hans had paid to make it worth her while. There he was, thinking that Ona was footloose but by comparison to this woman, he now knew she was a virtual nun. What a jungle of men Precious must roam in a year, turning a trick at the drop of a hat. What a hell of a way to earn a living, he thought sadly. He pined afresh for Kosi, wherever she was, sorry that she had to live a life like this too. Soon, they both fell asleep, she on her bed and he on the sofa.

He was awakened by the rays of the morning sun, which the chiffon curtains could not stave. He was used to waking up early, no matter how late he went to bed. He watched her as she still slept, sound as a babe. Amazingly, she even contrived to wear an aura of purity. Right now, she appeared like anything but a whore, which was incredible, since she was so actively one. In case of any doubt, he could even see some paraphernalia of the trade in a corner, garters, a whip and a pair of handcuffs obviously reserved for the kinkier clients. Nevertheless, she was warm, nice and human. She seemed normal in spite of everything and he liked her.

She was bestirred about noon by a knock at the front door and was not pleased at all. She obviously loved her sleep and why not, being a nocturnal creature. It apparently did her a world of good as well because for all the stress of her occupation, she was in excellent condition. She went groggily to the door rubbing away at her sleepy eyes but one peep at the door hole and she was all life.

"Peggy!" she shrieked and yanked the door open.

"Precious!" The visitor hugged her. She was clearly the less extroverted of the two, but her delight was unmistakable as well. "I missed you."

"Jus cum in an' tell me all 'bout Abidjan, love bird." They approached the bedroom but just outside the door, Precious paused and lowered her voice. *"Hey, I made me a new friend de other day. A cute, black, baby boy."*

"Precious!" Peggy shook her head incredulously. "You'll never change."

"It's nothin' like dat," Precious vouched, crossed her heart and added: *"Not yet."*

Peggy laughed but when she saw the cute, black, baby boy, she froze. He was seated on the sofa, turning to when he heard them enter the room. Though she had not seen him for four years, how could she mistake her own baby brother? The boy as well was at first rendered speechless by the utter surprise and rubbed at his eyes, the better to take in the sight of her. He almost lost his footing getting to his feet.

"Kosi?"

"Tito." She stumbled forward and clasped him in a long, dear embrace before pulling away to appraise him. He had grown, but the familiar dimpled grin still marked his face. Though she appeared neither overjoyed nor displeased at his sudden appearance, she was certainly nonplussed. She turned to her friend. "What is he doing here?"

"Y'all don' mean . . . ?" Precious stood transfixed at the turn of events. She gaped from brother to sister, bewildered at the unwitting part she had played in the reunion.

"Precious," rasped Kosi, who was apparently also known as Peggy. *"The cute, black, baby boy* is my kid brother."

"Oh, my God, let me explain, Peggy." Quickly, Precious went over the dramatic co-incidence of their meeting. She looked to Tito to corroborate all she said, which he managed with rapid nods and a wide eye.

"Yeah, right," Kosi said ascerbically.

"I swear," Precious protested, knowing that her friend would not trust her in matters of physical love. Kosi would easily decipher her attraction to the boy's good looks and shy charm. She was always given to impulsive flings with young and handsome boys, which had led to quite a few *contre-temps* in her life. Good that Fate had made Hans come calling when he did last night, she reflected. *She* could imagine what might have been had he not.

Soon, the young women were suitably reconciled and the reuniting siblings went back to rediscovering themselves. They recalled old times as much as they could, saying how much they had missed each other.

In the afternoon, they left Precious' apartment. In the taxi, Kosi disclosed that she had recently begun to live with an Englishman in the suburb and that they were planning to get married. She made this monumental disclosure quite casually, Tito noted with silent alarm. *Getting married to a white man!*

Shortly, they turned into an open gateway into a well-kept compound, in the gravel driveway of which stood a brilliant white Land Rover.

"My fiancé just bought me this jeep," she said. "But I haven't learnt how to drive."

A manservant in khaki hurried from within the house and up to them. He held open the taxi door, pandering to Precious in so deferential a manner that it could only mean she was the mistress of the house.

"Welcome, madam."

"Come on, Tito." She led her brother into the living room, watching him gaping about the large lounge with the clean walls, impressive appointments and expensive adornments. An Arabian sabre with a gilt handle, slid in a minutely detailed scabbard really caught his fancy. The armchairs of dainty soft white leather were so delicate that he was almost scared to sit in them.

What an agreeable sight Kosi now made, he thought. How so mature she had become; a far cry from how he remembered her. She had always been pretty to look at, to be sure, but had understandably been rather down-at-heel. Now she was unbelievably well kept, even threatening to look sophisticated.

"You live *here?*"

She nodded. "I want to give it a try."

"It is so beautiful," he said, though careful not to appear too overcome. After all, Kosi *a.k.a* Peggy had left them all these years and sent not a word and it might have stretched to forever if not for the fluky encounter with Mr. Taylor.

She did not need to be a psychic to read his mind and she seemed pensive and self-conscious. She knew he had almost certainly never been inside any house like this before, except in so far as they used to smuggle occasionally into the Kafaras'.

"How is home?" she finally asked, settling in a chair opposite him.

He shrugged. "Just the way you left it."

"Where are your things?" she asked, ignoring his petulance.

"Stolen." He related the events leading to that, after which she promised they would go shopping for clothes. However, he was itching to ask the question that really bothered him. "Why did you never come back?"

"Funny enough, I was planning to," she said, seeming unwilling yet to delve into the issue.

"You never wanted to see us again," he accused her.

"Don't be silly. I was coming. Soon even."

"Ma is very sick. She nearly died last month. Pa, too. He had a stroke."

"Oh," she caught her breath. "How are they now?"

"Ma keeps lapsing," he said, willing to extort as much penitence as possible. "Pa will never get better. His hands shake all the time and he can't speak properly anymore."

"Does he still drink?"

"Not a drop."

"Does he still jest at funerals?"

"He does not go out. He hardly can speak."

"Well, maybe that is just as well. They can now go find themselves a new village idiot."

"Don't talk like that," her brother chided, a mark of how grown up he was becoming.

"I'm sorry," Kosi said quickly, taking some moments to reflect on things. "A good doctor should do them a world of good."

"A good doctor charges good money," he reminded her, miffed at her annoying logic. "Don't tell me you have even forgotten how we live."

"How on earth could I?" she snapped. "Listen, Tito, I would have come back a long time ago but you know how Pa beat me up that last time. He hurt me so much and you know I was pregnant. You didn't ask about the baby."

"Yes, how's the baby?" he asked compliantly.

"I lost it. I was sick for a long time and in the end, I lost my baby. I could never forgive Pa."

"I'm sorry you lost the baby."

"And just as I was going to forget all that and come home, I get what looks like an offer of marriage, so I have to see what comes of it first. So, tell me. Everyone at home knows I am a prostitute in Lagos?"

He shook his head. "No one knows."

"No one knows?"

He shook his head again and for a fleeting moment, she appeared to him to look curiously disappointed. "I am the only one who knows—as far as I know."

She sighed and reached in her bag to produce a cigarette case, selected one and lit it. Tito watched raptly as she exhaled a lungful of smoke into the living room's conditioned air.

"Want something to eat?"

"Later."

"Drink?"

"Later."

He was disappointed that she smoked. Something did not commend itself about the sight of girls smoking. Then he reminded himself that Kosi was not exactly seeking admission into a novitiate. He recalled the wild girls at the Pub and the Mona Lido and forced himself to remember that those were her fellow professionals.

"Oh," she smiled. "I smoke a little these days."

He waved that aside. "You haven't asked after Elo."

"That crazy boy," she said dismissively but affectionately nonetheless, exhaling more smoke. "How is he?"

"He is dead."

She stiffened and the cigarette fell from her fingers. "Don't you joke like that, Tito."

"Elo is dead, sister."

"Oh, no."

"He was killed in August."

"Oh, God. Oh, my God." It was more than she could bear. Not even dashing herself to the floor and letting out a hair-raising cry or pulling at her hair or the avalanche of tears could stem the sudden grief. Her devastation was as heartfelt as it was contagious and Tito himself broke down and wept yet again as he had done countless times since that dreadful night. He still found Elo's death extremely difficult to come to terms with.

Memory Lane

Remember the day I ran away from home?" she asked him some time the next day.

He nodded. "You were wearing the blue frock that Ma bought for you at Christmas."

She smiled because it was true. "Pa had beaten the daylights out of me and I was pregnant by this man, Ben."

"I remember him. He used to drive up in a Volkswagen and wait for you at the top of the street."

Kosi laughed because Tito's memory served him well. "He told me he would take me away to Lagos and that I would be alright and that he would take care of the baby. He said he was going to marry me as soon as I had the baby, bla, bla, bla . . ."

Ben did make good the promise to take her to Lagos but that was about it. He kept her in a seedy hotel in a windswept part of Ikeja for a week and then said he had to go on a business trip to Lome for a few days.

Before he left, he took her to a friend's place in Surulere so that they could save the hotel costs. It sounded reasonable. She loved him and he was going to marry her. He was going to take her away from the misery of her abusive father and send her to a decent school. Therefore, it was a good idea to be thrifty.

However, no sooner had he left for Lome than his friend—Tommy was his name—began to get fresh. At first, she gave him the polite rebuffs, and then mild threats about reporting him to Ben. However, Tommy's overtures intensifed and one night he burst wild eyed into her room and raped her. In the morning, she bolted from the house. She finally suspected that she had been ditched by Ben but was confounded and shattered that it should be the case. Ben had appeared to love her.

She had very little money. Ben had promised to buy all she needed but had not got around to it. Now she was truly needy. She wandered about the strange streets for hours on end at a time. She had tears in her eyes, shame and guilt in her gait, afraid that she might even lose her mind, not to talk of the baby.

She was grateful when a dark, young man stopped in a beat-up Peugeot, offering her a lift. He inquired after her destination and being unfamiliar with anywhere, she pointed in a vague direction, which the streetwise man correctly recognized as the sign that she had none.

"What do you say we have a drink at my place?"

"Only a drink," she remembered replying tamely. She was grateful for the respite from her perambulation but nonetheless apprehensive about an imminent sexual advance. The man made an abrupt U-turn back up the road they had been cruising.

"Where are you going?" she had cried. Lagos was a big, bad place.

"My place is this way," the man replied, pointing ahead, which seemed enough explanation, since she knew nowhere in any direction.

Idris—that was this person's name—treated her well enough at first and bought her junk food. Then predictably, he later cajoled and ultimately bullied her into giving up her bruised and tired body. She stayed four days at this place, a ready source of gratification for him. She did nothing but lie in bed, watch television, eat junk food and gratify him. Her pregnancy was six weeks along and she felt sick, threw up a lot and ran high fevers. She hurt all over but her host did not appear deterred, only pre-occupied with taking his pleasure at will. He would leave her home alone most of the time, come back late and take her yet again.

On the fifth day, as she was wondering how long this would go on, he informed her that he had to travel to his hometown in the North.

"Why?" she asked, between relief and panic.

"My parents have found me a wife and I need to go take a look at her."

So, just like that, he was gone and she was back on the streets. In fairness, he did give her a little money, and with it, she initially intended to head back to Onitsha. She stood idly at a street corner on Masha for a considerable time, lamenting her life, riding the pain and the fever. She did not fail to notice how Lagos men leered. One man fairly jumped out of his car seat, arching his brows at her in flirtatious inquiry.

She was wondering how to set about the journey home to Onitsha, when four youths in a red Volvo stopped and called out to her. They said they were going to Apapa. Was she going that way? She regarded them warily and saw that they were all about her age, for which she was glad. She got in the backseat, once more happy just to be sitting in a car and taking the weight off her feet. The boy at the wheel was quite handsome and if he made a move on her, she might not mind. Since all males wanted the same thing, it was better to give in to those you fancied.

The boys decided to go to the movies and ended up at the Roxy. By the time the movie ended, dusk had gathered outside and the boy at the wheel was anxious to return the Volvo. His father would kill him if he came home to find his favourite car gone, he said. He had to hurry home before *popsy* returned.

The problem for her was where she would be dropped off, since she had nowhere to go and could not possibly go home with him. The thorn in the flesh for Jimi—the boy at the wheel—was where to have sex with the free girl. In a conspiratorial tone, one of the boys suggested the backseat of the Volvo and the others acclaimed this as if it was a brainwave of Archimedean proportions.

Jimi drove into the local amusement park. She was distinctly unamused because it was dark and deserted. She read their intent but was too weak and frightened to scream or fight or cry or beg them to spare her; which was just as well because the boys were too far-gone in their intentions. Even though Jimi had a little compassion in his manner, he was the ringleader, the pressure of his peers propelled him, and they all went to her one after the other. All this took just a few frantic minutes, after which they dragged her from the car and skidded off at top speed.

She lay there for what seemed a lifetime before she clambered to her feet and walked unsteadily back out the park.

She had not walked a great distance when she chanced upon a group of girls carrying on in the unmistakeably bawdy fashion of whores. They had such untamed manners as they chatted noisily in vulgar slang. They smoked cigarettes, something she had never seen girls do so openly up to that time. Some were about her age, though quite a number would be her mother's.

The intriguing scene absorbed her. For the first time in her life, she was among prostitutes and night crawlers. The vicinity of the Excelsior was very busy and as the night wore on, the prostitutes multiplied. They whistled and called out at men in passing cars.

"Darling!"

"Sweetheart!"

"Honey!"

They blew the men kisses, and then cursed and mocked them if they did not stop.

"Bastard!"

"Idiot!"

"Motherfucker!"

Many of the men however succumbed to the lewd charm of the night women.

Engrossed in the goings on, she was quite startled when a young white man approached her and made a proposition. He had an angular face, dopey eyes and stubble on his cheek, reeked of garlic and chewed gum. Although she could not make out all he said in the strange accent, his request was clear. She had never spoken with a white person in her life and the first time had to be in this compromising circumstance. Would she stay the night in his hotel?

"How much you want?" he asked.

She was hesitant, torn between the dreadful crudity and the dire straits. Moreover, she was not familiar with the scale of charges around there; or anywhere, for that matter.

"How much you have for me?" she fenced.

"$50 okay?"

She jumped at it. Her first *business,* as the girls referred to the patronage. Demis was his name. He was a junior Greek diplomat staying over at the Excelsior that night. He gave her an expensive dinner and red wine and she felt much better. He took her back to his room and was soon all over her. However, less than half an hour later, in a fit of unrequited desire, he was to throw her back out on the street. The reason was a request he made, which she was at a loss how to grant, so strange was it to her. In the staidness of her rural rearing, it had never crossed her mind that the anal passage of the female anatomy served any other purpose than passing on waste. That night, Demis the Greek insisted it had a sexual use. She did not think so. He was livid. And she was out. Life was different in the city.

From that day on, she would hang around at the fringes of the hotel and from there understudy the girls as they shadowed their preys. As time went on, she noticed how the white men seemed quite attracted to her svelte and willowy 'western' figure. They often complimented her discreet sexuality and felt flattered when they contrasted it favourably with the hard-hitting 'African' voluptuousness of many of the other girls. She learnt the ropes quickly. White businesspersons and diplomats were the prime market, followed by a motley mix of Arabs, Asians and sailors. Girls could get as much as $100 on a good night, even $200. Business was not always good, naturally. As with other economies, there were booms and recessions. Sometimes things could get pretty dismal and a girl would jump at $10. As a rule, local black men were to be avoided. They could never match the rates that the white expatriates paid. They would even send a girl away empty-handed in the morning, sometimes with a black eye into the bargain.

It was her luck also that many of her clients liked to play Romeo to her Juliet. Her men generally liked to treat her not like a lay but a lady, a damsel in distress that they were inclined to rescue. They took her to the beaches, movies, clubs, restaurants, casinos and malls, the way they would a proper girl friend. Many times, she felt as if she was truly being courted. Something about her apparently inspired tenderness and possessiveness in men. Several times down the line, she was to experience the emotional dilemma of having to be a faithful whore.

She felt very excited about her new life. For the first time, she was on her own, in charge of her own affairs and did not answer to anyone. Warming to her freedom, she gradually learned the skills she needed to maintain it and was soon making enough money to eat and clothe reasonably well. In keeping with the trade practices, she adopted the *non d' amor*, Peggy and an early return to Onitsha receded into the horizon. Her independence grew very quickly in the city and she ditched any nostalgic thoughts of going back to the insufferable restrictions of home. Since she had already embarked on the voyage of prostitution and was adrift in mid sea, she might as well make the crossing.

She lived in a 'guesthouse' on Calcutta Crescent. Guesthouse was a local euphemism for girls' hostels that came just a little short of brothels. There, she shared three contiguous rooms with a likeable girl called Precious. Precious was from Liberia. She met her one evening lurking around her favourite shade near the Excelsior. She was a stunning, dark, bold and buxom beauty with an infectious *joie de vivre*. They took a strong liking straight away to each other and soon became great pals despite being of quite different temperaments. Precious had actually trained to be a nurse, but having fled empty handed from the war in Liberia, she had very little option than to switch to the ancient profession.

One night about a year after they met, two white men pulled up to them in a Ford pick-up.

"Good evening, lady," the one in the passenger side leaned out and addressed Precious. "Could I have a minute with you please?"

"A one-minute man!" Precious sniggered in her charming patois. *"Aint dat jus' wha' I need!"*

The men laughed and warmed to them.

It turned out to be a fateful night, for that was how Kosi met Jim Stewart. He was a hydro-electrical engineer with a British firm working a massive dam project in Nigeria. The other man, Bill Harding was his friend and a ship captain. They volunteered in the looseness of later familiarity how they had traversed the hotel zone several times, revving up the courage to encounter them.

"Y'all needn't be so shy nex' time, darling," Precious said glibly. *"We're business girls! Ain't it so, Peggy?"*

Sometimes, Precious went overboard with the fizziness. Though not aggressive, she would not shirk a club fight, nor pull a punch if she got into one. She once stabbed a girl who tried to manhandle Kosi. Usually, however, they both went to great pains to distinguish themselves from the gum chewing, make-up-laden, pot smoking, slang slinging, fire-spitting whores of archetype. Nevertheless, Precious was certainly an extrovert and needed reining in at times.

Bill Harding had to set sail for Europe the next day and kept stridently to his schedule. They all saw him off to the docks and he gave Precious quite some money for her troubles.

Jim Stewart kept seeing Kosi afterwards. As time went on, he did so as frequently as thrice a week, which took some doing because they were both very busy professionals. He cared very much after her well-being, going to considerable expense to make the rooms she shared with

Precious quite liveable. He bought her a Persian rug and fashionable wrought iron lounge chairs. He bowled her over with a trendy Japanese compact disc player for her birthday.

As the relationship developed, she found that she could quite get by without having to stick religiously to making the nightly pilgrimages to Ikeja, Apapa or Victoria Island, the sex workers' shrines. This is not to say that she gave up hustling. Just that breakfast in the morning did not have to depend entirely on her working the night before. She could afford to ease up and not be terminally desperate for a dollar.

As time went on, she even began to experience a hint of guilt when she went out on business with clients other than Jim. Even though she would grit her teeth and get on with things, she was uneasy about the lack of professionalism that was creeping up on her. Jim *was* a client, she reminded herself repeatedly. She had a business to do and there was no room for anything but the hardest nose.

"We not in Lagos to look no white man face, girl," Precious reproved her more than once. She had begun to notice the budding love affair and was not impressed. *"We in de city to do a job, rememba?"*

"Jim is quite a nice person," Kosi said with fretful logic. "He has perfect manners. He treats me like a lady."

"All the same, baby," Precious snorted. *"Don' stub yer toe."*

"No shakin'," Kosi reassured her modishly.

Sometime later however, Jim asked her to move in with him. He lived at that time in a flat on Apapa's fashionable Park Lane.

"For how long?" she asked.

"For as long as you please."

That seemed impossible.

"Your wife?" she hedged. Jim did not say much about her but she assumed she was there, somewhere in England.

"If I wasn't divorced," he said sullenly. "I wouldn't be carrying on with you."

Other than a week or so to think it over, she gave in to the suggestion and moved into the flat with him. He made her comfortable and doted on her. He hardly got in her way, as he was often very busy with the dam project. He took her around and seemed very proud of her, even though much to her unease, she was known to many of his friends as a *business girl*. Many expatriates went to the same clubs and generally saw the same girls. She felt awkward when he introduced her as his girlfriend to some of his friends. Some of them had patronized her custom in the past and greeted her with enough insinuation to hint as much. Yet he did not appear to care. Last week, while they were in Abidjan to spend a few days, he popped the famous question.

"My parents would disown me!" she exclaimed in mock alarm. Traditionally, Africans balked at the idea of taking white spouses. This was quite paradoxical, considering the material disparity between the races in favour of the whites and the apparent financial benefits of the alliance to the Africans in general. For club girls, however, the great career move was making it down the aisle—or at least up the registry steps—with an expatriate ex-client. Perhaps the only greater career high was making away with a briefcase full of dollars belonging to a drunken, filthy rich, white john!

The more she weighed things up, the more she reasoned that perhaps hitching Jim was just the thing to enable her face the fastidious folks back home. Jim lived almost as comfortably as she recalled that the rich Kafaras ever did. Only last month, just before they went to Abidjan, they moved into this new detached house on Hinderer Road, not very far from the old flat.

Jim's firm was doing well. They had key Nigerians on their kickback payroll and gave massive bribes to politicians to influence contract awards. Jim had been in the country seven years and was the firm's expert at compromising Nigerian officials, which did not take much doing, to be honest. In fact, *he* learnt much of the ropes from the Nigerians, who were past masters in the art and science of corruption. They conjured one overblown contract after another for his firm and he too got quite personally rich as a result. He proposed they got married in the summer, for which reason Kosi was already planning to travel to Onitsha and introduce him to her family sometime in March.

"I want a real traditional Nigerian wedding," Jim enthused. "We'll both dress up in Onitsha clothes and dance to the jungle drums and drink palm wine!"

"You'll be quite a sight then," Kosi laughed.

"I can't wait to tell my brother Malcolm about all this."

"Will he come from England?" She hoped so. Jim always spoke of his brother. It would look strange from the African point of view if none of Jim's family failed to show up at the wedding. Marriage in Africa was not merely a union of man and woman but an amalgamation of families, tribes or—in this case—races.

"Of course, he will," said Jim. "He's my only brother *and* my best friend. He's got a very demanding job but I'm sure he will be able to get some time off in the summer."

Tito later got to meet his would-be brother-in-law. Jim Stewart was in his mid thirties but he looked considerably older. He had an almost solemn visage and an avuncular air helped along by a receded hairline. It would strike one that perhaps he worked too hard.

Jim was of the icy eyes but whenever they rested on Kosi, Tito was sure he saw a welcome warmth thaw them. That was an encouraging sign because his main apprehension concerning the couple was the circumstances of their meeting. Recalling the girls of the *Mona Lido* and *The Pub* and the white patrons, he was moved to wonder if the affair was genuine. Was the relationship merely firing on the cylinders of raw passion? Was stolid Jim only momentarily overwhelmed by Kosi's considerable sensuous charm? How long would it last before it perhaps wore thin? Jim seemed such a conservative, levelheaded, foursquare gentleman. Didn't people like that normally look on prostitutes with disapproval?

Meanwhile, the man seemed to have wrought such a tremendous change over her. She carried on now with quite a polished air. It was difficult to reconcile her with neither their unmannerly upbringing nor the desperate temperament of the society of sex workers she had enrolled in. Her English had improved beyond recognition. She had dropped out of school in fourth form and had not been such a bright student at that. Jim's shelves full of books and magazines were rubbing off on her. She was unbelievably comfortable with European cuisine, at ease amid the crockery, cutlery, silverware and serviettes. She was so expert at western table etiquette, which had never been a part of their lives. It was sometimes difficult to believe that this was she.

Jim was not someone to stand accused of joviality. He certainly did not go out of his way to be friends but Tito sensed that he was all right really, just reserved. On his part, he responded to the Englishman's taciturnity with some circumvention, for instance feigning a fever to avoid a dinner. In any case, he found it difficult catching the man's turn of phrase when they did speak. This was his first time being on conversational terms with an Englishmen and he was in no position to decipher the peculiar accent, Geordie in Jim's case.

Though he was dour and moody, Jim was quite a sociable sort of fellow and had a wide circle of friends. They were mostly fellow Englishmen, local contractors and Nigerian bank and government officials. At weekends, they usually would drop by and knock back large quantities of whiskey and beer. Kosi's cooking made things even more convivial. Although back in Onitsha, she was doomed to do most of the domestic chores, their low life never prepared her to be a hostess of western-style dinners. Very grudgingly, Tito admitted that the best of their mother's cooking now palled greatly besides Kosi's.

This Sunday afternoon, they had a meal of roast beef and steak and kidney pudding. Friends of Jim's came and went. Precious came by too, bringing along the windiness that Kosi adored, but about which Jim was eminently cool. It would appear that as wedlock with Kosi drew nearer, Jim became less and less enamoured of Precious, who he regarded as a standard-bearer in the legion of sex workers. Nevertheless, he was never impolite or improper with her and was adjusted to the fact that the two girls came some way.

"My friends and I are going to the park," Jim said to Tito. He had a bit of drink and was in a relatively light mood. "We play a spot of football most Sundays. Want to come along?"

"Yes, I would, thank you."

About four thirty, he left with Jim in the white Land Rover for the football park, if it could be called that. It was really just a bumpy piece of earth, which belonged to a neighbourhood primary school. Jim was dressed in replica football colours of Saxon Valley, the English football club. He was considerably out of shape and even though it was possible that he had played a little football in school, it was not very likely. *Most likely*, he would have been something of a swot at school, oscillating *ad nauseum* between the library and the classrooms. Just how Kosi had hooked up with so proper a creature as this man, he could not for the life of him fathom. She was such a tart by comparison. But, didn't they learn in physics that *'opposite poles attract'?*

"You play football?" Jim asked in such a way that it did not appear to matter one way or the other.

"Yes. All the boys play."

"I never could quite play but my brother Malcolm did. He even played a few times for the England Under 23s but he's retired now."

There was a handful of Europeans on the field already. There were also Lebanese. The players were all dressed in replica football colours of European and Middle Eastern clubs. He sat with Jim on a wooden bench on the sidelines, where some of his friends soon joined them.

The men fell into light conversation. It was all quite difficult for Tito to follow because of the peculiar English tongue. However, he understood enough of it to know that the football league of their native England was the dominant subject.

"Kingford are sure to win the title yet again," observed one Denis, a hunched, thickset fellow.

"Getting a bit boring isn't it?" another remarked. "Kingford winning it year after year."

"Well, someone does have to come and *take* the title away from them, haven't they?" Denis said, obviously a big Kingford fan.

"Westbury United is challenging strongly," mooted someone.

"Aren't they always?" chortled Jim, looking in the league tables column of the *Daily Mirror*. "But I can't see them closing a fifteen-point gap now. Not unless Kingford go to sleep."

"Not a chance of that," Denis said. "They are really going great guns, Kingford. The way they are playing in the Champions' league, they might nick even *that* this year."

A swarthy Lebanese came trotting over to their bench, a little short of breath already. The Lebanese side was a couple of men short, so he was going to ask a couple of the Europeans to play on their side. But it appeared that the Englishmen wanted to play on the same side. Jim decided he would just watch, the bit of tipple not having done him much good. Denis, his mate, was sitting things out too, content to follow the football in the papers.

"You play?" the Lebanese directed this to Tito.

"Yes, sir, but I haven't got my football clothes."

"Come. I find you something, if you can play."

He followed the Lebanese man across the field to a shade where they joined his compatriots, who were joking noisily. Someone handed him a replica green shirt of one El-Itihad Club of Saudi Arabia. Some previous, pot-bellied wearer must have distended the shirt and it hung on him as if on a peg, flapping freely about his slender frame.

He did not have football boots but he had on a new pair of training shoes that Kosi bought him the other day. He glanced at his teammates, stifling a laugh. What a contrast they made with the brawny mates he played with on Sunday mornings at St. Charles' in Onitsha. Only a couple of them here were in any sort of football shape. The rest would be more comfortable with meatballs. Nevertheless, it was a *foot*ball team and he was in it.

He enjoyed the surprisingly spirited game. The men soon huffed and puffed, their faces red with the effort as they chased and chased. He had not played for about two weeks but he could do so with ease against these men. He enjoyed himself, putting over on them some of the ball tricks his friends and he tried against one another at St. Charles'. He made some of them look quite hilariously stupid while at it.

His side won the game and he scored the winner to the delight of his mates. They splattered him with wet kisses and sweaty bear hugs at the end of it and he was considerably proud that he was something of a hero. He could keep the great green shirt he wore, they said. He was also welcome to freebies at an ice cream and *sharwarma* joint owned by one of the men on Bombay Crescent.

"That was really good, Tito," Jim said, patting his back, an intimacy that almost took him aback. "You know, you really can play."

Tito smiled shyly. "You can't really tell against this lot," he said modestly.

"True," Jim nudged him playfully. "But you play rather well."

As he later lay on his bed, his body aching sweetly from the work out, he re-lived the almost ridiculous game, relishing all the plays he made and the appreciation of the scant crowd. He went to sleep, a smile about his lips

A Bad day's night

As dusk gathered one Sunday early in March, Obi Tansi sat in his front porch, reclining in his well-worn whitewood chair.

When the white Land Rover pulled up, he put down the *Sunday Times* and peered owlishly over old, horn-rimmed glasses, cocking his head in anticipation of the expected party.

A can of some malt beverage was at his side, where in former days, it would have been a valiant bottle of gin emptying fast in the face of his onslaught. He was in his seventh month of sobriety.

A conspicuous trembling of the right limbs impaired his movement. However, he struggled bravely and as often as possible, propped himself up and sometimes hobbled about with the unaccustomed walking stick. His speech had been markedly slurred, an unkind blow to him, since his reputation was that of a glib, quick-witted fellow, albeit in an inebriated sort of way. His debilitation from the stroke was considerable but altogether not as severe as had been first feared.

Since Tito came back from Lagos last month and brought the news of Kosi's intended return, the family spirit was greatly lifted. It helped that Tito returned with some money and other presents from the runaway girl. As with most poor families, prodigal children could wipe away their transgressions with one good down payment. Needs were so basic that it was unrewarding for the offended parents to belabour the point after that. With some of the money, they had set about some paintwork, for which their house had stood in desperate need for so long. Now, the odd little place was looking bright, if nothing else.

When she saw her daughter alight from the car, Mrs. Tansi having impatiently awaited the return for the past couple of hours, sprang through the front doorway. Letting out a goose-bumping shriek of delight, she ran to Kosi, with hands outstretched, gazing at her in near delirium. Kosi, feeling alternately sorry and happy, found herself in the surprisingly forceful embrace of the frail woman.

"*Nnem!*" the mother sobbed from the relief. "My mother!"

"Mama!" the daughter cried to her mother.

"Where have you been?"

"It's alright, Ma." Kosi flinched at her mother's heartfelt tears and tried to wipe them. Her eyes went over the woman's spare frame. She had always been slender of build but now she was positively emaciated. She felt very guilty.

The man of the house cleared his throat rather loudly in the background, demanding attention from all indications. The women instinctively turned to. For an acclaimed ne'er-do-well, Obi Tansi ruled the women of his family with a steely fist. The reason was his domestic temper. He was accustomed to raising hell in his little domain, no doubt his only means of staking a last redoubt in a world shrunken for him by his low station. His reputation as the jolly neighbourhood drunkard disguised the manic depression that simmered just underneath. This condition was not helped by the proximity of old mates such as Kafara and Malife, with whom he was always unfavourably compared. Staggering home many a night, haunted equally by alcoholic spirits as by the spectres of his failures, he would ensure that his family physically bore some of his pain. He routinely beat his children, only sparing the rod when they became too big for him to manhandle, since he was not a strong man at all. Many nights, his feeble wife was at the end of his venom. Many times, a virtual rape followed a fierce beating, the woman bleating like a goat at the point of slaughter. Neighbours marveled at her capacity to take the assault and showed a dubious admiration for her resilience. Frequently, the neighbours predated by their windows, pricking up their ears for the expected commotion and the ensuing bestial union. Scarcely did they make any real effort to resolve the couple, because they took a twisted pleasure in the entire affair.

Now, sitting almost motionlessly and looking vacuously up at his daughter, Obi seemed to her nothing like the monster she used to know. It was apparent that his days of beating on anyone were over. For a warped moment, she felt a strange nostalgia for his old ways.

"Pa." She knelt in front of him and embraced him delicately. He was porcelain fragile.

He smiled, warmth filtering his staring eyes.

"What a big girl you have grown to be."

"I am sorry for everything." She swallowed a tight knot in her throat.

"It's alright. To see you makes all the difference." His eyes went slowly over her. "How well you look."

Tito was coming in at that moment from school, stopping by the white Land Rover to greet Jim. The latter was sitting at the wheel, unobtrusively witnessing the emotional re-union and biding his time to make an entrance. Kosi had no doubt notified him about the old man's prickly nature. Tito had mentioned nothing about the Englishman to their father, although he had done to their mother.

"Who is that white man?" the father asked, his gaze ranging to Jim.

Kosi spoke haltingly. "He is one of the reasons I came, Pa."

"How so?"

She looked solicitously from one parent to the other. "He is someone who wants to marry me."

"What?" Her father was startled. Some of the old fire sneaked shortly back into his eyes. "A white man?"

"Yes, Pa."

"What country is he from?"

"England."

"Ah, an Englishman," he said, curiously relaxing.

He beckoned to Jim, who presently proceeded to the porch accompanied by Tito. The intending son-in-law offered his hand, which was accepted and they shook.

"My name is Jim Stewart."

"I am grateful that you brought back my child from Lagos," Obi said, affecting his best English inflection.

"I will do anything for her," Jim avowed, nodding and smiling. "Peggy is a wonderful person."

"Who?"

Kosi spluttered. "That is me, Pa," she explained quickly. "That is what everyone calls me in Lagos. Peggy."

"Why?"

She shrugged and smiled effacingly. "They just call me that."

Her father seemed to accept that, which was unthinkable previously. In earlier days, he would have demanded a more satisfactory answer and being fussy at times like those, perhaps laid the rod on her. He would have wanted to know why she should exchange her meaningful African name for a silly one like that.

It was not long before their relatives and neighbours got wind of Kosi's return. She had been a well-liked girl in the area. She had those healthy good looks, which despite being low lifers, Tansi's children were blessed with. She would run errands for anyone. She was keen on school, even if she was not particularly brainy. She went to the local church regularly and was an alto in the choir. It had come as a bit of a shock when the news of her pregnancy broke and many of their neighbours had genuinely missed her when she disappeared.

She spent all that evening receiving the folks that visited her. Most of them came out of curiosity, about not only her sudden reappearance, but also the white man in her company. White men coming to Africa historically did so as superiors and certainly acted the part. The locals, who customarily played the inferior role, held them in the highest awe. A fishmonger from Bermondsey might easily have the red carpet rolled out for him in the misconception that all British men were blue-blooded. When white men hobnobbed with Africans, they only did so with *big men* like Chief Kafara, Chief Justice Malife and their like. It was curious therefore that one of them would have any business to do with peasants like the Tansis.

Kafara was in town, as could be attested by the steady drone of the big electricity generator at his place just up the road. Kosi knew she must make a mandatory visit to him. He was lord of the manor, to whom every knee in the area must bow. His wisdom and approval was always sought before embarking on any course of action. The logic was that he would not be so rich if he were not so wise. Therefore, this whole thing about getting married to Jim, she knew, would have to be sorted out with Karafa in the end.

Tito did not feel up to tagging along with Jim and Kosi to Kafara's. He had developed a deep aversion to their rich cousins since the night of Elo's killing, as if they had anything to do with it. It was illogical, he knew but he had made a firm decision how much he disliked them. He did not feel that anything had happened since then to change his mind. He had a much better idea what to do and that was to visit Ona. It was her birthday today and though he had earlier sent her a card, he had not seen her. It was getting dark but it was not too late to look her up.

Since he returned from Lagos, they had become closer. He had saved some of the pocket money that Jim and Kosi gave him, managing to buy her a couple of jeans and T-shirts. With little remorse, he had also pinched one of Kosi's better perfumes for her benefit. For that, Ona was very happy with him and she demonstrated this by the frequency with which she led him into temptation. Needless to say, he always succumbed without resistance or a prayer. His trip to Lagos and the nightclubs of Apapa had offered him a new perspective on passions, which now gave their relationship a physical intensity.

In spite of that, he retained some disparate feelings about her worldliness. Ona knew more about the facts of life in one nipple than he ever would in this entire life. With a gross sense of misgiving, he understood that the acquisition of that knowledge must have seen her pass through much tuition at the hands of men. Obviously one of such men was Skido, who was not even a real man yet, but had more money than many, which effectively made him more of one than most. Tito had come to adjust to the fact that Ona would never stop seeing Skido. He was very resentful of that but loved her too much and would rather have just a piece of her than none at all.

As he stood roadside waiting for the bike ride to Ona's, a black Peugeot went past, then stopped abruptly and backed up to him. The dark-tinted window of the rear side came down.

"Tito! Tito!" It was Francis in the back seat shouting over the din of the car stereo playing at full watts.

"Man, it's you," Tito smiled and shook hands with Francis, happy to see him as always. He leaned in and saw that it was Skido at the wheel, and then, the smile was wiped off his face by the sight of none other than Ona sitting in the passenger side. To make matters worse, she acknowledged him only curtly, which cut like a knife and caused him a bleeding heart.

"Your friend can come along if he wants!" Skido said offhandedly over his shoulder, seeming impatient to keep going.

"Come on," Francis said, making space in the back seat. "Skido's throwing a birthday party for Ona at his place."

He was numbed, but like a zombie, got in the car. He did so for one solitary, twisted reason: to have Ona somehow in his sights yet. In case he still had any lingering doubts, he was now certain that he was going insane with love and jealousy. It was not enough that he had a gaping wound in his heart; he seemed consumed by a masochistic desire to find out exactly how much salt she would yet rub into the injury.

At Skido's third floor flat, there was a fair crowd of youths partying in the living room. An assortment of drinks and foods was arranged on a long table and it appeared that the party had been on for a while. The youths seemed to be having fun and the sound of their voices and laughter carried far above the thudding music.

Tito took a seat, feeling sick. His eyes trailed Ona's every step but he kept a good distance. She, on her part, consciously ensured to keep her eyes averted from his constant gaze and made no attempt to talk to him.

Skido leaned at the kitchen doorway, looking around indulgently and swigging from a bottle of wine. Everyone called out to him or shook his hands. Every now and then, he went over to Ona, stroked her proprietarily for a few moments and returned to the doorway. He was the epitome of self-assurance, for which Tito felt blazing envy.

Then suddenly, there was commotion. Two young men burst into the living room, wild eyed and livid with fright. Something was happening downstairs. Tito looked out the window. There were four police jeeps in the compound, down from which a dozen menacing police officers jumped. They were armed with machine guns and looked eager to use the weaponry. Expertly, a number of them cordoned the block, while others surged into the building. In a few moments, they bounded into Skido's living room.

"Stop that music!" ordered the leader, a burly, fearsome mastodon of a man with tribal marks on both cheeks. He waved an *Uzi*. "Hands up, everybody! Where is Skido?"

A pair of the police officers went directly towards Skido's bedroom, as though they knew exactly where it was. Shortly afterwards, they came out looking very pleased with themselves.

"Sir, see wetin we find!" one of them said animatedly to their leader.

Tito watched horrified as the police officers showed two .38 revolvers and a packet of ammunition to their superior.

This was a serious situation. No one carried revolvers in Nigeria unless they were in the police, some other authorized security outfit or the underworld.

"Where is Skido?" demanded the leader again. He wore a bulletproof vest over denim shirtsleeves and looked extremely trigger-happy. His dilated eyes darted frighteningly about the cowered crowd. A deathly silence prevailed, broken only by the barking of Skido's Doberman.

Tito briefly caught sight of a mortified Ona looking anxiously in the direction of the kitchen doorway, where Skido had been shortly before the furore. The party host was not in sight. Neither was Francis, he thought with rising alarm. He had no inkling what this was exactly all about but with those .38s somewhere in the picture, they might all get charged as armed robbery accomplices.

The lights suddenly went out and the living room was plunged into darkness but it was not the usual general power cut because lights were on in the rest of the neigbourhood.

"Nobody move!" roared the squad leader as if sure that somebody would. The police officers cocked their guns. They seemed quite jumpy and frightened themselves.

A burst of machine gun fire came from somewhere downstairs, outside. It was followed by a succession of further bursts, punctuated by revolver reports.

The police officers downstairs yelled feverishly to their mates upstairs. More gunfire crackled the cool evening. Then there was a spooky few moments of silence.

"We don' catch dem!" one of them claimed at the top of his voice.

"Everybody *move!*" the leader upstairs barked at his hostage crowd of frightened teenagers. He flashed a torch that only made a wraithlike light, with which his men began to herd the silhouettes in a mild stampede down the stairs. Tito sought and located Ona's outline but she was well ahead of him and he could not reach for her.

By the time they got downstairs, the lights in the house were back on. Someone must have switched off the mains in Skido's block. Probably to facilitate his escape, Tito hoped. Perhaps it was Skido himself or even Francis, he calculated frenziedly.

The crowd of youths suddenly turned in horror as a prone figure was dragged feet first by policemen into their view. Without being morbid experts, they saw that the victim was dead and more shockingly, that it was Skido. His motionless eyes were fixed on eternity and half his entrails had tumbled gruesomely from his ripped gut.

Overcome by the sight, a cry escaped Ona. The dour, ill-tempered squad leader from upstairs turned sharply and slapped her hard across the face with a backhand.

"Shut up!" he spat. "Feeling sorry for a robber, you harlot!"

"That's his girlfriend," volunteered one cop. "I have seen them together a few times."

"Is that so?" the leader leered. He turned to another cop. "Handcuff her!"

Tito winced as Ona was jerked roughly about and a pair of handcuffs immediately fastened about her tender wrists. Reflexively, he stepped forward, remonstrating with her captor.

"Please let her alone, sir," he pleaded. "She only came for the party."

The squad leader swiveled to him, causing him to cringe.

"You came to make party with an armed robber!" he roared. He was a very highly-strung man indeed. "Arrest him! Arrest all of them. Take them all to the station!"

A uniformed corporal hit Tito at the back of his head with the butt of his rifle and he dropped to his knees stunned. A heavy service boot dug into his side and he fell prostrate, gasping. Though dazed, he came instantly to his senses when he saw Francis dragged by the feet along the stony red earth. Almost his entire groin had been shot away, a mass of veins and arteries exposed in a messy pulp. It was surprising he was still alive and surely a matter of time before he died from the ruptures.

He was yelping with pain, his glazed eyes staring up at his captors in terminal fright. The police usually finished off anyone if they made the slightest connection between them and a gun. He was obviously being left alive only briefly and for the usual theatrical reasons. The cops would soon send word to the television stations and he would be made to 'confess' his crimes in front of the cameras. The networks would show it later tonight at prime time. The police would get kudos for a great job and the Commissioner seize the opportunity to make a case for more funding from the politicians. The captive would later be killed in cold blood to bring the case to a close.

A police pick-up truck screeched up presently to the scene, raising dust and and the smell of burning rubber. The squad leader ordered Tito and a couple of the youths to toss Skido's body and that of the dying Francis in the back. While doing so, Tito's eyes locked with Francis'. The wounded boy was writhing from the awful pain, his face sweaty. He groped for Tito's hand. There was surprising strength in his grip still but a melancholy shake of the head conceded that his life was ebbing.

"I'm sorry." His voice could not rise above a whisper. "But I didn't do anything. Please tell my mother that. Promise"

"I promise." A streamlet of tears wound down Tito's cheek.

"I want you to believe me," Francis strained, clearly with all his strength. His weak gaze ranged to the police squad leader. "That Inspector over there, he always took payoffs from Skido. Last week, Skido said he didn't have money. So they had an argument. He threatened he would deal with Skido. I had nothing to do with it."

Tito nodded somberly, spitting aside a teardrop that had reached his lip. A police officer came literally breathing down his neck, prodding him with a rifle muzzle to move it. Two more police vans arrived at the scene. By now, there was a considerable crowd of curious and excited on-lookers from all around the neighbourhood.

Minutes later, the police officers packed everyone who was at Skido's party into the vans and whisked them off to the station. They were all twenty-eight of them, to spend that night in a cell not more than ten-foot square. The cell stank of the scores of in-mates that had passed before them, as well as of their own breaths. If anyone wanted to move their bowels, they only had to go to the corner to do so in a rusted bucket. And were there a lot of upset stomachs that night.

Some time in the dead of the still and balmy night, they heard two resonant gunshots. Without uttering any words to one another, they knew that Francis had finally been dispatched somewhere in the bushes.

Tito cried the rest of the night, notwithstanding his relief that Francis had thankfully been put out of his agony. He re-lived some of the times they shared together, especially the hours in Papa Joe's pits where they forged a bond based on honest, hard labour. Francis was not a bad lad and he worked very hard. He did not deserve to die this way. Papa Joe and everyone at the works would be stunned to learn of this. Even if he had done anything wrong, what were the courts for? If guilty, what were the prisons for? He felt a tremendous sense of loss. That night in the cell was the longest, most bizarre night.

Somehow, morning came. Relatives and friends of the detained partygoers thronged the station from very early, seeking the release of their kin. The police officers did brisk business trading bail. So much cash was transacted that the station seemed uncannily like a bank. Since the cops really had nothing on the youngsters, they were each released upon the payment of a handsome ransom. Kosi haggled over the ransom for Tito's release with an Inspector, who was actually sitting beneath a poster on the peeling station wall that proclaimed: *'Bail is free!'*

On the stony ground of the station front, the cops placed the corpses of the two dead buddies on public display. The stiffening cadavers were browned from the dusty haze off the red earth, while flies buzzed busily about their unsightly wounds. An arsenal of revolvers, shot guns and rifles was conjured and arranged beside the dead boys to leave no one in doubt that they were indeed a deadly duo. Such dramatic exhibitions were typical and most likely, the very same array of weapons would be displayed beside the next set of stiffs. Over the carnage stood an appropriately dog-eared flag of the police and a moth-eaten one of the country, both flapping from rusted poles.

The official word was that Skido and Francis had been killed in a shoot-out; that a car robbery had been traced to them. They had been running a crack car-snatching gang, the police *communique* said. Tito reflected hard on all this. It was quite possible that Skido stole cars. He certainly had more money than he could reasonably account for. But he did not believe that Francis was a part of it because he saw him most of the time and he wouldn't be as cash-strapped as he always was. Francis, he decided angrily, had merely paid the price for fawning after Skido.

It took the sight of Ona to wrench him to some composure. She was on her way out of the station, her parents having finally secured her release. They looked naturally none-too-pleased with her and would be having some strong words to say to the birthday girl when they got home. When their eyes met, she quickly looked away.

Jim looked on squeamishly as people came and went to view the gory scene. Not surprisingly, he was grossly uneasy. But chivalrous suitor that he was, he had to be at the side of his future bride. He had been in Nigeria seven years and had come to expect the unexpected, but no length of stay in the country would make anyone get used to this bizarre scene. The real outrage was that it was almost an entertainment for the public. Tito tried to put him at ease by telling him that it could have been worse for the two boys.

"What could possibly be worse than this?"

"Better it was the police than the vigilantes."

"How's that?"

A dozen vigilantes, he explained, dressed in all black and wearing red bandannas would have dragged the boys through the crowded streets. The vigilantes would be wearing brass chains around their necks with live turtles as pendants, their wild eyes aflame with intoxicants. A lusty crowd of traders, artisans, moped riders and children would trail after and cheer them on. Semi-automatic rifles in their untrained hands, their bodies wrapped in belts of cartridges, the vigilantes would end the procession at a suitable crossroads. With awesome, razor-sharp, double-edged machetes glinting frightfully in the wicked sun, they would decapitate the boys to the ecstasy of the demented spectators. Finally, the dismembered bodies would be drenched in petrol, ignited by gunfire and the macabre circus brought to an infernal end.

Jim shuddered at Tito's accounts of how vigilantes casually meted out the death penalty to mere pickpockets. For all his time in the country, he could never comprehend its people. If there was one last chance for him to have second thoughts about his marriage to one of them, he would suspect it was probably now.

At that point, Kosi emerged from the station and joined them, having sorted out the money matters with the police officers. She dabbed at her eyes with a kerchief meanwhile. It was all too much for her. Jim put a placating arm around her shoulder, bravely setting aside his own horror.

"You're sure you don't know anything about all this?" she prodded Tito during the drive back home.

"I swear," the boy deposed, catching Jim's incisive eyes in the rear-view mirror.

"But Francis *was* your friend," she somewhat charged.

"My *best* friend," he said defiantly. "And he wouldn't hurt a fly."

"You must leave this town, Tito," she concluded after a reflective pause. Francis was beyond all indictment anyhow. "This is a dangerous place."

"I can't leave Onitsha. I don't know any other place."

"You do know Lagos now," said Jim.

"I will be sitting for my exams in July and I can't leave the old people alone by themselves."

Kosi seemed to turn things over in her head. Tito always was a reasonable boy.

"Alright then."

She brooded a long time that day.

Man from the West

Never had there been a day in the lives of the Tansis like that on which the couple got married early in June. Tito could not remember ever having experienced any feeling towards his family remotely resembling pride. However, on the day that Kosi got married to Jim, his heart was nearly bursting with it.

Their small house was set in a tiny space of land and so the crowd of wedding guests, though by no means large, naturally spilt onto the street, creating an illusion of a big affair.

Kafara had at last become the state governor. He had won a landslide at the May polls, which everyone knew was thoroughly rigged. Only the most naïve Nigerians believed that the actual casting of votes really counted for anything at these elections. In this, the Nigerian people were strange accomplices in the manipulation of their destiny by cynical politicians. They accepted without much misgiving that what mattered was not the votes they cast at the polling booths but the wheeling and dealing inside the election commission offices. Preposterously, they even admired the politicians for this.

Previously, Kafara would have merely strolled across to the Tansis for the wedding if he were in town. He would have done so imperiously, to be sure, being the important man of the area. These days, however, a platoon of armed police and secret service men preceded his arrival anywhere, while he was trailed by a coterie of administration types. His large retinue took up much of the Tansis' limited space while the menacing guards shooed away a good number of humble guests.

Kafara had indulgently offered the Tansis the use of his spacious gardens for the event. Obi Tansi was going to jump at the offer, proud to be mates with a governor, but Jim had insisted against it. He said he preferred the tiny house that truly belonged to his wife's family. If Tito had any lingering misgivings about him, that act banished them forever.

Jim absolutely reveled in the exotic novelty of the African wedding. His costume was a blue brocade *kaftan,* in uniform with his wife. On his fair head, he wore a black fez and around his neck, a sequence of agate beads. He was thrilled that those were his wedding clothes and not a tailcoat or a tuxedo. About the only concession he made to white weddings was the white-frosted, four-tier, white fruitcake and the champagne.

A beam of absolute glee dwelt on his face, which was raddled not just from the sun but also the considerable drinking. African weddings were regularly marked by the imbibing of libations along with the ancestors, which he did not mind in the least. His brother Malcolm was in attendance, having arrived from London only the previous night. This contributed no end to his jollity.

His wife was dazzling in a wrapper suit. An elaborately contrived head tie crowned her braided head of hair, showing up her radiant, pretty, brown face. An intricate group of young native drummers goaded the couple on to the dance floor from time to time. The happy guests whooped and cheered as Kosi gyrated to the funky beats with the proverbial grace of a gazelle. Then they fell over themselves in mirth when Jim attempted to imitate her. He jigged merrily out of time and rhythm and achieved the most awkward steps they could ever imagine.

"You don't really *have* to prove that white men can't dance, Jim Stewart!" his wife ribbed him and then kissed his mouth, sending the crowd wild.

Precious was among the guests, as well as other girlfriends of theirs from the Lagos sex circuit. Obviously the bride was not about to turn up her nose at old friends of the sorority just because she was going into retirement. Rather, she was quietly amused that the girls made Malcom Stewart the object of much professional curiosity. Business girls would be business girls and Malcolm was the ideal proposition. He was a stranger, white and presumably well-off. He looked to be in his late thirties, of a good build and a headful of chestnut brown hair. His disposition bespoke a pensive person, who was not given to frivolity, though of adequate humour. He surely could not have failed to notice the flirty girls, discreet as they were in view of the formal circumstances and seemed to take it all in good temper, if nothing else. Tito thought he caught even Ona eyeing up the man.

"Your sister is *so* lucky," Ona remarked at one point.

"Yes," Tito agreed.

"Hooking up a white man, I mean," she specified and feigned a swoon. "All those dollars and pounds to spend!"

Tito considered this and nodded in agreement, though he had honestly not quite thought about the marriage in that stark light. But with the dollar being roughly two hundred times stronger than the naira, it was a pretty practical way to look at things.

"You're right."

His cousins, Charles and Peter Kafara were in town as usual for the summer holidays. They too attended the wedding though Tito knew it must have been with the greatest reluctance. Ordinarily they would not have come within a mile of the tiny Tansi shanty. He could easily picture their mother urging them grudgingly to the event. The incongruous blood ties would have tied her hands and their non-attendance correctly interpreted by folks as a sign of disdain for their lowly cousins. These days they were the Governor's kids and the gulf between them and the Tansis had grown infinitely wider. Tito resented them by that same measure; though it was not as if they would take any notice with everyone else falling over themselves, fawning after them.

Expectedly, Charles and Peter did not eat or drink anything that was on offer at the wedding. Normally they did not eat outside their home when they were in Nigeria. They were sure they would catch cholera or typhoid fever, if not get poisoned. They did however give the appearance of enjoying the gathering of their country cousins, much as they would that of exotic animals in London Zoo, Tito suspected.

At some point, Charles tapped Tito's shoulder. "That other chap," he asked, pointing out Malcolm. "Who is he?"

"Oh, that's my brother in law," Tito replied coolly. "Malcolm Stewart."

"Well, I'll be!" Charles exclaimed, turning to his brother. "It *is* Malcolm Stewart."

"You know him?" Tito asked.

"Yes. He used to play for Saxon Valley."

"Really?"

"Yes," Charles nodded. "He's now a coach at Valley."

Tito recalled Jim having said that his brother played football but did not recollect if he had said at what level. All the same, he was proud that for once, there was something about them that impressed their privileged cousins. The Kafara boys were crazy about football. Their rooms were festooned with paraphernalia of the avid fan—scarves, rattles, pennants, footballs and replica jerseys. They had all the latest football kits, though he would bet they could not get into a girls' side! They had mountains of football magazines, films and computer games. They followed the English league raptly and even more so the European game. They scoffed at what passed for a league here in Nigeria. Charles supported Westbury United, which was always among the leading clutch of clubs in England. Peter was daft about legendary Kingford.

Obi Tansi meanwhile was beside himself with happiness. Marrying off his only daughter—who he had actually *written* off—was quite a turn around. On top of that was the caliber of the groom, a middle class and well-to-do Englishman. He had always revered the ways of the English, particularly the quaint stereotype of colonial legend, complete with *toupeé* and tobacco, replete with culture and condescension. His adolescence was formed in the heady days of the anti-colonial struggle, when Dr. Azikiwe demanded independence from the Crown. However, his fascination with the British had a stronger hold on him than the popular aversion to their subjugation of Africans. He was one of those Nigerians who genuinely thought that the British should have been left alone to civilize the savages. Up till this day, decades after independence, he did not see any reason to change that view. If anything, he felt more vindication with each miserable, passing, Nigerian day. How he wished Azikiwe had not been so agitative against Whitehall, that he had left them to be brainwashed by the Brits. They might have achieved something better than the crude country of today. But who ever took the opinion of an inebriate seriously?

Jim Stewart was the sort of husband he would never have dared dream that Kosi would marry. Jim was infinitely more than she deserved but he was certainly not going to be the one to question his own son-in-law about his curious choice of wife! Kosi might so easily have ended up the hapless homemaker of some illiterate, local, petty Ibo trader. His low degree actually made it insane for him to have hoped for much more than that. Yet, here he was, presiding over her marriage to an Englishman of sufficient means. She would be well taken care of and not suffer any longer, one millstone off from around his neck. It was such a relieving turn of events, especially as Elo's death had devastated him. He grieved for his first son to this day and held himself ultimately responsible for his fate. *And* to think that just the other day, Tito might easily have gone the same way at Skido's birthday party.

He was very proud to be host to quite a few important men. He nodded to the beat of the drummers and looked on as expansively as he could manage, while Governor Kafara lent the prestige and urbaneness he sorely needed. A couple of old mates, now made out good, were gracious enough to come and be with him. One was now a minister in the Federal cabinet, who had once been expelled in their school days for rape! Another, a right old scamp, was now an Assistant Inspector General of Police! And of course, jolly good, profligate Jonas Malife, the state chief judge felt obligated to attend.

Later that evening, the hurly-burly done, Tito and Ona walked Charles and Peter up the road back to the latter's place. Not too far behind the youngsters trailed a pair of armed police officers detailed to mind the Governor's kids.

"Wish I could live here," Ona gushed when they were at the Kafaras' giant steel gates.

"Why?" Charles wondered needlessly.

"For one, to have everything!"

"Like what?"

"Like watch television all day, swim in the pool anytime I want, never worry about power cuts because I have a *big* electricity generator."

"Oh," Charles shrugged indifferently. The difference between him and the likes of Ona and Tito was equal to that between a Prince and peasants. "It's not the only big thing I've got, I promise you."

"She's only joking," Tito said glumly. "Ona's parents have an electricity generator too."

"You call that a generator?" she snorted with a self-deprecation that was either amiable or pitiable. "Can I swim in your pool sometime?"

"Anytime, sweetheart. Can't wait to see you in swimwear," Charles smiled at her, full of intonation. "And you can see my art room afterwards."

"I would love to!"

"I'll show you my etchings then."

"Your what?"

"Etchings."

"What is that?" She shot an inquiring sideways glance at Tito.

"I don't know," he shrugged sullenly. "One of those fancy English expressions, I suppose. I'm only an *area* boy."

The Kafaras laughed and Ona with them but Tito did not see the joke. They said goodnight and the brothers disappeared inside under the eagle eyes of the police guards.

His mood was grim as he walked her homewards. She had a habit of making him feel bad and it did not seem to bother her in the least. She always seemed to take more interest in other people than in he. Even that might have been tolerable if she did not usually appear to disregard him completely. She was an incorrigible flirt, but what could he do? He loved her desperately. He loved her with an intensity that approached insanity. She occupied his every thought, inhabited his entire dreams and colonized his whole mentality, all which he yet camouflaged for fear of rejection. Funnily, she frequently told him how much she loved him but he understandably had his doubts about her honesty. The certainty with which he was aware of her lack of chastity made it impossible for him to feel anything but paranoid about her sincerity.

"What's the matter?" she asked suspiciously.

He stole a glance at her and even in the dark, saw a naughty smile dancing in her eyes.

"You," he blurted.

"What did I do *now*?" she simpered.

He was mute for a few good moments, trying to organize his irritation.

"You always love to put me down," he managed finally. "You are always going with other guys, flirting with people in my face."

She stopped in her tracks. They were almost halfway to her place, which could be sighted in the near distance.

"But I love *you*," she stated and apparently, as far as she was concerned, that ought to be sufficient. He groaned with exasperation but not altogether without some elation as well. How he loved to hear her say those words, whether they were true or not: *I love you.* He squeezed her hands and looked wistfully in her big, deceptively forlorn eyes.

"But do you mean it? You're just saying it."

"I *do* love you," she said and looked him fixedly in the eye. "You are very handsome and gentle and everything; just that you don't have any money. You can't buy me things."

"Like what?"

She shrugged. "I am a girl and I need things. I need shoes and bags, jeans, jewellery; I need bras, undies, and tampons. I have to be like the other girls. I want to be like your sister."

"What do you mean?"

"What do I mean? I mean, I know what all the girls do in Lagos, how they go with the white men. Your sister didn't meet her husband by sitting around in Onitsha with a black boy her own age. That white man is old enough to be her father."

"Why are you saying this to me?" he was crestfallen again. She always took him on these roller coasters.

"Because I love you." She kissed his cheek and hugged him dearly, rocking his senses further. "But don't give me too much close marking."

She sniggered and he found himself smiling despite being so depressed. For him, such was the force of her personality.

"No close marking," he nodded pliantly. It was a current slang among teenagers in the town. *Close marking.* "I suppose I have to take it or leave it?"

"Since you put it that way, darling," she purred in his ear and then brushed his lips with hers. "I suggest you take it."

"Alright," he sighed listlessly. "I guess I *will* take it. I could never leave you."

"That's my baby," she whimpered. She snuggled up to him and laid her head on his chest and began to encourage him by body language to take the initiative with her.

There were quite a few advantages to the frequent power cuts that plagued the country. Naturally, it benefited those craving the cover of darkness for clandestine reasons. Being temporarily in that category, they kissed, cuddled and groped there on the street corner, with little of the usual apprehension about passers by. There was a strong hint of urgency in her manner as she led him literally by the hand and he followed almost tamely. Shortly, they disappeared into an alley that was even darker than the street.

The next day, Charles paid a thoroughly unaccustomed visit to Tito. The purpose was to show him a copy of an English football magazine. The splendid full-colour publication showed page after page of gripping football stories and pictures.

In this particular issue, which was about two years old, there was a story of Malcolm Stewart. Avidly, Tito discovered that his brother in law was quite a notable figure in English football. He had been a useful player before retiring prematurely about eight years ago owing to injury.

"No wonder I never heard of him," Tito said, attempting to make an excuse for his lack of knowledge. "I was only eight at the time."

"So was I," Charles rejoindered, steering his attention back to the article.

"*You* live in England," Tito insisted petulantly.

He learnt that the last club for which Malcolm Stewart played was Saxon Valley. He had been player-manager in his final season there and when he finally retired from playing, he was given the acting manager's job.

Saxon Valley was one of England's oldest clubs but their best days had been before the Second World War! They however still achieved snatches of post-war success and were always in the upper half of the old first division. They even reached the final of the old European Cup some thirty years ago but in the last ten years or so, they had become a fixture in the lower division. The job of turning around their fortune was apparently too much for Malcolm and a new manager named Neil Carpenter was appointed recently.

Tito now took a lot more interest in his brother-in-law. He stayed close to him for the rest of his two-day stay and tried to ingratiate himself with him. He ran any errands and took him on walks about the neighbourhood. With the wedding done, Malcolm's sights were set on watching an international game between Nigeria and Zaire in Lagos in a few days.

"I've never been inside the National Stadium," Tito said obliquely.

Malcolm turned to him with a smile. "Not every boy I know has been inside Wembley either."

"I would love to watch the match," Tito said more directly. Whenever Nigeria played, the whole country stayed glued to the tube. How exciting it would be to watch the game live from inside the stadium itself. "Can I come along with you, sir?"

Malcolm shrugged. "By all means. My word, there'll be one or two fine players on that pitch."

Of course, Malcolm would be familiar with some Nigerian players such as Kingford's Bashir Hassan, who played in England. He would certainly be conversant, as indeed everyone was, with Zaireoise superstar, Oye Bolingo, who also played for Kingford. There were a couple of other players on both sides also well known in European football.

"I play football too," Tito said to him with a careful sidelong glance.

"As I understand everyone in Nigeria does."

"I hear you are a coach."

"How did you come about this profound knowledge?"

"My cousins told me. They school in England. Look."

He produced from the deep pocket of his *Ankara* jumper, the magazine that Charles had given him. Malcolm flipped through it, seeming to be familiar with the piece.

"I admit. That's me," he said.

"Will you coach me, sir?"

Malcolm chuckled. "Why would I?"

"We're brothers in law, sir," Tito replied and this quite amused the Englishman. "Will you coach me?"

"Wait a minute," Malcolm said, affecting some seriousness. "Just how am I to do that?"

"It says here that you are a coach with a club."

"Uh-huh?"

"Can I play in your team?"

"No, I don't think so."

"Why not?"

"There is a way for getting into clubs. There are scouts. There is the academy. There are trials. There is the transfer market, alright?"

"Give me a trial, sir," Tito implored with an air of desperation. "We are brothers in law, sir."

Malcolm chuckled with a confounded shake of the head. The insistent young man seemed to have a decided idea what he wanted out of their infant relationship.

"Alright. I'll see what I can do. I might get you into the trials assuming you actually can kick a ball."

"I can," vouched Tito, missing any humour. "You can ask my games master or Jim."

"Okay."

"You will give me a trial, sir?"

"Well, seeing how you twisted my arm."

"I'm so sorry, sir."

"It's okay. We'll see," Malcolm Stewart said, dismissing him. "And you can call me Malcolm."

"Oh, thank you," he said breathlessly. *"Sir Malcolm."*

He went along with Jim, Malcolm, Kosi and Precious on their trip back to Lagos. He could not wait to see the football game. At last, he would get to see a live game in the famous National Stadium!

The Nigeria-Zaire game, though a friendly, was something of a grudge event. There was a current rivalry between the two sides concerning which was the best in Africa. That issue would probably be settled next January at the Nations' Cup, but this was a great sneak preview.

As was expected, it was a keen contest notwithstanding being played under the cruelest sunshine. The star-studded, green-shirted Nigerians had the early advantage but the red-clad visitors defended well and even looked more likely to score. Their star player Bolingo was not at his best but he gave the Lagos fans glimpses of why he was so highly rated in the lucrative European game. So many rich clubs were in the hunt for his signature but Kingford would keep him at all costs.

Bashir Hassan scored for Nigeria late in the first half, sending the home fans into half-time wild with joy.

"Brilliant stuff!" Malcolm applauded. "He's such a fine player. He is moving to Spain at the end of the season, you know? He's going to Conquista."

"I know him. He used to play with my brother," Tito shouted over the din.

"Your brother? I don't recall that we met."

Tito nodded. "That's because he's dead."

"Oh."

"He died a few months ago."

"Sorry to hear about that."

Bolingo equalized for the visitors a few minutes to time with a superb free kick to end the exciting game in a fitting draw. The rivalry between the countries was even more heated as a result and the home crowd trooped testily home, looking forward to the Nations' Cup for the real showdown.

They saw Malcolm off to the airport the following evening. He was effusive about what a wonderful week he had and how he would love to be back again sometime. The past football season had been most frantic and they could not guess how grateful he was for the African break, short as it was. His club Saxon Valley had narrowly escaped relegation to the second division. A last-gasp home draw had enabled them cling on to the Championship by a whisker. The fans were furious. What they wanted was promotion to the Premiership, not dangling at the end of the Championship. Now, there were rumours of a take over. The week in Nigeria had briefly relieved him of the stressful condition but now he was on his way back to face reality. If he did not lose his job, he would count himself lucky.

"Tito," he said as he was taking his leave. "I'll try and get you into trials at the club if I can."

"I'll be waiting, Sir Malcolm," Tito gulped. He looked excitedly at his sister. "I will call and remind you."

"Jim put in a good word for you. He said I could take a chance, but remember," Malcolm wagged a finger. "I'm not promising anything. I do have to see if I still have a job."

"Thank you, Sir Malcolm."

"And one more thing, old chap," Malcolm said as he turned. "I don't have a bloody knighthood."

"Thank you," Tito mumbled, while Jim and Kosi laughed.

He only half-remembered Malcolm disappearing towards the boarding gates, waving. He was already day dreaming about leaving on a jet plane himself. He was only vaguely aware of the drive back from the airport and snippets of the chitchat that went back and forth between Kosi and Jim. The rest of the evening was one glorious blur.

Cold feet

The British Airways Airbus touched down at Heathrow one icy cold morning in October. As it taxied to a stop, Tito scowled. He was none too impressed with the sight of men on the runway in ordinary overalls working regular forklifts. This *was* fabled London and though he had not immediately expected to see a colony of the famous beefeaters about, neither was he quite prepared to be welcomed by the sight of grubby workers like the late Francis and himself.

He followed tentatively after the other passengers out of the craft and down the chute, hoping he was going in the right direction. He picked up his suitcase from the belt, set it on a trolley and rolled towards the exits. According to the arrangements that Malcolm made, someone would be at the airport to fetch him.

He emerged into the arrival hall, where there were so many more passengers and so many anxious faces behind the barricades. He guessed this must be where his man would be waiting.

He caught sight of his name in purple ink on cardboard. A small man wearing a woollen tartan cap and scarf was holding it up. He had a hard, lean face and wore thick bifocals.

"Tansi?" the man arched his brow. Tito nodded and he stepped forward and extended his hand and a warm handshake. "Terry Morgan. Mr. Stewart sent me. Let's go to the club, where he is working."

"I am Tito Tansi," he said superfluously. Obviously, Malcolm had not lost his job, as he had feared. Outside, a gust of cold wind made him cringe.

"You are advised to put on your coat, son," Morgan said genially. He was a middle-aged man with ingrained facial wrinkles suggesting that he had not had an easy life. They walked out of the terminal to the car park. "I'm a trainer at the club. Mr. Stewart is at training with the reserves. We'll meet him there."

They left Hearthrow and headed into the deep frozen city. Inside Morgan's car, the warmth of the heating provided relief that was hard to imagine. On the streets, people tried to bury their heads into the upturned collars of their coats, their hands plunged deep into the pockets and their breaths coming in mists. He could hear the clip clop of their shoes as they walked briskly on the concrete sidewalks. Here, people scurried. Back home, people strolled. The women here walked hastily as if racing against time. At home, they lolled and rolled with time to spare. Obviously, the difference between people had a lot to do with the weather.

"How old are you, son?" Morgan asked.

"Eighteen."

"Real age?" Morgan winked conspiratorially. The word was out that African players were not always on the level about their age. Apparently, the desperate need to leave their poor native hands usually led to one or two falsifications on the passports. "Heard the one about the African teenage sensation who went to Belgium, ready to conquer the world? But he was really *thirty* and by the time the club thought he was ripe for the seniors, he came down with the arthritis."

"I am eighteen, sir," Tito insisted, though thinking Morgan a nice, funny fellow.

"Just joking. Malcolm recommended you," the trainer revealed.

"Yes, sir." He was intent on the odd, big, black cab in the next lane and the curious red double-decker bus in front of them. He was also struck by Morgan's words: *Malcolm recommended you.* The striking thing was that Malcolm had never seen him play.

"Saxon Valley has got a handful of promising lads your age coming through from what passes for our academy, so it won't be easy. You will work very hard."

"Yes, sir."

It was about nine when they reached Saxon Valley Football Club. It was a big edifice with a rose pink colour scheme on Allen Lane. *1899* was inscribed beneath the club escutcheon, the year it was founded. It was most impressive and Tito gaped at it, finding it hard to believe that this was a club in trouble.

The training ground was further up the road. There was a field of young players playing a serious practice game on a lush, elm-bordered field. Morgan and he sat on the sidelines with a handful of other players and watched the session. Malcolm was embroiled in it, seeming not to take any notice of them. It was a frenetic game. Someone would punt the ball up field and players would chase after it like hare, putting themselves about with great determination and poise.

It was a wonder that he managed to follow the game at all. The cold was indescribable. It bit at his ears and nose and made his eyes smart. He did feel some warmth however, when one of the players scored with an astonishing thirty-yard volley worthy of the World Cup. Everyone applauded and congratulated the scorer, a statuesque youngster with long, golden hair held in place by a bandanna.

Not long afterwards, Stewart blew his whistle and ended the practice session. Everyone went toward him in the centre of the field.

"Great shooting, Charlie," he said to the scorer of the lone goal.

"Thank you, boss," replied the fine looking lad.

"I would like to introduce someone to all of you," Stewart said after a length of football talk. "His name is Tito Tansi. He's from Nigeria. He's come to try out for a while. So please give him the best treatment you can."

"Is 'e a forward, boss?" asked a big, chiselled, stubble-cheeked fellow.

"Yes," Tito offered, as Stewart seemed shortly at a loss, since they had not even gone over those details.

"Then I promise to give 'im the best treatment *I* can alright," the big fellow said, and sniggered.

"Not *your* sort of treatment, Jimmy," Stewart grunted. "You'll soon be fit enough to go maim 'em in the league, anyhow."

The big fellow, a defender named Jimmy Cummings, laughed a bellyful and soon after that, the meeting broke up and players drifted gradually away.

"Hi, mate. I'm Billy Blair." One of the players stepped up and offered Tito a handshake. He was young; about nineteen, pleasant, handsome and smooth-faced, and had a head of raven-black hair.

"Good morning," Tito responded a little nervously. He was in very strange company.

"Mr. Stewart said you're to share our digs."

"Your what?"

"I made arrangements for you to stay in a club house not far from here," Stewart explained. "Rest up for the day and be at training tomorrow."

He turned and left him in the company of the lad called Billy Blair. He was a little taken aback by the perfunctory manner of his brother-in-law. A little deflated, he followed the other youth, who was doing his best to put him at ease.

Their *digs* was the top floor of a grey brick apartment building up the road from the club stadium. It was called *Potter House,* after an earlier Chairman of blessed memory, who bequeathed it to the club. A couple of apartments in it were temporary housing for young or passing players.

"Listen, mates," said Blair brightly to a group of other youths in the lounge. "Say hi to Tito."

"Hi," said a sandy-haired youth. "Robbie. Quinlan."

"Scot Ryder," said another, a strapping young lad, who had been impressive during the practice game.

"Tomas. Ohlin," smiled a stocky bleached blond.

"Charlie Jones." The youth had scored the fine goal at training. Up close, his good looks were extremely striking.

There was a living room and five rooms in the apartment. Great French windows afforded a magnificent view of the club ground's rose pink façade in the near distance. Blair showed him to a room down the corridor, helping him carry his suitcase there.

"Not quite The Dorchester," he remarked good-naturedly.

"Uh?"

"It's not as bad as it looks," Bliar smiled. "Get settled in, alright? I'll see you later."

The new comer sank into his bed, looking around the surrounding after his friendly new acquaintance had left. The room was Spartan but cool, carpeted in flowery red, with an armchair in one corner and a dressing table in another.

He unizpped the suitcase, a brand new one that Kosi had bought the other day. He brought out from a corner of it, a framed picture of Ona's, which he had specially requested her to make the previous week. He looked yearningly at the fresh charm of her young face smiling up at him and it dawned on him how far apart they now were. She was not just down the road anymore, and he would not be seeing her around; not even by chance in the passenger side of a car with a strange guy at the wheel. He groaned at the yawning distance that now separated them and flopped face down on the soft bed, fighting back tears without success.

•

Training was tough. Malcolm Stewart and Terry Morgan were real taskmasters. Sometimes it seemed impossible to carry on. He had never had to take himself to such limits of physical endurance or been subjected to any meaningful training regimen. Football was not just all about the Saturday afternoons. That was only the tip of the iceberg. The real work was done behind the scenes on the drab training ground; and because it was wet and miserably cold, it was unattractive if you asked him. Yet, as difficult and unfamiliar as the conditions were, he was always found stregth whenever the apparition of going back home to Nigeria reared itself in his mind's eye. If he failed to impress the club, he would be handed his return ticked sooner than later and it did not all depend on Malcolm Stewart.

Though he was dreadfully home sick, he was even more fearful of making the journey back home. He knew how all too easy it was to encounter a fate similar to Francis', Skido's or Elo's. With every passing day, he felt more bitter the way those boys had come to their sorry passing. The vile country *did* after all make it easy for kids to give in to the temptation to steal. Wasn't crime on Nigerian streets the result of the crime in high places? Didn't the ultimate culpability lie in the corridors of power, among those crooked men who ran the country? God should never forgive those rich slobs, who robbed the nation blind, cheated the old, fleeced the sick and then had little boys killed for picking pockets. How were poor people to survive, since those nabobs in government deprived them of the means for survival? The young and the poor were the scapegoats for the Nigerian system failure. They were free to starve but must not to *feel* hungry; they would be whipped but must not cry; they would be bereaved but should not grieve. The worse their leaders became, the more good citizenship was demanded of them. They would get lynched for the least misdemeanour, while the foul leaders strutted like peacocks and got away with the grossest felonies. When he thought of all this, he put his head down and worked furiously at his game.

•

"What do you think, Terry?" Stewart asked at training and then winced as big Jimmy Cummings felled Tito with a hefty challenge.

"Tough little lad if I ever saw one, Mal," chirped Morgan, chewing gum. "He's quick and he's not very afraid of the big fellas."

"He likes the ball a little too much," Stewart suggested.

"An African affliction, I'm afraid," remarked Morgan. He had had a stint in the past as a trainer with the Ugandan national side. "But nothing a few knocks from the likes of Jimmy shouldn't cure him of."

Even at that moment, Tito went crashing to turf yet again, from Jimmy Cummings' hacking.

"Easy on the lad, Jimmy!" Morgan called.

"It's a man's game, Terry!" the sinewy defender called back almost merrily. "Not the bloody ballet."

Cummings was a defender of the old mould; a medieval hacker. Still, he was probably the player most central to manager Carpenter's approach. He was coming out of an injury and working his way to fitness with the reserves.

The club captain, Bob Stone was in the reserve game too, working off an injury as well. A right-sided defender, he had been at the club forever and had a paternal air about him. He came trotting up to Tito, who was tenderly feeling his shin.

"Are you alright, kid?" he asked.

"Yes," Tito lied, riding the pain while grimacing up at Stone. It was true what Cummings had said, though. This was a grown man's game and he was going to be no crybaby.

By the turn of the New Year, he had a feeling he had wormed himself into the club books, at least sufficiently not to have his name stricken off immediately. He was therefore reasonably happy, even though nothing much was really happening. He was fast getting used to the routine of training and finding some warmth in the company of most of the lads at Potter House.

Billy Blair was naturally his favourite, being the friendliest. He was a genuinely helpful fellow, adequately sensitive to the fact that he was a fish out of water. Robbie Quinlan, Tomas Ohlin and Scot Ryder were decent lads too, even if they were nowhere near as warm as Blair. Quinlan was very aggressive on the training field, very hard into the tackle, a real terrier but he was calm and introverted off it. Ohlin, a Swede, was like that too. Ryder was a useful striker and though he had a rather ungainly gait, most likely had a good career ahead of him. He was a jovial character but could be moody and read quite a bit.

The exception was Charlie Jones, who treated him indifferently, to say the least. He in fact had a suspicion that Jones did not like him at all, which was a pity because *he,* on the other hand, thoroughly admired him. Then, almost everyone adored Jones and he probably took that fact for granted. He had a very attractive, if somewhat cavalier personality. A desperately handsome face was highlighted by deep azure eyes and crowned by a leonine shoulder-length mane of golden hair. He was blessed with truly confounding football talent. He was a superb athlete, aided no doubt by a near perfect physique. He had stunning pace, good balance and great technique. He was very strong on the ball and most difficult to dispossess. He packed the kick of a mule in both feet and had a towering aerial power. He was probably a complete player, if there was such a thing and being only eighteen, everyone, not the least the lad himself, had a gut feeling that he was destined for big things.

"Charlie's so brilliant!" Tito overheard Morgan exude one day over Jones.

"Oh, yeah. *That,* he is," Stewart agreed ebulliently and he was not a usually gushy man. "He's so brilliant, you could go blind just watching him!"

"I think that's what must have happened to Carpenter," Morgan said dryly. "He's gotta *be* blind not to see what we see."

Malcolm Stewart shrugged with resignation. It appeared that Carpenter would always favour thirty-six year old ex-England international, Ron Race over young Jones.

Still, Carpenter could not help but give Jones a run-on now and then and whenever that happened, the kid seized the opportunity to show what an astonishing prospect he was.

The club floundered in the relegation zone of the table and there were not too many happy faces around Allen Lane. That much was illustrated one miserable afternoon in April. Ramstoke, one of the division's best, came to the lane and hammered Valley by 5-0 right there. It was a little too much for the long-suffering home fans and at the end of the game, they hurled missiles at the manager and the players as they left the pitch, really having a verbal go at them.

However, one afternoon, almost at the end of the season, Valley beat runaway leaders Oakfield Albion 3-0, which ensured they would not go down. Though Albion had probably taken their foot off the pedal with the title in the bag, the Allen Lane fans thoroughly enjoyed the rare win. Jones capped an incredible personal performance with two goals and had the fans chanting at the end: *'Jones-y! Jones-y!'*

Blair scored the third with a free kick worthy of the best specialists. He always worked hard in training at the set pieces and he was understandably pleased with himself. The fans marveled that their team had it in them to play this well.

The season ended poorly for Valley, which was normal. The only consolation, if possible, was that it was not as desperate as last season when they had only managed to escape the drop with virtually the last kick of the campaign.

About this time, the great Sir Johnny Hastings bought control of the club. The corporate fencing over the buy-out had been on for quite a while. The multi-millionaire had initially stalled at the enormous cost of acquiring the tottering, old club. He also had an attractive opportunity to buy a substantial stake in profitable Premiership side, Westbury United.

In the end, he was swayed onto acquisition of the club by the clamouring Valley supporters and so it was more of a decision of the heart than of the head. The reason was that Johnny Hastings, while a player at Saxon Valley, was one of the legends of English football. His playing career at Allen Lane spanned seven seasons, during which he attained cult status and passed into folklore as a prolific centre forward. Thirty years ago, he inspired the club to the European Cup Cup Winners Cup final. It seemed such a long time now, but at the club, it was still like yesterday. Though Valley lost that final to Spain's Conquista, the feat was still the club's great watershed and every one pined for those halcyon days. Following that, Hastings had moved, for a then world record fee, to Italian giants Bellona, where he ended his glorious career after two successful seasons.

He was not the run-of-the-mill, working-class lad fortunate to beat a path to the good life through football. On the contrary, he was a scion of a landed lineage and heir to a prosperous family business dating back to the turn of the twentieth century, the highbrow Baronet international store and property chain. After his football career, being equipped with family, fame and fortune, he concentrated on his heritage of big business and high finance. Being naturally astute, he propelled the Baronet business to increased profits. In a few years, he added to the chain, new high-rise stores and property in Johannesburg, Los Angeles and Tokyo.

Still, football remained his real love and now, as owner of his beloved Saxon Valley, he got down to work just before the season ended. He met with everyone, directors, administrators, football managers, grounds men and even ball boys. Everyone he could talk to at the club, he did. He felt a savoury nostalgia for the club where he had made such a name.

He was familiar already with the directors. John Fisher, Bill McDougan, Philip Wark, George Finley and Alex Cooper were all successful men in their chosen fields. They were quite knowledgeable about the game and the business of it and were generally regarded as having the best interest of the club at heart.

"But we're in a great conundrum here," confessed Wark, 56, a droopy-eyed dairy merchant. "We just don't seem to know what to do."

"That's not entirely correct," protested McDougan, 53, a portly, jowly fellow, appropriately in the junk food business. "But yes, we do have our handicaps."

"Thankfully, our stadium is not one of them," shrugged Cooper, 59, a builder. He was literally one of the architects of the improvements carried on at the stadium by the club about a decade ago when they were still in the Premiership.

"It will be if the fans keep staying away," said the arcane George Finley, a well-heeled descendant of wealthy colonial merchants of India and East Africa.

"I wonder how much longer we can keep Midlands Bank away with the dwindling gates," agreed the sardonic Wark. "We can't compete in the transfer market and we don't have many players we can get good money for."

"Just the young man, Jones," Finley said cagily.

"Yes," nodded Fisher, 50, a rather taciturn but reputed solicitor and influential local politician. "Westbury have asked questions, so have Oakfied Albion. One million pounds. Can't be sniffed at by Valley."

"Unfortunately," lamented Wark. "Especially for a gem like Jones."

Sir Johnny looked at the men with studious detachment, acutely following the disclosures. He could detect the lines along which the board was divided and was quietly convinced that Finley and Fisher were out of their minds about selling Jones.

"It is youngsters like Jones and Blair who will give us any sort of future," he said.

"Carpenter doesn't seem to think so," Wark remarked dryly. "Jones will have to go elsewhere or be twiddling his toes until Ron Race goes into an old people's home."

"Ron Race is still crucial to the club," asserted Finley rather testily. "Even if he may be getting on in years."

"Getting on in years!" Wark exclaimed. "*That* is putting it most kindly."

Finley went on sourly: "His mere presence at Valley still keeps the turnstiles turning quite a bit and we do need whatever crowd we can get."

"What we need to bring the fans back is a winning team."

"People still wish to see the great man, whatever anyone thinks."

"*I* think he's more suited to the Harlem Globetrotters than to an English league side," said Wark unremittingly.

"Gentlemen," Sir Johnny cut in. He had had enough of the subtle bickering. "Saxon Valley is very dear to me, as I'm sure you all suspect. What I desire is to get it back on the road to recovery so that in the next two or three seasons we might start challenging for promotion. I intend to put a lot of money into this club. I have always had a good feeling here." He swiveled in his armchair to take in what view of the grounds could be had through the French windows behind him. "You're right, look at the grounds. It is beautiful; first class. Valley deserves better than the first division. We belong in the Premiership."

"Aye," said Finley dourly.

"I shall be proposing three things to you as a matter of urgency, gentlemen. One: that a replacement be found for Neil Carpenter."

Finley looked askance, being a trifle sensitive about the topic. He was the manager's chief backer on the board, for which he felt some justification. Carpenter had won promotion to the Premiership with *two* different clubs. Although he was replaced both times once the clubs were promoted, he was logically something of a promotion specialist. Because Finley was very close to Harry Bates, the immediate past Chairman, it had been possible so far to resist the swollen clamour for his sack.

"What do *you* think, Mister Finley?" Wark asked, tongue in cheek.

"I will take no notice of your impishness," Finley claimed with some vehemence.

"Gentlemen, please," Sir Johnny moderated. He looked with a blasé expression from man to man. "Two: I want your approval to replace Carpenter with a first class manager and I have in mind Gianluca Mellini."

"*Gianluca Mellini!*" The exclamation around the oak table was almost in concert, any previous dissension notwithstanding.

Mellini was until only just a few days ago, the coach of Italian champions Bellona, Sir Johnny's old club. The club's famous billionaire president, Cesare Palazzolo had recently axed him after losing the Champions' league final to bitter Spanish rivals, Conquista. Palazzolo, globally indulged as a charismatic eccentric, apparently needed to exorcise a few demons. Otherwise, Mellini was a very successful manager. He had a great domestic and continental club record and had managed the Italian national side. He was a respected international player in his days and a teammate of Sir Johnny's at Bellona.

"We have in fact been constantly in touch since he lost his job," Sir Johnny told his rapt board. "I have a feeling he will be persuaded to accept the challenge."

"I'd be more worried how to pay his wages," Finley remarked cautiously.

"Naturally," Sir Johnny agreed quickly. "A man like Mellini will obviously come at a cost. It is an expense we must bear, gentlemen, even if it means breaking the bank."

The directors took some time to ride the surprise. They had known that Sir Johnny would come in with a few ideas as any new owner would but were not prepared for the caliber of the proposed new manager.

"You did say you were proposing *three* things," Wark prompted, seeming the first to recover from the concussion.

"The transfer market," Sir Johnny said. "New players. We must give at least the appearance of new life, gentlemen. As I said, I have been in consultation with Mellini and he has a few players in mind. Like Roberto Di Salvo . . ."

"Di Salvo!" Finley's eyes popped fairly out of their sockets. "First, it's Mellini, now Di Salvo. You really do mean to break the bank."

"We really do."

Roberto Di Salvo was arguably Italy's best striker of the past decade. He had been at Bellona his entire career, having broken through the ranks as a starlet of seventeen. Now at 32, he was no spring chicken and on the last lap of his career but millions swore he was still as good as ever. He still started many games for Italy in the face of fierce competition from much younger rivals. Like Mellini, he had just suffered an ignominious public censure from Cesare Palazzolo after Bellona lost the Champions' league final. He missed a late penalty in stoppage time that might have won the game for the Italian side. Instead, Conquista nicked it in extra time. In any case, Di Salvo's contract at Bellona was up and since Palazzolo 'punished' him with its non-renewal, he was a free agent.

"You really think we can land someone like Di Salvo?" asked Cooper incredulously. "You think we can make him pass up on all the big clubs that must want him and come to little Allen Lane?"

"Mellini has considerable influence on him and might bring some of it to bear, I believe," said Sir Johnny noncommittally. *"And* I am well aware of the financial implications of bringing him here."

"I trust you do," Finley grunted.

"And in any case," Sir Johnny demurred. "It is by no means certain if he will come here. He needs time, I believe, to sort himself out after the upset. If the deal does happen, I think it will lift the club."

Mellini, he went on, had made a few other recommendations concerning the acquisition of players. He would ask the board to consider them very favourably. It was clear that Sir Johnny would impose his will on an obviously irresolute board. He had the greatest respect for Mellini and the two of them had been more seriously in touch than he had let on. They had been very good buddies in their days at Bellona and had remained quite close since then.

•

It was Billy Blair's birthday in late July and that evening, he took his housemates out for a sip and a bite, cramming everyone into his Vauxhall estate car.

Tito was still very much struck by the glut of merchandise and humanity in busy London town. There was so much to be seen in the shops. It was not an easy place to live in if you were not well in pocket. Every imaginable thing that money could buy beckoned wickedly at one from behind ubiquitous plate-glass shop windows. Anything from edible G-strings to stately Bentleys challenged the swooning passers-by to possess them or eat their hearts out.

Yet for all the glitz, he observed with some perverse pleasure that there were people who seemed almost as out of sorts as the Tansi family of Onitsha. Well, at least in a manner of speaking! Even as a cool couple considered a sapphire and diamond ring at a Belgravia jeweller's, a lonely busker with a busted guitar drooled hopelessly at fish and chips in a shop window down Seven Sisters.

Mean time, talk among the lads soon turned to the recent developments at the club, the future and the coming season.

"If I don't get a decent run of games," Blair complained. "I'll look elsewhere."

"Me, too," agreed Robbie Quinlan. "And with all the talk about a new manager and new signings, I'd say going elsewhere seems pretty likely."

"I think I like the idea of a new manager," said Charlie Jones in the passenger side.

"Not if he's coming in with an Italian team," Scot Ryder snorted.

"For me, I'll have to seriously consider the move to Sweden," Ohlin said ponderously. There was a chance for him at Stjarna, a first division club in his native country. "It's not the same as here in England but it's better than rotting away at Valley."

"I hope the rumour about Mellini coming here is true," insisted Jones. "A real top class coach, that's what we need."

In his short time here, Tito had keenly followed the conflicts and divisions at the club. There was on one side, Malcolm Stewart with the young players from the academy; and on the other, Neil Carpenter with the senior ones. There was undeniable acrimony in the air at Allen Lane and now there was going to be even another line of division with the introduction of a foreign coach, assistants and players as rumoured.

Piccadilly Circus was agog with its endless stream of tourists, the usual exotic blend of people of different races. Watched impersonally by Bobbies in curious helmets, they shuffled about the crowded square and sidewalks. On Wardour Street, they passed a girl in a perfectly short skirt duck tailing in the general direction of nowhere.

"What's up, pussycat?" Jones leaned out and called to the sexy walker.

The girl turned to the slow-going car, took a good look at Jones and gave him an appreciative smile. She was a very busty girl and flaunted that fact. Her make-up was a little heavy and she wore grungy black lipstick. Her ample lips moved sensuously as she chewed gum and her eyes drooped in professional inquiry, which all did give her a peculiar charm. Even if this was not Soho, she might still be easily marked out as a hooker, Tito thought; so much did she conform to the stereotype. It seemed they were the same all over the world.

"You don't want to go with *that*," Tito exclaimed with put-on alarm. "She's a prostitute."

Jones turned slowly to look over his shoulder. He pulled his designer shades down the ridge of his delicate nose and regarded Tito with some put-on alarm of his own.

"I see we have an altar boy here!" he said and the others laughed.

"I'm sorry," Tito said quickly. "Forget it." He really only wanted to strike up some conversation with Jones, whose unwillingness to be friends often frustrated him. What right did he have anyway to moralise about prostitution, from which he would appear to have benefited? He would not be in London today if Kosi had not been a hooker.

"Party pooper," Jones muttered. He turned back to see that the girl had moved on down the road, as no real overture had been made to her. Behind his cool façade, he seemed clearly annoyed that Tito had distracted him.

Blair laughed uneasily, trying to dissipate the brief tension. "You got no girl, Tito?" he asked inoffensively.

"I do. She's back in Nigeria. Her name is Ona."

"Uh huh. She's the looker on your dresser."

Ona's framed picture had sat there since the day Tito came to Potter House.

"And now that she's not here?" Quinlan asked, sounding like he really wanted to know.

"Nothing," Tito shrugged.

"Thank God for hands," Jones chortled, while his eyes picked out the girl, who had turned into a side street. "I presume your girl back home's got a chastity belt on, then."

She's faithful to me," Tito lied. "I'll wait for her."

"Touching show of affection, I must say," Jones sighed wearily. He jerked his thumb in the direction of the girl, who had walked some way down the side street. She turned to glance coyly at them, aware of their attention. "But *this* one, I can't wait for."

The car resounded with rocking laughter and Tito was miffed. Jones was a natural leader of boys, so unabashedly admired by his peers. He was the sort of person who would get away with murder. Mainly to humour him, they trailed the hooker down the street with its peppering of topless bar signs sticking out of basement doors. They were shortly to catch up with her and Jones get his girl, as Tito would learn with time, he invariably did.

•

The atmosphere at Allen Lane rippled with expectation when the new season began in August. There was a sense of change at the club naturally, with a new owner, a new manager, his assistants and a bunch of new signings.

Some of the old players were offloaded in a bid to help balance the books, which was in vain, as most of the new players had been acquired for considerable sums. No other club in the first division went into the close season transfer market with quite as much single-mindedness as Sir Johnny did.

Nino Lanzarini, a twenty-six year old Italian international wide midfielder was bought from *Serie A* side Ancologna for £10 million, a fortune by any standards, let alone Valley's.

Tall, blond, twenty year old Fritz Fuchs, a central back came from *Bundesliga* side Hansbrucken for another £5 million.

"Here's a good boy," Mellini said about Fuchs in urging on Sir Johnny to the market. "I first saw him in Venezuela at the FIFA youth championships; very strong. For me, best in the world one day."

Lazslo Kutcka, a strongly built twenty-nine year old Hungarian defender came from Croatia Dravajek and had once played for Bellona under Mellini. He cost Valley a further £3 million.

"Maybe a little rough," Mellini had said of him. "But is sometimes what you need."

Tommi Peltonnen, a lanky Finnish goalkeeper was purchased from Swedish side Varnenborg for £2 million. He was young but experienced and had played in the UEFA Cup. He wanted to play in England and since Premiership clubs were not exactly falling over each other for his signature, he would settle for modest Valley with its world-class coach.

The big acquisition, however, was superstar Roberto Di Salvo. Few people believed he was really coming to Valley until he actually showed up at the Lane in flesh and blood. He put pen to paper in a blaze of publicity and brought the sort of pre-season attention to Valley that was only commanded by top Premiership sides like Kingford and Westbury United. For his formal presentation, the stands were almost half-full with curious and excited fans. The younger ones had certainly never seen that caliber of player at the Lane. Only their fathers could claim they had, recalling the seasons that Johnny Hastings graced the pink rose and grey colours.

For the opening game of the season, the ground was full to the rafters. Visiting them were Ramstoke, who had achieved the famous 5-0 win here last season and had only narrowly missed promotion.

Of last season's first-string players, only two were starting today for Valley: Bob Stone the captain and dreadlocked *Rastafarian* left back, Zion Livingstone. Blair, Quinlan and Ohlin were starting in midfield along with new signing Lanzarini, while Di Salvo and Jones were paired in front.

The game was not quite twenty minutes gone, when the young Ramstoke centre back, reacting at being given the early run around by the veteran Di Salvo, lunged recklessly into a late tackle, studs up. Players immediately around heard the horrendous sound as Di Salvo's leg broke at the shin and he let out a chilling cry. It was a bizarre breakage, the leg twisting grotesquely, and there was blood on the turf.

"Oh, il mio Dio!" Mellini cried and ran crazily onto the pitch, cursing in his native tongue. He had a shock of jet-black hair, considerable for his fifty-eight years, which lent him a very avant-garde front.

"Off you go, sir!" the ref rapped at him but Mellini lunged at the Ramstoke defender. He seemed intent on a scrap and was being restrained by his own players! The ref saw red and indignantly flashed a card in his face—the red one understandably. So, as Di Salvo was getting stretchered off in agony, Mellini was striding to the dressing room, still no less stiff-necked with rage.

"Fotterla!" he cursed on his way out, jabbing the air with a stiff middle finger in the direction of the Ramstoke defender, who the referee had only shown a yellow card! *"Lei il figlio di una femmina!"*

He knew as well as the most casual spectator did, that Di Salvo was out of action for most of the season at the least.

Stewart stood in for Mellini on the sidelines and sent on Ryder for Di Salvo but that was only moments before Ramstoke got a goal to rub things in.

However, a moment of individual brilliance from Jones near the end salvaged the draw for the home team and the fans went home with mixed emotions. There was a definite quality about the new team, they felt, and everyone had given Jones a great ovation at the end but Di Salvo's accident was a dark cloud over the bright afternoon.

After the opening day draw, Valley would get into a good rhythm and run up a surprising string of wins that soon saw them in an unfamiliar position at the top of the table.

Mellini had tightened up things at the back with Kutcka and Fuchs giving very little away. Fuchs was exceptional and became an instant favourite at Allen Lane. A strapping, blue-eyed lad with a physical presence to intimidate a number of forwards, he was particularly strong in the air and read the game very well.

The fans were pleasantly surprised at their team. Last season, the defence let in the most goals in the first division. Cummings, Whitehouse and Livingstone, the hard men, gave away free kicks and penalties like Santa did gifts at Yuletide. Nowadays, it was a relief for the fans being able to sit through games without the threat of heart seizure.

They marvelled at what a fine player Billy Blair was and wondered how he never got more than a walk-on under Carpenter. Some of his passing was quite breathtaking and he was hitting it off straight away with the crafty and speedy Lanzarini.

The cynosure of eyes, however, was Charlie Jones, who was in sensational form. Playing with total commitment, he hit the net repeatedly and by October, he was the leading goal scorer in the entire football league with sixteen goals in eleven games. His charm did him no harm and the media was getting to like him very much. He was good, he was glib and he was photogenic. He was getting almost as much attention as the stars of the Premiership. Wayne Starr of Kingford was arguably the most popular English player in the land and Fernando Montego the Argentinean of Westbury United, the most expensive import but young Charlie Jones was getting the best start to the season of anyone.

At the end of October, Valley played an away game in the Midlands against Barrowfield. The home team had a good defence and did a good job keeping Jones and Ryder quiet on the afternoon. In the second period, with the game still without a goal, Jones was involved in a clash of heads going for a ball and had to be taken off with a mild concussion.

"On you go!" Stewart said with an exhortative slap to Tito's behind.

It was amazing how a player always fantasized about a debut and when it was upon him, he was nonplussed. His pulse raced as he limbered up on the sidelines. He looked briefly up in the stands, listened to the baying of the unfriendly crowd and felt the fluttering in the stomach that anxiety caused.

"Scot is pushing up," Stewart instructed him over the din as the ref checked with his assistant. "You're wide to his left. Try getting the early ball to him at the near post."

He ran onto the Barrowfield turf and despite his nervousness, there was nothing to describe the exhilaration he felt playing for the first time in Valley's strip of rose pink shirts on dark grey shorts. Though he did not get more than a couple of touches on the ball, he ended up on the winning side. The game's only goal came late from Ryder at the near post from his early ball!

Valley were still unbeaten in the league after thirteen weeks and apart from that opening-day draw with Ramstoke, they had a 100% record. Their fans rubbed away at their eyes in disbelief.

Shooting star

He scored his first goal for Saxon Valley at the end of October. It was the fifth time he was appearing in the rose pink since Barrowfield, always as a sub for Ryder.

It was a game against Milton Town at Allen Lane and he would remember it forever. Valley had gone ahead through Lanzarini but Town equalized. The dogged visitors were holding on to the draw when he blasted a spectacular overhead volley into the top corner. The ovation might have brought the roof down.

"Meraviglioso, il mio ragazzo!" Mellini punched the air from the dugout, delighted with the scorer, who charged insanely into his embrace. He wet Tito's brown face with quick kisses. *"Ciò era fantastico!"*

"Why, you old son of a gun!" cried skipper Stone. Tito had a feeling the skipper liked him very much. Mellini had retained the thirty two year old as right back and captain, keeping faith with the past, it seemed. Stone was a strong and likeable character and a great club man.

"Wicked, *buoy!*" Livingstone exhorted, his dreadlocks falling about his chiselled face.

"Not bad at all," said Charlie Jones, jogging up and rapping the back of his head. He was having another great afternoon despite having the Milton Town defenders all over him like a rash.

"Thanks." Somehow, it was Jones' compliment that Tito craved the most. However, even as Jones trotted off, he could not mistake the coolness. How he wished he knew the password to his friendship. Since the beginning of the season, he had been captivated like everyone else with the blistering form of the golden haired boy wonder. Jones' power and precision, passion and predation went well beyond his young years and limited experience. Increasingly, the feeling gained ground that he was the best young player in the Championship. Out of nowhere, he was even being touted as perhaps the most impressive player to emerge this season, the best all-round player in the entire country *pound for pound,* as they say in boxing. He was a serial goal scorer and *goals* was the name of the game. Tito thoroughly enjoyed playing alongside him whether in training or now in league games. He always daydreamed about what a partnership they could make some day.

The huge Championship fixture of the Christmas was Valley away to second-placed Southbank Rangers. Rangers were managing to stay close on Valley's heels, which obviously meant they were doing excellently themselves. They too had spent quite some money in the close season, which seemed to be paying off for them so far.

It was a testy match played in an absolute downpour, at the end of which the travelling Valley fans were the ones singing in the rain. Two goals from Jones and Tansi signalled the beginning of the lethal strike partnership. They were frighteningly in-form for that game, and in the football community, the talking point for much of that week.

"Absolutely amazing stuff from these two youngsters!" the *Sky* commentator growled with wonder. "Just where have they been all our lives?"

"My word, you'll never see better finishing than from these two Valley strikers!" his fellow analyst gushed. "And this in spite of the miserable conditions here."

Mellini stayed with his combination and things kept going Valley's way. The fans nicknamed him Mellini the Magician. On Boxing Day, Tito scored a hat trick in a 3-0 home win against Midhampton as Valley opened up a nine-point gap at the top.

It was a very happy Christmas as far as he was concerned. He had scored five goals in four starts and it felt good to be useful to the club. Malcolm Stewart was pleased and that was very important to him. Mellini paid more attention to him these days than previously and that was very exciting. Jones and he played very well together for and off each other. They synchronized so well lately that on these wintry surfaces, they might well be a champion ice skating pair. Still, off the park, they rarely spoke and what a downer that was for him.

He missed home and tried to picture life back in Onitsha. Funny how its very disarray now seemed almost picturesque; incredible how those monumental garbage heaps and smelly drains now assumed the status of endearing landmarks in his homesick mind. His parents obviously were never far from his thoughts. Their faces, inbred with long suffering, were ingrained in his consciousness like the works of a master engraver. Then, he missed Ona beyond all measure. How he wished she were here. How he longed to hold her in his arms, to feel her warmth in this miserable weather. *'London cold!'* one reggae singer cried in a hit song. He agreed.

"I saw you on TV," she told him on the phone, referring to the watershed performance against Southbank Rangers. "I watched it at a friend's".

"Who would that friend be?" he asked suspiciously. It was not difficult, unfortunately, to think of her without imagining lecherous young men on her tail, or she in their arms.

"A girlfriend of mine you wouldn't know."

"Why wouldn't you watch it at home?" he asked grumpily, full of insinuation.

"Because, silly boy, we don't have cable TV at home."

"Oh."

"You'll buy one for me?"

"Of course I will," he gladly promised, even though he had already sent her some money and presents. Nothing was too much for her. He was not paid too much at Valley but it was weirdly comforting that the little he managed to send her converted to a small fortune in much-devalued Nigerian money.

"I wish I was with you in England," she purred.

"We'll be together as soon as I am settled, darling."

"How long will that take? You've been gone over a year now."

"A little more patience, girl."

"You know I can't wait to be with you. I'll be the envy of my friends then."

He sighed dolefully when she hung up and his eyes misted over. He could not wait to have her come to London yet was apprehensive about anything coming between him and football just now.

In January, they were drawn in the fifth round of the FA Cup against fellow Championship side, Maidenheath. The Cup-tie took on a grudge character because Neil Carpenter was managing Maidenheath now. Predictably, he would like to demonstrate what a mistake Valley made by ditching him. Apparently, there were still a few sides in the division also convinced of the qualities of the former Valley boss.

Jimmy Cummings, having faithfully gone with his master, was in the Maidenheath side as well. The new arrangement was not working out yet, however because Maidenheath were struggling in the lower table as Valley had done the past seasons. Nevertheless, they were good enough to grind the first leg to a goalless home draw, and go two goals up within twenty minutes of the second at Allen Lane, stunning the home crowd into stony silence.

Valley hopes were raised just before half time when Jones won a penalty after Cummings pole-axed him in the box. However, Lanzarini shot wide from the spot and Mellini was livid.

"Nino! Nino!" he cried, sinking to his knees and shaking his fist, his disheveled hair flying about his face. *"Che ha fatto lei?"*

"Calm down, boss," Stewart said to him with feeling. He was getting familiar with how easily Mellini flew off the handle and had come to accept it as artistic license. A maestro was entitled to his peccadillo. He was the first to tell anyone how much he was learning from the Italian. For him, it was a breath of fresh air after working with the drab Carpenter.

In the Valley dressing room at half time, there was a desperate atmosphere, which had not been common this season. Apart from the opening day draw against Ramstoke, they had won *every* game at Allen Lane. The dressing room had generally been an agreeable place since Mellini arrived.

"We've got no business being two goals down," Bob Stone berated his men. "Let's go back in there and give 'em hell!"

"If only Zion would calm down," complained the usually humorous 'keeper Peltonnen with considerable justification. The first goal had been an own goal, a miscalculated back pass from Zion Livingstone; the second was from a penalty after Livingstone tripped someone in the area.

"Was only a mistake," Livingstone mumbled contritely.

"Was *two* mistakes," Peltonnen quipped.

"Hey, man, stop picking on me so," the Rastaman snarled.

"Cut it out, you blokes," snapped Stone. "We have a game to win or we are out of the Cup!"

Valley went hammer and tongs at the visitors in the second period. Jones immediately thundered against the crossbar. Thrice inside ten minutes, the Maidenheath keeper had to be at full stretch to deny the league's top marksman.

Expectedly, Jones' persistence paid off when he pulled one goal back into the final five minutes and the Valley fans roared expectantly at the top of their voices. They knew they could count on Jones even with time running out. Sure enough, in stoppage time, he slipped his marker, rounded the keeper and served a glorious pass Tito's way. However, the latter tripped in front of the open goal and watched in dismay as the frantic Maidenheath defence cleared their lines gratefully.

Tito held his head, distraught as he well should be, while the rumbling of the crestfallen crowd compounded his misery. He saw Mellini collapse to the turf and knew it was not mere theatrics. He wanted to burrow the earth and bury his head.

"It was the grass!" he cried to Jones. He could swear he had stubbed his toe on a rogue tuft of grass. However, if he expected any empathy, he figured, he might have looked anywhere than in those blue eyes. Damnation was all he thought he saw instead and for the first time, he really loathed Jones. Despite his disconsolation, he managed to glower impudently back at him.

Making a bad day worse, Livingstone soon fouled someone at the Valley end and the visitors scored from their second penalty of the afternoon to hand Valley their first defeat of the season.

A very pleased Neil Carpenter led his victorious team into the tunnel, while most of the home fans stayed glued to their seats long after the end. Only Valley's awesome league form might have stopped Carpenter having a thorough gloat over his old club.

In the dressing room, with long faces and heavy heads, the Valley players sullenly peeled off their strip. Today, it was a very weighty chore indeed, where lately it was a pleasant ritual. Tonight, their boots might have been made of lead and their shirts of iron.

"You played not so bad," Mellini said, much to everyone's surprise. A thorough ticking off from the stormy petrel would not have been out of place. "Not so lucky today."

"I'm sorry, boss," Tito muttered, agitated at the sitter he had missed.

"Wash up and go home," Mellini said dismissively and left.

Peltonnen put a comforting arm around Tito. "They had a bloody good 'keeper and he had one of those days. *And* we backs had a bad day."

"We in front might have stuck in one in anger."

"I did stick in one," Jones riposted. He was probably the only player, whose mood was not fatally overcast with gloom. There was, in fact, some complacency about his manner. Apparently, he could not do much more than score once, hit the crossbar twice, force half a dozen fingertip saves from the 'keeper, win a frittered penalty and provide a perfect assist that was miraculously botched.

"At least *you* had a great day," Tito blurted testily to him in the mirror, fighting hard to keep his cool. This was one game he either would forget or never would.

Jones turned slowly to him with a little smirk.

"Maybe I did," he said and ran his hands through his great tassel.

"Yeah, right," Tito said, tongue-tied with resentment. His anger and frustration furiously sought a vent in the golden boy. "The team lost but I suppose *you* won, right?"

"Stop being stupid, you two," said the normally civil Billy Blair. The budding confrontation was attracting some of the other players.

"Hey, what exactly is your problem, *dumbo?*" Jones said jabbing a finger at Tito. "I am not about to apologise for doing my bit and if *you* missed a sitter, that is *your* problem. You didn't think football in England was as easy as swinging through them trees back there, hey?" Jones took his bag and slung it elaborately over his shoulders, making to leave. Tito stared at him, trying in vain to stem his spiralling rage. He was confused. Was he merely envious of Jones? Still, whatever it was, Jones, for some reason, was not going to be the first player out of the dressing room, if he could help it.

"Listen, Charlie." He placed an impolite hand on Jones' shoulder but was taken by surprise when the latter reacted with a flash backhand that caught him flush across the face. Stung, he lunged at Jones, sending him crashing to the tile floor. They flailed at each other for a good few moments and both got in one or two decent blows at the other before being separated by their teammates.

With Peltonnen and Livingstone off to another corner having a verbal exchange of their own, the Valley dressing room had never been this acrimonious even during the worst years.

The Maidenheath loss was an ominous portent and the rest of January saw Valley to three successive defeats in the league. They even lost, to the dismay of their fans, to early relegation candidates, Barking.

This situation made Tito very anxious. He had not scored in four weeks and even though Mellini seemed to favour him alongside Jones, he wondered how much longer that would continue. He did not forget that Scot Ryder was fighting hard to take that spot. Even old Ron Race was not entirely out of contention. He had come on as a late sub against Scarlingham and scored two goals in a 2-3 loss!

As for Jones, he never seemed to have a bad game. He would get on the score sheet even in defeat, with only the odd exception such as in the loss against Scarlingham, where he had limped off early with a calf strain. For sometime now, there had been indications that the England manager, George Windsor was a keen admirer of his and might consider handing him a senior England shirt sometime. Adding grist to the rumour mill, the England boss was at Allen Lane when Valley played Eastoak Athletic in February.

Eastoak were in contention at the top of the table as a result of Valley's recent recession but Valley showed breathtaking quality, knocking out the visitors with an impeccable performance. Jones and Tansi, the young firm, was at its very best, displaying an uncanny understanding on the pitch that totally belied their animosity off it. 2-0 was the score line, Lanzarini scoring both.

A couple of good results came after that, which was timely because the gap they had opened up earlier at the top was now substantially diminished. Ramstoke, Eastoak, Barrowfield and Coltshire were not too far behind any more. Now, every game counted. There was great excitement at Allen Road as anxiety heightened about either a dream return to the Premiership or a dreadful diasappointment.

Charlie Jones got a call-up to the England Under-23 side for a match against Finland in Manchester and scored in the 1-1 draw. Tommi Peltonnen was in goal for Finland, so it was a proud night for Saxon Valley FC.

As far as Tito was concerned, if Jones was previously merely cool towards him, he was now a solid iceberg. Even though he had tried in so many ways to make up for the post-Maidenheath game bust up, he may as well have been romancing the proverbial stone.

"Can I buy you a drink, Charlie?" he said to him one evening after a rewarding home game. He knew Jones was not averse to the odd pint or a glass of bubbly.

"No, thanks." Jones' eyes were a blue blank.

"Let's go to a club later then," Tito suggested rather uncharacteristically. Jones was known to crawl nights and he to tuck in early but he was eager to humour the golden boy if that would win his friendship. He would gladly hang out all night in Soho or Leicester Square, if it came to that. "We could meet some girls."

"Some other time, mate," came the po-faced reply.

"Why don't you want to be my friend, Charlie?" Tito asked directly, looking searchingly at him. "What is it about me you don't like?"

"Lay off me, man, alright?" Jones said and with that, wrenched himself away. He felt hurt and humiliated, and did everything to avoid him after that, which was not very easy because they saw a lot each other at Potter House and at training. The only consolation was that the grueling hours practicing together every day seemed to be paying off on Saturdays.

Before the season, Ramstoke had been the bookies' favourites to win the Championship. They were a well-managed club focused on getting back in the Premiership, from which they had been relegated only the other season. Now, as the campaign came gradually to a finish, they were battling furiously with about a half dozen others to catch up with surprise leaders, Valley, who had restored a respectable lead once more over everyone.

Live on *Sky Sports*, away to Ramstoke, Valley outplayed the home team, Jones heading from a corner for a first half lead. Ramstoke clawed back into the game in the second period, equalising midway through and hanging gamely on. As the game wound down to a draw despite Valley's superiority, Lanzarini crossed hopefully into the area and the crowd watched spellbound as Tito whacked in a venomous volley for the crucial away win.

It was regarded widely as the goal of the season and Tito got not a little attention for it. Anywhere from Land's End to John O'Groats, people watched endless television replays of it that weekend. For the first time, he felt real attention being turned on him. Here and there, perfect strangers walked up to him, beaming at him, effusive about how they had seen *that* goal on TV. Despite being in Jones' shadow, he was becoming very recognizable himself and it was not an altogether unpleasant experience.

With that win, Valley fans seemed assured once more that their incredible promotion dreams were not far fetched. They had a six-point gap over second-placed Barrowfield and with every week, it really appeared to them that they could make it to the Premiership as the division's champions. Jones got a hat trick against relegation certs, Burbank, while Tito scored four times in the cold-blooded 7-0 demolition to keep the momentum.

When they beat Coltshire United at home with two games to go to the end of the season, they knew they were home and dry. They had won the Championship and promotion to the Premiership with some time to spare and even if they lost their last games, they still would not need to go to the play-offs. The fans could now erupt in celebration, their joy absolutely unconfined. They cheered and clapped and stomped and whirred and waved and jigged. They hugged the nearest persons and kissed perfect strangers and very many wept for joy, while the players trotted round and round in victory laps. It had been an incredible campaign and it seemed that all around the country, they got a standing ovation. They had generated as much national excitement during the season as the big Premiership sides.

The slaphappy players carried Mellini aloft and tossed him recklessly in the air. They genuinely loved the wacky coach. They had stuck to the Italian's tough regime and strict work ethic. They had worked hard, kept their heads, passed the ball well, moved methodically, played safe and absolutely taken their chances mainly through the rare pair of Jones and Tito.

In his viewing suite, Sir Johnny pumped hands with those of his directors there that day, Wark, McDougan and Finley. Champagne and glasses popped up from everywhere. Sir Johnny indulged his occasional habit, stoking up a Havana, whose smoke rose in threads and spirals and filled the booth with a rich aroma.

"I can't believe this has happened in my lifetime!" said the usually acerbic Wark in a broken voice. He was awash with emotion, as was everyone who had been part of Saxon Valley in the last decade. This turnaround had been so sudden and so complete; it took the most ardent optimist by total surprise. It sure would take some getting used to. They almost not dared think it was really happening.

"Accept my sincere congratulations, sire," Finley said with exaggerated formality, though with no less exuberance. He raised his glass to the chairman and to Wark. "To Valley in the Premiership."

They sipped, bantered and carried on with a thoroughly justified sense of achievement.

That night at the digs, the lads drank a bit of champagne themselves. Jones even smoked a cigarette, which no one had seen him do previously!

"The Premiership!" they yelled and shrieked.

"*Ya—hoo!*"

"Here we come!"

They were so light headed and that was understandable. Just the other day, none of them was sure of getting more than a spattering of games in the Championship. Now, they were headed for the prized Premiership as seasoned performers, if they could be regarded as such based on *one* season's performance!

Over the hilarity, Tito wondered fleetingly if his parents would understand the significance of what he had helped Valley achieve. He decided not. Even if they understood the vague notion, the enormity of it might be lost on them and that caused him a little deflation if that was possible. Still, he wished someone from home were about; quite preferably someone like Ona. It was rather depressing being in the middle of all that jubilation with no home person to share his joy or pride. He was lonely in the crowd.

Billy Blair, the closest he had to a friend, was pre-occupied these days with a girl called Nicki. She was one of those girls so in love with love and who truly worked at a relationship. She was that type who assiduously followed the romantic tips to be found in *Cosmopolitan* and the like. As a result, she made it quite difficult these days for the other lads to spend much time with him. Jones was usually in stitches about the proprietary manner that Nicki had with Billy. She, on her part, thoroughly resented Jones' philandering and thought him a bad influence on her bloke. Blair would not spend a moment more with him than was absolutely necessary, if she could help it.

They drank and talked until deep into the night. Jones had a few of his girl friends drop by and he seemed incredibly comfortable with *all* of them. He was the envy of his mates, who constantly shook their heads in amazement, wondering how he managed it. His young life was already littered with the broken hearts of lovelorn girls and it was certain there would be many more volunteers still.

The Golden boy and the Godfather

He wished he might have travelled to Nigeria for the summer holidays. His cousins, Charles and Peter had called to find out if they could make travel plans together. The fact that they did so showed that he had attained some stature in their eyes and despite his dislike for them, he found it significant.

He was desperate to see his parents again. He longed to see the old neighbourhood too. He was surprised how much he missed the sorry old place. Incredibly, he pined for its deprivation and unwholesomeness, its very savagery of subsistence. He was learning that people usually yearned to be where they were not, that the grass was truly greener on the other side.

Above all, he wanted to be with Ona. She had written him a nice long letter just before the end of the season, even though they spoke all the time on the phone. He saw that she took a lot more interest in him now. Stories about him appeared in the Nigerian papers and she had seen him in the tube a number of times. She seemed proud of him and he was ecstatic about that.

Yet, he was still insecure enough about his future at Saxon Valley not to travel home. Sure, he had had a decent season and reasonably justified his inclusion in the squad, especially during the exciting final run-in but anything could happen in Nigeria, he feared, and decided to stay back in London over the summer. Who knew, there might even be a *coup d'etat* to trap him back there and that would obviously change everything.

Everyone knew that Sir Johnny would go to Europe and make some major signings in the close season. The Premiership was a different kettle of fish. The standards were sky high and many of the clubs were studded with big stars from Europe, South America and Africa. Valley would have to be ready for a baptism of fire and would need to work twice as hard if they were not to drop straight back to the Championship like many a promoted side before them.

Di Salvo's broken leg had healed. He had even begun training towards the end of the season. It looked certain that with the Italian superstar fit again, Mellini would always pick him over any one. On the other hand, there were offers coming in for Jones, although nothing as such was concrete. If Jones left, he contemplated, it might make things a little less difficult for him but it did not appear as if the club was daft enough to let him go yet.

"Tell Ona I love her," he said to Charles, handing him an envelope addressed to her, in which there was some money as always. If she exchanged it at the money market in Onitsha, she was going to be happy for some time.

"I see you really care about her," Charles observed

"You can say that again," Tito nodded. "I *love* her."

"You do know she sleeps around? Charles asked innocuously.

"She *what?*"

"Everyone knows she sleeps around."

"Well, I don't," Tito lied, peeved at how his cousin always managed to take the wind out of his sails.

"Of course, it's not my business."

"You *are* right. It's not."

"I'm sorry."

For a week or more, he agonised over Ona, his mind tormented by images of her in steamy situations, in which he did not feature. If it continued like that, he was sure he was going to run mad. He decided it did not matter if she did sleep around, which he was not so dumb as not to know. Hell, he knew about Skido and a couple of other fellows he would be blind or daft not to. Besides, she was not too hypocritical about the whole thing, he recalled. She always tried to justify her behaviour and made sense in her own sort of way. Moreover, she always gave him the choice whether to take it or leave it. He concluded obstinately that he still loved her and loathed Charles as a result. It was his duty to whisk her from that life. It was all right for Charles to sneer at their sort. What did he know about suffering? They had Mummy and Daddy and played with expensive toys. Daddy was now Governor as well and with his finger now in the state pie, he would only get richer. Mummy was the First Lady and that was the *last* thing she would let anyone forget. They were a secure, happy family. Ona's father, on the other hand, was a disposable civil servant. His month's paycheck would barely feed his family for a week and was diminished constantly by the notorious Nigerian inflation. His hope of keeping starvation at bay lay in picking after crumbs off his boss' table, as he was not highly placed enough to get to the slices. He would usually be too busy pilfering petty cash to contemplate, for instance, how Ona got her tampons. A few days after the Kafaras got to Nigeria, she called.

"We can talk for five minutes," she said brightly at her end.

"I miss you," he croaked.

"Me too. Thanks for the money. You really made my *birthday*."

"Your birthday?"

"I got the money right on my birthday."

"Oh?" He had not remarked her birthday, come to think of it, though he ought to have, being that Francis died on that fateful date. "I'm so happy."

"I had a party at *Macky's*."

"A party at *Macky's*?" he frowned. He could just picture it. Young Nigerian boys and girls would be shaking to rap and ragamuffin music. They would be aping the speech and style of Jamaican and African-American dance hall gangsters and molls. They would pierce their ears and noses with rings, wear dreadlocks, bandannas and back to front baseball caps. Girls were not merely girls but *bitches or hoes* and proud as hell of it. Boys were cool with being *niggers and motherfuckers* and you called your friend your *dog*. They would be yelling over the bedlam and chomping away at *Macky's* burgers and grilled meat, waiting for their turn at the pool tables, immersed in their unwitting parody of the black Diaspora.

"It was nice. All my friends are still talking about it. The money was useful. Thanks, Tito."

"So how's school?" He wished to change from the party subject.

"Fine." She answered perfunctorily and did not sound so enthusiastic about the school subject.

"How's Charles?" he wondered.

"He's alright. In fact, I am calling from his place, but I have only five minutes before his mother comes downstairs for tea." She giggled.

"What on earth are you doing there?" he demanded angrily, and then got a grip on himself. "I mean, *what* are you doing there?"

"I came to use the phone," she giggled again much to his trans-Atlantic irritation. "He said I could use the phone if I wanted to call you."

"That is so nice of him," Tito said mordantly. "You said you'd get a new mobile."

"I've paid for it and will get it soon."

"Where is he? I mean Charles."

"In the balcony."

"Listen, Ona," he addressed her urgently. "I hear you sleep around, but I don't want you to ever do that with my cousin."

"Tito! You surely don't think?"

"I love you, Ona," he moaned. He did not want to dwell too much on the painful subject. "Please don't hurt me any more. I will arrange for you to come to England as soon as I can."

"I hope that will be very soon, Tito." She sounded excited. Most Nigerian youths would kill to come to America or Europe, lured as shark to blood by the deified dollar and the powerful pound. "I want to be with you. I want you to keep me under lock and key if that will make you happy."

"I will do everything. You don't know how much I miss you. But you must be faithful to me."

"I promise."

"Don't make promises you won't keep. At least don't go out with my cousin. *That will kill me.*"

"I promise."

"I will send you more money soon," he pledged, knowing that a couple of thousand quid in the black market was a fortune to her.

Charlie Jones was a surprise last minute inclusion in England's Nation's Cup squad. Even though his performance in the past season had been astonishing, England managers did not normally go outside the Premiership to pick their senior players. Even though it was widely whispered how much the manager admired him, it was assumed that he was merely eyeing him up for the future.

An influential columnist in The Daily Mirror wrote on the eve of the England squad's departure for Spain:

> **I would have thought Windsor had enough proven Premiership strikers raring to give Starr and Buckingham a stiff challenge for their shirts. A lot of people are surprised, for instance, that Jeff Cope is not going to Spain."**

Most fans and critics thought it unfair to exclude Cope, who had been outstanding in the Premiership for Doverham. The fact that he was black only added to the uproar.

"Unfortunately," responded the England manager, a respected gentleman of unflappable temperament. "I cannot pick every player I would love to, since there is a limit. Cope is a lovely player and what a great season he's had, but I have great faith too in young Jones."

Everyone at the club was naturally happy for Jones although it was a little different with Tito because of the frostiness between them. Tito was still as puzzled as ever about the reason for Jones' attitude. It was not as if they shared the limelight. Jones was far and away the undisputed star of Allen Lane. There was no question at all about which one of them was the better player. Everyone knew Jones was special. A charming charisma complemented his unique talent and extreme good looks. A certain libertinism was thrown in for good measure and a generous dose of self-conceit was perhaps the cutting edge that gave him his distinct personality. In Tito's opinion however, *that* was his great flaw.

"After this," Tito remarked barely in humour to Blair. "I hope he will accept for me to be in the same club as he. As it is, I'm like something he just stepped in."

Blair laughed, amused that Tito was picking up some colloquial English expressions.

"Charlie's not a bad bloke at heart, really. You will sort yourselves out one of these days. But I agree he does get a little big for his boots sometimes."

England's opening game of the tournament was against Croatia, who went into half time with a 2-0 lead. The England boss threw caution to the wind mid way into the second period and sent on Jones, who obliged him with two quick goals before Westbury United's Buckingham struck a late winner.

In the subsequent group games against Spain and Turkey, there was a suggestion of pre-destination about Jones' performance. He got both goals against the hosts in a 2-0 win and another two in a 4-2 victory over the Turks. People took instant notice of the free scoring, golden-haired English sensation, sensing that an explosive product was in the offing.

On hindsight, the quarterfinal against Italy was arguably the defining moment of his meteoric rise. Italy's defence was the best in the tournament, having got to that stage with a spate of clean sheets. Massimo Strazza, Claudio DiBari and Franco Russo were probably the most uncompromising back trio in international football. The twin centre backs Di Bari and Russo had a reputation as the brawniest man-markers in the game. They had such charming nicknames as *Il Cannibale*, *The Butcher of Rome* and *The Italian Assassin*. Russo was distinctive in his Van Dyke beard and a head that was bald but for a crescent of strands that reached almost to his shoulders. The shaven-headed DiBari was a menacing giant with a genuine air of malevolence, and a rookie's nightmare. They were past masters at clipping ankles, tripping, pushing, kicking, tugging and elbowing. However, in the second minute, the English rookie left the both of them groveling in his wake to score with an exceptional individual effort. He was in such rare form that he went on to complete a hat trick inside fifteen minutes! There was a sustained protest to the referee by Russo that Jones had elbowed him in scoring the third, something that the world audience found quite fresh and ironic. It was not often that *Il Cannibale* whined. The referee would have none of it and the fans loved it.

The Italians however clawed back into the game and mid way into the second half pulled two goals back. England were not just desperate to cling on to their lead but to their credit also tried to increase it with great attacking play. In the process, there were a good many tussles between Jones and Russo.

The ball was miles away from both players when the rookie inexplicably kicked the veteran in the groin! Russo collapsed frighteningly in a heap and the crowd was quite perplexed because no one could guess the cause of it. The referee consulted urgently with his lineman and promptly the English greenhorn was shown the red card. He was livid at himself and left the field in tears but got a standing ovation as he did so, which was presumably a bit of a consolation. Russo clambered to his feet, a canny grin on his face as boos resounded around the arena, but that was most likely music to his ears.

With eleven men a side, England had had it all to do against the difficult Italians. Now down to ten, they really had their work cut out for them. Jones watched the rest of the game in the dressing room television, heart in his mouth, kicking himself. It was a giant relief therefore when, an eternity later, his first half goals ultimately proved enough to take England to the semis by 3-2.

Shortly, he heard the stampede of football boots and the happy tones of voices as the English team returned from the battle. He ran into some passionate embraces from his grateful new teammates, by whom he rightly ought to have been overawed. Just a while ago, he only used to read about these famous people, Wayne Starr, Joe Hutchinson, Kevin Smithson, Barrington Bramble and the rest of them! Now, he sensed that *they* were the ones who seemed slightly in awe of him. He had spoken the correct password and gained entrance into the crypt.

At the customary post-game press conference, journalists expectedly made an issue of the sending off.

"Why did you kick Russo?"

"First of all," he said contritely. "Let me just say how sorry I am for acting the way I did. It's no excuse but he had been fouling me all night. Being the foxy old pro that he is, he obviously drew the reaction he wanted from me and got me sent off. I owe everyone an apology, my boss, my team mates and the whole of England."

Back at the team's hostel, George Windsor asked him up to his suite. The England boss was quite a formal and impersonal man. Therefore, informal and personal moments with him were highly valued by his players.

"Good game again, Charlie," he said, pouring a drink. "Shame you'll miss the semi-final."

"I am sorry, boss."

"What exactly made you lose your temper out there? Did I miss something?"

Jones looked away briefly and then into the boss' quizzical eyes.

"He said something I didn't like."

"What might that be?"

"He asked me if I was going to be his *girlfriend* and winked at me, you know."

Windsor laughed and shook his head incredulously.

"That was it?"

"I don't like gay jokes, boss," Jones tried to explain.

"But you *are* a fine-looking lad, Charlie and you know what, don't you ever feel guilty about it. Besides, Russo plays dirty. That's his stock in trade. He would tell you your mother was a whore just to work you up."

"It will never happen again," Jones promised. "It's just that I never liked gay jokes."

"You must be strong, Charlie. If you stay out of trouble, you are going to the very top."

"Thanks, boss." He was flattered and relieved.

Windsor released him and he went back to his room. The England boss would write much later in his autobiography that he had never been this taken by any player before or ever since. Jones came just short of perfection, he was to exude. As for the steamy side of things, he did think the lad had a sexual quality that straddled the genders and could not reasonably expect to be free of some gay curiosity. *He* frankly harboured a little himself, although that was certainly not contained in his book. It would remain forever in the closet.

Jones had to sit out the semi-final, in which England edged out the strong Ukraine side on penalties. Against Germany in the final, England fell behind to any early goal from Bellona's Carl Jurgens, who had come to the tournament with the most awesome reputation. His club mate Klaus Krebs put Germany further ahead early in the second half and England were made to struggle. Though Jones and Wayne Starr scored in the second period to draw level, Jurgens decided the game with a late strike.

In spite of England's defeat, Charlie Jones stole everyone's heart with his brilliance and charm. He crying his eyes out after the nail-biting final was to remain the most enduring visual image of the tournament, making the Spanish public even more enamoured of him. He was nicknamed *El chico* by the Spanish media, and with his ten goals, was not only the top scorer but also the player of the *fiesta.* Young people readily related to his youth and pin-up look. His gorgeous face would adorn and sell mountains of tabloids. Glossy posters in dripping colour reeled off hot presses. His azure eyes captivated teenage girls everywhere the way his prodigy did *aficionados* in every land. In one fell fortnight, Charlie Jones had attained the status of a pop star. It came as no surprise when the cream of Europe's football clubs came after him, besieging Allen Lane on-line and in flesh, persuading Sir Johnny to let him go. Everyone wanted him and it was a hectic time for the Valley chief.

Bellona, the Italian champions, were the most insistent after his signature. Its president, Cesare Palazzolo was practically living on Sir Johnny's hotline. Everyone accepted Palazzolo's peculiarity and indulged him almost to the point of pusillanimity. Of course it did help that he was the world's third richest man according to *Forbes.*

He came from Palermo but commanded a cultish reverence throughout all Italy. He was an enigmatic fellow, largely inscrutable and reputedly possessing equal portions of benigness and meanness. He was the *real life* godfather, everyone said, the high priest of the fabled Sicilian cabal of friends. He was endowed with an inventive intellect and a Midas touch, which also made him a major captain of legitimate international industry. He was everything.

He owned *Avanti Corporazione,* the world's latest automobile giant. The pride of his assembly lines was the Madonna limousine, which many predicted would soon take much of the luxury play away from the traditional likes of Cadillac, Mercedes and Rolls-Royce. His limo designs were perfect fusions of high sports car performance and private jet luxury. The target market was the richest auto connoisseurs.

Palazzolo had controlling interests in a dozen top-flight international banks. The most important to him was the untouchable *Dio Banca di Italia,* touted quite unguardedly as the mafia's biggest money laundering institution. Another of his multinational companies was *Italoleo,* which had widespread oil exploration licenses. It had especially massive concessions in Nigeria because of his close friendship with a brutal ex-dictator of that country. He also did in Venezuela.

His hands were full with diamond hauls out of Angola and Sierra Leone. He took Uranium out of Niger and had never fully extricated himself from a scandal linking him with alleged clandestine North Korean nuclear activity. He manufactured arms and ammunition in factories in Switzerland, for which he always found huge markets in the world's trouble spots. He was an extraordinarily gifted and outstanding man of influence and it was intoned in high circles that no one became the Prime Minister of Italy if he did not give the nod.

Soaring far over all his numerous persuasions, however, were a devout Catholicism and an extreme passion for Bellona Football Club. He would never miss mass on Sundays. No priest ever failed to keep a mass date in his private chapel. Not only was he a papal knight, but a bosom pal of *Il Papa* himself.

"If Jesus Christ was alive today, he would be a great friend of mine," he once joked at his birthday banquet. "Why? First, I suppose because I am a cripple and you know how he just loved the sick!" He laughed and his friends *and* friends of friends laughed with him. Palazzolo did not encourage any one to feel sorry about his condition. He did not indulge in any self-pity himself and was very well adjusted to his disability. "Secondly and *most importantly,* because I own Bellona, the greatest football club in the world!"

As with mass, he never skipped a Bellona game. He followed them almost everywhere in his Lears, limos and chair mobiles. It was an incredible feat for anyone, let alone someone of his age, disability and work schedule.

The club had been in the Palazzolo family for five decades. He was determined that in his time, the great club was to become the greatest in the world, preferably of all time. The zeal with which he committed himself to the goal was obsessive, usually leaving his lieutenants and subordinates feeling that they performed well under par.

Unfortunately, Spain's super club side, Conquista regularly upstaged Bellona on the European stage. That had been the case well before Cesare Palazzolo took control at Bellona, following the retirement of his ailing older brother Antonio fifteen years ago. Even at that time, the continental rivalry with Conquista was very keen but still quite a healthy one. The two clubs held sway over European football. They had won between them Europe's major football laurels almost more times than all other clubs put together. Their trophy rooms were choc-a-full with prestigious silverware dating back to the old European Cup, Cup Winners' Cup and Fairs Cup.

The same year that Cesare Palazzolo took control at Bellona, the club reached the final of the European Cup, in which they were pitted against the dread rivals, Conquista. The best players of the time played for both sides and it promised to be a classic encounter. However, shortly before the great day, Palazzolo made the unsavoury discovery that his wife had been unfaithful to him. She had been photographed poolside by a dare devil *paparazzo*, frolicking in a Malibu love nest with none other than Modesto Delgado, the playboy president of Conquista! In the photos, she wore not a stitch on to guard her virtue and Delgado was kissing her in frame after frame. It was the scoop and scandal of the decade. Spread all across Italy's gossip magazines the way they were, it dealt a near-fatal fatal blow to Palazzolo's immortal ego. He later confessed that he almost had a seizure that day.

The *paparazzo* was found dead in his apartment a couple of weeks later, his head bludgeoned to a messy pulp, his blood and brain splattered all over his living room walls. Even babies could make a connection between the Palazzolo *exposé* and the gruesome homicide but everyone looked askance, most notably the *polizia*. Still, for Palazzolo, the alleged vendetta was insufficient to ameliorate his discomfiture for long. To make matters worse, Bellona lost the final, despite having led most of the game through a goal from a prodigious eighteen-year old named Roberto Di Salvo.

To take his mind off that miserable week, Palazzolo decided to go home to Palermo. In his words, contained in his best selling autobiography, *Il Ragazzo da Palermo:*

I sorely needed to breathe the native air, clear the head, and be with the humble folks.

But even that Spartan wish was ungranted. His Lear suffered a blown tyre while taxiing, careened off the runway, hit a shed and almost got ripped in two. The pilot and his crew died but Palazzolo managed to hang on to life, though at the expense of both his lower limbs.

After his recovery, he devoted his life even more, if that was possible, to Bellona. He was secure in the knowledge that his other businesses could run on their own steam and spared no expense to achieve the club of his dream. No club paid its players as much as he did his. The club's new *stadio* would soon be ready, an architectural masterpiece modeled in ingenious detail after the coliseum in Rome. It therefore rankled him that in all these years, Conquista still dominated the European football landscape the *very* way that he dreamed that Bellona would.

In that time, the Spaniards had won the Champions' league four times, including the last two editions. Next season, if they kept on the way they were, Conquista stood a chance of clinching a distinguished hat trick of the title and Bellona could give up catching up with them in the glory stakes any time soon and probably forever.

Last season, Bellona emerged *Serie A* champions yet another time. They were clearly a cut above the rest in Italy. That had never been the problem. The important thing was that they were once again in the Champions' league. For him, that meant yet another chance to play catch-up with the Spaniards as a prelude to overtaking them. This English youngster Charlie Jones, was just what he needed. He had been extremely impressed with him at the Nations' Cup. A young and lethal finisher like that to lift his side with passionate commitment would be a splendid addition to his crack side.

"I need Charlie Jones," he demanded of Sir Johnny over the line for the umpteenth time.

"So do I," the Valley Chairman retorted politely, amused at the man. He had the manner of a spoilt brat accustomed to having his way.

"I need him more," insisted Palazzolo. He was not joking, for he was not a very playful person. "I am in the Champions' league."

"On the other hand," said Sir Johnny. "I must stay in the Premiership."

"Tell me, my friend, how much you really want?"

"I am not thinking of selling."

"Forty million pounds?"

Sir Johnny flinched. That was ridiculous. Jones was a youngster, still wet behind the ears, with less than two seasons' worth of experience and had *never* played in the Premiership. How could he inspire such a wild bid?

"I am not selling," he repeated perhaps with less conviction, snapping out of his rumination with more effort than he wanted to make.

"Forty million pounds," Palazzolo said again. "You know he is young and not very experienced. No one will offer that for a *cadete.*"

"I will think about it," Sir Johnny promised, meaning it more than he meant to.

"I give you a few days," Palazzolo said, comfortable with authority.

Predictably, Conquista were also in the queue for Jones. After all, Spain had been the stage on which his prodigy was formally unveiled to the world. The Spanish public was probably the most afflicted with *Jonesmania*. He would be a most popular addition to the European champions' star-studded squad.

Inter Cosenzaro, another top Italian club and Spain's Real Baracoa were also in the front running, with offers that were not easy to overlook. In England, Kingford and Westbury United came asking too, cheque in hand, waiting for Sir Johnny to give his nod.

"You tell me how much it really cost for *El chico*," Conquista's Delgado urged the Valley Chairman repeatedly. He was a radiant, warm and expansive man in his late fifties. He had suave, classic, Latin good looks, down to the pencil line moustache. He knew every step of Palazzolo's bid to grab Jones. In their version of the cold war, they had a good spy network worthy of the original.

"I will," Sir Johnny assured him. "As soon as we decide to sell."

"Before you decide anything," Delgado stressed. "Remember to tell me first."

Major fashion houses were not left out of the race for Jone's signature. Dior, Armani, Largefeld and Versace courted him since after the Nations' Cup. With his striking looks, a super modelling career should not be long in coming, *Vogue* suggested.

The whole football thing was getting crazy, Sir Johnny thought in wonder. The money in it these days was obscene, even insane. It was definitely nothing like in their days. Nevertheless, he was going to get used to it, he assured himself wryly.   ●

"Charlie Jones," said Mellini to a group of football correspondents staking out the Jones developments. "He is *not* leaving the club. He will stay here for many years."

"But a move to Bellona, your old club, is possible," he was prodded by a correspondent from *Gazzetto Dello Sport*. From all indications, it was most likely that Jones would go to Italy.

Mellini shook his head firmly. "Not possible. I need Jones here at Saxon Valley. He is important to my plans."

A fortnight later, Jones was sold to Conquista. For an incredible sixty-five million pounds, he was second only to Conquista's Brazilian ace, Hannibal as the most expensive player in the world. At 19, and with less than sixty league games into his career, he had hit the authentic big time. It was absolute dreamland and would be pardoned if he never again came down to earth. Yet he proved surprisingly at home with the attention. It was as though he was born to the buzz and the lights. Effortlessly, he turned on the charm in front of cameras and everyone was taken by his affable self-effacement.

"I still think he's a nasty guy," Tito muttered one evening late that summer. He was looking in the tube at Charlie Jones being hounded by frenzied fans outside Conquista's *Estadio San Diego*. It was a common sight these days and frankly, he could not deny some brazen envy on his part. It made him a little uncomfortable with himself but he did feel he had a genuine axe to grind with the new hero. He was disappointed that he could not really share in Jones' glory. He felt deprived of so much reflected glory and would not forgive him for that.

Blair furrowed his brow in thought. "It's really happening so fast for Charlie," he said.

"I wish him all the best, I guess," Tito shrugged. "Not that he cares, though."

Sir Johnny, with some money to spend off the sale of Jones, went after a few players that Mellini wanted. The manager had been somewhat embarrassed by the sale. He had really planned to have Jones for another season at least, although aware how difficult it was for Sir Johnny to turn down such money for the rookie. For all the young man's talent, this was football and anything could happen. A dramatic loss of form would downsize his worth. An accident could wipe it out. Sir Johnny had thought it wise to take the crazy money and run like mad all the way to the transfer market.

In the Premiership these days, the emphasis was on deep squads, enlarged teams capable of surviving the long rough and tumble of the modern season. Valley would be coming up against sides like Kingford and Westbury United, whose squads were a stockpile of top quality internationals, many of who had won the highest honours in the game. As the new season drew nearer, Valley fans, dejected by the exit of Jones, were considerably lifted by the news of a player influx.

Johann Kronberg, a vastly experienced Dutch sweeper arrived from Spanish club, Camponegro for £10m. Some thought it a curious signing, as he was getting on quite a bit at thirty-three but it was a major signing in the European transfer scene and Allen Lane was abuzz with activity over the event. Iordan Panev, a twenty-eight year old right-sided defender arrived from Russian club, Novopetsk for £3m. Although he was not wildly famous, he was an experienced regular international for Bulgaria and had been in *three* World Cups.

Twenty-year old Peruvian Marco de la Luna came from Resistencia in Brazil. He was a left side defender and had made a great impression at the Copa America. It appeared as if Zion Livingstone would be working overtime for his shirt this season. Everyone at the club suspected that Mellini was not exactly in love with the spirited but reckless dreadlocked defender. Oliver Temba, a twenty-six year old black South African forward came for £2m from first division Scarlingham, who had beaten Valley 3-2 at Allen Lane last season thanks to his hat trick.

Valley's biggest signing was Radu Mihailescu, the exciting, twenty-four year old Romanian midfielder, bought from Italian side, Pescarleno for £20m. Kingford had made the initial overture to him but as they prevaricated, Sir Johnny was quick on the draw with his chequebook. The skilled Romanian was eager to play in the Premiership.

Valley fans were happy at the additions. They liked the fact that the club was fast shedding the outback look and at least simulating the cosmopolitan air of the fashionable Premiership sides. Though some conservatives like director Finley thought there were too many foreigners in the side; that the English character of the club was going, if not gone, voices like his were increasingly lonely these days.

Di Salvo's broken leg had healed and he was probably automatic to get the top striker's shirt, leaving the support slot a slug-out among Tito, Ryder, Temba and surprisingly, the age-old Race, who still had a year of his contract to go.

Such a beautiful game

Charlie Jones was all the rave back where the rain fell mainly in the plain. *Estadio San Diego* was just under half full on the day of his formal presentation to the fans. Since the famous stadium sat seventy thousand, it was the size of crowd that made full capacity at a number of top club grounds around Europe.

They roared when he made his appearance in the company of Modesto Delgado and the club's iconoclastic German trainer, Herman Meissner. He held up his new shirt in the club's famous white and gold colours. Inscribed at the back was his name, *JONES* and his new number, 25.

'El chico! El chico!' The crowd cheered him wildly and in the giant screen, he flashed them his winsome smile, his great mane gilded further in the summer sun.

"*Viva, Conquista!*" he cried, his voice breaking from emotion.

The fans responded to him almost as one and there was a cathedral feeling in the *San Diego*. They were used to their club signing the world's best. They were once again the defending club champions of Europe and the world, going for a possible hat trick of those titles this season. They worshiped their idols, who had brought so much pride and glory to them.

In creating the Conquista playing strip of white and gold, the designers surely had in mind the matadors' suit of lights. It was perhaps a deferential gesture from Spain's favourite football club to Spain's favourite traditional sport. Conquista's celebrated team consisted of players that could certainly be likened to such immortal matadors as Joselito, Manolete and yes, the great Montez, even if he did die by way of a bull's horn up his posterior orifice.

The fans *knew* without a shade of doubt that the club captain Vasco Santamaria was the *best* midfield player on the planet; that Klaus Krebs was the *best* winger there could be; that the goal-crazy Brazilian, Hannibal was the *best* of the best, probably the greatest of all time. They adored the other greats in the side almost no less—Garcia, Sukic, Girard, Van Holten, Scala, Rojas and the rest. Yet there was already a special sentiment about Jones. They were impatient to see if the youngster would continue his Nations' Cup form here, in which case he was destined for all-time greatness.

He was deluged by invitations to grand openings, movie premieres, fashion exhibitions, art shows, talk shows, musical concerts, everything. There was a much talked about concert of *Los Mininos*, the Spanish mega-star all-girl pop group, who had a haul of platinum hits and worldwide sell out concerts. *Los Mininos* sang mainly in Spanish but their musical and sexual appeal crossed all *genres,* tongues and borders. A heavy, driving American-style beat characterized their best hits, while a sultry lead voice over *salsa*-like vocal harmonies was their trademark.

They had just recently returned to Spain coming off the high of a Grammy award in Los Angeles. Tonight, Jones and his new friend and teammate Luca Scala were in the packed theatre in Barcelona, which throbbed with the group's great music. Along with everyone else, they were bathed in ethereal lighting and spellbound by the big *mininos*. Girls gaped, while boyfriends drooled as all fantasized at their sexy stagecraft.

"*¡Buenas noches,*" a man's voice said. "*El Señor* Jones, *el Señor* Scala?"

"*¿Sí?*" Jones said, wrenching his eyes from the stage with some effort.

"*¿Le podemos ayudar?*" demanded Scala.

"*Las invitaciones para usted, señor.*" The man handed them cards.

They took the envelope from the faceless man and looked at its contents, absently at first, then with great interest.

"Thank you," Jones said. "Thank you very much. *Gracias,* right?"

He nudged Luca Scala. In the envelope were two invitations to a post-gig party the *Los Mininos* girls were throwing back at their hotel. Scala and he had fallen into a natural friendship. They shared two obsessive interests, playing football and hanging out with girls. Scala was a star midfielder of the dark, good looks. He was a devout Casanova but at twenty-two, already a permanent fixture in Italy's national side and arguably on his way to becoming great. The two playboys were not going to miss the prized party for the entire world.

Later at the hotel, the girls attended dutifully to their roomful of privileged fans. There was a good spattering of film, sports and music stars, society journalists, models, designers, politicians and people of general interest and upward mobility. When Jones and Scala made their entrance, the *Los Mininos* quartet turned to them with unconcealed enthusiasm, quite brusquely breaking away from a cluster of devotees.

"*¡Damas y caballeros!*" Alfreda, the lead singer announced playfully in her famously sultry voice. "We have the honour of having with us, *Señor* Charlie Jones."

She was even prettier in the flesh, which was more than could be said of many famous faces. She really was a tall, dark, steamy, tan-skinned, high-cheekboned sex bomb. Commentators said that she had something of all the world's most beautiful women in her look; that she was Lollobrigida, Taylor, Loren, Welch and even Cleopatra in one unbelievable package. They were not so far off the mark, improbable as it sounded. She slithered when she walked and Jones was instantly weak at the knees. "*Señor* Scala, it is so good of you to find time. Please meet Nina; Estella; Gloria."

"As if we didn't know," Jones smiled shyly while his pulse raced. "We are your biggest fans. I will not leave here if I do not get your autographs.

"Ah, you will get *more* than that," Alfreda pledged dubiously. Her English was good and she had sung a few hit songs in that language. She led Jones off in the direction of the suite's balcony, while Nina, a svelte brunette, engaged Scala, to whom she seemed to take an unveiled liking. Estella and Gloria, markedly less striking than the other two, left quite reluctantly to circulate among other guests. "You like it here in Spain?"

"*Sí, lo quiero tanto.*" He liked to exercise his frail Spanish. "I think I am going to have a great time here."

"*Puedo ayudar,*" she said with thinly veiled insinuation. "I like your country too. I wish I could see more of it some day."

"I'd be honoured to show you round."

"I'll be happy if you could. All my time is taken. Travel, rehearsals, concerts, recordings; God, I pray I get a break some day."

"Well, it sure beats hawking your demo around and getting turned down by one A and R after another."

"You know, I tell the other girls exactly that," she laughed. "It is the same for football players, I suppose; the lack of time, I mean."

"I guess so. Yeah."

"Conquista is a great club."

"Maybe the greatest."

"My father would die for them. I remember he used to take me to *Estadio San Diego* to watch the games. I think he wished I was a boy so that I could maybe one day play for Conquista!"

"Well, am I glad you *are* a girl!" Jones laughed, very smitten by her. She was *the* bomb.

"*¿Más champaña?*" a waiter asked courteously.

"*¿Por qué no?*" Alfreda smiled as she and Jones helped themselves to the champagne. "*Gracias.*"

The aroma of marijuana soon tinctured the air. He crinkled his nose, though he was mindful not to show distaste or disapproval. This was the hip world.

"Smoke?" Alfreda asked him. "Not good for football players."

"I don't have anything against it," he said quickly. "A number of players I know smoke."

"It's alright, Charlie," she said dismissively as the song playing in the background faded and the strains of another commenced. "We have better things to do."

"*Ah, si. ¿Podemos bailar?*" he asked haltingly for the dance as the slow salsa picked up some tempo.

"*Querría eso tanto,*" she smiled and slid into his embrace as easily as if they were old lovers. Under the starry sky, they smooched sensuously on the balcony to the lilting song, a current hit of theirs called, appropriately enough, *El amor está en el aire.* A famous romance had begun.

•

Saxon Valley began their time in the Premiership with an away derby against Westbury United. United's famous Penn Street ground was not too far downtown from Allen Lane. They had an awesome home record and Valley fans could certainly think of less difficult places to test the waters.

Mellini's changes came in the form of Panev, the Bulgarian playing in place of ex-skipper Stone at right back; Krohnberg in for Kutcka as sweeper and new captain; and de la Luna in Livingstone's slot at left back. It appeared as if Quinlan's central midfield position would generally now belong to the highly rated Mihailescu. Di Salvo was back in the side, which was great news for the fans and a big fillip for Tito, thrilled to be starting in his support.

The veteran Italian marked his return with a well-taken goal to put Valley in front after ten minutes, but Montego levelled for the home side soon after. Tito twice came close to scoring in the second period but Westbury's Nigel Powers was not England's first choice goalkeeper for nothing.

In the very last minute, Mihailescu clipped the Westbury bar with a great drive to give the home team a real scare but the match ended in the draw. It was a fine performance from Valley's point of view and it gave them a lot more confidence to face the fabled challenges of the Premiership.

They strung together consecutive wins after that, managing an amazing nine before losing to Liverton City. It gave the fans so much satisfaction beating teams they only previously read about: *Normanhill 0 Saxon Valley 1; Saxon Valley 2 Queensbridge 0; Saxon Valley 3 Millchester 1 . . . .*

Tito scored quite a few times in those opening weeks—six in ten, which was not a bad return. Overall, he felt he was doing better than he had in the first division, which quite surprised him. He put much of it down to the invaluable presence of Di Salvo. Whereas Jones was pre-occupied last season with being top gun, the veteran Di Salvo was more of an avuncular influence and took pains to help his game. If Tito made a mistake, Di Salvo usually had a kind word and tried to show him what to do. Encouraged by the great Italian, he got settled in more quickly than he might have hoped. The way he was going, he might have been playing in the Premiership all his life and considerable notice of him was soon being taken.

Some English purists still resented the ever-increasing number of foreigners in their football. Even though most acknowledged the extra quality they brought along, a few archconservatives like Finley still moaned about how local lads were suffering as a result. A few influential columnists still grumbled that the Englishness of the league had become a thing of the past. The good, old, down the middle, harum-scarum English game had lost out to the cool calculation of the European style, they groaned.

"I'm afraid our game has always needed a jolt from these foreigners," Sir Johnny once remarked. "Our mule has occasionally required a kick in the backside."

Sir Johnny's observations were not entirely shared by dyed in the wool supporters of the old English way. However, not even men like Finley could dispute that Sir Johnny knew the score, being an old war-horse of the English game himself. Who did not remember Belo Horizonte in 1950, where the minnows of the USA had embarrassed the English superstars with an unthinkable victory at the World Cup? That was at a time when Americans were hard pressed to tell a football from a cabbage. No one needed reminding of Wembley in 1953 and the 6-3 humiliation at the feet of Puskas and the Magyars.

'Well, let's talk of 1966,' the staunch conservatives contended stiff-neckedly. *'Didn't Ramsey win the World Cup with his wingless wonders?'*

'But that was only a fluke,' the revolutionaries conceded conditionally and pointed to the indifferent standards since that glorious year. They insisted that the local talent had been, in general, ordinary, despite the passion, fury and tradition of the English way. Of course, there would usually be a Charlton here, one Moore there, a Keegan now, a Barnes then but it was all desperately insufficient. The best of them still palled next to the outrageous continental and Latin talents.

Any English youngster who showed promise, however dimly, was instantly the Great White Hope, the object of so much goodwill and optimism. Not surprisingly, many would-be prodigies had fallen by the wayside, unable to fulfil the early promise. English football had always known its John Sissons and Peter Marinellos, hopeful meteors but with a life all too brief to make a difference in the firmament. Usually, the expectations were too high and weighed heavily on the objects of it.

Now, to most people, it looked as if Charlie Jones was the real article and as a result, an enormous outpouring of goodwill trailed the youngster. Here at last, was an English lad to match the exotic stars of world football, someone to prove that the game was born here after all. Jones was making all of England proud like no one had since they gave the world the beautiful game.

The English nation was very curious about his move to Spain and keen on his progress there. They closely followed his every step, game and goal, only slightly regretful that he was playing abroad, not at home. They watched him cut his teeth among the most distinguished company.

The quality of players at Conquista was a spur to, as well as a rein, on him. He had to work harder than the proverbial dog to get in the side for the *La Liga* games. He quickly made the humbling discovery that the massive transfer fee did not automatically translate to a regular place in the side. Away from the flash bulbs and his pop appeal, life at Conquista was a tough grind. He had to battle for places with the likes of Hannibal and Rojas, two of the *very* best the world had ever seen. His breaking-in was no fairy tale and he was really made to work.

"He's still very young," Herman Meissner, German coach of Conquista tersely assured impatient Englishmen, who wanted to see the world quickly at young Jones' feet.

Valley went into the most daunting and prestigious fixture of their young Premiership life, an away game to league champions Kingford. For their fans, it fully underscored the fact that they were in the big time.

Kingford were England's biggest club. They enjoyed fantastic funding and their basis was a solid, corporate style. It was a mammoth business with an incredible world wide following fuelled by unrivalled merchandising. It was a club with driven people working assiduously behind the scenes in every department. It was the most successful and efficient football *corporation* in the world.

Several years ago, it was taken over by enigmatic British media mogul, Lord Philip Baden-Goode. The peer owned *Solar Network*, which fiercely challenged *CNN, BBC* and *Sky* for the lucrative global satellite television audience. The take over had not been without resistance. There had been widespread public outcry at the bid. Kingford was, to the English, more of a national than capitalist symbol. Lord Baden-Goode however was a patient player, a pig-headed and shrewd manipulator, who had a reputation for getting his way. Ultimately, Kingford became the flagship of his entertainment fleet.

Although Kingford's business standing was the best, they always trailed the likes of Conquista and Bellona in football terms. The two latter clubs had won between them six of the last ten editions of the Champions' league. Kingford had managed it just once in that period. Even though they were perennial top contenders, it was not what they would.

On the other hand, they totally dominated the English league, where it seemed no one could challenge their monopoly. They had won eight of the last ten Premiership titles, accomplishing the prized double *thrice* in that period. What was more, they managed all this using more British players than most top English clubs did these days.

As usual, they were in pole position this season, but had not opened up the yawning gap over the field that had become customary at the corresponding point of most campaigns. A big early lead always helped them, especially when they became bogged down in their fixture-laden mid-season and faltered occasionally.

This season, newly-promoted Saxon Valley were surprising everyone by giving the perennial champions a dogged chase, coming up just the odd few points behind them. The impertinence of the newcomers served as an impetus to a handful of other clubs as well. So, Kingford were being made to sweat a little more early in the season than they were lately accustomed to.

They took the early lead at their posh Prescott Park ground through Scottish centre forward and captain, Gerry Logan but Tito drew the teams level with a brave diving header just on the break.

Bolingo, Kingford's winger posed all sorts of problem for Valley on the afternoon with his repertoire of outrageous skills. The dreadlocked Zaireoise possessed an array of turns, flicks and party tricks, which he used to practical effect. It was perhaps inevitable that *he* got the winner for the home team five minutes from the end. Overwhelmed by admiration, Tito trotted over to the fellow African at the end of the game.

"I wish I could play like you, Bolingo," he said without guise. He remembered it was not terribly long ago that Malcolm Stewart and he had watched the Zaireoise in Lagos.

"You are very good yourself," Bolingo replied with a warm, gap-toothed smile. "You will teach me some things too."

For Kingford, the win against the upstart Saxon Valley was a perfect tonic ahead of their Champions' league first phase game against Conquista. For English fans, the mouth-watering prospect of seeing Charlie Jones was the week's whole reason for existence. It was quite incredible that the golden boy of English football had never kicked a ball in the Premiership!

The Spanish champions did not play with much adventure, seeming as if a draw was good enough for them. They showed more than adequate respect for Kingford and duly went behind when the diligent Logan headed home. But they picked up the pace in the second period, needing to come out of their shell. In flashes, they showed what a sublime side they could be, although they were still not at their best.

The Brazilian, Hannibal equalized after some pressure and then Jones came on as a sub in place of the Mexican, Rojas to grab the winner with a penalty in the final minutes.

The newspaper headlines the next day were more about Jones' goal, ordinary as it was, than the game itself. The local press seemed curiously more elated that the English lad had scored the Spanish winner than sorry that the English team had lost the important game!

•

This was a great time for football connoisseurs, who sat back and relished it all. The world's top sport was living up to its billing. The players were turning in top quality performances, sponsors were pumping in fat money, the voracious crowds were swelling still and even ordinary clubs were building quite extraordinary grounds.

Great players from the past such as Sir Johnny could scarcely believe the transformation from their days. Even though some of them had earned what was considered fantastic wages back then, it was nothing compared to what transpired these days. Now, big money was not such a big deal anymore and financial security was taken for granted, at least at the top of the game.

Some great new players were coming through the unending mill: Carl Jurgens of Bellona; Zizinho, the latest Brazilian sensation, of Real Baracoa; Charlie Jones of Conquista; and many more. Despite the fantastic new salaries, some of these new players were in a way, refreshing throwbacks to the old days. Performers like Hannibal and Jurgens were still like the gladiators of Sir Johnny's time, when primordial pride in his performance was primarily what powered the player.

Late in April, Kingford visited Allen Lane for another league fixture. Valley had been audaciously at their heels all season, snapping at them the way few teams had done in the last decade. Kingford, as usual, were having a marathon season, having to play what many considered too many games. They were in the Champions' league, the FA Cup and the League Cup and many of the players were regularly on international duty for their countries.

Valley were still in the FA Cup too and by their previous standards, certainly considered themselves very busy as well. They played with black armbands in honour of Ex-Chairman Henry Potter's widow, who died earlier that day at 82. Potter had been legendary at the club. He was Chairman when Sir Johnny had been in the books and Valley *almost* won the old European Cup.

Under floodlights, they inflicted on Kingford only their third defeat of the season and in such stellar style. A splendid team performance upset the league leaders and presumably lifted the mournful mood at Allen Lane. Everyone in the Valley side might have been man of the match. Tito picked up the champagne however, his two goals and Di Salvo's one making a famous 3-1 win.

"It's my turn to congratulate you, Tito," Bolingo said gracefully to him at the end of the game.

"I learn many things watching you," replied Tito.

"Now," Bolingo grinned. "*You* must teach me some too."

"What could you possibly learn from me?"

"Oh?" Bolingo shot him a look of mock-disbelief. "Like, where do you get your speed from, man? And the power in your small feet, eh? *And* how do you jump so high for a little man?"

•

Spanish club Real Baracoa made inquiries after Tito and would pay £5million if Valley would let him go. That he was worth such a fortune came as a surprise to him, even though he was gradually acquiring the professional equanimity that came from knowing the football racket.

Looking back only a short way down the road of his young life, he had known only misery and poverty, fear and uncertainty. Now, he had to agitate his mind very hard just to be able to recall it with any vividness. Suddenly, he was in the unfamiliar situation of having enough money for his needs; too much even, if he was asked. He had acquired a comfortable home, a detached Tudor in Golders Green. He was in the newspaper pages a great deal these days. He was one of the top goal scorers in the Premiership. Life was not bad.

He had gone to Nigeria in March for a World Cup qualifier against Sudan. People were very familiar with him back home and it was a little strange at first but they saw him regularly these days on television. All the local stations showed European games, especially those that had Nigerian players in them.

Though the Nigerian team's trainers generally favoured the older players to keep their shirts, much of press and public opinion was in favour of Tito taking over the top striker's slot from Westbury United's Ehime.

"I hope you have thought of protection for yourself," Obi Tansi counseled his son in Onitsha.

"What kind of protection?"

"Native protection. African medicine."

"Juju?"

His father sneered. "That is a derogative name that white people call our religions because they don't understand them."

Understandably, the father's pride in his boy knew no bounds. The man had never had it so good. His health and that of his wife had improved immensely thanks to the sophisticated medical care they could afford these days. A storey building was in the pipeline, to be in place of the little old house that would be knocked over soon. They would be traveling to England next summer for a vacation. Tito's football earnings had made it all possible but also made them a little paranoid concerning his safety. They imagined that he would be the envy of every witch and sorcerer in town.

"You have rivals in the Nigerian camp," his father said. "Those other players will come along with their charms and the like. Some will stop at nothing, you understand? *Nothing.*"

"I don't think so," Tito said dismissively at length. It was not the first time he would be hearing about these things. "We are all friends at camp. The senior players are quite friendly."

His father grunted and was not pleased with his attitude. He was sure that the most sinister ends could be achieved by these voodoo means. He was certain that the undoing of his own life was inflicted by just such means.

Was Tito glad to see Ona! To sweep her into his arms and kiss her tasty lips was the climax of his trip, not the brace he scored in the 2-1 win against Sudan. Now they did not have to snatch their moments in dark alleys. She stayed with him in the comfort of a Lagos Sheraton suite a couple of extra days, for which he would have to account to Mellini when he got back to England!

"I'm almost a star myself," she told him, pirouetting playfully in front of the dressing mirror. "Everyone in town knows I'm your girl!"

"Oh yeah?" Tito smiled pliably.

"I can't wait to go to England," she moaned.

"In the summer, darling," he assured her. "I have everything worked out now. But there is one thing I would like to know first."

"What?"

"Will you marry me?"

She seemed to freeze and fix him a puzzled, rather than the delighted look he was anticipating.

"Marry you?"

"Yes." He seemed somewhat piqued that she did not jump at the proposal. "Is there something wrong with it?"

"I mean, we are both young," she suggested level headedly.

"At nineteen? In England, the streets are full of girls half your age pushing prams."

"Really?"

"Babies are having babies over there, Ona. And we are *not* babies."

"You will have to talk to my parents about this," she said finally and then lit up his world with a smile. "I suppose they can actually now sit and talk with *you*. My father is crazy about football."

"I will talk to them," he said self-importantly and nibbled on her lips. "After all, I can take care of you. Remember all those things you always wanted? Well, I could buy them for you now. I could buy Skido's workshop a hundred times over."

"God, I'm so impressed. Tito!" she cooed and nestled into him.

"So you don't need all those guys in your life anymore now."

"No," she agreed. "I don't."

•

Kingford clinched the Premiership title for the seventh season running. It was yet another predictable ending to the season, except that this time, they achieved it by the skin of their teeth. The photo finish with newly promoted Valley was a helping of humble pie. That they nicked it by the odd goal difference was the scariest domestic episode in their recent history.

In late May, the two sides squared up once again. This time, the occasion was the FA Cup final. Valley, the heckling upstarts stood between Kingford and their fourth consecutive double. It had been a long season for the champions, during which they had crashed out of the Champions' league in the quarter final, leaving them wondering if they were jinxed in that competition. They were quite tired and demoralized going into the FA Cup final, but it was still a great tradition, and it would always contrive to be a special game.

They made all the early play, although Valley had a couple of good chances too. Jacobssen, the great Dane in Kingford's goal was outstanding, keeping off great strikes from Di Salvo, then Tito. His saves buoyed his mates and on half time, Starr drilled a low shot past Peltonnen to put them in front.

Valley piled on the pressure in the second half, forcing Kingford to defend with uncharacteristic desperation. Mihailescu struck the post before Di Salvo had a goal disallowed for handball.

Kingford hung on, taking a pummelling from the underdogs and having much of their ego severely dented. Neutrals loved this development, for they had long thought Kingford's thorough dominance of the English game bad for it. To thrill them further, Tito took Lanzarini's cross on his chest and volleyed in the equaliser with ten minutes left on the clock.

Spurred the more, Valley stepped up the pace. Blair's free kick was destined for the top corner but for an incredible save from Jacobssen. Lanzarini's effort skimmed the top of the cross bar. Everyone sensed the upset coming as Valley waxed and Kingford waned. Then Livingstone, in place of de la Luna, scored an own goal to hand Kingford a stunning last-ditch winner and send his teammates and fans into despair.

•

In Spain, Conquista finished their campaign in the manner they were accustomed to, *La Liga* champions for the fourth consecutive season. More significantly, they were in the Champions' league final for the third consecutive time, going for a hat trick of the title. What was more, for the second time in four years, Bellona were their opponents, giving yet more dramatic flavour to the event.

Jones had a niggling calf strain, which was not so grave but bothersome enough to engage the chief physio's close attention and to make Modesto Delgado come calling one morning at the physio's room.

"*Buenos días, señor,*" the elderly physio curtsied.

Cortes was a tall, suave, man. He had the healthy radiance expected of someone who had had a lifetime of the good life. He was from one of Spain's wealthiest families, centuries-old wine merchants, ancient courtiers and confidants of Spanish kings. He was of a manicured appearance and dark Latin charm, affable and flamboyant and fell easily into conversation. A Gablesque moustache edged his sensuous mouth and enhanced a classic Casanova's reputation that he did nothing to downplay. A lawyer by formal training, his apparent *joie de vivre* masked a shrewd business savvy.

"*¡Hola,* Charlie! *¿Todo bien?*"

"*Estoy bien,*" Jones said quickly. He was not about to miss the Champions' league final for anything. He was the joint top scorer in the championship with Carl Jurgens, both of them going into the final game with eleven goals apiece. If he bested Jurgens, it would be another feather in his cap and he fully intended to accomplish that.

"Charlie must be fit for the game," Delgado told the physio and it was an order.

"*Si. Será conveniente para el juego, el Sr. Presidenté,*" the physio affirmed.

"You have done well, Charlie." Delgado placed a hand fondly on the player's shoulder, favouring him with a very warm smile. "I am extremely proud of you."

"*Gracias.*" Everyone was proud of him. He had heard those words from a million people in the last year; from royalty, from peasantry, from industry, from screaming teenage fans. Girls swooned and fell over; they bared their breasts and begged him to autograph them; they ripped their thongs, flung them at him and fainted. Hell, he thought, he had become more popular than the Beatles, to borrow an irreverent, famous old phrase from the fab four themselves. Still the compliment was most important coming from *el presidenté*.

His mind flashed to Alfreda. She said she would be at the game in Athens. Everyone in the world knew by now how crazy she was about him, she the sexiest, most sought after female pop singer in the world. It was sometimes frightening how far he had come.

"You must win this game, *si*?" Delgado said with almost hypnotic passion, as though it all depended on him.

"*Si,si,*" He still was dismal at this Spanish language thing, though he got by.

"To lose to Bellona," Delgado stressed in an intense near-whisper, beating a clenched fist into the other hand. "To lose to Palazzolo ees impossible. You must win *this* game. *¿Entiendes?*"

"*Si,*" Jones responded woodenly. What more could he say? He understood the whole passion behind the Conquista-Bellona thing, knew the history of it. For Delgado and Palazzolo, it was more than a game. It was a duel, almost medieval in its viciousness. That same curious, dubious honour was at stake that made jousting lancers charge furiously at each other with fatal intent.

"Good, good," Delgado nodded and appeared satisfied, after which he shortly left, rich, powerful cologne trailing him.

The physio gave Jones a wan look and went back to the calf. He had been around the club for ages and his smirk implied that they were all poor passengers in the roller coaster of *the* feud.

The deepest cut

Cesare Palazzolo simmered inside with the mounting tension of the coming Champions' league final and so his attempt at seeming *blasé* might have been quite laughable if the matter at hand wasn't so grave. Least fooled was his eighteen-year old daughter, Serafina, who everyone regarded as his closest companion.

Serafina was approaching early womanhood but she was only four years old at the time of her mother's infamous episode with Modesto Delgado. Palazzolo had had no choice but to go through with the divorce. It was indescribably painful, for he had worshipped the very ground on which his wife Rosa walked. He might conceivably have let her get away with another crime such as murder but the indiscretion with Delgado of all people was unforgivable.

Rosa was only nineteen when Palazzolo began to court her after they were introduced in Milan at an *haute couture* event. She was already a supermodel by then, walking the world's glitziest runways and gracing its glossiest magazines.

He knew her by reputation, since he took a keen interest in fashion and sartorial matters and even fancied himself as a competent amateur designer. He sometimes toyed with the idea of opening a line of garb himself and no one who knew him treated his versatility lightly. Lagerfeld, Versace and Armani all paid respects and socialised frequently with the beneficient billionaire.

The young and vivacious Rosa did not resist his advances with any vigour, notwithstanding the thirty five-year difference in age or his eccentric reputation. They both fully understood that money was his sole romantic asset and he courted her expensively as a result. He still recollected with strong emotion the bliss of those best first days. He still relished the memories of those sublime early months of the famous romance; how he lavishly submerged himself in her peculiar mix of *naïveté*, guile, purity and passion. He married her after the hurricane affair, for he had been unmarried long enough by then. His first wife, Constanza had died four years earlier, the victim of a rumoured Sicilian vendetta.

Constanza had died without child and since he lost the appetite for marriage after the divorce from Rosa, Serafina was the lone object of his extravagant affection. She was his sole heir and he dotted obsessively on her. He spared nothing in the pursuit of her happiness. She was all he considered he truly had.

All the while, he worked hard to consolidate his expensive clubside. After he sacked Mellini, he hired Paolo Mossi, an intelligent and successful coach, who had previously proved his mettle in Serie A with Inter Cosenzaro and was a former national team manager of Italy. He bought even more top quality players, adding to a squad that was already spilling over with the cream of the world's best. On his payroll were great players of the day such as Costas, de Souza, Baccanale, Jurgens, Strazza and so on. His only regret was being unable to snap up Charlie Jones, having been caught off guard by Delgado's hostile bid and Hastings's vacillation. Now, Jones had proved to be an invaluable asset for Conquista and would no doubt pose a grave threat in Athens.

Engrossed in his ruminations, his glass of whisky dropped from his grasp and shattered on the shiny *parquet* floor.

"Papa!" Serafina rushed to his chair. She dabbed at his cheek and hands with a kerchief.

"Il mio angelo," he smiled self-consciously and composed himself for her benefit. *"Sono così spiacente."*

"You must relax, Papa," Serafina said kindly to him. She was a beautiful young woman although not in a striking way like her mother.

"Sono bello, sono bello," he insisted. "I'm alright, my dear."

"You are not." She was mildly reproachful. "You are thinking of the game with Conquista and you have not been yourself all week."

"No, I don't think so," he mumbled bravely. "I don't think so at all."

"Papa, it's only a game." She leaned over and kissed his wrinkling forehead, letting him be.

•

Bellona lost the final to Conquista, conceding the Champions' league title to their arch foes for the second time in three years. It was a game of the highest quality, correctly reflecting the high standard of the players on both sides. Both sides were impeccably organized with hardly a wrong foot or a stray pass all night and it was not surprising that it was decided by the one goal in extra time. Timing a blistering run to perfection, Jones tamed a pacy pass from Santamaria and chipped the advancing Carnera in Bellona's goal for the picturesque winner.

Watching the victory ceremony, Modesto Delgado was beside himself with joy. Gritting a panatela in his smiley teeth, he pumped hands and backslapped with his cronies. Palazzolo, on the other hand, sat immobile in his suite, so obviously broken and only barely held together by the tender arms of his daughter. His aides hovered around but kept a mournful distance. His suite was like a funeral parlour and *he* was the corpse.

•

Charlie Jones was the definitive toast of European football and top goal scorer of the Champions' league with twelve goals. He seemed like a born champion, a serial winner, one of those children of fortune who always found themselves on the victorious side. He would later be voted European Footballer of the year and then World Player of the Year. No player in the world made the impression that he did that season, but for a rookie, it was particularly astonishing. Everyone agreed he was the most important new player to emerge on the world scene and knowing the quality of the field today, it was no mean honour. The world literally was his, at least for today. It lay at his feet and still sprawled ahead of him. He was very happy at Conquista and Delgado made it astronomically worth his while. He laughed and laughed all the way to the bank.

Over the past months, he had also been making a reputation as a model. The way he was going, with the press he was getting and the enormous goodwill that trailed him, he was well on his way to becoming a super model. He recently signed an exclusive contract with Versace and had lately begun walking the runways as much as he worked the football turf. Hollywood beckoned too with a science fiction movie, in which he would appear alongside Jackie Chan and Angelina Jolie. He was going to play the character of a footballing alien from some distant planet, which seemed altogether quite appropriate. He would get megabucks for it.

"Son of a bitch!" exclaimed Tito only half in jest.

"Charlie's sure got there," whistled Blair, whose own career had recently received a boost by him getting a call-up to the England squad for the World Cup qualifiers. "He's got a charmed life. I wonder what's next."

"Perhaps England will win the World Cup."

"I wouldn't bet against it with his sort of luck. He's a talisman."

•

Jones came to London during the vacation. He had bought a house in Essex that was set in sprawling grounds and there he had a party one mid-summer night. A colourful crowd was gathered, a good smattering of celebrities and very important personalities.

Tito attended the party with Ona, who had finally arrived in England a few days before. She turned heads with an indigo Lycra mini skirt, which was so form hugging that it might have been painted on. He was very proud that she was so remarkable even in this sophisticated crowd. Predictably, she gaped wide-eyed at the cascade of *beautiful people,* her eyes popping as Tito pointed out one famous person after another. People came over frequently to chat with Tito and she realised with some bemusement that *he* was a famous person too.

A willowy, doe-eyed, blonde commandeered Jones' attention for a while but he soon extricated himself with some effort and circulated breezily among the guests. His shirtsleeve was loose fitting and sheer, revealing the silhouette of a taut torso underneath, allowing a peep at a field of tender golden hairs on his chest, among which nestled a gold neck chain and crucifix pendant. All the females gave him an eye full and he was very conscious of it.

"Hi."

"Hi." Ona turned to see that it was the host himself, the famous Charlie Jones. She was on her way back from the toilets, where she had gone to scrutinize herself. Naturally, a Third World country hayseed like her would feel self-conscious amidst such an array of glamorously appointed people.

"You are Tito's wife," Jones said.

"We're not married," she offered quickly, struck by surely the most handsome male she would ever set eyes on. His eyes might have been emerald gemstones and the golden locks gave him a kingly air. A gold ring adorned his left ear, lending him the *avant-garde* groove.

"Will you walk with me?" he asked her with disarming politeness. "I am curious to know you more."

They walked down a few stone steps and into a fresh-scenting garden.

"Where's your girlfriend Alfreda?" she asked him.

"Alfreda?" He shrugged. The love affair was such public property that it had a website. "Brazil. She's always on the road."

"I always read about the both of you back in Nigeria."

"Don't believe half the things you read," he smiled. Then to her surprise, Jones pulled her suddenly but gently to himself and planted a kiss on her cheek. She pulled away reflexively but he drew her back again and kissed her mouth for good measure.

"I want to make love to you," he whispered quite matter of factly.

"Just like that?" she frowned. "You don't even know my name."

"I do. Ona."

She was surprised; not to mention flattered. "How?"

"Back at the digs, I saw your pictures and I thought you were very beautiful. Now I see the pictures didn't even do you justice."

"You like black girls maybe?" she theorized, trying to conceal her ecstasy at his flattery.

"I've been with a couple, but it's not just *that*."

She followed his eyes as they went desirously over her. She was aware that she was growing into a fine young woman, filling out very nicely in the right places.

"You are very direct," she observed, not entirely with disapproval.

"I always was an honest bloke, I think," he smiled reticently, which was a curious habit, for he was so clearly a conceited fellow.

"You are very handsome," she said with unabashed admiration. "You look like a pop star."

"I suppose that is because I *am* a pop star," he smiled, and then leaned to her. He kissed her lightly again and laughed impishly. "I don't believe I said that. How conceited you must think I am."

"Well," she smiled as prudishly as was possible in the impassioned circumstances. "Maybe you have every right to be."

"Come on, baby," he said to her, a telltale thickness in his voice. "Let's go where we can be alone."

"No," she demurred, though with a noticeable shortage of resolve.

"Come on now," he urged, appraising her with rising passion and shortening breath.

"But Tito . . ."

". . . is with friends." He caressed her with practised urgency and saw through his dilating pupils that though she was indecisive, she was pliant.

"Oh, Charlie," he heard her whimper, the soft cry of imminent capitulation, which was familiar music to his ears. Sensing expertly that he might seize the moment, he preceded her boldly along a cobblestone path, turning around occasionally to watch her follow tamely after. Moments later, they disappeared into the large house.

Tito soon began to take notice of her absence. The crowd was considerable but not so much that she should get lost in it, while her sexy gear made it improbable for her to be inconspicuous for long. He was standing among a cluster of celebrities from various occupations, many of whom he honestly did not know. He took a lot of comfort from Billy Blair's being there with him and holding fort for both of them with his wit, charm and plain good nature.

He became uneasy and soon disengaged himself from the company to go discreetly in search of Ona. He picked his way through the thicket of guests, his progress impeded by the greetings he had to acknowledge along the way.

Worried that he did not see her after a good look around, the thought struck him quite curiously that he had not seen Charlie Jones either. Instinctively, his pulse quickened and he was conscious of some apprehension, about which he was frankly embarrassed but considerably anxious nonetheless. He could certainly do without the coincidence of his girl *and* Charlie Jones going missing at the same time.

He went down the stone steps to the lawn below, looking for any sign of the both of them. Impulsively, he followed the cobblestone walk and reached a door that was ajar. He peered around it, his imagination beginning to run away.

He saw a staircase and followed it with some trepidation. Upstairs, he then went through another door and into a passage. He had not crept ten paces or so when he saw Ona and Jones through an open door in that most intimate manner possible to find a man and woman. Oblivious of him, their clothing barely off their bodies, each was demanding raucous but clandestine loving from the other.

He wrenched his eyes from the sight. He was unable to look on for longer than the few moments it took for him make sure what he had seen. He turned quickly back the way he had come. Rage, hurt and shame brought stinging tears to his eyes. Even as he tiptoed away, he could still hear Ona's muted feline squealing and Jones' low guttural grunts as their liaison picked up intensity and tormented him.

He staggered out of the building in an indescribable daze, gulping the cool air outside like someone who had been drowning. He somehow groped his way to a new Jaguar that he had bought for her benefit. He left the grounds, sobbing and cursing as he drove home, beating the wheel in terminal despair. The fact that Ona did not always have her chastity belt on was nothing new to him. Yet, this time, she had finally crossed the line. He had put up with enough of her indiscretion and this would have to be the end. He finally had to accept that she would never change, that she would never be his. He felt very exhausted.

Ona came home about an hour later, leaning forever on the front doorbell. He wondered what to do with her. Suddenly, there was nothing to live for, as his mind swirled with frightening ideas, one of which involved the meat cleaver in the kitchen. He did not see how he could regain the will to love or even live, let alone play. After an eternity of irresolution, he reluctantly decided to simply open the door and let her in. It just was not in him to commit murder, which he thought was a great pity.

He confronted her with the most distasteful look he could muster but to his surprise, she scowled back at him before pushing brusquely past into the living room.

"Can you explain why you left me at the party?" she demanded angrily.

"What?" he blinked in disbelief.

"You sneaked out with a girl, that's what, didn't you?" she accused him with such conviction that in spite of his great sadness, he almost laughed.

"Good try, you lying bitch," he hissed. She cringed, but ever so slightly. "You cheating nymphomaniac!"

"How dare you?" she spat, still with enough conviction.

"I hope Charlie Jones will keep you, because *I* will not."

"What are you talking about?" she shot back, but her expression admitted the first uneasy sign.

"I saw what happened," he managed. He could yet kill her, he thought with some fear. "And it's over between us."

"You are out of your mind!" she cried, stepping back from him in ostensible horror. "So, the party host shows me the way to the toilets and you think . . ."

"The toilets my arse!" He stepped menacingly towards her and she quickly back-pedalled. "I saw you with my own eyes, bitch; in a room upstairs; on a *green* sofa. You didn't even shut the door. You couldn't wait to get laid by the great Charlie Jones."

He had backed her up right against the wall. Her eyes were wide with fright, finally realizing that she had been caught literally pants down. Cowering in the face of his rage, she attempted to slither sideways out of his range but he caught her in his angry grip. She shrieked and flailed at him in self-defence. Out of his skin with anger, he flung her furiously aside, causing her literally to fly all the way across the room. Thudding into the wall with the back of her head, she let out a shrill cry and fell instantly quiet, crumbled in a lifeless heap.

•

He was charged with assault and released on bail. He was overwhelmed by the entire episode as well he might. First was the initial fear that he had killed her, then the relative relief that he had not. She had suffered only a cranial injury, though there was considerable internal haemorrhaging. Then there was the humbug of the media, the embarrassment of his private parts made public.

In the end, the lasting emotion he felt was no longer anger or despair at her betrayal but gratitude that she was alive. He did not really wish her dead, though he had come perilously close to doing so. He would gladly suffer a footloose wife all life long than have guilt over a manslaughter trail him forever.

•

The new league season began with the cloud of the Ona case still hovering over him. Saxon Valley, being last season's league runners-up, were in the Champions' league and had gone shopping in the transfer market.

Marc Dedieu, a veteran French striker who had been in the World Cup, came from Chastelbleu; and John Thomas, an Irish defender came from Premiership side Queensbridge. Ron Race finally left Valley to become player-manager at second division Stanleigh Town.

Mellini did not pick Tito for the opening day clash, which like the season before, was against Westbury United. The new signing, Dedieu seemed to hit it off straight away with Di Salvo as they each scored in the 2-2 home draw.

Sir Johnny came out with a much-orchestrated public show of support for Tito. He went to great pains to aid the youngster, lending him the weight of his legendary name. Tito had proved a tremendous asset to the club over the past season, he said. Although he was still learning the ropes, he had already shown some exceptional qualities and the entire affair would unsettle him.

"It makes me remember my own ordeal," he told a press conference at Allen Lane. Thirty years previously, as an England player, Johnny Hastings had been falsely fingered for stealing a Rolex from a jeweller's prior to a World Cup game in Zurich. "I totally sympathise with Tito Tansi and am sure he will come through it just like I did."

Reference to the Rolex incident struck a sensitive chord in English hearts. There had been such public solidarity with Hastings at the time, an unequivocal conviction about his innocence. The episode had ended in sweet vindication when a contrite pageboy confessed that he had been paid to plant the watch in the player's hotel room. The plan, hatched by a syndicate of betters, was aimed at rattling Hastings and of course, the English team.

Sir Johnny invited Tito to lunch at his magnificent house, an Elizabethan juggernaut set in endless Essex parkland that had been in the Hastings family since the eighteenth century.

"You just keep your head, son," he counseled.

"Yes, sir."

"*I* nearly lost mine in Zurich," he confessed and it was obviously an experience that gave him no pleasure re-living. "Would you believe it, a *bloody* Rolex?"

"Very preposterous, sir," Tito said, looking around the daunting abode. The drawing room was a virtual Chippendale gallery, from whose walls illustrious forebears of Sir Johnny's looked benignly down from gild-framed portraits. A natty butler with impeccable manners tended them all the while. He did not know if he was more cowed by the superior station of the Chairman or by the personal simplicity he conveyed in the worn cashmere over faded Wrangler. Sir Johnny was of the upper classes but had been a workingman's hero and his long fraternity with everyday people showed in his casual manner. Still it was quite challenging reconciling his innate nobility with the rather proletarian image of chasing after a football for a living, let alone filching a watch.

"You must not let it get to you." Sir Johnny wagged a finger, and then lit a pipe. "Concentration is everything."

Saxon Valley were in European competition after three decades and it was a thing of special significance for Sir Johnny. He could not afford to have a player such as Tito playing at half cock. Valley were a good side these days. They had proved it with two consecutive seasons of high performance and good results. However, he did not think they had the depth of squad needed for the Champions' league. The big time had come upon the small timers rather suddenly. When he took over as Chairman, not in his wildest dream did he reckon on playing in the Champions' league even in the next decade. It never entered his head at the beginning of last season that Valley would be preoccupied with anything besides acclimatizing to the Premiership. That alone would have been feat enough. It was probably not until the New Year that the notion began to filter into his mind that they might be challenging for honours.

•

Valley were drawn in Group C of the Champions' league first phase alongside Spaniards Real Baracoa, Holland's Argos and French side, Charlotte. It was deep waters indeed, especially for the incredulous fans still marooned in Neverland. Thankfully, a number of the players were not total strangers to European competition. Di Salvo was a Champions' league veteran and every one of the other players would be looking to him to draw confidence and inspiration. He had played in the final an incredible five times with Bellona, winning the title thrice. Lanzarini had been in the semi-finals with his former club Ancologna. Krohnberg had been in it with both Argos and Inter-Cosenzaro, as had been Mihailescu and Thomas with Pescarleno and Queensbridge respectively. Marc Dedieu, the new French forward won a UEFA winners' medal with Charlotte five seasons ago. Dedieu was a curious signing, by the way, as he was considered over the hill by observers, but Mellini insisted on his experience.

Tito made his season's Premiership debut against Milton Town and scored a brace to hug the back page headlines. Like last season, Valley were immediately in the front running, bunching up with Liverton, Millchester, Westbury United and of course, Kingford, who were straight away at the top as usual. He was among the leading goal scorers after the first few weeks, along with more likely names like Starr, Montego, Buckingham, Di Salvo and Cope and although it was early days yet, it was still gratifying.

The court case did not appear to be weighing him down unduly and he really had Sir Johnny to thank for that. Mellini seemed happiest when he played him in attack alongside Di Salvo, who was really beginning to endear himself to the Allen Lane fans with some very influential performances.

They travelled to Spain for their first Champions' league game, a special and significant occasion for the fans. Real Baracoa were the favourites to win the group. They were a great club with so much tradition and last season's runners up in *La Liga*. They lived in the shadow of Conquista, which they thoroughly resented and were forever doing everything to shed, though quite unsuccessfully. They had not been in the Champions' league for a while, only the UEFA Cup. Though that was also a great competition, it was decidedly inferior to the Champions' league where Conquista lived a dream.

Like all the big European clubs, Real Baracoa boasted a galaxy of top international stars. Their biggest players perhaps were young Brazilian, Zizinho and the Mexican, Diaz, who was a revelation at the last World Cup.

Diaz shot Baracoa into the early lead, putting the home fans in a good mood. They went on to play some excellent football, demonstrating why they had been getting results lately. Valley came close to levelling before half time but Di Salvo headed just wide from Blair's cross. The Spaniards were difficult to break down, though shortly into the second period, Tito struck the post on the end of Lanzarini's cross.

Krohnberg, Thomas and Fuchs had their hands full with Diaz and Zizinho. The Real forwards were both in splendid form but the Valley backs managed to hold their own with some excellent defending. Just before the end, after some sustained Real pressure, Livingstone gave away a free kick from which Zizinho's swerving shot wrongfooted Peltonnen for the second goal. Valley were beaten squarely by a class team and they took it in good faith because they felt they had given a good account of themselves.

Gain the whole world

Charlie Jones stirred from sleep, stretched and yawned. He blinked against the daylight that filtered through the cheesecloth curtains and rubbed at his eyes to gather his wits to the present.

The party last night had been rather wild, though there were not more than ten guests, all young, fashionable *and* all girls except for Luca Scala and him. They had drank and danced until the early hours, and the smell of marijuana hung heavily still in the air.

He looked about the room. It was like a desolate battlefront just after the guns had fallen all quiet. Articles of clothing were littered and scattered about like shrapnel and debris. Young sexy female bodies were sprawled or slouched on the needlework rug like rubble on the day after.

On the wall above the mantelpiece was a large mirror picture of Marilyn Monroe smouldering eternally from between silvery satin sheets. Under a poster of Che Guevara, an acoustic Fender guitar leant against a Steinway grand piano. On top of it stood a near-empty bottle of Southern Comfort and an ashtray full of cigarette butts and roaches. The whole atmosphere had just the right amount of the bohemian air, which he craved.

He peered bleary-eyed at some lines of cocaine on the terracotta tile floor. Someone had forgotten to shift *those* up their snout. He surveyed the body to his left on the wrought iron bed, cleverly recollecting that it belonged to Juanita, a pretty, young brunette, who was the most insistent after him all last night. He had always had a way with women but these days, they wanted him wantonly. Every one of them, it seemed, demanded a right to a piece of him for keepsake. It was little wonder, though, with so much fuss made about his *body* in the never-ending magazine spreads. By now, every woman knew every last muscle of his torso by name; knew every blue-green vein snaking its sexy course under his golden skin; knew the remotest detail of the erotic tattoos that now adorned his front and back.

In August, *Cosmo* readers had unanimously voted him 'The Sexiest Male Alive.' He had even been made to bare much of his sunbrowned buns for the lens, for which he was heralded by *Playgirl* as "The Guy With The Tightest Arse On Earth.' Because of all this, Alfreda was driving herself to fits with jealousy. She did not seem to see the joke in her man being on top of *Hustler's* 'The Horny Hoe's Most Wanted list,' for instance.

She did try to be broad-minded about everything. After all, there was no business like show business. *She* was away most of the time herself and was aware that Charlie was a bad boy at heart. A pop idol like him could fend off only so many groupies. She really tried to be levelheaded about things. However, passion and prejudice usually triumphed over reason, forcing her into wild mood swings and manic depressions.

Anywhere in the world where *Los Mininos* played, word always got to her about Charlie's capers. She would call him on the phone raving or sobbing, and he would generally pander sweetly to her in that modulating voice of his. She might relax for a while because deeper down he was really such a nice person. Nevertheless, something was always bound to happen soon after to trigger the vicious cycle of her possessive passion.

As Jones scrutinized the blonde in bed to his right, the telephone rang. He surveyed the permissive scene around him with some guilt, wondering if by some telepathy, Alfreda had sensed it.

"Hello."

"Charlie?"

It was not Alfreda's rich Spanish tenor.

"Who's this?"

"It's me."

"Who?"

"Ona."

"Oh," he said with a hint of relief. "Tito's girl. Hi."

"Hi."

"Where are you?"

"I'm in Nigeria. Lagos."

"You're alright now?"

"I can't say that."

"How's Tito?"

"We've broken up. Officially."

"I'm sorry to hear that." It was not so surprising and he knew he had played no small part in bringing that about. Although he felt some sympathy or guilt, he silently assumed a perverse kind of credit as well.

"It was a terrible mistake what we made, Charlie. I don't know what to do."

"I'm sure you'll both settle this," he suggested tamely. He did not know what else to say.

"I am certain we will not. He was very hurt. I feel so bad, Charlie. I have lost everything."

"I'm really sorry," he repeated with a strain of impatience as Juanita stirred. "I wish I could help."

"*You wish you could help!*"

"Really."

"But you *can*, Charlie," she charged.

"How?"

"Don't leave me alone," she pleaded.

"What?"

"Please stand by me. I am so alone. Everyone here hates me. They hate me for getting Tito into trouble. They write such horrible things about me in the papers, Charlie!"

"But *what* can I do?"

"Take me away from Nigeria. Take me to Spain or anywhere."

"That is not possible," he declared quietly.

"At least, take care of me," she cried. "I am so lost. You know Tito was going to marry me."

"You should have thought of that, shouldn't you?" he all but snapped.

"He used to send me money and to my parents too. You know things are so difficult in Nigeria. I can't face my friends. I'm pregnant." She was discomfited and incoherent.

"Alright, but we'll talk later," he said, meaning it. "I've got to go now."

"Please, Charlie, don't hang up!" By now, she was sobbing without much control and she could not be putting it on.

"I've got to go now. Talk to you later, alright?"

He dropped the receiver with some will power. He did not think he was at all a bad person and if anything got to him, it was a crying girl, but he felt genuinely at a loss what to do. He owed Tito an apology as it was and didn't think the wisest thing for him to do was get more involved with the girl, break-up or not. Still, if she needed help, he would be obliged to respond. He would be generous to her with money but that was about it. He would send her a couple of thousand quid right away by Western Union. She was a fine girl and he had liked their short few minutes together.

Juanita was awake now. She sat up and stretched lazily, her linen cover down to her waist. He could see that she was proud to show her peachy bare tops. She leant over and kissed him, hungrily snuggling up against his famous body. She got up from the bed, sauntered over to a white leather sofa and sank in it, hugging a chintz-covered cushion. She bent over a line of cocaine on the glass-top table and expertly made it all disappear up her nostrils.

"I guess that passes for breakfast?" Jones commented with thinly disguised reproach.

"Want some?" she asked in reply, bending over the next line.

"Nah."

"Go on," she urged. "Have some."

He did a line or two occasionally but was glad that he was never going to be hooked. He was only a social snorter and rarely so at that. His unequivocal loyalty was to football and he was never going to do anything to diminish that God-given talent. His only real vice—if it was that—was girls, but that did him no harm. He was not one of those puritanical players like Tito, who believed that sex and sports did not mix. Tito thought that a tryst in the hay took its toll on the turf, he recalled with unexpected fondness. As for him, *he* always followed a Friday night romp with an athletic *tour de force* on Saturday afternoon. And the proof of that was the fact that he was the scourge of European defences. Nothing could stop him playing the way he was. He was the rampant lion of world football and defences packed up under his power, pace and prodigy. Only last weekend, he had scored four times in *La Liga* against rivals Real Baracoa, who were very much in form this season.

In the Champions' league, Conquista had opened their campaign well, winning at home by a comfortable 4-0 over Croatia Dravajek, and he had scored twice. Along with them in the so-called group of death, were the Italian duo of Inter Cosenzaro and Bellona. It promised to be a tough campaign.

Being grouped with Bellona was something he—and perhaps most of the players—could do without. Frankly, he did not mind if the two sides never ever had to meet. Their encounters were never ordinary, coming with so much emotional baggage. Football, for him, would never cease to be a pleasure, a release. He would quit the game the day it did. However, football was also a business, he acknowledged and business was business. *And* Palazzolo and Delgado made it their business to feud.

"OK," he said, capitulating playfully to the charming Juanita. He knelt over the glass-top table and put his nose to a line.

•

By December, the first phase of the Champions' league was ending and each of the groups had produced the expected portions of passion and action. Saxon Valley were topping their group and surprising everyone. They were making an impression, not with pluckiness but great football.

After their opening loss to Real Baracoa, they had made a remarkable recovery. A 3-1 win over Charlotte, in which Tito scored the hat trick, had given them confidence. They followed that with a gritty performance against Real Baracoa at Allen Lane, an epic 4-4 draw, in which Tito scored yet another hat trick. An excellent away win against top class Dutch act Argos then sent them to the top of the group, upsetting the pundits no end.

Impetuously, they went on to a 3-2 win in Charlotte's newly built gold-domed citadel in front of 80,000 frenetic French fans. The new stadium was called *Le dome des dieux* and should one day become as much a *Parisien* cultural icon as the Eiffel Tower and the Arc d'Triomphe. Much to Tito's disappointment, he did not play in that game, owing to a sprained toe. However, Ryder in his place scored the winner, indicating Valley's strength in depth.

By Matchday 6, they were two points clear at the top, needing only to draw at home against Argos to progress to the next phase. A loss would be inauspicious. Third-placed Baracoa certainly had enough guns to beat a demoralized Charlotte in Spain. If they did so and should Argos win at Allen Lane, the Spaniards would nick the second spot and Valley were out. Football was a funny old game, as everyone knew.

Allen Lane was agog for the huge fixture, the home crowd astir with excitement. The big time was around and they were living every minute of it with all the anxiety that accompanied it. To think that just two years ago, they were mired in the doldrums of the lower division, churning out grinding, drudging, tedious, showings. These days, their team was giving them so much to be happy about, playing some really excellent, sometimes flamboyant football and getting great results. But Argos numbed them with the early lead, a tenth minute strike by Dutch international, Vanderbilt, who intercepted from Livingstone and swiftly swept a sweet left past Peltonnen. Valley equalized before the break however, the superb Mihailescu supplying a cross for Tito to head in.

At half time, Mellini rang the changes, betraying a trace of panic. Therefore, off came Livingstone and on did young de la Luna, who loved to get forward. The Peruvian was coming back after a lay off. Off came Di Salvo too, who was rather unfit, making way for Ryder. Still, Argos quickly regained the lead in the second half, Goosen heading past Peltonnen to stun the home fans. Stung, Valley responded with some intense attacking play and since Argos reciprocated, there was some fiery end-to-end stuff to delight the neutrals at least.

Tito was very feisty on the night, bothering the Dutch with his mazy, lightning runs at the defence and his energy soon gave rise to the equaliser. His cross dropped perfectly for Ryder, who volleyed home and went crazy with joy. Then near the end, Krohnberg, forward for a corner, out jumped the Argos defence and headed the winner! The veteran sweeper was scoring for the first time in the Valley shirt and the players swarmed to him, almost suffocating him with felicitation. As a result, Valley were into the second phase and Allen Lane was a good place to be that night if you were a fan of theirs. Real Baracoa were through also, squeezing ahead of Argos by having hammered hapless Charlotte 4-0.

•

A fortnight before that, Conquista won their penultimate group game at home against Scottish champions, Strathnock Rovers. They were comfortably on top of Group B and would be cruising into the second phase. They had won all their games quite handily, except for a 2-2 draw away to Bellona in October.

Cesare Palazzolo was most uneasy as his team went into the last game of the first phase. After five games, Bellona were in an embarrassing third position behind even unfancied Strathnock Rovers, who were originally meant to be canon fodder. The Scots had shocked Bellona with a 1-0 win in the opening game of the campaign and the Roman giants had never really recovered their poise since then. Bellona's only chance of averting a shameful first phase exit depended on them winning their final game, which so happened to be against Conquista in Spain! The stage was thus set for yet another gripping episode in the Palazzolo/Delgado saga.

•

"*Autógrafo! Autógrafo, por favor!*" A group of coquettish Spanish girls stepped up to Jones at the airport in Madrid. He was arriving from a flying mid week Versace photo shoot in Milan.

"*Si, si.*" He smiled flirtatiously, signing up, kissing some of them and sending them into raptures. He was enjoying his life. He was every football fan's favourite player and every teenage girl's choicest heartthrob. He was fully engaged with offers and deals of all descriptions and certainly could not complain about much. His latest project was to make a CD sound recording. He could strum a Spanish guitar and finger the primary chords. He was so idolised that even if he recorded *Man on the Flying Trapeze,* chances were it might hit the Top 100 and ship platinum!

So far, he had chalked up seven goals in the Champions' league but was miffed by having to share that distinction with Tito of all people. The Nigerian's back-to-back hat tricks in the group games had made him a major player. The Spanish press had gone to town about him after Valley's game against Real Baracoa. Tito was a wet blanket if you asked him, he thought with a naughty, private smile.

Apart from that, things could not be better. He played for the world's greatest club side and despite being in a squad of the most outstanding football players, he was probably the top gun of them all. That logically made him the greatest player in the world, he permutated.

"*Signor* Jones."

He turned just before reaching the waiting limo and saw a small, dapper man in a blue suit approach.

"Yes?"

"I wish to see you very urgently, *Signor* Jones." The man spoke politely in English but betrayed the fact that he was Italian. "Confidentially."

"Journalist?"

"My name is Pizzi," the Italian said. "Stefano Pizzi."

"I am sorry but have we met?"

"No," the man answered. He was of a very engaging nature and looked well heeled. "But I have an interesting proposition to make to you."

"You're not an agent?" Jones shot his brow inquiringly up. "Because I have no intention of leaving the best club in the world."

"I am not an agent," smiled Pizzi indulgently and handed Jones a card. "I am General Manager of Bellona."

"Good to make your acquaintance, Mister Pizzi," Jones said, impressed by the small man, but shrugged. "Still, I don't see the point because I am not leaving Conquista."

"I am a great fan of James Bond's," Pizzi smiled. "And I like the idea of never saying never. However, I am not here to talk of you leaving Conquista. I have some other business."

"I can't imagine what."

"I am staying at the Grand Hotel. Can we meet there, tomorrow evening at seven?"

"Why not?" Jones said, taking a shine to Pizzi and his direct manner. "It better be good."

"It *will* be good," Pizzi promised.

"Alright then," Jones shrugged, flashing a final steamy smile at the squad of star-struck *señoritas*. "I think I can make it."

They shook hands firmly and Jones disappeared into the limo and left.

They met punctually the next evening. The cosiness of the restaurant encouraged some intimacy and there was some conversational rigmarole. It was Pizzi's favourite eating-place in Madrid, so he said. Such good cuisine, he vouchsafed. Unfortunately, he did not visit the country as much as he would have wished, about which Jones was quite indifferent and soon grew a little impatient. Alfreda was in town and he was looking forward to seeing her tonight.

"What's all this about, then?" he asked Pizzi.

The Italian cleared his throat. "It's about the game."

"What game?"

"The game against Bellona." He leaned closer confidentially. "The second leg."

"*What* about the game?"

Pizzi's piercing eyes locked into Jones' and held them.

"Bellona *must* win or they go out of the competition."

"That's pretty obvious, ain't it?" Jones said. "I'm sure Conquista fans won't lose sleep over that."

"Bellona must win it," Pizzi said with courteous but unmistakeable emphasis. "I am asking your assistance."

"In what way?" Jones inquired with an appraising frown.

Pizzi seemed to hesitate but only briefly.

"Conquista have nothing to lose. Even if they lost the game, your team is already into the next phase."

"You're out of your bleeping mind," Jones cut in, getting Pizzi's drift and making as though he was leaving.

"Please, Signor Jones," the affable Italian spoke urgently. Quite elegantly, he made a restraining gesture. "Two million dollars."

Jones froze to hesitant attention and sank slowly back down in the seat. He looked quizzically at Pizzi.

"*Two million dollars?*"

"Yes."

"Who the hell are you really?" Jones demanded warily.

Pizzi produced a business card different from the one he gave Jones the previous night. This one was of the world-renowned conglomerate, *Globo-Italiano,* Cesare Palazzolo's mother ship corporation. Pizzi had a meticulous manner, which might be impressive or annoying.

"I am also a director of Globo-Italiano. I am a nephew of Don Cesare's and a most trusted assistant."

"What you're saying is that Palazzolo sent you to bribe me to throw the game?"

"Oh no," Pizzi said quickly. *Too* quickly, Jones adjudged. "That is a little dramatic, but I have plenty of—shall we say—latitude, *Signor* Jones."

"What am I supposed to do, anyway," Jones asked guardedly. "Score a hat trick of *own* goals?"

"It is nothing as complicated as that," Pizzi replied with a pleasant smile. "You are the leading scorer at Conquista. If you don't score . . ."

"Hannibal will or Rojas or Scala or Krebs or a whole bunch of other blokes."

"You will be interested to know that a few of your team mates are willing to do us this favour," Pizzi revealed. "I will take care of everything. All you have to do is *not* play to your capacity. In other words, do not score against us and you will get the fee."

"I can't," Jones muttered indecisively, worried that he could. It was a lot of money and it was coming easy. Conquista were already in the next phase. Two million dollars was a lot of money, even to Bill Gates.

"You have nothing to lose," Pizzi assured him quietly.

"I am not too sure about that." He was a little frightened. Pizzi was looking alarmingly like the devil offering Christ the world. Delgado would do anything not to lose the home fixture to Bellona. Any victory against the archrivals was worth a dozen *La Liga* wins, apart from which Meissner, the head coach did not suffer anyone under-perfoming. At Conquista, there was such a competition for places among the squad of superstars that no one dared perform below his best. Besides, he wanted to increase his Champions' league goals haul and distance himself from Tito Tansi. Every game counted therefore. "I will think about it."

"You must decide now, *Signor* Jones," Pizzi insisted. He seemed to sense he had game and was circling for the kill. "Half of the money before the game and the other after. You understand, of course, that this is an agreement between gentlemen; a matter of honour."

Pizzi did not relent until he felt he had obtained Jones' commitment. He then more or less released him from the restaurant. His sense of mastery was that palpable and he watched pensively after the superstar, who virtually staggered into the night as if punch-drunk. Jones would naturally be wondering if he was making a mistake but Pizzi was sure he would get around to doing the deal. The obligation was relatively small, the remuneration pretty massive.

•

As far as club fixtures went, Conquista-Bellona was the hugest in world football. The two finalists from last year were already set to replay the unending drama so early in this year's competition. Usually each encounter had a peculiar *denouément* and this one was no different. Conquista were through already to the next phase and had looked in devastating form doing so. On the other hand, the Italians would have to be at their very best to attain the win they *must* in Spain. Absolutely nothing less than a win would do for the Italian *colossi* and they knew more than any other team the hostile atmosphere of Conquista's *Estadio San Diego*.

The *San Diego* was a most daunting football basilica. For over half a century, millions had come there to worship the gods with the leather balls at their feet. Though it was an old monument and stood in need of some modernization, it was for their multitudes of fans, a beloved haven where they congregated to make life hell for unbelievers.

Jones was to find that his name was not in the starting line up. That was unusual these days but all right with him today, because he had developed a serious case of cold feet about the deal with Pizzi. Pizzi had wired the money barely an hour after their meeting while he still reeled from indecision, but he later decided it was a big mistake and made up his mind to refund the downpayment. Now the idea was forming in his mind that if Meissner did not pick him to play at all, he might yet eat his cake and have it. The payment of his balance should not be prejudiced by his non-inclusion in the side. It was not his fault if he was not picked. And what better way to ensure that he did not play to his capacity than to *not* get picked?

"I'm not playing?" he checked anxiously with Meissner.

"May be you might," replied the legendary German coach guardedly.

"I am fine," the player hedged. "I need to score more goals, Professor."

Meissner fixed him an owlish and reproachful glare.

"The game is not about Charlie Jones scoring goals. It is about Conquista winning."

"I am sorry, Professor."

The thin and bespectacled German was a club icon. Elderly and heuristic, he was appropriately nicknamed *Herr Professor* back in his country. His god-like status at Conquista dwarfed the stature of even his biggest superstars. He had been a great player in his days, which was very helpful with so many modern-day greats in his charge. He had captained Germany to a World Cup win. He had also *coached* Germany to win both the European Nations Cup and the World Cup. He had taken three clubs from three different countries to the European Champions' league title. This season, he was attempting to take Conquista to their fourth *consecutive* Champions' league title. Only recently, he had concluded a new five-year deal with the club. Since he was sixty-five years old, it surely meant he would be staying there until the end of his glorious career. He was without a shade of doubt, the most successful coach in the world.

The first half of the game ended 0-0. It was a very cagey contest, characteristic of most of their encounters. Still, there was some really brilliant stuff on show expectedly.

Bika, Conquista's goalkeeper let slip a back pass from Garcia soon after the restart. It might have resulted in a bizarre own goal but for a desperate clearance by French back, Girard.

Conquista came closest to going in front from set pieces, where Hassan's height and strength posed a great threat. Then quite uncharacteristically in the 60th minute, Garcia miscued a clearance and the ball fell to Jurgens, who did not miss the chance to put Bellona ahead.

On the touchline, Meissner stood immobile, pulling fretfully on a pipe, his habit whenever he was displeased with affairs on the field. It was not long before he substituted Garcia and Bika, who had both been unusually shaky tonight. A few minutes later, he had Hannibal come off and sent on Jones. The prolific Brazilian had been eerily quiet by his very high standards and had failed to threaten the visitors.

The fans roared restively in the stands, while Delgado fretted in his suite. They were not going to easily accept a home loss to their fiercest rivals, even if the game did not have strategic significance for them.

Bellona's centre back, Franco Russo materialised at Jones' side as soon as he came on. This was their first meeting since the Nations Cup.

"We meet again, Jones," he intoned with a leer.

"Yeah. Small world, Russo."

"Just call me Franco, *darling*."

The Spanish champions raised their game and with a quarter of an hour left on the clock, Santamaria's free kick rebounded for Hassan to steer in the equaliser. Minutes later, Jones took a pass in a great position from the outstanding Santamaria but was felled by Russo. Jones complained but did not get the free kick and was sulky.

"What a lovely arse you've got, Charlie," said Russo affecting a lecherous look up Jones' famous bottom, which was partially exposed as they scrambled to their feet. Jones adjusted his shorts but not in time to prevent a close up by the television cameras. That thoroughly delighted the naughtier fans, for who it was the best *shot* of the night. Trivia journalists were later to have a field day showing the pictures under witty captions.

"You're right, Russo," Jones responded dryly. "Lots of people do love my arse and I expect that would include faggots and sons of whores like you."

"*Mama mia*! You insult my mama!" Russo's eyes flashed with anger.

"Yeah, Russo. I know your mother is a whore." Jones was surprised but pleased with himself that he had scored the upset.

Moments afterwards, he took another pass from Santamaria and from the corner of his eye, saw a raging Russo stampede after him. From all indications, *II Cannibale* would maim him if he could. The dreaded defender was very quick for his size and pounced on him with a murderous, two-footed tackle. Jones felt his legs caught as if in a vice and crashed to the turf, thinking he might need an amputation. The referee was as decisive about giving the penalty as showing the red card in Russo's face.

"Your turn for the early bath, Russo," Jones said in an undertone as the big Italian strode without protest on his way out of the pitch.

"*Fuck you.*" The furious Russo turned and spat at Jones full in the face. The latter fell on the turf and play was held up while assistants from the bench washed the spittle off with much elaboration. Russo was later to receive a five-match European ban from UEFA and a hostile release from his contract by Palazzolo.

Meissner gestured from the sideline for Jones to take the penalty. With a number of players making some bizarre errors tonight, Herr Professor was perhaps counting on the reliable English lad. And moments later, the idol of the San Diego stroked the ball adeptly into the Bellona goal for the winner.

So Bellona were out of the Champions' league in the very first phase. He had blown his part of the deal with Stefano Pizzi and realized immediately that he would have to pay the money back. He would be happy to do just that. He had never been comfortable with the transaction anyway.

The result of the game was a monumental embarrassment to the peevish Palazzolo. He would find it hard to live down.

•

Tito had promised his folks he would visit home at Christmas but he had reckoned without Valley's crowded fixtures. On Boxing Day, he was in a league game against Doverham at Allen Lane, Valley losing it at that, to make a miserable Yuletide. All the same, things certainly could have been a lot worse at the club. There was a bunch-up at the top of the Premiership with no runaway leader and there were only six points separating Valley in fifth place and uneasy leaders, Kingford.

In the Champions' league, they were still hanging tough with Europe's best, second behind Ukrainian side, Torpedo Krivnev in their group. They won away in Portugal against Santa Isabela, Temba scoring a priceless winner from a Blair cross. A fortnight later, however, they lost in the Ukraine to Torpedo 1-0.

Personally, it was dreamtime for him; he was making a definite reputation with his unfolding prowess in front of goal. He was joint top scorer in the Premiership, along with the illustrious duo of Fernando Montego and Wayne Starr. Amazingly, he was replicating the same form in Europe, where he was performing like anything but a novice. He had nine goals so far in the Champions' league, one ahead of Jones, which gave him considerable pleasure.

•

By the time he got to Onitsha on New Year's Eve, the new house was completed and his parents had moved in. He was impressed with the space of it, glad at having induced a neighbour into parting with an abutting lot of land.

'I want you to live in a house with enough room,' he had written to his father some months back. His father initially had a draughtsman draw up a plan for a much humbler bungalow, which Tito instantly rejected. He wanted a real house, modern and well appointed and so he had an architect design something of impressive size and quality.

"It's too large," his father had complained to his wife.

"I agree," she had said. She had always meekly toed his line. "People will turn their eyes on him."

But their son was adamant that they should live in a very good house. He remembered how he always ogled at the palatial home that John Kafara made available to his family. He remembered the sinking feeling he always had returning home after a rare visit there. He wanted to forget that miserable, humid, mosquito-infested hole they used to call home.

"I can afford it," he had told his mother quietly when she fretted. Sir Johnny had installed a hefty new pay structure that put him among the club's highest earners.

Except for the Kafaras', he thought the house was the prettiest in the neighbourhood and even beyond. It was a handsome, white-painted mansion, given a colonial character by the red tile roof, *jalousie* windows, colonnaded verandas and leafy banana plants. The compound was florid with soft grass, roses, lilies, hibiscus and bougainvillea. A jeep he bought for the old man and his wife sat in the gravel drive, gleaming in the sun.

News of his presence in the neighbourhood soon spread and it was not long before callers invaded the new house. Everyone wanted a glimpse of him. He had not realised he had that many childhood friends, old classmates, cousins, aunts and uncles. Among the callers was old Mr. Dazie, who was very suitably proud of his old boy made out good. So was the fastidious school gamesmaster, who he never would forgive for leaving him out of the school football team. He was very happy to see Papa Joe, who he had kept steadily in touch with and would always have a special place in his heart. He could not say quite as much about the crooked old school gatekeeper, who fleeced him on countless occasions when he came late to school and even did so on this visit. It was amusing how everyone remembered some episode in the past that he had figured in, which for the life of him, he could not recall.

Everyone pretty well had an idea how much money he earned and the emphasis was on *much*. They learnt all the figures in the sensational local press and when they converted those earnings into the local currency, it boggled their minds. Of course they did not know how much the Exchequer withheld or what it cost just to live in England, and they frankly could not care.

"Please give us something, *Brother* Tito," a group of youths begged. He knew them all. They were much smaller when he left, all fellow members of the fraternity of the deprived, from which he was just narrowly escaped. They would have learnt long ago how to stave off hunger by lying on their stomachs. Now they were in their teens and getting nowhere fast like most others before them. For as little as picking pockets, police guns would soon mow down many of them. For as commonplace a misbehaviour as shoplifting, Vigilantes' machetes would dismember the remainder. He pined anew for Elo, Francis and Skido and the hundreds more like them, and the many more there would be.

"Here." He gave the youths a wad of bills and they rejoiced so much, it made him mourn. They would spend it quickly on drinks, smokes and tarts, jeans and basketball pumps. Then they would need even more. He gave away a lot of money that way during his visit. While in England, he often daydreamed about the things he could do to make a change back home to help even a precious few in the old neighbourhood at least. He had thought of a small factory, a bakery, a gaming arcade, a library, a machining shop and so on. However, he found that people preferred what he could hand them straight out of his pocket. Folks were still battling to put something in the belly and were understandably more eager for a coin at hand than a castle in the air.

Almost everyone here was up to the minute with the European Champions' league. They knew all the players, all the scores, the coaches and the permutations. Even here in his hometown, while Tito was a hero, Charlie Jones was a god. Certainly, there were more pictures of the English lad about than his. Nothing gave him the gripes more than the sight of Jones grinning out of a giant fluorescent Pepsi billboard directly across the road from their new home.

"Can you get me into a football club, Brother Tito?" one of them asked anxiously. "I am a good player. Like you."

"Yes," one of his mates suretied.

"I believe you," Tito said. With supreme ease, he could put himself in the youth's place. He shut his eyes briefly and it was *déjà vu*. It was only a couple of years since he had put the same wide-eyed question to Malcolm Stewart. "But it's not very easy, you know?"

"*You* made it," said the youth snappishly.

"I had a bit of luck, I imagine," he replied with candid reflection.

Adeze, Ona's old friend from Rosary College, came calling one afternoon in the company of three girls. The last time he saw her was at that fateful birthday party Skido had for Ona. It was not so terribly long ago, but she had transformed from a mere trendy teen into a promising woman.

"You should not have hit Ona like that," she reproved sometime during their conversation. "I don't remember that you were a violent boy."

"You're right," he said, inwardly grateful that the whole episode had petered to this. He had been so relieved when the magistrate dismissed the charges. He had put it all behind him, though with some pain. "I didn't really hit her."

"Will you make it up to her?"

"No," he said with an emphatic shake of the head. Ona did not live in Onitsha anymore, anyhow. Not that he cared, he told himself. She did now in Lagos, where she reportedly ran a restaurant. The restaurant was supposedly a popular one. She had a giant screen, where football showed most of the day. She would appear to have converted her period with him to some profit. People were curious, it seemed, to know the young girl who had been at the centre of that international imbroglio.

She could—and obviously did—claim a measure of stardom as a result of everything. A couple of months ago, he had been in Lagos to play for Nigeria in a World Cup qualifier against Ghana. He had played a good game, scoring in the 2-1 win. The day after the game, as most of the papers touted his exploits, *ENCOMIUM* published an interview with Ona, where she claimed she was pregnant with his child.

"That poor, innocent child," Adeze said of the unborn baby. "You won't take care of it?"

"I don't want to discuss this, please," he said. He was still doing his level best to get over Ona. He sensed the other girls in the room prick up their ears for some authentic gossip material to be used later. He would have none of it and shortly was steering them subtly in the direction of the front door.

"Me and my basket mouth," Adeze cried in mock self-reproach. "I hope I have not offended you."

"Not really," he mumbled but held the door ajar.

She stepped up close to him and lowered her voice.

"I only want you to know that I am there if you want me."

"I'll remember that," he promised spuriously, while avoiding her warm, searching eyes. Like hell, he would. She would not be the first girl wanting to help him get over his hurt but how could he get involved anyone now? He had never been at ease with girls at the best of times. Now he was positively running scared of the creatures.

Ironically, he got a surprise visit from one of the more petrifying specimens of that species. Precious turned up at the front doorstep the following evening. Even at worst, she was a stunningly attractive woman but that evening, she had clearly gone the extra mile to look her best, wearing a short, frilled, silk dress that played up her all earthy charm.

"*Sorry, my man,*" she smiled and touched her cleavage in a playful *mea culpa. "I kno' I really shouldna cum' bargin' in like dis.*"

"It is so good to see you," he said, gulping at the sight of her. "Come in."

He took her travelling bag and watched her walk to a sofa. She was as always very much aware of her primeval attraction. She was probably *too* aware of it, Tito thought harmlessly and that was perhaps both her pitfall and her appeal. She was an obvious narcissist, so in love with her beautiful body and apparently enslaved by its simmering passions.

"*Ya mus' be wonderin' why I've cum all dis way, from Lagos,*" she said.

"Five hundred miles *is* quite a distance."

She shrugged. "*I jus' fel' like to see ya, dat's all. Is da' aw' right?*"

"That's actually nice of you," he said haltingly. "But then, you always were nice to me."

"*A few things ha' changed since ya came by da club lookin' fe yur missin' sista,*" she laughed.

"By the way, I just got off the phone with her."

"*I was at her place las' night. I stayed till quite late.*"

"Did you tell her you were coming to Onitsha?"

"*Are ya kiddin'?*" She affected fair alarm. "*She'd kill me!*"

"I'm a big boy now," he claimed.

"We shall see," she intoned snugly. From all indications, she meant to attend to some unfinished business, and as his eyes went over her, he was not averse to the prospect. He had this particularly enduring image of her. The sheer evening gown sliding gloriously off her body on that misted-up night back in her room in Lagos was forever secured in the vault of his sensual fantasies. Still he was nervous. He was still very much a novice in the art of love and here he was, face to face with a legend of the art form. It was the equivalent of an amateur boxer making his pro debut against Mike Tyson *circa* '88.

"So how's life with you these days?" he asked, to downplay his anxiety.

"*Got me a small bi'ness goin' down now,*" she said. "*An In'ernet café.*"

"You still go to the clubs?"

"Cos I'm used to it, not 'cos I gotta," she said. *"When I go, I hang out wid ma girls; we drink, dance, y'kno'? Dat's all."*

"Yeah, right," he agreed, tongue in cheek.

"Whatever," she shrugged and smiled facetiously

He enjoyed her company more than he might have thought he would. She was very vivacious and her bubbliness so contagious. Even though Ona had almost put him off the female sex, he felt an ironic sense of security with Precious. Precious was older, so bad and corrupt that nothing could possibly come out of their relationship. She stayed two memorable, fun-filled days.

•

He returned to England soon after the New Year and found it a curious relief to be back to the grind of professional football. It was bitter cold and the turfs were heavy but he did not seem to mind this anymore. He plodded along with the rest of the team, getting good results in the end, which was all that seemed to matter in life. They stayed among the leaders of the Premiership and kept in the FA Cup running just like last season. They were largely consistent but it was excruciating. It made him find great respect for teams like Kingford, Westbury United, Doverham and Liverton, who maintained that tempo season after season for decades.

They continued in the Champions' league with a home tie against Kaiserheim, the German champions. There was little to remark a drab first half and the sterile game badly needed something to bring it to life, which was finally provided when Tito got on the score sheet with an acrobatic volley. The subdued crowd came alive and the game picked up pace. Wagner, the visitors' six-foot nine forward predictably bothered the Valley back in the air, and soon equalised from a corner. Soon after, he again headed past Peltonnen from close range to put his side ahead.

The giant German international became the emphatic hero, completing his hat trick late in the game with another headed goal. His grateful coach substituted him after that and Kaiserheim eased up, which was ultimately not so profound, as Di Salvo, then Blair from a penalty, clinched the draw to the relief of the home fans. The incredible six-goal half was the European game of the night.

A fortnight later, the teams met again. This time, the circumstances were a little tenser. It was the last game of the second stage. Torpedo Krivnev had been in awesome form and were comfortably through to the quarterfinal with eleven points, five clear of Valley and Kaiserheim, who both had six. Valley's slight advantage lay in a goal difference of one. Porto Isabella of Portugal were effectively out of it and so their game against Torpedo was only a formality. Kaiserheim-Saxon Valley for the second quarterfinal berth was the crunch game of the group.

From the opening minute when Blair's shot struck the bar, a fierce encounter was on the cards. Valley were without the services of Di Salvo and Lanzarini, the two Italians having been sidelined by cautions. Kaiserheim battled hard in front of their vocal fans but the deadlock was broken by Tito's goal. Minutes later, Dedieu scored to put Valley two up and in the driving seat. The German fans were suddenly subdued but Wagner pulled one back just before half time with a towering header.

Early in the second half, Fuchs hacked down the difficult Wagner, giving away a penalty and getting an expulsion. Their captain, Reinicke scored from the spot to equalise.

"Come on! Come on!" Mellini screamed, looking furiously from his watch to the referee. Every minute was an eternity. Valley were tiring with one man short. Then, Kaiserheim's Helman beat the offside trap and slotted coolly beyond Peltonnen. The Valley players hounded the referee, furiously contesting the goal, to which the official responded by expelling Krohnberg, who already had a warning.

It was getting to be the most dramatic game of the Champions' league. The fans were on their feet, their hearts in their mouths. As the game drew to its closing moments, Valley pumped all balls hopefully to Tito, demanding one moment of goal scoring magic from the tournament's leading scorer. He was coming close to indispensability.

However when the next goal came, it was off the foot of Dedieu and then all hell broke lose. The Kaiserheim players crowded the referee in protest but the fastidious man pointed resolutely to the centre for the restart.

Big Wagner, perhaps underestimating his own strength, shoved the official, who fell to earth as if pole axed. Not surprisingly, the man went for his red card and flashed it at Wagner. At his tether's end, the big striker snatched the card and flung it furiously aside. He bounded angrily toward the tunnel and showed the booing Valley fans a stiff middle finger just before he disappeared to the baths. Surely, he would be hearing from UEFA. Meanwhile, Dedieu's equalizer had sent Valley into the quarterfinal as runners up to Torpedo.

•

In March, *Los Mininos'* concert in Rome, like everywhere else, was a sell-out. The girls were promoting a phenomenally successful new album, *Adore Explosión* and were at their impeccably choreographed best. Alluring in sexy costumes, their earthy vocal harmonies coasted with a life of their own over the beat of the well-drilled orchestra.

Alfreda was in the foreground, the big spotlight on her, fuelling the fantasies of a million males. She was great tonight, like she was most nights. On stage, she totally obscured her vulnerabilities beneath a façade of sexual confidence. Watching her, no one would suspect the depression she suffered over Charlie's famous incapacity to give her the undivided love she craved. On stage, her eyes smouldered with breathless promise. Off it these days, they were usually bleary from crying and from substances.

"*Te quiero hasta el fin de tiempo,*" she sang wistfully to the downbeat.

Jones was in the crowd. He was bursting with pride, seeing the whole audience on its feet acting as if they would literally die for her. To think that she was *his* girl. He looked smugly about him and lapped up the lasciviousness on the faces of men. They would do anything to possess her, whereas she would do anything to have *him* possess her. It really was a funny, old, world.

All this made it a rather peculiar time for his mind to turn to Tito. The Nigerian and he were getting to be something of a fated pair and he hated that. He hated the comparisons that had been lately made between them by the impressionable football press. Much had been made of their so-called time together in the Saxon Valley youth system, their precocious talent and now their continental goal-scoring prowess. Tito had chalked up an amazing eleven goals for Saxon Valley going into the quarterfinals of the Champions' league.

Conquista were in the quarterfinals too, not surprisingly. Last week they beat Inter Cosenzaro to round off an impressive second phase showing. Jones had ten goals to his name and even though that was prolific enough—some of the best strikers would usually manage roughly half that tally in the entire competition—he did not fancy coming second best to the Nigerian. He did not mind contesting for the goal crown with the likes of Jurgens or Karpenko, Diaz or

Hannibal, hallowed aristocrats of goal conversion. Tansi was too much of a commoner to be the goal king and he merely one of the knights!

There was the usual after-concert party at the hotel suite, to which much of Rome's hip society gravitated for the privilege of hanging out up close with the *mininos*. A slim, young woman soon entering the suite attracted Jones. She had a somewhat regal manner and appeared a little proper in the laid back and essentially maverick gathering. Her dressing was quite subdued in comparison with the largely avant-garde gear of the majority. She was wearing a sober, pink, knee-length frock.

She was in the company of a big, rough-edged man, who vainly sought to smooth himself over with a handsome grey suit. A nose flattened at the bridge gave him the look of a gym boxer who had journeyed the sparring circuit. He would bet he was her minder and not her consort.

"Who is she?" he asked, nudging Scala.

"Ah, that's Serafina Palazzolo," Scala replied, starry-eyed himself. "Cesare Palazzolo's daughter."

"Yeah?" Jones looked closer. Though she was a celebrity, she was extremely sheltered and secluded by her father. "She is cute."

"And she is going to be the richest person in Italy one day," Scala added helpfully. They watched as Alfreda and Niña met the young woman and her escort. She appeared much bowled over by the girls and they in turn seemed extremely delighted for her presence at the party. She got autographs from each of them right away and acted just like any star-struck girl her age, gushing all the right things.

Young as she was—eighteen and a half—she was reputed to have a wise head, which she needed if she was to run the Cesare Palazzolo Empire some day. She was a known patron of the poor and needy and gave away a lot of her father's money to charity.

Next, a young man made his entrance into the bubbling assembly. Debonair and fresh-faced, he would not be more than twenty-three, was very good-looking, his jet-black hair slicked meticulously back.

"Look who's here," Jones said to Scala with a sidelong smile. "Claudio."

Claudio was Modesto Delgado's first son. He had a reputation as the black sheep of the family. A famous *roué*, he took very little interest in the family business, only just enough to ensure he could pay for a frolicking life style crammed full of fast cars, jet travel, cruises and other expensive pursuits. He worked the circuit of Europe's top resorts, where his charm and family name won over dozens of well-heeled women. He had eyes for Alfreda, with whom he had reportedly dallied briefly before she became the megastar she now was. Since then, she had rebuffed his constant entreaties for a re-entry. Now he had a real obstacle in the formidable Charlie Jones, who the whole world knew she was crazy for.

But Claudio Delgado would not be accused of lack of persistence and had never given up the pursuit. He strode confidently over to where Alfreda and the other girls stood chatting with Serafina. He engaged them in some lively talk but even as he courted Alfreda, his dark eyes flirted at Serafina. Shortly, the latter's big companion put a reverent hand about her slender shoulder and although he did not quite steer her away from the group, delicately prompted her eventual disengagement from them.

"*Si fa tardi, la principessa,*" the big man said. "Don't you think we should be leaving?"

"We still have a little time, Lorenzo," Serafina spoke in a hushed tone to the big man but he seemed politely adamant that they depart. "*Parla in gergo stiamo un po' più lungo?*"

"Ah, the feud," Scala said, enjoying the little scene. Serafina's minder was obviously well mindful how Palazzolo would throw a fit if his daughter as much as spoke with a Delgado. Moments later, Serafina excused herself from the party and started for the exit, not looking very pleased with the big man, who trailed apologetically after her.

With some nifty footwork, Jones manoeuvred himself into her path, sleek as the original lounge lizard.

"You're leaving so early, Signorita Palazzolo," he said to her in his most solicitous manner.

"I am afraid I must," she replied wearily.

"You must?"

"I'm afraid so." She was about to move on when she appeared to look closer at his face. "I *know* you."

"My name is Charlie Jones," he said with exaggerated modesty.

"Of course. Charlie Jones." She looked at him with an admiration she did not attempt to disguise. "I am happy to meet you. I have read so much of you."

"I'm really flattered."

"*You* put Bellona out of the Champions' league," she kidded.

"I'm awfully sorry about that," he smiled with an intention to infect.

"I forgive you," she laughed, infected. "Even though you ruined my father's birthday."

"I can imagine it wasn't the present he hoped for. I hope I can make up for it somehow."

The season had been a near disaster for Bellona, but they had miraculously turned around at the brink, with the result that they still had something to play for. Having exited shockingly in the first phase of the Champions' league, they had shown great character and were now in the quarterfinal of the UEFA Cup.

"May be one day you'll play for Bellona," she suggested. "Then you will have a chance to make up for it."

"I can't imagine refusing you anything," he said with a flirtatious intonation that was inoffensive from the look of things.

"You will sign an autograph for me?" She produced a leather-bound book and turned a vacant page to Jones, who scribbled eagerly: *To Serafina, my new friend. Charlie Jones.* "I will treasure this. Thank you."

She took her leave and Jones stared after her with a strong liking forming in him. Here was one of the world's real heirs and she was just a wide-eyed child.

•

Saxon Valley won the first leg quarterfinal Champions' league tie against Inter-Cosenzaro 3-1 at Allen Lane They therefore went into the away leg in a strong position.

Inter were a strong team and this season they had the added strength of Franco Russo, who had come from Bellona in the summer. Tito had experienced his tough minding during the first leg and now knew why people called him *Il Cannibale.*

Inter knew *they* had to chase the tie and an irascible crowd fired them on. They had gone out of the competition at the same stage last season and were no doubt looking to go one better this time. Their fans jeered every time Tito touched the ball. He had scored twice in the first leg, which was very naughty of him by their reckoning.

Peltonnen needed to go full stretch thrice in the first period, as Inter's dangerous forwards threatened, especially the Argentinean, Buenos.

Some racist chanting directed at Tito picked up decibels in the second half, which was curious because Inter had a black player too, the Nigerian, Efosa.

"They don't like you, *amico*."

"Huh?" Tito turned to see Russo towering next to him.

"I mean your black monkey face." Russo bared his teeth in a mirthless smile. "They don't like it, the fans."

He smiled jadedly up at Russo. If the big man thought a little racist ribbing would rile him, he was mistaken. He took racism for granted and expected it. In Nigeria, everyone took *tribalism* for granted and expected it. Every Nigerian tribe loathed the next, every little hamlet the other, so why would he get touchy if a white man hated a black man?

"If I score," he grinned impishly up at the big man. "They'll shut up."

"If you score," Russo persevered with a low, ominous chuckle. "You might not leave the *stadio* alive."

At some point, the chanting got so bad that a disenchanted Mellini asked Ryder to get ready to go on in Tito's place. But with Valley defending deep in their half, Blair played a long ball out and Tito slipped ahead of Russo to shoot Valley into the lead. The crowd fell quiet for the first time since the beginning of the game and stayed that way until the end, which was just a few minutes afterwards.

At the final whistle, Tito dashed half way across the field to the front row of one of the stands. During the game, he had seen a boy seated there, a young crippled Inter fan in a wheel chair. He had made a mental note of him even in the heat of the game. The boy had been cheering his side as vigorously as his condition allowed, waving a club pennant all the time. Now the game was over, his side had lost, and he was not waving it any more. He sat despondently and his eyes glazed over with imminent tears. His father was trying to comfort him, saying some words in his ear.

"Please have this." Tito handed the boy his boots and shirt and the boy's fallen face brightened with a smile of such profound gratitude. It was obvious he was never going to lace the boots but the on-looking Italian fans knew he was going to treasure it for the rest of his life and they applauded Tito.

"That is so kind of you."

It was not the boy or his father but Franco Russo, who had materialized somehow at his side. He was not looking mean at all now but oddly restrained.

"It's nothing."

"Thank you," Russo said warmly. He walked with Tito to the changing rooms and was very polite and friendly. It seemed the infamous *Il Cannibale* was probably a cordial fellow at heart and Tito was ironically disappointed. Somehow, it did not quite accord to the script.

The next day, Tito, who had sent the Italian side out of the competition, was the unlikely toast of the local tabloids.

•

The breakneck season hurtled on through its shuddering finale. By April, with only a few weeks to the end, the Premiership title was in real contention for the first time in a decade. Usually at this stage, Kingford were reasonably assured of the championship. This season, however, it was eerily different for them. Doverham sat at the top, though precariously, while Liverton,

Kingford, Saxon Valley and Millchester stampeded after them. No one was sure by any means, which would win the title this season. It would likely go to the wire.

Valley were in the semi-final of both the FA Cup and the Champions' league. Kingford were in exactly the same position and it seemed almost fated when they were drawn against each other for an all-English, Champions' league semi-final tie.

The season had provided a crammed programme for both teams. Many of the players had also been in internationals for their countries, especially qualifiers for the next year's World Cup in Australia. Kingford however looked the fresher of the two sides because they had a bigger squad and more reserve of power and quality.

However, with the Allen Lane fans in full voice, Valley won the leg, the veteran Dedieu clinching it with a late header. The Frenchman was proving to be a plucky match winner and Mellini could be justifiably proud of his acquisition, which many had criticised.

"We might well have kept old Ron Race," Finley had sniggered about the Dedieu deal at the time.

Kingford had won the UEFA Cup thrice in the last six seasons but the Champions' league continued to elude them, increasing their craving for it. This was a crucial season for them. They stood in real danger of finishing without any silverware, just as easily as they had a rare chance to achieve an incredible treble. Sir Gordon Elliot, Kingford's manager, felt his job threatened for the first time in over a decade, no matter how slightly.

"If Kingford fail to win anything," Chairman Lord Baden-Goode said in a testy mood after the Allen Lane loss. "We may look for new managerial direction. But mind you, we're still in good contention for all *three* major titles."

"Yes, we are still in with a chance of making the treble," vouched a sullen Sir Gordon in an interview the same night. "The Premiership, the FA Cup and the Champions' league are still within our reach. But we are taking things one game at a time."

Amazingly, Saxon Valley could technically say exactly the same thing.

Kingford had it all to play for and were fired up for the crucial second leg at Prescott Park. The game was played at a cracking pace in a great atmosphere. Peltonnen had to save desperately from Logan, the Kingford captain, then at Bolingo's feet but couldn't stop Starr's drive from twenty yards. Almost immediately, Logan fired past him and Valley were two goals down. They were suddenly the ones having to chase the game.

Tito was labouring under a muscle strain and apart from an early attempt on goal, had hardly had a look in. Mellini had to take him off for Dedieu in the second half.

Kingford held their lead doggedly. Valley fought gamely but ultimately began to ebb, tiring from the racy pace of the frustrating game. As time ran out, they were, as they say, bloodied but unbowed. The lads knew they had given it everything. Getting this far in their first-ever Champions' league season was a bonus no one had seriously expected and they could look back to a relative fairy tale season. Their travelling fans had tears in their eyes, contemplating what might have been, as Kingford wound down a great performance. Therefore, Di Salvo's goal at the end of stoppage time left them totally numb with joy as it sent them into the final on the away goals rule. Words could never express the gratitude those fans felt towards the great Italian.

Candle in the wind

The Champions' league final was uncharted territory for the Valley players with the exception of Roberto Di Salvo, who had won it *thrice*, and Marc Dedieu.

For their opponents Conquista on the other hand, reaching the final was getting to be a birthright. *Winning* it was becoming a habit. All of their players had been triumphant in it at least once, most of them repeatedly. Santamaria, their great captain and talisman had won it thrice and made ninety-five appearances in the competition.

Even new boy Jones had already won it once and was playing in the final for the second consecutive season. He was again the *goleador* of *La Liga* and had contributed hugely in propelling Conquista to this year's final with a haul of fifteen goals. He was once more the tournament's leading goal scorer going into the final, having overtaken Tito, who was now running-up three goals behind.

•

In Mid-May, Valley won the Premiership. They achieved the feat by the solitary point, pushing past Doverham and Kingford with a last gasp effort away to Keynesbridge. Tito clinched it with almost the very last play of the season, a headed goal in the final seconds that tied the game and denied Kingford the title that would have been theirs if Valley had lost. That goal was to be engraved in the annals of Saxon Valley, the name Tito Tansi assured a place in the club's sun.

Still in dreamland a week later, they met Kingford again, this time in the FA Cup final. Incredibly, they added that hallowed silverware too to their long-vacant trophy room. There was some violence after the game. It was more than some Kingford die-hards could swallow, being licked yet again by the upstarts at the last hurdle. The police broke up the fights but there were a few broken heads and one young man died later from stab wounds. Blair scored the only goal of the ill-tempered game, not surprisingly, from a penalty.

Sir Johnny looked sanguinely about his large office. He found it still hard to take in. Valley had won the fabled double and would make it an incredible treble if they won the Champions' league final in a few days' time. It was an overwhelming achievement for any club, let alone humble Valley of the backwaters. His cell phone rang.

"Hello."

"Cesare Palazzolo." The patriarchal drawl was famous. "How are you, my friend Sir Johnny?"

"How nice to hear from you, Mr. Palazzolo," the Valley Chairman said less than truthfully, wondering what the matter might be.

"I wish to pledge a bonus to your players if they win against Conquista."

"Really?" Sir Johnny chuckled.

"Two million pounds."

"You really want Conquista beaten."

"I do," the voice came back at the other end, without amusement.

Just last week, Bellona had concluded an astonishing recovery by finishing the season as UEFA Cup winners, beating Sweden's Varnenborg in the final. However, if Conquista lost the Champions' league final to Valley, Sir Johnny suspected Palazzolo would find *that* more satisfying.

"Will some ethical questions be raised?" the Valley Chairman wondered. A free two million pounds was nothing to be sniffed at. The players would give it some serious consideration if they got to know about it.

"You know it is perfectly alright," Palazzolo said. "I am not asking you to lose the game. I am giving you an incentive to *win*. What could be wrong with that?"

"Hmm."

"You want to win the game? You want the championship?"

"Of course," Sir Johnny frowned. What sort of question was that?

"So what do you say? Two million pounds bonus to your players from nowhere if they win."

"I'll think about it."

"No need to think about it," Palazzolo snapped.

"I'll see. I won't promise anything now."

"*Madonna*!" Palazzolo cried in fair alarm. "But I am the one promising anything."

After a little small talk, the men hung up.

Sir Johnny mused over the conversation, working out the ethics and the mathematics of Palazzolo's offer. In the end, he decided he was not going to distract his players with the information. What if Palazzolo did not come through? But if Valley won and he coughed up, what a pleasant surprise it would be for them.

"Bloody lunatic," he muttered with an incredulous shake of the head, and went on to other matters.

It was only a matter of days to the big game and the great media hype was in full cry, as if the natural fever of the event was not enough.

Somehow, all the focus had narrowed down to the old firm of Jones and Tansi, now pitted against each other. Pictures of the two forwards dominated the back pages of Europe's major tabloids. In *News of the World,* they were depicted like a pair of medieval knights. Black knight, Tansi; white knight, Jones. Both were going head to head for the golden boot of the championships. Football was a team game but it was ultimately all about goals and the goalscorers were the kings.

"I wonder where the rest of us fit into all this?" Quinlan snorted one day at training. He had largely spent all season in the dugouts but although he fancied a move, he still enjoyed being part of the overall success at Allen Lane.

"I don't pay any attention," Tito said modestly.

"It's impossible not to," riposted Quinlan. "Your mug stares at you everyday in the papers, and in the tube everyone's talking about you and Charlie. Just promise it won't go *too* much to your head."

"Oh-kay!" Tito said a little nervously and Quinlan sensitively left him alone.

As for Charlie Jones, he was *very* comfortable with the hype. He was secure in the knowledge that he was not merely a media creation. He was truly one of the best players on the planet and relished that fact to the point of narcissism.

Inevitably, the meteoric development of his near-cult status led to some personality conflicts in the Conquista dressing room. Even the great Brazilian, Hannibal was incredibly living somewhat in his shadow now, where he had previously been the undisputed king of the San Diego. While Hannibal's acclaim as the world's best player perhaps still stood, Jones was a new icon of a pop culture that transcended football. It was no secret that the Brazilian would seriously consider a move on from Conquista, something previously unthinkable. Bellona had expressed a hostile interest but the Spaniards were bound to resist it with all they had.

Jones looked eagerly forward to the final against his old club. It should prove some re-union, he thought excitedly. If he had any iota of regret about his dream career so far, it was perhaps that he had not been a part of Valley's success in the Premiership. It was honestly amazing what the lads had achieved in such a short time. The double was every great club's fantasy and you could not call Valley a great club. Now they were unbelievably going for the Champions' league title to make a terrific treble! *That is,* not if he could help it. Nonetheless, he *was* impressed with the audacity of their ambition.

His season had been punishing. He had been in so many games for club and country. He had also had to honour the numerous engagements and appearances in far-flung places. For months now, he had been sporadically on the set of *Unidentified Soccer Object,* the sci-fi football movie he was making with Jackie Chan and Angelina Jolie. Last week he had made the tedious Hong Kong trip for the opening of a new Versace outlet. Sometimes, he feared he might be stretching Delgado's indulgence a little but his instinct told him correctly that the Conquista owner had a soft spot for him. The coach, Meissner was not quite as charitable but playing the way he was for now, he could still count on some license.

His mind never strayed far from Alfreda, who was in the United States as *Los Mininos* continued the never-ending world tours, playing to sell-out crowds. She was always on the phone, calling him sometimes as much as four times a day, so it was never as if she was very far away.

For all his ardent lifestyle, deep down he loved her fiercely and couldn't really imagine parting ways with her. All things being equal, he had a feeling he was going to walk her down that dreaded aisle one day. She promised to fly to Paris for the final. It was always an extra spur whenever she was in the stands watching him play.

But right now, she was a couple of thousand miles away and he needed to unwind. He wanted to take his mind briefly off *even* her as well as the furiously spiraling build-up to the final. He called up Juanita, who was always fun to be with and took her to a disco, where they partied anonymously in grotto-like, multi-coloured dimness. A while later, a girl he knew passed by their table. Her name was Mona, a pretty television presenter, with whom he had had a recent tryst.

Juanita was having a whale of a time, beaming at dancing couples as she nursed a cocktail. He got up off his seat, his eyes surreptitiously following Mona.

"Excuse me, darling," he said to Juanita with a winning smile off the top drawer and kissed her forehead. He waded through the crowd after Mona, who he soon caught up with. He startled her slightly, twirling her playfully around.

"Charlie!" she cried with pleasant surprise and melted in his arms.

"So glad to see you, Mona." His eyes went smotheringly over her and he kissed her lightly. She obviously evoked some sensual nostalgia in him.

"But *I* never get to see you, Charlie," she pouted with coquettish reproach, seeming like she may have knocked back a few tequilas. "Too many girls. Charlie's Angels, *no*?"

'Don't be silly, Mona," he laughed facetiously, still smooching her. "What are you doing tomorrow night?"

"*Anda, mi amor.* What's wrong with tonight?" she drawled saucily. "I am here alone."

He shook his head regretfully. "I am *with* someone," he explained.

"Ah," she arched her eyebrow and quite without warning, slapped his face as hard as she could, which was not a great deal, to be honest but enough to draw some attention. "Then you should stay with her!" She flailed in vain at him and Jones was restraining her almost playfully, when Juanita strode up to the scene.

"*¡Ah mi Dios!*" Juanita gasped. She took in the apparent lovers' tiff and her face fell. She spun around and made stridently for the exit.

"Juanita!" Jones called after her. He was momentarily torn between the two girls but then shortly appeared to opt for the departing Juanita, and went after her. Party people recognized him and looked on with star-struck interest. Tongues began to wag. It was not everyday they got a close up on the famous love life of *El chico*, the pin-up Prince of pop football.

Juanita burst onto the street, gulping a lung full of the cool night air in the manner of a drowning person just surfaced. Frantically, she flagged down a taxi, with which she presently receded down the neon-lit street. Jones was seconds late, gaining the sidewalk only to see the retiring taillights of the taxi.

He thought briefly of going back inside to Mona but decided to stay on Juanita's case instead. There was something about her that made her one of his favourite favourites. He tried calling her mobile phone but she had switched off. He reckoned she was going back to her apartment and so decided he would go there and make things up to her. He had no doubt she would forgive him. After all, she knew he did come with a reputation. He would buy her a bouquet of flowers and a box of chocolates. He quickly crossed the street to his tomato red Ferrari and turned the ignition.

He must have not had enough time even to be startled by the rocking explosion, with which his young life was blown away. A swollen orange envelope of fire gave surreal illumination to the night and remarked his early exit from the face of the earth. The blast sent people scampering in all directions but soon they began to gather themselves back, drawn like magnets to the flaming Ferrari. Soon the wailing of sirens seared the night but the police and the fire fighters were too late to do anything.

It was not long before the stunned on-lookers learnt the identity of the cremated victim and it was to become one of the most mournful nights in Spanish football history. The Spaniards had taken him deeply to heart. In their adulation and now their grief, it was the easiest thing to forget that *El chico* was not Spanish.

Millions of people around the world were stunned at the monumental disaster. The universal grief felt that night assured Charlie Jones a place in the constellation of the world's most beloved stars. Most people would forever recall the minutest detail of what they had been doing when they heard the horrendous news, as was usual when death cut down the world's finest in their prime. His death devastated the hip world as Marilyn Monroe's did, John F. Kennedy's, Jimi Hendrix's or Bob Marley's.

In a matter of hours, suspicion concerning his death was steered towards ETA. The blame sat very conveniently, if inexplicably, on the Basque separatists.

Tango in Paris

Under silvery lights, the impeccable turf of Charlotte's *Le dôme des dieux* shone like a giant emerald. The fans filled up every space of the masterpiece and the atmosphere crackled and popped. The excited hum of the crowd came in tidal waves as the players stepped almost daintily out of the tunnel, decked out in fashionable strip. Camera lights flashed out of every cranny like electric fireflies as spectators struggled to capture for eternity, something of the world's greatest sport. A cosmonaut from another planet touching down on earth over Paris would relay home an account of surely the most surreal scenes imaginable.

Only the dark cloud of Charlie Jones' death last week flawed the great day. The players on both sides wore black armbands, most of them pensive with genuine personal grief as they observed the minute's silence for their late playmate.

Despite the heavy gloom, it was a highly entertaining game. Santamaria, the Conquista captain was extraordinary and his ingenious passing prodded his teammates on, while Hannibal and Rojas kept Valley's backs at full alert with intelligent running. Peltonnen had to leap fairly out of his skin to palm over a twenty-yard scorcher from Scala.

Thankfully, for Valley, Mihailescu was also in great form, pulling the strings in the middle of the park. It was always a head start for the English side when the Romanian was on song like that. Lanzarini and de la Luna made a lethal combination down the left side, with Tito and Di Salvo trying hard to get on the end of some great service.

The high quality first half ended goalless but ten minutes into the restart, de la Luna worked hard to get to the bye line, cutting back a cross, which Blair headed in with some splomb. But the ref disallowed it.

Conquista, fired by the reprieve, fought back and Peltonnen saw Hannibal's header flash just wide. Almost immediately, Bob Stone, the old captain, in Panev's place, was tripped in the Spanish area after some valiant running.

"Penalty!" the Valley players claimed.

The referee agreed and pointed to the spot, resisting the heckling protests of the Conquista stars, who were relieved however when Mihailescu's kick was saved by Bika. As if that was not enough, Di Salvo had a goal disallowed shortly after, the referee ruling offside. *Then,* Tito's header ricocheted off the crossbar's underside and bounced surely behind the line but the referee did not give the goal. The Valley players protested in vain and were very obviously disappointed because teams didn't get too many chances against Conquista.

"*Ole! Ole!*" the travelling Spanish rooted for their heroes. Their team began to assert a marginal superiority over the fired-up English side, which now had much of the wind knocked out of them by the rash of ill luck. Santamaria, with only minutes left, obliged their fans with a superbly taken free kick, which flew into the net way beyond Peltonnen. It seemed however that someone in the Valley wall had been tripped and the referee disallowed it too.

"*Ringrazia un milione!*" muttered Mellini with ironic gratitude, still mad at the ref. "*Stronzo di fottere!*" As far as he was concerned, the official was merely trying to atone for having denied Valley three legitimate goals. *Three disallowed goals* in the Champions' league final! He punched his palm in anger.

His bad mood was worsened when, with four minutes left on the clock, Scala, who was having a brilliant game, chipped Peltonnen for a wonderful goal.

"*Eso fue para usted, Charlie, mi amigo bueno!*" Scala sobbed as he charged about in celebration. Tears streamed from his eyes and he was being comforted rather than congratulated by his teammates. He had come to be regarded as Jones' best friend and was certainly more devastated than almost anyone was at his death. Even the referee, a highly rated man with a reputation for sternness, was very subdued in ordering him back to the restart. Kneeling, the emotional Scala looked skywards. "I know you are in heaven, Charlie. This goal is for you, my friend."

Valley fans were overcome with relief, however, when Tito headed the equalizer almost within a minute, sending the game into extra time.

Conquista had to pick themselves up from the disappointment of surrendering their late lead almost on full time and they seemed pondersome at the restart. On the other hand, Valley were the ones with a little more spring in their steps, not surprisingly, having come back from the dead.

The dramatic game was decided six minutes into extra time. Santamaria's pass intended for Scala was intercepted midfield by Bob Stone, who hefted a hopeful kick that caught Bika completely off guard and dipped into the Conquista net!

It was an incredible, fluky, anti-climax, which stunned everyone in the *Dome*, not least the scorer himself! Stone was the least likely to get on the score sheet, let alone grab the winner. He had been largely superfluous to Mellini's needs, retained only perhaps for sentimental reasons. He had only been on for a few minutes as substitute for Panev, who twisted an ankle. Even the oldest Valley fans could hardly recollect he ever scored for the club. But what a time to do it! The players crowded around him and buried him under their embrace, his face wet with tears and sweat. It was the greatest moment of his life. A largely undistinguished career had incredibly managed a fairly tale ending. When it was his turn to hold aloft the trophy on the victory podium, he took it very personally

The New Coliseum

The biggest clubs in Europe queued up for Tito's signature, offering amazing sums of money for that privilege. For Sir Johnny, it was *déjà vu* relatively so soon after the same deluge he had experienced in Charlie Jones' case. It seemed like an eternity ago. So much had happened at Saxon Valley since that time, the most important thing now being that they were champions of Europe.

"How much would we miss Tito?" he mused aloud to Mellini.

"Oh, very much," the coach replied candidly. He was clearly basking in being the most successful coach in the world the past season. He was understandably chuffed at having put one over his old boss Palazzolo, who he reckoned should be eating his heart out at that moment. He had accomplished at Saxon Valley in two seasons, what the old man would give the last breath of his entire lifetime for: he had won the Champions' league *at the expense of Conquista!*

"These offers for him," Sir Johnny said confidentially. "They are difficult to pass up. And Palazzolo is willing to set a new transfer record if he has to."

"No problem," Mellini shrugged. Sir Johnny had sold Jones at a time when he seemed indispensable and yet he had made a success of Valley after that. He was confident he would do the same in Tito's case. Football was a team game. Usually the media blew the individual out of proportion. He reeled off the names of some players that interested him as candidates for Tansi's replacement: Karpenko of *Torpedo*, Vanderbilt of *Argos*, Wagner of *Kaiserheim*, Bandeiras of *Isabela*, Romanova of *Novopetsk,* Cope of *Doverham.* He was not sure *Real Baracoa* would let go the highly valued Zizinho.

•

Meanwhile, the game of football was still riding the crest of the big wave. Like the world itself, it was without end and just like life, it was never monotonous despite its repetitiousness. On the contrary, the more one got of it, the more one craved. What a wonderful world; such a beautiful game.

The summer saw the World Cup in Australia. The best players were once more on call, this time for their countries. In many cases, club comrades were at unremitting war against each other at the world's greatest fiesta, segregated now by their national colours. Tito inspired Nigeria to the quarterfinal with his marksmanship. He notched up six goals before they went out against eventual finalists, Italy. The Italian side included Di Salvo and Lanzarini, his fellow Euro champions of only a few weeks before!

He was in Nigeria soon after the team's exit from the World Cup. The entire nation welcomed them with almost as much commotion as if they had won it. Even the country's notoriously unfeeling President fawned after them and treated them like royalty. Of course, he was not so numb as not to know that with the corrupted economy finally on the brink of collapse, football was the people's only source of good cheer. Therefore, like a gluttonous infant, he would milk the football team's achievement for all it was worth. The pompous little man even made the ridiculous claim that Nigeria was robbed of the Cup and lavished ridiculously extravagant gifts on the players, hoping by that to reverse his unpopularity! Tito had scored two memorable goals in a draw with Brazil but the virtuoso South Americans had deservedly gone on to win the Cup yet another time, inspired by the great Hannibal and the young Zizinho.

Now back in London, Tito was putting up his feet, contemplating his future in the light of the scramble for his signature. The phone rang. It was from his agent, Tim Banks.

"There's someone who would like to have a word with you," Banks said.

"Who?"

"The General Manager of Bellona. His name is Stefano Pizzi."

"Sounds like an important man alright."

"He's a nephew of Cesare Palazzolo's," Banks said. "I believe you will be interested in what he has to say."

"O.K." He liked Banks, a well-mannered middle-aged man, who had quite a few well-known clients to his credit. They met the next day at the Halkin, where Pizzi was staying.

"Mr. Pizzi here has Mr. Palazzolo's ear," said Banks quite ingratiatingly.

"I *am* Don Cesare's ear," Pizzi said rather superciliously but with an ameliorating good cheer. The neat, little man had a very cordial manner, conveyed subtle power and was impressive. "And he has asked me to make you an offer you cannot refuse, as they say."

"I am all ears," nodded Tito, sensing the drift, for which he need not be a genius. And *did* Pizzi have an earful for him. It was indeed an offer he could not refuse; an offer that would make him by far the highest priced, highest paid player in the world. Palazzolo would also provide him a palatial villa set in grounds, a Cessna for his air travels, a limousine, and a long-term advertising deal with *Globo-Italiano Corporazione*. It was an outrageous offer that had the primary goal of beating Modesto Delgado to the deal. It also had the aim of making Hannibal eat his heart out. The Brazilian had turned down the bid from Palazzolo, persuaded by Delgado to renew his contract at Conquista.

It was an incredible, eccentric offer, and even as Tito thought that the football business was mad and Cesare Palazzolo even madder, he was glad he was right now a part of the whole madness. There was no other madness he would rather be in.

There was not a chance of Valley matching those sort of terms, not even in their eagerness to please the fans and make him stay. Sir Johnny's head ruled his heart in these matters. Therefore, to the dismay of Valley fans, the transfer was concluded relatively quickly and Tansi would be leaving the Lane. Bellona paid an astonishing—some said insane—£80 million for the Nigerian meteor and he was on his way to Italy and the *Calcio*.

The fans were not impressed with the money, rather dejected that they had lost a second gem in three years. They lamented that the caliber of Jones and Tito did not happen along as regularly as Sir Johnny seemed inclined to disposing of them. This was not to say that they did not appreciate Sir Johnny's dilemma. Trying to keep Tito at Allen Lane, they knew, would have been a losing battle in the end. The unreal wages he would be earning at Bellona were unmatchable if Valley were not to bust the bank, let alone team spirit. *The Guardian* commented:

If people think the football wage system has gone haywire in England, they need to visit Bellona, where Cesare Palazzolo is furiously plotting to rule world football with his unlimited funds.

Shortly before he left, Tito went up to see Sir Johnny and came away with the impression that the great man was genuinely sad to see him go. He told the Chairman how much he would have loved to stay, and meant it. He was however satisfied that he had done his bit for the Saxon Valley cause. Though he was a foreigner, he understood what the recent renaissance meant to the local people and the long-suffering fans. He had helped them to see the rainbow.

"I will never forget all that you did for me," he pledged emotively.

The Chairman clasped his hand warmly, feeling a rush of emotion himself. It only remained for him to dab at his eyes.

"You can be sure I'm indebted to you as well, old chap," he smiled. "You've given me great service on the turf. And just look at the difference you made in the old bank balance!"

They both laughed. The sentimental meeting over, Sir Johnny walked him to the door.

"Thank you," Tito said one last time.

"You take care of yourself in Italy. Mind the defenders. *But especially the paparazzi.*"

•

Pizzi and an unruly herd of journalists met him at the Rome airport. Rapid questions came at him from every direction and the first thing he knew was that he would do a crash course in the language. They glided into the city in a sleek, roomy Madonna IV limousine, to which a stately chauffeur added grace with some suave handling. To think that Palazzolo himself designed this moving luxury apartment.

"Heaven on wheels!" Tito whistled.

"It is yours," said Pizzi casually. "From Don Cesare."

Overwhelmed, he sank afresh into its soft cream leather and looked out through the silver tinted window glass at the ancient city.

"I would like to see the Vatican and St. Peter's," he said excitedly. He had been in Rome a couple of times with Valley but really seen nothing of it, not being a great tourist.

"You'll see everything," Pizzi assured him.

They swung through the wrought iron gates of a large ground some half an hour later. An impeccable landscape, relieved by classical statues, scenic gardens and an artificial pond undulated before a white marbled villa that sat gleaming in the near distance.

"I hope you like your home, Signor Tansi," Pizzi said. "Don Cesare holds you in the highest esteem and assures you he will do anything for your well being."

"I am lost for words." He took in the large grounds. This surely was the Garden of Eden. The old apple tree had to be somewhere out there. The only thing missing was Eve. It was really absurd that all he had to do to earn this opulence was kick and chase after a football, something he would gladly do for nothing.

"There's a swimming pool at the back, a squash court, a sauna, gym and Jacuzzi," Pizzi reeled off. He appeared to enjoy titillating the African, knowing fully well how very different this was from the famous thatch and mud huts of his native land. "Anything else you require will be provided. Anything."

Cesare Palazzolo welcomed him with a private dinner at his imperial Villa Palermo. The first thing anyone noticed after recovering from the villa's magnificence was the gallery of gold-framed portraits of famous football stars. There was such a memorable collection of legendary players from through the generations on Palazzolo's white walls. The great Johnny Hastings in the colours of Bellona looked down at mortals from a pride of place over a mantelpiece. There were faces from more contemporary times, such as Carl Jurgens and Roberto Di Salvo. Football mementos stood or hung from everywhere—trophies, pennants, medals and standards. Only his eminent good taste saved the place from a certain gaudiness. The man was daft about the game, no doubt about it.

He was an intriguing figure just to look at. Lean faced, bushy-browed and of the thin brown hair, a grim set to his chin marked him out as an obstinate individual. He was inventive and eclectic, largely reclusive but most influential in the realpolitik of Italy and Europe. He was said to be quite intemperate and mean but with a converse capacity for prudence and magnanimity. He gritted a cigar in his browned teeth and squinted to keep the smoke from his cagey eyes. Except for his receded hairline and some rather deep facial lines, he didn't seem to have taken undue beating from the years.

He finished his dinner and reclined in his gold-plated, custom chair mobile.

"I hope you enjoyed the food," Serafina, his daughter said to Tito.

"Oh, yes, Miss Palazzolo," Tito smiled. "Thank you."

"You like Rome?" she inquired.

"Yes, I do. But I must learn the language."

Palazzolo touched a button on the control panel of the chair mobile. A compartment whirred open in the side of it, from which he took a decanter of scotch, a glass and some rocks. He poured some and threw it back with some relish.

"Drink?" he asked.

"No, sir," Tito declined, admiring the custom chair mobile.

"I designed it myself," Palazzolo said off handedly and raised his glass, which he had refilled. "Here is wishing you a happy stay at Bellona." He again threw back the drink and poured yet another.

"He doesn't always drink," Serafina said self-consciously aside to Tito. "I think he is excited because of you."

"I venerate great players, Tito," Palazzolo said, eyeing his row of portraits. "That is my *Wall of Fame*. Every one of those players you see on that wall has personally unveiled his portrait in my house. Every one of them has been my guest at this very table. You must try to get there, to unveil your own portrait one day."

"I shall be greatly honoured when that day comes," Tito said, careful to eye the wall with sufficient deference. Palazzolo certainly made it sound like the ultimate honour and maybe it was.

"*If* that day comes," Palazzolo said poignantly. "You still have some distance before you achieve greatness. But you are lucky, you have potential."

I merely have potential and you cough up £80 million for me? Tito thought incredulously but said, "I think there's someone missing from your wall."

"Who might that be?"

"Hannibal."

Palazzolo waved his hand dismissively. "But he plays for Conquista"

"He is the greatest, sir."

Palazzolo grunted impatiently and appeared moody.

"*But he plays for Conquista,*" he repeated painstakingly. "The first thing you must know, Tito is that at Bellona, the mortal enemy is Modesto Delgado and his Conquista. Perhaps you don't know what you did for me by beating him in the final of the Champions' league."

"I have a little idea, sir," Tito affirmed dutifully. The Valley players knew where the added winning bonus had come from.

"I was willing to pay anything to have you come to Bellona after that game." Palazzolo moved the powered chair in an idle back and forth, the equivalent, presumably, of pacing about a room. "I paid more than you are really worth. If I hadn't, Delgado would have had you at Conquista, like he did Charlie Jones. He took me by surprise over Jones and I regret it forever."

By the time Tito left Palazzolo's presence, he was literally reeling from the effect of his peculiar personality. The man was probably not insane but his obsession with Delgado and Conquista surely stood at the outer limits of sanity.

Serafina, walking him to his car, was not oblivious of his unease and tried as much as she could to steer conversation along other lines.

"I have a request to make," she said.

"I will do anything you ask," Tito responded chivalrously.

"I should like you to visit young Giorgio Pessotti."

"Giorgio Pessotti?"

"The young boy you gave your shirt and boots after the game you played against Cosenzaro."

"Ah! I would love to, Miss Palazzolo."

"I was really touched by your gesture," she said. She seemed extremely genteel and very humble for her lofty circumstances. "Your behaviour that day was very civilised. Unfortunately there is too much racism and hooliganism coming into football."

"I am afraid you're right."

"Giorgio Pessotti is a student at a school for disadvantaged children, of which my father is patron. His parents died last week in a car accident. It would be a great lift if you visited him."

"You only have to instruct me when," Tito said loyally.

"You are so very kind. I shall arrange a time suitable to everyone and inform you."

"Goodnight, Miss Palazzolo."

"Goodnight."

•

A football correspondent in the Times wrote of Cesare Palazzolo and the magnificent new stadium he had just completed for Bellona in Rome:

MIGHTY CESARE RESSURECTS THE COLLISEUM

Bellona's new stadium, *II Nuovo Colliseum,* will be ready in time for the new scuddetto. Aptly named, the edifice is a striking modern adaptation of the ancient Coliseum and will seat 80,000 of the club's ever-increasing Roman legion of fans.

"Paris' *Le dome des dieux* will pale next to *Il Nuovo Colliseum,*" remarked Bellona General Manager, Stefano Pizzi. He however refutes the suggestion that the desire to outdo the Parisien icon was the main motive that prompted the famously competitive billionaire club president, Cesare Palazzolo to building it.

Be that as it may, the air conditioned *Il Nuovo Colliseumo* will be the world's best football stadium. All 80,000 seats are cushioned and games will be played in any weather owing to its retractable roofing. Its massiveness may be matched only by the mammoth ego of Palazzolo himself.

Apparently, mighty Cesare is Emperor of Rome, *Il Nuovo Colliseum* his playground, his expensive players the gallant gladiators, while the fans are the original mob goading the performers on to glorious gore. From *Il Nuovo Colliseum,* the Emperor will conquer the world of football and give it the Pax Bellona.

He was determined to do just that, namely, give the football world the *Pax Bellona.* Last season could have been disastrous but his gladiators had shown incredible character to claw back and take the UEFA Cup as well as the *scudetto.* This season, they would set tracks yet again in search of their ultimate aim of being the world's undisputed champion club. They would be better suited for that title in the majesty of the new stadium.

Tito Tansi's record transfer was very much the hot topic of world sports and rather obscured the fact that the club had acquired a couple of other great players as well. Remarkably, Bellona had managed to steal Bolingo away from Kingford, Karpenko from Torpedo, João Filho from Baracoa, Uwe Herbst from Kaiserheim and Antonio Buenos from Inter Cosenzaro. With the acquisition of Filho and Herbst, the entire Bellona defensive quartet now consisted of players who were captains of their countries: Filho (*Brazil*), Herbst (Germany), Strazza (Italy) and Sazanovic (Serbia) all captained their countries at the World Cup! Even Bolingo was captain of his country Zaire. It was an excellent collection.

Tito's *Serie A* debut was a home game against Pescarleno, last season's runners-up. It was difficult for anyone to live up to a £80 million price tag and he had been quite anxious before the game. However, two illustrious strikes from him either side of the break gave Bellona a 2-0 win and had the fans instantly rooting for him, much to his relief.

The media deluged him and *paparazzi* staked out his place. There was a microphone or ten stuck in his face every time he ventured out of his villa and cameras followed him everywhere, many secretly. Last week, a popular opera tenor had been photographed sitting in his toilet and was not too pleased about that. These fellows would go to any lengths for their scoop.

"In Italy, when you are a football star, you are public property," Serafina told him with pert wisdom. They had fallen into a natural friendship, cemented the day of the visit to the boy Giorgio Pessotti. They took the boy to the park, bought him presents and even though they had desperately sought to avoid reporters, the creatures were ubiquitous.

"The visit to Giorgio was supposed to be private," Tito complained at yet another tabloid account of it. Now, the poor boy had his wasted legs in every paper.

"Maybe Giorgio enjoyed seeing himself in *Gazzetto dello Sport*," Serafina said hopefully. "Everyone likes to be a star, perhaps except you, I think."

"Me?" He was surprised. "Why do you say so?"

"You don't seem like many of the players I know," she remarked. "You are the best player in the world, but I don't think it matters to you."

"The costliest, not the best."

"It comes to the same thing."

"I never dreamt I would come this far," he said with stony reflection. "Not in my wildest dream. Maybe I'm not used to it yet. Sometimes it is hard to imagine that this *is* me, you understand?"

She nodded. "In Africa it is very difficult, I know."

"You don't *know*," he chortled. How could she know? She may have read a few tit bits on the 'Dark Continent,' seen the usual footages of famine victims of Somalia, refugees of Rwanda, child soldiers and war casualties of Sierra Leone and Liberia; but her world was so removed from it that she would never really *know*. He shook his head. "You don't *know*, Serafina."

"I have had some difficult times myself," she proffered.

"Like?"

"My parents breaking up."

"I know."

"I was about four," she said. "I didn't really understand it but as I grew up, it was very upsetting. The scandal was very depressing for me."

"Fortunately, you don't show it," he said and their eyes met briefly, then disengaged. "Your mother, where is she now?"

"She lives everywhere." A smile played about the corners of her full lips and he could discern the fondness. "New York, Cape Town, São Paulo. She loves to travel. I don't think marriage was really meant for her."

"Do you see her often?"

"Not so often but no matter what, I always see her in August of every year. Since I was a child, I always spend August 14th with her in Sardinia. She comes from Sassari and there is a festival on that day called the *Il Candilieri*. You know Sardinia?"

"No," he answered, more interested in knowing her.

"Oh, it's fun," she said. "Would you like to come? I mean, for *Il Candilieri*?"

He looked at her unbelievingly. "Me?"

"Of course, you," she laughed.

"With you?"

"Yes,"

"Why, yes. Yes, yes."

●

Bellona opened the Champions' league campaign at home against Swiss side FC Garrone, and in accordance with the formbook, they won, though by a margin of 5-0 not altogether forecast. *Il Nuovo Colliseum* seemed to have cast a spell over the visitors and the chanting of the fans took on a mystical, primordial character. The throaty Romans yelled for the blood of the

Swiss lions and the gladiators of home obliged. FC Garrone were no Conquista but the slaughter was a morale booster nonetheless.

Coach Mossi had five excellent strikers at his disposal, a great luxury no doubt: Tansi, Karpenko, Jurgens, Buenos and Castellani. He usually started with Tito and Jurgens. Both got a goal each against the Swiss and the team's overall quality was reflected in the fact that players from other departments got on the score sheet, midfielders Bolingo and Baccanale, and defender Herbst.

There were so many great players at the club but unlike at Saxon Valley, there was no real warmth among them, not much personal fellowship. The big names of Bellona generally kept to themselves but did what they were so highly paid to do. In spite of the steep upswing in his personal fortunes, Tito deeply missed the chummy fraternity of Allen Lane. Except for Bolingo, he rarely had any off-the-game interaction with his fellow players. The Congolese player came around to his place quite often and he to his and they were getting to be great pals. Now that they were in the same side, Tito truly came to appreciate what a maestro Bolingo was, grateful that he could only get better with such a man playing behind him in midfield.

He left Rome on the thirteenth of August bound for Sardinia. Serafina was already in Sassari but would be at Elmas Airport in Cagliari to pick him up. He had been thinking of her rather obsessively these past days. He felt sure that she liked him. He thought he detected genuine warmth in her manner with him but resolved not to ruin it with any presumptious advances.

She wore a pleated, long, olive skirt and a sheer white cotton blouse. As usual, she had little make up on and her full head of auburn hair cascaded to her shoulders and beyond.

"I am so glad you could come," she said and offered her cheek for him to kiss. "We will drive to Sassari and see a little of the island."

She powered her cherry red SUV expertly down the winding miles of the *strade statali*. Chestnut and oak forests and vast wastelands of vegetation rushed picturesquely by as they sped on their way. The ash, yellow-trimmed road unfurled like a ribbon released by some unsure traveler to remark his route through the strange, hilly country. They stopped briefly at a mountain village and ate *fregula succa* and *porchetto alla sarda*. He was delighted with the local soup and spit-roasted pig. With Serafina in the driving seat, he had never enjoyed a ride better.

He met Serafina's mother in her modest white-painted part-stone house on the outskirts of Sassari. She was a strikingly beautiful woman and at thirty-nine, was not at all over the hill. In fact, she was still very much with the youthful ways. Serafina did not inherit her vivacity or glamour and to him that was perhaps welcome. With two characters as apparently strong as both her parents, it was a great achievement on her part to have attained a distinct personality of her own, succeeding seemingly without effort in being quite like neither.

The next day was *Il Candilieri*. It was a musical festival to celebrate the deliverance of the people of Sassari from some deadly plagues that afflicted them in medieval times. It was a mammoth party with the whole town involved. Tito and Serafina mingled in the crowd of flute players, folk dancers and drummers. Taken by the widespread gaiety, they cheered, clapped, danced and laughed along with scores of other people. They acted like carefree children. The world of heiresses and big time football stars seemed so far away, banished temporarily by the crashing of cymbals and the brilliance of brass.

They followed the procession of dancers and musicians through web-like back streets and alleyways, which emptied like tributaries into the *piazza*. The square was agog, bathed in a myriad ribbons and buntings of countless colours.

"More of the wine!" Tito shouted over the din. He was not a drinker at all but he had had quite a good quantity of *Vernaccia,* the local wine.

"Are you sure?" Serafina asked in merry inquiry, her face flushed from exertion. Their bodies were close against each other in the crowd.

He nodded. "Yes, I think I'm getting drunk and I think I like it!"

"Today is special," she said permissively. She pouted her lips and narrowed her eyes, which she probably presumed was as clear a come-on as her conservative nature could manage. "Maybe you can lose your head today. Just today, *si?*"

He felt a rush of blood to the head and a weakening at the knees. He made bold to kiss her, his natural reserve yielding to the dry wine. He was having the time of his life with an enchantress on a quaint Mediterranean evening straight out of a medieval fairy tale.

His head swirled. It was not with the wine, he would swear, but with a great liking for her. He pressed his body next to hers, wanting her to feel his rising passion. All around, people were gorging on the veal and the wine, oblivious of them. There was not a *paparazzo* in sight. No one cared who they were. They were free to be themselves.

"You want to tell me something?" she teased with feline self-assurance.

He nodded almost solemnly. "I love you," he blurted.

"Those words! Careful with those words." She closed her eyes and briefly rested her head against his chest.

"I'm not a child," he said quietly. "I know what they mean."

Her eyes lingered in his for many moments.

"I love you too," she finally decided. "*Ti amor troppo*, as we say."

They sealed the monumental mutual proclamation with a perambulating kiss.

•

In November, it was wet and cold again. He was determined not to bother anymore with the European weather, only to get along with his job. Sometimes the conditions were so bad, it was almost an impossibility to run with the ball especially at the blistering pace that had become his trademark. Hard work and endless training had turned him into a frighteningly quick player. In good conditions, he could trouble any defence. However, at £80 million, he was obliged to *destroy* them in any condition.

Bellona were through to the second phase of the Champions' league, although the going had been tough. They had barely squeezed out of the first group stage, which pitted them alongside Kingford, Real Baracoa and again, Scottish upstarts, Strathnock Rovers, who this time surprisingly finished tops.

On a grim, cold night in mid-November, he returned to Allen Lane, where Bellona were kicking off the second phase campaign against Valley. It was a special feeling going back to the good old lane. He only wished that it had been on a better night; that the game was not played in these difficult conditions. It was impossible to put in a satisfactory performance in the driving rain, swirling winds and slippery turf. The untidy tie was decided by a lone goal scrambled in for Valley by Di Salvo near the end.

It was not a disastrous result for Bellona however and he was quite happy to see his old mates again. He followed Valley's progress studiously through the English papers that he regularly bought for the sole purpose. He was delighted that they were once more in the front running of the Premiership and that Di Salvo was in the form of his life. The veteran striker had shown great resilience to come back from the broken leg. Incredibly, he had gone on to pick up a Champions' league title and a World Cup silver medal within two months of each other in the late twilight of his career! It was incredible. He now had a new strike partner at Valley, Oleg Romanova the Russian star, who had come from Novopetsk after Tito's departure. Blair was playing brilliantly with the fluidity and efficiency that had now become his hallmark, also having come off a satisfactory outing for England in the World Cup.

"Can't say we've done badly, our class," Blair remarked when Tito and he got together after the game. Many of the Bellona players had gone off into the London night but the two ex-Potter Housemates preferred a languid, ruminating conversation in Tito's cosy Belgravia hotel suite. Tito nostalgically called the roll:

"*Robbie.*"

Quinlan had gone to Doverham for 5 million pounds and was enjoying great form there as they challenged Valley and Kingford at the top of the Premiership.

"*Tomas.*"

Ohlin was now with Varnenborg, the Swedish champions, who were in the Champions' league. He had also been a useful member of Sweden's World Cup campaign.

"*Tommi.*"

Peltonnen had grown into a world-class goalkeeper and a great Allen Lane favourite. He had just signed a new contract at Valley that was forced by offers he was getting from Conquista and Charlotte.

"*Scot.*"

Ryder was still at Valley, a credible alternative to the top strikers. Though he was threatening to be a serial substitute, he always got goals and surely, a lot would yet be heard of him in future; if not at Valley, somewhere else.

"*Charlie!*"

Blair groaned. "How I miss that son of a gun."

"Me too," Tito nodded glumly. "*You* know how much I wanted to be his friend; but he never gave me a chance."

"*God!*" Blair winced at the reflections. "Still such a mystery. You know I never bought that story about the ETA. Why would they blow up best player in the world? Even the craziest terrorists have a point they are trying to make. It didn't make any sense to me."

"They denied it but that doesn't mean they didn't do it."

"Makes you think about life. Charlie was going to be the greatest. Then he literally goes up in smoke, wiped away completely."

"Fortunately, there's a lot of video tapes to remember him by," Tito sighed and then lowered his voice, rather needlessly. "Besides, Charlie had a child."

"He did?"

"Yes. A Nigerian girl he made pregnant."

"You're not putting me on?"

"A girl named Ona."

Blair shot him a look of near alarm. "Ona? *Ona?*"

Tito nodded sombrely. "Remember the night of his party; the assault case?" he said and then went over what really happened.

"Christ!" Blair was wide-eyed.

"I saw them with my own eyes," Tito said haltingly. He had not told this to anyone before now. He had thought the episode too painful. It was better to stoke the impression that Ona had attacked him in a fit of jealousy, to which he had overreacted. The recollection of that event brought back the hurt anew. "Charlie's child is about nine months old now."

"You've seen him?"

"Yes," Tito nodded with an arcane half smile. "Half caste, blue eyes and all; his child, no doubt. Before she gave birth, she thought it was mine."

"So, how's she? I mean Ona."

"She's alright, I guess. She's back in Nigeria. You know I really loved her but *she* knows she crossed the line."

"I'm sorry."

"No, I am alright now," Tito said, retrieving himself from the sad flashback. At first, the pain had been unbearable and almost every night he wet his pillow with bitter tears. After an eternity, the agony somehow subsided to a dull ache. Then he found Serafina and miraculously now felt nothing for Ona anymore. In the end, it was not a bad exchange at all—trading an uncouth African tramp for a cultured European heiress. He felt warm comfort and his big, sunny smile belied the wintry night. "I am alright now."

Almost as soon as the team stepped off the plane on their return to Rome, he saw that the big news was not the loss last night in London. Instead, it was the colour pictures of Serafina and him blazing forth from newsstands. On front pages, Serafina was leaning against him and their lips were touching. He recognised instantly the *piazza* in Sassari and even recalled a couple of flushed faces in the bacchanal crowd. '*L'erede italiana ed il principe nero*!' The Italian heiress and the black Prince! screamed one heading.

"Oh, shit!" He swore under his breath as eyes swiveled to him at the lounge. He wondered with real panic what Serafina must be feeling now. Being essentially prim, she would be grossly embarrassed by this.

"You're doing it with the boss' daughter, boy?" Bolingo teased.

Tito gave him a reproachful look. "I'm not *doing* it. I love her."

"O.K."

As he turned into the gates of his villa, Pizzi was right behind him. As always, he was impeccably turned out in an expensive suit but his usually deliberate manner betrayed agitation.

"Don Cesare is very angry about this," he announced. "He has gone into himself and will not speak with anyone."

"I am sorry," Tito mumbled. "I did not mean to upset him"

"It is a terrible mistake."

"I will apologise. Please, how is Serafina?"

Pizzi ignored his inquiry and spoke irritably.

"There is one thing you must understand about Don Cesare. Serafina means everything to him and he is preparing her to inherit all his life's work. Do you understand me?'

"Yes, yes."

"And he is very displeased with me," Pizzi grumbled and eyed him in such a way as to make it clear how much *he* deplored that state of affairs.

"How are *you* to blame for anything?"

"He thinks I should have known the *paparazzo* hawking the pictures and should have done something about it. He thinks I should have got wind of it."

"You didn't?"

"I did. I tried to stop him but he double crossed me," Pizzi said pensively.

"What can I do to apologise to Mr. Palazzolo?"

Pizzi glowered at him and fingered his perfectly made tie. "First of all, you must never see her again. On no account must you be seen with her ever!"

"Alright, but can I talk to Mr. Palazzolo?" Tito was worried about the old man. A black person obviously did not figure in his plans for Serafina and he could understand that. Parents from his hometown usually took the same exception towards their daughters' suitors if they were natives of towns merely five miles down the road. Besides, Palazzolo had given him the best service conditions of any player in the world and that included tested multiple-World Cup veterans. Much media speculation had gone on as to Palazzolo's real motive for setting his value so high, some putting it down to spite, some to plain madness. His arrival at the *Nuovo Colliseum* had accounted for quite a few long faces and bruised egos in the dressing room. Palazzolo had been extremely extravagant with him, appearing unmindful of any cleavages it might cause in the player ranks, which was perhaps not altogether very sensible of him. The last thing he wanted was to upset the man.

"I shall reason with Don Cesare," Pizzi promised after a lengthy pause. "My uncle *usually* listens to me."

The weather in Rome was not so hostile for the return leg of the Champions' league fixture with Valley, though conditions were still far from good. Tito could at least turn on some of his electrifying pace, outrunning Fuchs to gun past Peltonnen in six minutes. But Valley were not European champions for nothing and quickly drew level through the impressive Romanova after a spell of pressure.

Bellona battled hard and in the last quarter of the game, had Valley pinned backs to the wall. Valley had won their first two games of the stage and a draw was all right by them. Bellona, on the other hand, had only one point going into this match day—a draw at home to Varnenborg—and would get into a good position with a win today. But it was Valley going in front near the end when the great Di Salvo muted the *Nuovo Colliseum* with a diving header.

Valley held on until the final whistle and achieved a welcome away win, causing not a few glum faces in the home stands. The Bellona dressing room was deathly afterwards, the players grim and taciturn. They were very professional, though, and did not usually barter blames or bicker between themselves. They knew they had it all to play for in the remaining group games. They also knew they could still pull the chestnut out of the fire.

Since the Valley team was not leaving until the next day, Tito was happy to play host to a good number of them, who in turn seized the chance to ogle at his palatial pad. Blair, Peltonnen, Ryder, Temba, de la Luna and Di Salvo made the stag party, throwing back quite a few drinks. The animated chitchat was interrupted by the ring tone of Tito's handset, a pentatonic blues scale played on a marimba.

"Hello."

It was Serafina.

"Pity about the game," she said. "You played well. A draw would have been fair."

"It's going to be tough," he acknowledged. Now Bellona were lying in third place behind Valley and Varnenborg. The next game against Racing Skopgrad would be crucial, a win imperative.

"But let's not talk about the game," she said.

"If it's possible," he laughed with a little irony. She was after all more or less his boss and had a real interest in the outcome of the games.

"I hear voices in the background."

"Some of my friends from Saxon Valley. About four or five of them."

"No girls?" she asked suspiciously.

"Just boys."

"Billy Blair is there?" she asked.

"Yes. And Di Salvo."

"Uncle Roberto! I should love to see him. Can I come over?" She sounded very excited, just like any other youngster her age struck by the stars of the era.

"I don't think so," he suggested warily. The truth however, was that he wanted nothing in the world more than to see her walk through the front door. He had not seen her in months, although they always spoke on the phone.

"I shall come. I'm on my way."

She sounded like she was dying to see him too. He could tell in her undertone. Maybe the game tonight got her adrenaline flowing. Football was an elixir. Some would even say it was an aphrodisiac. The players were, if not quite gods, at least supermen inhabiting the fantasies of men, women, and children.

About half an hour later, she joined the party. Tito was thrilled at the sight of her. He was chuffed to bits at the look of disbelief on everyone's face. They had all read about the little 'scandal' in Sassari. Now, they were seeing it for themselves, it seemed. He had really moved up in class, they would no doubt be thinking.

"Serafina!" Di Salvo gathered her in his arms very affectionately.

"*Roberto di zio!*" she sniffled.

"*Come buono per vederla, il mio bambino!*" He had known her since she was a child, when he was the praetor of Rome, when he too had been the apple of her father's eyes.

"Why have you made it a habit to score against Bellona?"

"Maybe it is because Don Cesare treated me badly in the end," he smiled. "*Ma io farò di te una promessa.*"

"*Quale promessa?*"

"For your sake, next time we play Bellona, I promise not to score."

"*La promessa?*"

"*Si*. I will pass the ball to someone else, who will!"

She threw back her head and laughed heartily.

"You know my father," she said. *She* knew her father and how he habitually stepped on people's toes. She could not possibly atone or even apologise for everything. "But he does not always mean harm."

•

Apart from making Bellona the world's greatest ever club side, Cesare Palazzolo's pet dream was starting a World Champions' League tournament in his own name. To achieve this, he aimed to fully take advantage of his influence with the game's top bureaucracy. FIFA president, Claudio Franchetti had a respect for him that approached reverence. Palazzolo's *Dio Banca di Italia* had once bailed Franchetti's construction company out of financial ruin and this obviously fuelled much of this loyalty. That was as it should be, as far as Palazzolo was concerned, for whom to dispense favours was to purchase loyalty, an item that could never be obtained free. Therefore, Franchetti ensured that Palazzolo's plan was always near the top of FIFA's current agenda.

Palazzolo had it all worked out: The champion club from each of the six continental federations comprising FIFA would be eligible to play in the annual league championship. The teams played a home and away tie with one another so that each team played ten matches. He was sure that football would be better for it, even though there was the problem of fitting it into the already crowded programmes of the top clubs, who complained of too much football. He had no doubt that their boards would find a way to get around that difficulty, unable to resist the money. It would be an enormous boost for teams from the lesser-developed federations. Though ultimately, the title would rightly go to the better-organised clubs of Europe or South America, it would still prove to be a profitable experience for the others.

It was a project he wanted dearly to be remarked for, by which to leave his imprint in football's sands of time. He wished to take his place among such immortals of football bureaucracy as C.W. Alcock, Lord Kinnaird, Jules Rimet, Hugo Meisl, Henri Delauney, and so on. He would in fact surpass them, no thanks to his phenomenal personal funds. He could and would literally put his money where his mouth was.

Palazzolo was poring over the details of his sublime plans, going through a speech he intended to deliver at an imminent FIFA seminar here in Rome, when Bellona trainer Mossi entered his office. He had summoned the coach, who could not readily guess what the matter might be and was always a little uncomfortable in his presence. The beefy, balding man had been at Bellona for four seasons since replacing Mellini. Although in that time, he had won the *Scudetto* thrice, the *Coppa Italia* once and most recently the UEFA Cup, he knew it all still fell short of the club president's ambitions. Palazzolo wanted Bellona to dominate not just Italian, but European football, by winning the Champions' league repeatedly, ideally back to back, as Conquista had done. In addition, when the World Champions' League ultimately materialized, Bellona should dominate that too.

"*Sedersi,*" he mumbled to the coach, motioned him to a leather armchair and then seemed to forget he was there.

"*Padrone,*" Mossi began nervously after a while. "I know you must be disappointed with the loss against Saxon Valley."

Palazzolo cut him short with an imperiously raised palm. The coach then re-adjusted himself in his seat, bracing for the worst—a mid-season sack.

"I wanted to see you about Tito," Palazzolo said some minutes later.

"Tito?"

"You will drop him from the side immediately."

"Pardon?" Mossi was bewildered. The Nigerian was his best man now, doing a good job in the circumstances, drawing crowds to *Nuovo Colliseum*, scoring some vital goals in *Serie A* and the Champions' league. Though it would always be difficult to live up to his sort of price tag, he was succeeding overall.

"From now on, he will not play any games for Bellona," Palazzolo said for clarity.

"*Ma ciò non è possibile, il padrone!,*" Mossi protested, emboldened that he was not here to receive a sack. "I am depending on him to get to the quarterfinal. We have a difficult game against Skopgrad in Belgrade."

"I do not repeat myself, Mossi," Palazzolo reminded the coach. "And if you do not do as I say, another coach will. *Lei mi capisce?*"

"Si, *Padrone,*" Mossi nodded obsequiously. "*Capisco.* We have many good strikers after all."

"Good," Palazzolo nodded, satisfied. After many moments, he realised that Mossi was still present and turned absently to him. "*Lei potrebbe andare.*"

•

Pizzi was, in post-modern parlance, pissed and had for once thoroughly lost his trademark cool.

"I asked you to stay away from Serafina!" he cried, passionate as an opera tenor. He was in a restaurant with Tito on Via Veneto on a cold and drizzly afternoon. Tito had even been late for the appointment, which did nothing to soothe Pizzi's nerves, as he was a punctilious person.

"I did as you said," Tito proclaimed with justification.

"Look at this," Pizzi said sourly and pushed an envelope roughly across the table to him. Inside it were some photographs. There was one of Serafina arriving at his place and another one of them holding hands, smiling. Tito thought they were ordinary enough pictures of platonic friendship, not exactly the Vallachi Papers! Besides, she had come visiting of her own volition. He shifted the envelope back across to Pizzi, who added for emphasis: 'Don Cesare gave me these pictures himself."

"How did *he* get them?"

"That is a silly question."

"He has my place watched?"

"He watches everywhere."

"I will not accept that," Tito declared boldly, even though Pizzi was making Palazzolo seem unnervingly like God. "He can't invade my privacy that way. I think he has a very wonderful daughter and perhaps he should try not to ruin her personality by over-bearance. She was at my place because she wanted to meet a few heroes of hers especially Roberto Di Salvo. Just like anyone her age."

"Listen," Pizzi said, lowering his voice. "Serafina is my cousin. I know she is a nice girl but she does have a rebellious streak too. Her father, you must understand, is very sensitive about scandals since the one involving her mother."

"Let me ask, Mr. Pizzi," Tito responded with equal seriousness. "What makes it a scandal for Serafina merely to be seen with me? I know it's a little something for the gossip columns. But *scandal*? That's taking it a bit too far. We have a few things in common, Serafina and me."

"Like what?"

"Like we are more or less the same age and we are both famous, so maybe we understand each other a little."

"Wrong, Signor Tansi. You have nothing in common, you and Serafina. You are black and she is white. You are poor and she is rich. You are wrong for her," Pizzi told him levelly. "You are a good football player and Don Cesare knows that. That is why he pays you so much, may be *too* much. But one day you will stop playing and you will go back to Africa and Serafina has a life here in Italy, a future, and an inheritance. She has a great responsibility since Don Cesare has no other child."

"So this is really just about my colour, Mr. Pizzi?"

"Considerably."

"Then, it is Serafina you have to talk to," Tito said retiringly and braced the edge of the table signifying his intention to leave. "If she wants to visit me, there is no way I can prevent that. I should actually feel honoured that she would."

He left Pizzi at the table and strode out of the restaurant with righteous indignation.

One of the most frustrating things for a top player was watching the course of games from the dugouts, dressed in playing kit and being inconsequential to their outcome. It was worse still to be watching from high up in the stands, dressed in a Giorgio Armani suit.

Tito found himself successively absent from the team sheet. He nursed no injury and in fact had never been fitter in his entire life. He was the top scorer at the club and second in the entire *Serie A*. Only the Uruguayan, Ceinfuegos of Pescalerno was ahead of him in the goal stakes.

"Is there something I have done wrong, Mr. Mossi?" he asked one day after training.

"No. I am experimenting," the genial coach had replied but Tito doubted his candour especially when his name was absent for the crucial Champions' league fixture away to Skopgrad. Mossi could not possibly be experimenting at this stage of the campaign. If they did not win the game in Belgrade, they could blow a goodbye kiss to the Champions' league. He wondered how Mossi could afford to leave him out with Jurgens also ruled out from a recent double hernia operation. There was more to it, he suspected.

To the relief of their fans, however, Bellona won the tough away game. Bolingo and Karpenko scored the two goals that capped a gritty performance on the night to grab the three valuable points that kept them in the running.

Catch a falling star

Valeria loved her sleep and usually got as much of it as she could. She knew she was not a raving beauty but then made up for it with a radiant freshness. She put this down to getting sufficient sleep.

Earlier this evening, she had thrown herself about quite a bit, riding her favourite horse, Hugo. She imagined she had exerted herself sufficiently, yet she could not sleep tonight. For over an hour, she squirmed in her bed, turning fitfully this way and that, unable to get thoughts of Tito to leave her mind.

It was mid-March and she had not really been with him since December. She had not even had the consolation of watching him play in the *Calcio* because Mossi had dropped him completely from his selections. She did not have to be an undercover agent to know that the coach did this on her father's secret service. The official line was that Bellona was spoilt for choice players and that any combination of them was as good as the other. It was quite true but still, the more incisive fans wondered about their eighty million-pound man.

She talked with Tito on the phone now and then but that made her feel worse, if anything. The cellular conversations only made her miss him the more. She felt extremely guilty. The world's most expensive player was naturally eager to justify his ranking, which in Tito's case had been the subject of some debate, but he was being denied the opportunity to do so. How it must rankle him, and it was all because of her.

As far as the love affair was concerned, she was the guilty party, according to her own judgment. She it was, who had led him on. Otherwise, she did not think he would have mustered the nerve to seduce her. He was a meek and levelheaded African, very reconciled with his humble station in life. He was very modest about his stardom and thankful for the European system that made football such a money-spinner, making it possible for him to be a millionaire for indulging in his hobby. For having seduced him, she sought absolution in the church. To the priest at confession time, she bowed her head and beat her breast. Still, no number of *Hail Marys* could set her at ease.

She had been furious at first with her father but always knew how futile a course that was. Papa was a headstrong man and she had to capitulate and stop seeing Tito. Still, he was being left out of Mossi's selections. Some of her friends, trying to cheer her, teased her a bit, wondering jocosely what Tito had to complain about, earning all that money for doing nothing. Life could certainly be a lot worse than being paid a fortune just for sitting around! But *she* knew better the inner workings of the professional player's mind. She had been living in her father's obsessive world of football since she was a baby. Playing football was the player's greatest joy. Notwithstanding the cold-blooded economics of the game, despite the high-wire finance, the big-money transfers and way-out salaries, the game was still very much about the boy inside the man. For the goal scorer, the whole point of the business of football was *scoring*. It had to be the most sublime feeling, the thrill of planting the ball into the pliant netting, running to embrace a whole arena, which would in turn rise to greet him with an awesome roar of barbarian affection.

She got off her bed and walked to the French windows. She parted the blinds and peered outside as if she might find him there. How unadvisable to nip love in the bud, she thought. Forbidden love was always prone to ginger the lover to love the more. Adam and Eve just may have left the fruit in the garden be, if it was not forbidden. She had spent these past months forced to withhold her love, only to achieve deeper feelings than she perhaps might have had.

She hugged herself tightly as if she was hugging him. Her hands ran haltingly over her body through the luxuriant silk of her nightdress. Her delicate fingers caressed her slender shoulders, cupped her pulpy breasts and roused her own passions until her gasps turned to sobs. She could bear it no longer. She walked unsteadily to the table where her phone lay and called his number. It seemed to ring for an eternity before he picked up at the other end.

"Hello." His voice was thick.

"Are you alright?"

"Sort of. I was sleeping on the couch, bored to it by CNN and the endless suicide bombing."

"You're lonely?"

"Like hell."

"Like *me?*"

"More."

"You don't know how much I miss you."

"You can't imagine . . ."

"How I want to be with you."

"You know you can't."

"I *can.*"

"But, you know . . ."

"I want to see you."

"Please, Serafina."

"I need you."

"We can't."

"We can."

"Godfather is watching."

"I don't care."

"Damn . . ."

She cut the phone.

•

Palazzolo spoke very captivatingly at the FIFA seminar in Rome. The subject was his pet proposal, the World Champions' league. He spoke passionately and painted the picture in vivid images. There was no question that the idea was a genuinely exciting one. He compelled them to imagine the inter-continental league fixtures of the future. Bellona, for instance, traveling to São Paulo to play Resistencia in a league game, was an intriguing prospect. He was rather eager to visualise Conquista, for example, losing at home to Club Mupenzi of the Democratic Republic of Congo! Everyone laughed and listened.

It was quite possibly a boy's dream but the hard-nosed, septuagenarian *Forbes* frontliner dreaming it made all the difference. He would commit both *Globo-Italiano* and *Dio Banca di Italia* to its realisation and the FIFA brass knew the significance of that solitary detail. They made favourable notes.

"It is a matter of time," Palazzolo proclaimed. "I, Cesare Palazzolo will donate the trophy for this ultimate club championship. I promise it will be the most beautiful, most expensive trophy that the world has ever seen. I shall design it with my own hands."

A great ovation greeted this and from all indications, the FIFA World Champions' league would become a reality at the soonest possible time. President Claudio Franchetti would see to it.

Next week, Bellona would play at home against Conquista. They had squeezed through the second phase of the Champions' league and into the quarterfinal against their Spanish arch-foes. It was a rather sobering prospect for Palazzolo, coming from the high of FIFA's virtual adoption of his proposal.

Coach Mossi was understandably apprehensive about the game. Though he knew Conquista were having a difficult campaign as well, he also knew that the Spaniards were better than their results suggested and the games against Bellona traditionally brought out the best in them. He was without the services of Bolingo, Karpenko and Herbst through cautions, while Jurgens was doubtful for the tie.

He would talk to Palazzolo about Tito. The Nigerian made a hell of a lot of difference and it was honestly insane to voluntarily dispense of his precocious services. Though Bellona had made it this far, it was very likely that the course might have been less arduous had he been playing. How ridiculous it was to bench the world's best player at a time like this. How absurd splashing £80 million pounds on a player and paying him a record salary only to have him sit in the suites up in the stands.

"I have come to make a request, Don Cesare," he said as calmly as he could.

"I have an idea what it might be, Mossi," Palazzolo responded graciously. He seemed in a good mood and this encouraged the coach.

"*Se lei per favore*, I would like Tito to play in the game against Conquista. Bellona must be at her very best, Don Cesare."

Palazzolo appeared to consider the request and Mossi could imagine him shuddering inwardly at the thought of Conquista coming to the *Nuovo Colliseum* and getting a result.

"*Signor Mossi*," he said affably and the coach was heartened. "I am sorry if I interfered with your job in the first place. I wish I hadn't had to."

"*Capisco, il Padrone*," Mossi muttered gratefully. He correctly put down Palazzolo's expansive mood to the prospect of the FIFA World Champions' league.

"I give him another chance," Palazzolo decreed and dismissed the coach.

Mossi passed Pizzi on his way out of Palazzolo's office. They exchanged curt greetings and moved on. Mossi was a thorough football man and stuck to football matters. He did not have much to do with the busy Pizzi, whose duties were nebulous but obviously top priority with the boss.

Pizzi, on his part, was worried, although Mossi did not notice this, not being the most discerning of men. Pizzi was very angry, as well, behind the dapper exterior. He loathed double crossing with a religious passion and as it seemed there was no shortage of it these days, he had a lot of loathing to do.

"Don Cesare," he curtsied when in Palazzolo's presence. He handed him a package. Inside the envelope was a videotape. "*Qualcosa di terribile è successo!* Something unfortunate has happened."

"*Che è la questione ora, Stefano?*"

"An ugly sight, Don Cesare," Pizzi warned. "You may wish not to see it."

"Then, why do you give it to me to see?" Palazzolo was irritated by the suspense.

"It is a recording of Serafina and the Nigerian," Pizzi stuttered. Palazzolo wheeled around urgently to slot it in a video player in a rack behind him.

As the moving pictures soon filled the large screen, his hand went to his throat as if he was going to choke and the colour drained from his face.

"*Madonna!*" the old man croaked "*Madonna!*"

In the video, there was no mistaking Serafina his daughter, or Tito his employee, or the adult and intimate game at which they were playing. They were on a large bed in what was presumably the player's bedroom. He shuddered at the union of the white body and the black one, wheeling around in a daze to shut off the machine. His breathing came in frightening gasps.

"*Zio! Lei stanno bene?* Are you alright?" Pizzi rushed to his side. For a moment, he thought Palazzolo would suffer a stroke.

"*Come? Come questo è successo?*" the old man managed after a while. "How, Stefano, how?"

"I hired Guido," Pizzi explained slowly. The detective was an old customer he had used a number of times in the past particularly for blackmail duties. This time, he was to snoop on Tito and find out if Serafina was still in the habit of visiting his villa. Unfortunately, the man had done more than that.

"Now there is a problem."

"What more?"

"He is now blackmailing us with this tape. He is in great debt as I gather and is asking a lot of money."

"How much?"

"Ten million dollars."

"*Quell'animale!*" Palazzolo spat. He had some of his wind back now and his breathing had started to come to passable normalcy. A sense of quiet rage was replacing the sense of wild panic. This was the scandal to end all Palazzolo scandals. Other eyes must never see that sordid video. "Stop him! Take the money to him quickly!"

"*Pardone?*" Pizzi protested. "*Parliamo in gergo fa ciò!*"

"You heard me!" Palazzolo snapped and banged the desk.

"*Si,* Don Cesare," Pizzi said, still with misgiving. "Is that all?"

"Of course not," Palazzolo answered in a near-whisper, his face contorting with a portentous sneer. His hand came to his throat, where it made a slow, slitting gesture. "*Ed uccide poi il bastardo!*"

Pizzi nodded firmly and there was a spring in his step as he left the office.

•

At Bellona's five-star training facilities, *Campo Serafina*, the players went really hard through their paces getting ready for the crucial weekend quarterfinal tie. Mossi and the trainers worked furiously at the preparations. At this level, it was as much a mental as physical thing. Mossi was rueing the loss of Herbst, Bolingo and Karpenko, all through suspensions as earlier said. The German, Herbst was the best libero in the business. The front men would sorely miss his piercing long balls from out of defence and as for Bolingo's artistry in midfield, he had few peers in the modern day.

Thankfully, he now had Tito available, so he could count his blessings. Jurgens, Karpenko, Castellani and Buenos were all excellent forwards but for his money, Tito had the edge. His pace and sharpness in front of goal could usually be counted on. When it mattered, he would always get on the score sheet. The coach called him aside.

"You will start the game on Sunday," he told him confidentially.

"Oh, thanks, Mister Mossi!" Tito said with gross relief. He had not found his lengthy exclusion easy to bear. Nor at first had the fans of the *Nuovo Colliseum* but as time went on and the team seemed to be getting along well enough without him, they seemed to adjust to it.

There was a young local lad coming through the Bellona ranks called Vittorio Ghini. He had made a couple of decent outings and impressed the fans, who were as fickle as the original Roman mob. They rooted as throatily for the gladiator who had just made a kill as for the lion that next ripped his gut. Fickleness, Tito now understood, was part of the fans' stock-in-trade. He had to learn how transient their adulation could be and never to let it get to his head. It was altogether deflating but it never stopped him from working hard at training, never shirking the responsibility he bore as the club's costliest acquisition.

He had just bought a new car, a Lamborghini, which he was still ecstatic about and liked to gun about in the hellish Rome traffic. On the car radio, it was all about the Bellona-Conquista game, arguably the world's most prestigious club fixture. There was well over a half billion pounds worth of players on show anytime that both teams took the field. It was amazing to imagine.

Sometimes it got very lonely, especially in that huge villa of his. He was thrilled therefore, that Kosi was around for a few days. She was now doing a successful import business in Nigeria, which usually took her to Rome and Dubai. On his way home, he stopped on Via Barberi to buy her some gifts—shoes, perfumes, chocolates and the like. He could never give her enough. Everything he had he owed to her.

When he turned into his gates, he noticed that a car was right behind him and wondered idly who it was.

Serafina was watching the evening news on television, reclined on a delicate, chintz-covered *chaise longue*. Her pet poodle, Silvio, sat pertly on her lap. By the groovy lampshade that shed muted gold lighting, she flipped idly through a magazine she had just picked off the top of a pile.

She was not in a very good mood lately, as her attendants could testify. This was of some concern to them because her good cheer and modesty were her most endearing qualities as far as they knew.

Her father had been rather gruff with her of late and she could easily fathom why. It must have to do with Tito, even though she did not see him much by any means. Thankfully, sex was not very high on his priority, since she herself was no Aphrodite. His love for her was emotional, not impassioned, and she felt very comfortable with it.

She was startled shortly by the news and pictures on TV of the gruesome murder in Centro di Roma, of a private eye named Guido Montini. He was found inside his car trunk, his eyes gouged out and throat slashed. The *polizia* had yet no clue as to the incident but were working round the clock, as usual. Montini was aged 47.

"*Scusarsi, la Signora,*" a voice spoke from the doorway. It was Concetta, the matronly Sicilian, who worked for her. She was in her late thirties and brought to the urbane setting, a rustic edge that appealed to Serafina. She was married to big Lorenzo, her father's chief bodyguard.

"Concetta. *Entrare,*" Serafina motioned her in. She immediately noticed some tentativeness about her manner. "What is it?"

She inched closer. "There is something I want to tell you, *la Signora.*" She spoke hesitantly, visibly battling some procrastination. "You know how much I am devoted to my husband; since when I was still a child back in Palermo."

"*Si, si,*" Serafina acknowledged patiently. She knew the story of Concetta's betrothal to the local enforcer, who was well connected to Don Cesare.

Concetta warmed with the thought of her husband.

"Lorenzo can be crazy sometimes. He once said to me a long time ago that he loved me more than he loved his mother."

"Surely, that's quite possible," Serafina smiled indulgently.

"But," Concetta stifled a snigger. "He later confessed to me that he *never* knew his mother. She didn't want the baby and cast him away in the street. If it hadn't been for some good Sicilian folks, the little creature would have died a miserable death."

"Why are you telling me this *now*?" Serafina interjected. She knew all these stories. There was precious little, probably nothing, that her father did not tell her about his life and that of those around him. Her father knew the minutest details of the puniest *domestici*.

"I know you love *Signor* Tito, the African," Concetta blurted suddenly. "I know this because I am a woman and have known you since you were a child."

"And what if I *do* love him?" Serafina frowned.

"Then I must tell you this, though my husband would kill me for it." She looked furtively and lowered her voice somewhat unnecessarily. "He is in grave danger."

"*È venuto come?* What do you mean?"

"You must alert him at once. I think some harm might be coming to him."

"Lorenzo?" Alarm went off in Serafina's head.

"*Si, signora,*" Concetta nodded gravely. "I hope it is not late already."

Serafina got quickly to her feet, cursing Concetta for taking so long to come to the point. Big Lorenzo was not big for nothing and even *she* knew that he had crushed the life out of many a man in her father's service.

She reached for her phone and called Tito's number but no response came from his end. In a flash, she was out of the house, screeching off in her Madonna II Coupe. She was soon hitting the floorboard in a panic, headed towards Via Cavour.

A baseball bat crashed for the fourteenth time at Tito's fallen form. On the other hand, it might have been the *fortieth* time. He had lost count of the deadly blows. He was crying like a baby, never having felt this much pain in his life.

He felt all the bones in his body crack, *heard* them break. He could barely make out his assailants. With every second, his eyes were swelling out of their sockets from the brutal beating.

He was pleading, coughing, splurging blood through his battered lips but they would not let him go. When it dawned on him that the men really meant to bludgeon him to death, he wept; with pathos more than from pain.

Kosi was in the bathroom and had not known when her brother drove into the grounds. She was on her way downstairs when she heard the dogs barking. She went to the window only to see the horrifying sight of Tito surely dying under the hail of blows. Gripped by fear, she wondered what she was going to do. Scream? How to reach the police in Rome? Surely, Tito would die before she figured that.

A pair of headlights swung through the gates. The car devoured the driveway like a jet taxing for take off and then came to a grinding halt a few metres from the lynching. The powerful lights seemed to freeze the mugging scene in mid-action.

"Lorenzo!" Serafina cried, darting out of the car "*Partirlo solo!* Leave him at once!"

"*Signora*, stay out of this," big Lorenzo replied in a rough but deferential tone of voice.

"Stop at once!" she shouted again and drew a revolver, which she levelled at the big man.

Lorenzo was big indeed, about six foot six and chasing two hundred and fifty pounds. He was an intimidating man and a good one to have on one's side. Puny by comparison, Serafina did not look too convincing training the gun up at him but he was apparently taking no chances. In any case, he was made irresolute by the conflict of allegiance to his master and his master's sole heiress. He knew that under no circumstances would Palazzolo accept it if any harm should come to Serafina.

"He sent you to do *this*?" Her eyes flashed wildly, taking in the sight of Tito, who was crumpled like a rag. "I regret that he is my father!"

"*Signora*!" Lorenzo remonstrated. "It is blasphemous to speak of Don Cesare so."

"*Uscire!* Get out! Out!" Serafina shouted at him and his cohorts, close to tears. She could not believe this was happening. It belonged only in the cheapest, most gruesome Mafia movies. She pulled the trigger twice as if to attest that the gun was loaded and Lorenzo and the others scampered almost comically to their Lancia. No one was hit but it was not because she was not a good shot. The driver quickly turned the car around and they sped away. She fired another shot in anger after them, taking out a taillight. She *was* a good shot.

She kept the gun aside and bent urgently over Tito, who was not even writhing by now. He was all pulpy, bloodied, and still. Only the faintest breathing escaped his gaping mouth. She called an ambulance just as Kosi reached the scene. Kosi saw that her brother was barely alive, but even that was something to be thankful for. She turned tearfully to the rescuer.

"You must be Serafina."

"And you Kosi."

They had never met, but Tito had filled in each with accounts of the other. Along with his mother, they were the only women in his life, he often said.

The ambulance arrived very quickly, siren wailing. The medics went about gathering the broken body onto a stretcher. As to the gravity of the injuries, their faces were inscrutable and the on-looking women could not detect anything. Hearts in their mouths, they drove behind them and sped towards the hospital. They muttered prayers and said nothing.

The Italian nation and other people around the world were gripped by news of the Tito Tansi mugging. There was a great consternation, particularly in international sports circles, especially as the obliteration of Charlie Jones was still fresh in everyone's memory. An eerie feeling grew that there was a serial killer on the prowl after football stars. People everywhere stayed with the breaking news as the networks monitored his progress or lack of it. He was in very intensive care and critical condition.

On the day of the quarterfinal, however, the fans of the *Nuovo Colliseum* sounded in very high spirits. The dark cloud of Tito's mishap seemed to give way temporarily to the unbelievable atmosphere of the crucial tie with Conquista. The two teams never played ordinary games. All their meetings were dramatic encounters.

The progress of either team in this year's championship was practically poised on this game, even though there was a second leg to contemplate. A win today was almost imperative for either team, as that would be the ideal booster with which to go into the return leg. A win by Conquista here would practically ensure the Spaniards a semi final berth. They had not lost a home game in two and a half years and would be most unlikely to give up the advantage in Spain.

Mossi was still staggered by the loss of Tito, on whom he had banked so much. On the other hand, Conquista looked re-organised after last season's traumatic loss of both Jones and the Champions' league title. Zizinho had come to them from Baracoa and was enjoying a great season with his fellow World Cup winner, Hannibal.

Bellona started the game with the pair of Buenos and Castellani in front, but they could not have got off to a worse start. Castellani was stretchered off in the fifteenth minute with a twisted knee and no sooner had Mossi sent on a half-fit Jurgens than the visitors went ahead, Hannibal hitting the net with an awesome shot following a superb build up. Then just before the break, Scala put Conquista further ahead, scoring from the penalty spot after Strazza had fouled Zizinho. The *Nuovo Colliseum* was like an old graveyard.

Serafina stormed into her father's presidential suite high up in the stadium. She saw from the TV monitor that Conquista were 2-0 up but could not care less today. At another time, she would have been faithfully at his side, propping up his spirits, which would be very low at this point.

"Papa." Her eyes glowered with hostility at the men seated with her father in the suite, and they sensed correctly that something was amiss in the family. Palazzolo gestured woodenly to them and they excused themselves.

"You are still upset," he grunted, though with some feeling. This was the second time he was seeing her since the Tito incident.

"Papa, *how* could you be so cruel?"

"I have told you I don't understand what you mean." He denied any foreknowledge or endorsement of Tito's near-murder, but his indifference was suspicious.

"It was Lorenzo," she said. "There was Flavio, Gualtiero and Guillermo too. I saw them myself."

"I don't believe you," he declared illogically. He had not even told her about the videotape, which mercifully was out of existence now. He looked at his watch. "You know we are losing a game here. The next forty five minutes means everything to me."

"All you think of is your stupid hatred for Modesto Delgado," she said deliberately to hurt him. "I am beginning to understand why my mother did what she did."

"*Madonna!*"

"I suggest, Papa that you think of that poor black boy you almost had killed."

"He is in good medical hands. What can I do? He will be alright." He looked down at his leglessness. "Even *I* am alright."

"Papa!"

"Can't we talk after the game, my dear?"

"That game you love so much, Papa," she was sobbing, despite a valiant attempt not to. "Do you know Tito might never play it again?"

"Are you sure about that?" her father asked and she could not tell if it was out of distress or delight!

"The doctor told me in confidence that it wasn't likely he will ever play again."

"*Sono spiacente, il mio angelo.* I am sorry to hear that. He will get insurance anyhow."

"That is all?" she wondered wide-eyed.

"*Che altro, il mio amore?* What else can I say, my angel?"

"I feel ashamed to be your daughter."

"Don't say that to me again," he said, pained.

"I will say it to the whole world."

"You will not!" he snapped quietly. "You love me too much, just like I love you. We are all we both have."

"If that is true, Papa, you have just lost the only thing you have." She wiped away a travelling tear. "You are all alone now."

"There are things you don't know," the old man protested, remembering the video in which she was an unwitting porn star. "I have to protect you. One day, I will leave everything to you." He waved his hands about him. "Everything I have is yours, so don't let a mere Negro ruin it for you."

Horrified by his lack of feeling, she hurried indignantly out of the suite and headed back to the hospital.

Bellona worked hard in the second half, but they hardly threatened the Conquista goal, whereas Hannibal soon had Carnera beaten again, only to see his shot bound off the bar. Mossi was frantic on the sidelines. Jurgens was ineffective. Buenos was working furiously but also getting nowhere and he soon took him off and sent on young Vittorio Ghini.

Minutes later, Ghini slid through to scramble a cross over the Conquista goal line and cut the lead. Sensing a comeback, the home team threw everything forward but counter-attacks soon had Carnera going full stretch to stop the lighting-quick Krebs and the wonderful Zizinho stretching the visitors' lead.

A well-timed run into the box gave Ghini the chance to rifle in the equaliser from close range and suddenly, the *Colliseum* came back to feverish life. Conquista rallied to guard their result, while Bellona piled on the pressure, sensing the possibility of a win. The anxiety was nothing for the faint-hearted.

The winner came a few agonising seconds from the end. Ghini strained and fought off the big Yugoslav Sukic, then stabbed past Bika for a dream hat trick. Half the Conquista players collapsed to the turf in dismay. They would not easily forgive themselves at having blown the two-goal lead.

The home fans released one last monstrous roar that seemed to shake the very foundations of the *Coliseumo*. Every one of them rose to salute Ghini, the hero of the day, giving him a sustained ovation. He was only seventeen but what a night it was for him, the stuff of dreams and legends. His name would be on every Italian lip that night and in every paper the next day. Every football *aficionado* would be likening him to the great Di Salvo, who had made a similar impression at roughly the same age. Vittorio Ghini would be the latest arrival on the big stage.

There was the usual post-match conference where the managers and some of the players did a spot of soul searching or breast-beating, as the case may be. Mossi was expectedly elated and uncharacteristically effusive in praise of his team's performance, their discipline and mental strength. Old Meissner was elegant in defeat and very gracious to the victors, with many good things to say about young Ghini. Of course, it was not over yet, he reminded everyone. Conquista had the insurance of the two vital away goals and Bellona *did* still have to come to the *San Diego* for the return leg. *That* was certainly something for the victors to think about.

About the same time, another press conference was taking place at the Villa Palermo. Serafina sat at a long table behind a battery of microphones. Some of her close attendants flanked her. She wore a sweater over faded denims and her fine auburn hair was all over her face and shoulders. Her visage was strained and she looked a trifle older. Her eyes were puffy and while she usually wore little make up, she wore none at all today. All the reporters were very curious indeed at her state.

"I know Bellona fans are still celebrating the victory over Conquista a short while ago," she said haltingly and fidgeted a little. Though she lived in the public eye, she would rather not do much public speaking. "I regret that I missed the game but I had to be at the side of someone I love and who needs me desperately at this moment, one of the world's best football players, Tito Tansi."

Everyone in the hall seemed to catch their breath at the same time and reporters scribbled furiously. Certainly, this was something for the pages. This was the first time Serafina Palazzolo was being officially linked romantically to anyone and it was coming straight from the horse's mouth.

"Can you tell us more about his condition at this moment?" asked one journalist.

"Yes, I can." She cleared her throat and her voice trembled despite an obvious effort to keep it under control. "To begin with, doctors think it is extremely unlikely that he will ever play top level football again."

The audience groaned.

"Is that absolutely so?" someone asked.

"Yes. Fractures almost in every bone."

"There must be some clues as to who was responsible and why," suggested the same man.

"Do you think the motive was racism?"

"Were there no witnesses to the beating?"

"There were none," Serafina said, pulling on a trendy pair of shades. "I arrived the scene a little late and his sister here was upstairs and did not see anything."

They had agreed like blood sisters on the lie, namely that Serafina would not finger the mobsters. Kosi was relieved that Tito was not going to die and she agreed readily to the sealed lips.

"How is Don Cesare taking this? It is not too long ago that he spent a fortune on this player."

"Devastated," she lied yet again. "He is devastated but he is taking it well. Thankfully, Bellona won tonight and that should lift his spirit."

"You are taking this very personally, Signorita Palazzolo," said an elfish reporter from *La Stampa*. "Do you feel in any way responsible for what happened?"

"What do you mean?" Serafina responded hedgily. "Of course, I am taking it very personally because I love Tito, if that's what you mean."

"Well, everyone knows your father does not approve of your secret affair with Tito and Don Cesare has a loyal following among nationalist radicals."

"What are you insinuating?" she asked with some trepidation. The reporter was uncomfortably close to the fact of her father's complicity. "And I don't think you can call the affair secret now."

"You are a national icon, Signorita. Many nationalists would think you *belonged* to Italy. You confirm that you and Tito are lovers?"

"Yes."

"Could it be infatuation?"

"Let me just say," she cleared her throat, straightening and adjusting her seating. Her body signals suggested that this was the main point of the press conference. "We are so very much in love, that on behalf of the two of us, I am announcing our engagement."

A buzz of excitement ensued, sustained by ripples of undertones. Reporters worked their note pads eagerly. Some hurried out of the room, no doubt to send the juicy scoop to editors ahead of others.

"Accept my congratulations," the man from *La Stampa* said ambiguously. "But the timing of the engagement is curious. Your fiancé is in critical condition."

"I love him in sickness and in health," Serafina said.

"Does it have the blessing of your father?" the man insisted.

"Not at the moment."

"Is he aware of your intention?"

"Maybe," Serafina replied obliquely.

"You stand to inherit his fortune," a woman interjected. "Your marriage will be of great importance to him, even to all Italy."

"But most importantly to my fiancé and I," she said cuttingly but wondered silently if she had not gone overboard with this press conference thing. The idea had come to her as a capricious tantrum meant to embarrass her father but now it was spiraling out of her control. "Parents—even parents like Cesare Palazzolo—must learn to respect their children."

"The attack on Tito," the *La Stampa* man went on doggedly. He seemed increasingly like the only one there. "Would it perhaps have been meant to stop this engagement?"

The whole room turned to reappraise the little man. Serafina was flustered but managed to look levelly at him. He had certainly proved more inquisitive and fastidious than the rest; a right little ferret, if you asked her. A male assistant consulted her and shortly spoke in the microphone.

"Gentlemen," the assistant said in a deep voice. "I am afraid the press conference has come to an end. Thank you."

"Please let her answer my question," protested the *La Stampa* man. "Signorita Palazzolo . . ."

But Serafina was already on her feet. With a weary smile in the direction of everyone, she left the room amid a mild commotion and heated conversation.

"I think there was something about the timing of this announcement," the *La Stampa* was saying to some of his colleagues. "*That* Serafina Palazzolo is not as soft as she looks."

"How do you mean?" asked one of the others.

"I can discern an obstinate streak in the young woman," the man remarked. "She is standing up to old man Palazzolo, which is more than you can say for a few Italian Prime Ministers I have known."

She got home much later, having gone by way of the hospital after the press conference. Tito was in relatively better condition, considering everything. Though his limbs were still encased in plaster, much of the facial swelling had subsided. The gash over his eye and cheek had been sutured and would hopefully be mere scar tissue some day. There would be no damage to his sight as it had initially seemed in her lay calculation. Minor abrasions and lacerations were already responding to the first class attention he was getting. His mouth was not speaking much yet but his eyes were alive and eloquent, which made her happy.

Her phone buzzed and she picked it up. It was a surprise call from Alfreda of *Los Mininos*.

"I saw your press conference on TV."

"Oh?"

"You left some things unsaid," the superstar said stingingly.

"Like what?"

"Like the really important things. Like who did this terrible thing to your guy."

"I don't know who did."

"I suspect you do, Serafina."

"I am very tired, Alfreda."

"I can understand, though, if you don't want to tell on your father."

Serafina stiffened. "What?"

"I know what it feels like to live with a secret. I had the same problem after Charlie died." Her voice was breaking at the other end. "I still cry for Charlie to this day. I will cry for him forever, Serafina."

"I am sorry, Alfreda."

"Thank you." Alfreda tried to compose herself. "You'll never guess who killed Charlie."

"The ETA, I heard."

"Oh, sure," the singer sniffed. "If it's the KGB that mugged your boyfriend."

"Who did it, then? Who did kill Charlie?"

Alfreda sighed. "Someone paid Charlie to help make sure Conquista lost a game. Two million dollars. But what does crazy Charlie do?" She chortled ironically. "He actually scores the *winning* goal!"

"He took a bribe?" Serafina was horrified.

"He made a mistake," Alfreda cut in defensively. "But he *didn't* throw the game. He was a true professional, Serafina. When it fell to him to score, he did."

"He shouldn't have—"

"He wanted to give the money back almost immediately he took it," Alfreda championed, sniveling. "He told me everything shortly before he died. He was very worried about it. He wanted to give it back."

"I am so sorry to hear this," Serafina said after a sensitive pause. It was not everyday that a pop megastar cried to you.

"Then," Alfreda continued, starting to cry. "After he scored the goal that actually *won* the game for Conquista, they planted the bomb in his car and ended his beautiful life. Cesare Palazzolo had Charlie killed, Serafina. Your father killed him."

"*Gesu Cristo*! How can you say that?"

"He sent someone to bribe Charlie and some of the other players. Hannibal, Bika and Sukic, I think. I remember his name. Stefano Pizzi. He came from your father. He told Charlie so. Charlie told me."

Serafina froze. She held a hand to her forehead and spoke haltingly. "I am sorry but I have to go now, Alfreda . . ."

"Serafina, please wait—"

"I have to go. Good night . . ."

She cut the call, collapsed in the *chaise longue* and stared in a daze at nothing.

•

Cesare Palazzolo looked glumly out the tinted window of the Madonna V stretch limo, the latest model off his assembly lines at Avanti. He frowned with boredom at the perennial tourists of Piazza San Pietro. He had just come from audience with his good friend, the Pope but it had done no magic for his mood as he had hoped. During the meeting, he had even felt a certain pity for the frail *Papa*, who seemed like he stood in need of more propping up than he did.

Fate had a way of pulling the rug from under your feet, he ruminated. What a time Serafina had chosen for revealing her innate deviance. How so much like her mother she seemed now; so reckless in carnal matters that she would trade an empire for an orgasm.

Ironically, he had lately been quite a contented person, not easy for a fastidious character like him, who had a finger in every pie. He had acquired the feeling that he had done his bit, run a good race and contributed something to humanity. The aesthetic and cultural quality of the *Nuovo Colliseum* would ensure his immortality. As the name of Caesar still echoed from the past, so would Cesare's resonate down the ages.

Bellona was an immense organisation, even though his perfectionism often gave his subordinates the impression that he did not appreciate their massive efforts. They were the top club side in Italy, and dominance over the European landscape, he knew, was only a matter of time. He just knew that some day, they would get there. For everything, there was a time and season. They were in the quarterfinal of the Champions' league and he had a gut feeling that this year, he would take Delgado's scalp. It would be an indescribable satisfaction for him.

The big wigs at FIFA had finally kowtowed to him as far as the World Champions' league was concerned. Very soon, the giant 24-carat gold, diamond encrusted Cesare Palazzolo trophy would come off his design room and be cast by the very best goldsmiths in the world. Overall, therefore, he had cause to be reasonably satisfied with himself. He had the world's best football stadium, owned the world's greatest clubside and would soon be patron of the world's foremost football tournament. All his entrepreneurial and inventive genius, as far as he was concerned, played second fiddle to football. He had surely given—as well as received—enough from this game that he loved so much.

Then Serafina had to come along to poop his party. For the first real time, he lamented that he had not fathered a son. Up to this point, his devotion to her had been total and left him no room for any regrets over primogeniture. On second thoughts now, a son would have ensured that the rewards of his life's labours stayed in the family. A son might have gone back to Palermo one day, to the pastoral pleasures that he had passed over early. He would not then have been confronted with this horror; the ugly likelihood that his massive fortune and all the sweat of his brow would ultimately end up in the hands of a pack of Nigerian *mulattos*. He could quite imagine them even now: grinning, woolly-haired, bulbous-nosed, bow-legged, blinking pickaninies, parading as Cesare Palazzolo's offspring; with logical proof of the progeny at that, DNA and all!

Serafina had irretrievably damaged her standing with him. Head bowed, he grieved as the limo sailed down Via Barbieri. The pedestal on which he had set her was ultimately undeserved and this he decided desolately but with resounding finality. She was just like her mother and so had to go the way of her mother—out of his life! She would soon discover as her mother did, that his capacity to love was the equal and opposite of his faculty to begrudge.

Even though he could not totally disinherit her, he would remake his will and leave her only what was sufficient for her barely to maintain her station. Since he had no son, he would now have to bequeath the bulk of his fortune to his late sister's son. Stefano Pizzi, was an intelligent, shrewd and adequately ruthless young man. What was left, he would dispose to any number of charities and to a World Champions' league trust. His mind made up, he put a call through to his lawyer, Arturo Carlo, who would handle the painstaking legal re-engineering of the will.

"Yes, Don Cesare," the *avocatto* spoke deferentially at the end of the line. Carlo was the best in the country. "Of what humble service may I be, *padrone*?"

"I want you at my place nine a.m. tomorrow."

"I shall be there punctually."

"It is most important. Cancel all appointments. We will not be in a hurry."

"I shall do as you wish," Carlo said submissively.

Late that same night, however, Palazzolo suffered a massive coronary and the *avocatto* was never to find out the reason why he had been summoned to Villa Palermo.

The Final

In late May, Tito, Serafina, Kosi and Jim departed Rome in Serafina's Falcon, bound for Munich. Tito was not about to miss the Champions' league final, even though he still hobbled about on crutches and needed his painkillers to the point of addiction. He wanted to be at the *Olympikstadion* in person, not watch the game on TV.

His life had been a nightmare since the night of the beating. The fact that he would never play again confounded him the more he struggled to come to grips with it. He was only twenty-two and he liked to think that the impossible was yet possible, that the bones might rise again. He believed in miracles. Had the past five years not been a miracle? One day he was an incurably obscure rural West African urchin and then the next, he was one of the world's foremost athletes. Without having to do any real wooing, had he not won the love of Italy's most eligible spinster, making him the envy of the worthiest suitors from Europe's cosmopolitan aristocracies? He thought of all these as the Falcon glided through the golden skies. He leant over and touched her cheek with a kiss so light yet so heavy with endearment.

"I love you," he said, declaring this yet another time. She rested her head on his shoulder and smiled an unspoken but audible response.

She had come into her astronomical inheritance and at twenty-one, was at once one of the world's wealthiest people. She was the only female football club president in the world and the youngest as well. *And* she was well liked.

Bellona had clawed a hard way to the final of the Champions' league and she was obliged to be there as the new president of the great club. There was an almost religious belief among the faithful of the *Nuovo Colliseum* that everyone owed winning this final as much to the late president as the new one.

The shock of Palazzolo's death had seemed to galvanise the team to superhuman effort. Incredibly, they had destroyed Conquista 3-0 in Spain in the return leg of the quarterfinal, thanks to *another* hat trick from the amazing Vittorio Ghini. It had been a glorious night for Bellona and everyone close to Palazzolo deeply regretted that the old man had not lived to witness it. Humiliating Conquista right in the *San Diego* and seeing Modesto Delgado come close to tears might have added more years to his life.

After that, they had managed to edge out the tough Ukrainian side, Torpedo in the semi-final on penalties. Tonight in the final at the *Olympikstadion,* they were up against the English champions, Saxon Valley, who were still on a roll. They had just been crowned champions of the

Premiership for the second year running and had they not lost the FA Cup final to Westbury United, they would have been here in Munich to defend the treble! Sir Johnny and Gianluca Mellini had achieved a boys' adventure book miracle back at Allen Lane.

Both sides were at full strength, which meant that some magnificent football was on the cards. The teenage starlet Vittorio Ghini had been in headline-grabbing form since the night he came on as a substitute in the game against Conquista at the *Colliseum*. With an undeniable measure of cynicism, Tito noted that Ghini was the new hero of the Roman plebeians, reminding him again how flighty fans were. 'Football is an infinite but fleeting drama,' he reflected, indulging in stoic pretension. 'The scenes are short, the cast endless and the actors have but a little while to strut the perennial stage.' All the same, this was today, the stage was set for the latest scene and the new entrant Ghini was a handful for the Valley defence. Just before half time, his enterprise paid off when he was fouled by John Thomas and won a penalty, which Bolingo converted.

Early in the second period, however, Romanova levelled for Valley with a headed goal and the scintillating game picked up even more brilliance. Jurgens put Bellona back in front with a quarter of an hour to go, only for Blair to level things up again with a trademark free kick almost immediately.

Olympikstadion brimmed over with fever-pitch fervor as Mihailescu and then Ghini, scored within one minute of each other to make the scores 3-3 with five minutes on the clock. For most neutrals, it did not really matter by now who won. The palpitating game, which no one would ever forget, had been of the very highest level and that a victor should emerge seemed curiously secondary. Yet a victor did emerge when Di Salvo broke Bellona hearts with the stoppage time winner.

Tito was beside himself with the thrill of the classic game. Upstairs in the suite, well after the final whistle, he gave a standing ovation to the sweaty men, who were now swapping shirts and mingling on the field far below. The pulsating final had sapped him mentally almost as if he had been in it himself. The long faces, of course belonged to the Italians and the sunny ones to the Valley players, but somehow he felt like one of the neutrals, as both sets of players were one to him. He had played on both sides and it gave him a great deal of nostalgic pleasure to remember that. But it also clouded his mood, because was nostalgia not evidence that something was gone?

"I'm sorry, my dear," he said to Serafina, snapping back to the present. He pulled her close and squeezed her comfortingly.

"It was a great game," Jim remarked, not exactly displeased with the outcome. His brother Malcolm would be picking up a second consecutive winners' medal in a few minutes. He hugged Kosi. "It could have gone either way."

Serafina smiled bravely and sighed, looking into Tito's face.

"I know one day Bellona's time will come," she said. "One day our season will come. My father always said that."

"But *our* season has already come, darling, you and I," he replied, looking in her big, brown eyes and kissing the engagement ring on her slender finger. "We'll be together for all seasons."

THE END